Too late, **Spock knew.** ***Too late.***

He stood quickly from the low stool in the alcove that he'd set up for his meditation. He turned toward the wall, where he had hung an "infinity mirror": a black octagonal frame held a perimeter of small lights between a transparent piece of glass and a mirror, causing a series of reflections in the mirror to resemble a tunnel of lights receding into the distance.

Spock put his fist through it.

The front glass shattered and fell in shards to the floor, the pieces landing with a clash. The mirror splintered but remained relatively intact, only a single thin wedge falling free. The tunnel effect of the reflected lights vanished.

As Spock pulled back his hand, he saw lacerations in his flesh, his blood flowing green from them. He wrapped his other hand around his injured fist and fixated on the physical pain. He needed something—almost anything— to help him pull his emotions into check.

But Spock had no control. He had no quietude. And he mourned.

He understood the logic of the situation, but logic failed him. Emotion alone drove him.

And the time had come for him to do something about it.

ALSO BY DAVID R. GEORGE III

NOVELS

The 34th Rule (with Armin Shimerman)

Twilight (*Mission: Gamma, Book One*)

Serpents Among the Ruins (*The Lost Era, 2311*)

Olympus Descending
(in *Worlds of Deep Space Nine, Volume Three*)

Provenance of Shadows (*Crucible: McCoy*)

The Star to Every Wandering (*Crucible: Kirk*)
[Coming soon]

NOVELLAS

Iron and Sacrifice (in *Tales from the Captain's Table*)

STAR TREK®

CRUCIBLE: SPOCK
THE FIRE AND THE ROSE

David R. George III

Based upon STAR TREK®
created by Gene Roddenberry

POCKET BOOKS
New York London Toronto Sydney Shi'Kahr

An *Original* Publication of POCKET BOOKS

 POCKET BOOKS, a division of Simon & Schuster, Inc.
1230 Avenue of the Americas, New York, NY 10020

This book is a work of fiction. Names, characters, places and incidents are products of the author's imagination or are used fictitiously. Any resemblance to actual events or locales or persons, living or dead, is entirely coincidental.

ISBN-13: 978-0-7434-9169-3
ISBN-10:   0-7434-9169-6

This Pocket Books paperback edition December 2006

10 9 8 7 6 5 4 3

POCKET and colophon are registered trademarks of Simon & Schuster, Inc.

Cover art by John Picacio

Manufactured in the United States of America

For information regarding special discounts for bulk purchases, please contact Simon & Schuster Special Sales at 1-800-456-6798 or business@simonandschuster.com.

To Audrey and Walter Ragan
—Audrey Ann and the Navy Man—
two of my favorite people,
who welcomed me into their family
with extraordinary love and support

FOREWORD

The Fire and the . . . Well, Not So Much Fire

So I've got my approach for this *Star Trek* trilogy that is intended to help celebrate the fortieth anniversary of the show. First, I will base it solely on the original episodes and the films (and maybe a little of the animated series, just for good measure). Check. Second, though the novels will include all of the familiar faces—Scotty, Sulu, Uhura, Chekov, and others—I will focus each book on one of the three main characters of McCoy, Spock, and Kirk. Check. Third, I will tie the stories together through this one event, this crucible, that I have posited had a significant and abiding impact on the lives of those three. Check.

I finish the outline for the McCoy tale and move on to that for the Spock story. And as I did with McCoy, I ask myself what we don't already know about Spock. Amazingly, I quickly devise an answer. The last time, chronologically, that the character appeared in the *Star Trek* universe, he dwelled secretly on Romulus, working toward reunification of the ancestrally related Vulcans and Romulans. But how did he get there, and after being seen in *The Next Generation*'s two-part episode "Unification," what happened to him? Moreover, was there some way I could tie this into my notion of the crucible? As it turned out, yeah, there was.

So I wrote a long and detailed outline. It contained

complex politics, roaring action, and more than a little character exploration. In the end, I thought that I had constructed a pretty good story.

I then scrapped it.

After thinking about it for a while, and after mentioning some of my ideas to my valiant editor, Marco Palmieri— who had yet to receive the outline—I decided that my tale did not really fit in with celebrating the Original Series. Spock would be the main character, yes, and there would be a series of flashback scenes that took us back to Kirk and McCoy and the rest of the *Enterprise* crew, but still, it seemed wrong to set a *Star Trek* anniversary novel fundamentally in the *Next Generation* era.

So now what? Well, again I asked myself what I didn't know about Spock—and in particular, what did I not know about him from the series and films? I pondered the question for a while, mulled it over, cogitated about it, and then, as had happened with my exploration of McCoy, I saw something hiding in plain sight. Spock had done something in his life—something big—that remained completely unexplained. I wanted to explain it, but I didn't necessarily want to do so by looking at that precise event. Maybe, I thought, Spock could decide to do something big again, and I could then explore that, while at the same time harking back to the first big event, finding parallels between the two.

Okay, not bad. But would the notion of the crucible tie in? It did, and in a way I especially liked, one that would provide some significant overlap with the McCoy novel. Things really seemed to be falling into place.

Once more, I was off and running.

We shall not cease from exploration
And the end of all our exploring
Will be to arrive where we started
And know the place for the first time.
Through the unknown, unremembered gate
When the last of earth left to discover
Is that which was the beginning;
At the source of the longest river
The voice of the hidden waterfall
And the children in the apple-tree
Not known, because not looked for
But heard, half-heard, in the stillness
Between two waves of the sea.
Quick now, here, now, always—
A condition of complete simplicity
(Costing not less than everything)
And all shall be well and
All manner of thing shall be well
When the tongues of flame are in-folded
Into the crowned knot of fire
And the fire and the rose are one.

—T. S. Eliot,
Little Gidding, V

Leila: We're happy here. . . . I can't lose you now, Mister Spock.

Spock: I have a responsibility. . . . To this ship . . . to that man on the bridge. I am what I am, Leila, and if there are self-made purgatories, then we all have to live in them.

—"This Side of Paradise"

OVERTURE

Left of the Pointed Peaks

As he regained consciousness, his head pounded and he felt—

Nothing, Spock told himself, the thought by now reflexive. *I feel nothing.* Not emotionally, at least, though pain suffused his physique and fatigue clouded his intellect. The energy bolt that had slammed into him, that had evidently sent him sprawling unconscious to the floor, had left a residue of deep aches buried in his muscles and joints, and a fog of exhaustion blurring his thoughts. But he had no time even to will away his discomfort. Recalling the urgency of the situation, he would simply have to ignore the throes of soreness throughout his body, the mists of weariness throughout his mind.

Keeping his eyes closed for the moment, Spock sought to focus. When he'd done so sufficiently, he listened closely to the sounds of his surroundings. The low hum of the force field had gone, he noted. He heard no voices, no footsteps, no movement of any kind, except . . . there, near the limits of his perception . . . not here in the corridor, but somewhere nearby, the quiet rhythms of somebody breathing.

But not Mitchell, he thought. Spock recognized the pattern of slightly labored respiration and knew that it belonged not to the *Enterprise*'s mutated helmsman, but to the ship's elderly chief medical officer. He heard no one else.

Spock opened his eyes and saw the glow of the lighting panels in the ceiling above him. He pushed himself up from his supine position, his arms throbbing, his equilibrium slipping. He paused, clearing his mind by concentrating on a single set of sensations, that of the concrete—solid, porous, and cool—beneath his hands.

Ahead of him, what he could see of Mitchell's cell stood empty, the frame that edged the entryway and generated the confinement field now dark. Rising to his feet, Spock peered about the area, then moved into the makeshift brig that the *Enterprise*'s security staff had improvised here on Delta Vega. The small, rectangular room contained only a bed, a basin and mirror, and a lavatory. He saw no sign of Gary Mitchell—or of whatever the lieutenant commander had become—nor did he see Captain Kirk or Dr. Dehner, both of whom had been present when Mitchell had struck. Despite being imprisoned behind a force field, the increasingly powerful officer had attacked his jailers, creating and controlling a jagged web of energy, toppling first the captain and then Spock.

Now, as familiar footfalls approached, Spock walked back out into the corridor. There, he noticed also missing the phaser rifle he'd ordered sent down from the ship. He'd wanted to keep it on hand for defensive purposes in the event that Mitchell managed to escape his captivity. Unfortunately, though Spock had brought the weapon to bear, he'd been unable to fire before being knocked out.

Dr. Piper emerged into the corridor from around a corner. The grizzled, craggy-faced human carried his black medical bag on a strap across his shoulder. "Spock," he said, "when did you come to?" He swung his bag around in front of him and began looking through it.

"Just now," Spock said. "Have you seen the other members of the landing party? Or Mitchell?"

Piper peered up at Spock with a grave expression on his face. "Kelso's dead," he said, referring to the *Enterprise*'s first-shift navigator. "I found him in the control room, strangled with a length of cable."

A twinge of sadness rose within Spock, a reaction to the loss of life—particularly to the *unnecessary* loss of life—and he tamped it back down. Kelso had just finished leading an effort here at the automated lithium-cracking station to scavenge the equipment needed to patch and reenergize the *Enterprise*'s main drive enough to allow it to reach the nearest repair base. Along with the captain, Dr. Piper, Dr. Dehner, and Spock, the lieutenant composed the last of the landing parties still on the planet. The five officers had been on the verge of transporting back to the ship, stranding their prisoner here, when Mitchell had staged his assault.

"What about Captain Kirk and Doctor Dehner?" Spock asked.

Piper looked back down at his medical bag and extracted a small pouch from it. "When I came through the control room and saw Kelso, I spotted Gary and Doctor Dehner walking out across the valley, toward the left of the pointed peaks," he said. "After that, I found you and the captain here." He gestured down at the floor, then took a white pill from the pouch. Holding the medication out to Spock, he said, "I revived Captain Kirk and gave him one of these. You should take one too."

Spock accepted the pill, but did not at once ingest it. "Where is the captain now?" he asked.

"He took the phaser rifle and went after Gary," Piper said, and Spock noted that Mitchell must have become so powerful that he hadn't felt the need to commandeer the weapon, either to defend himself or to keep it from his pursuers. "The captain wanted me to wait until he'd gone before bringing you around. He left orders for us to go back to the *Enterprise* immediately. If you haven't heard from him in twelve hours, he wants you to take the ship to the nearest starbase and deliver his recommendation that this planet be blanketed with lethal doses of neutron radiation."

"Yes," Spock said, understanding Captain Kirk's rationale. Given Mitchell's growing strength and abilities, as well as his commensurate and amoral ambitions, he had to be stopped here, at the outskirts of the galaxy, far from any population centers. As Spock considered the situation, pain and weariness overtook his thoughts. The doctor must have noticed his momentary distraction, because he pointed at the pill he'd handed to the Vulcan.

"You really should take that," Piper said. "I know what you're experiencing. Whatever Gary hit you and the captain with, he hit me with it too."

"What is this?" Spock asked, holding up the pill.

"An analgesic combined with a mild stimulant," the doctor said. "It'll help you concentrate."

Spock placed the pill in his mouth and swallowed it. "How long has it been since Mitchell attacked us?" he asked.

"Ninety minutes," Piper said. "And it's been half that long since the captain came to and went after Gary and Doctor Dehner."

"Could you ascertain whether Mitchell took the doctor with him as a hostage?" Spock asked. It made sense that Dehner had been taken against her will, but because of her obvious interest in Mitchell—both in his transformation and on a personal level—Spock allowed that she might have gone along willingly.

"No, I couldn't tell," Piper said. "She was walking alongside him, but that doesn't mean that he wasn't forcing her to go with him."

Spock nodded, then pulled his communicator from where it hung at the back of his waist. When he unfolded the gold grille that functioned as antenna and activation control, the device chirped, indicating its functional status. "Spock to *Enterprise*," he said.

"I've been trying," Piper told him. "I can't get through." As though in confirmation of the doctor's assertion, the communicator emitted a burst of static. Spock closed the device and placed it back on his belt.

"In that case," he said, "since we are unable to follow the captain's orders and return to the ship—" Unexpectedly, his communicator beeped twice, signaling an incoming transmission. Retrieving it once more, he again opened the grille.

"Enterprise *to landing party*," came the voice of the ship's chief engineer. Fourth in the crew hierarchy, Lieutenant Commander Scott had been left in command with Kirk and Spock away from the ship and Mitchell relieved of duty. He sounded insistent and concerned.

"Spock here."

"*Mister Spock*," Scott said, a note of surprise in his tone. "*We've been trying to reach the landing party for more than an hour. Is everything all right?*"

"Negative," Spock replied. "Lieutenant Kelso has been killed. Mitchell has escaped and fled the lithium plant, taking Doctor Dehner with him, and Captain Kirk has gone in pursuit." Scott uttered a Gaelic oath. "Doctor Piper is here with me. Transport the two of us back to the ship at once."

"*Aye, sir,*" Scott said. "*Right away.*"

"Spock out." He replaced the communicator on his belt, his mind already turning to the task of utilizing the ship's sensors to search for both the captain and Mitchell. As he thought about what other actions he could take, the whine of the transporter grew in the corridor.

*   *   *

The sky burned.

Spock bent over the hooded sensor monitor at his sciences station and studied the dramatic atmospheric effects. A cavity cleft the ozone layer, he saw, allowing the ultraviolet rays of the Delta Vega sun to penetrate through to the troposphere and the planet's surface. But the perforation of the jacket of trivalent oxygen ensphering the world did not adequately explain the stratum of fiery matter hovering above the cloud cover.

Below it, he knew, Captain Kirk might already be dead.

Standing up straight, Spock looked toward the front of the *Enterprise* bridge at the main viewscreen. On it rotated the reddish brown planet about which the ship still orbited, the remote site of the uncrewed lithium facility, where years passed between visits by ore freighters. Bands of gray white clouds swept across the globe, and in one location, Spock could see the brilliant orange patch of plasma that floated in space above the valley containing the mining and processing plant.

Until four hours ago, the swath of superheated, ionized gas hadn't existed. According to Chief Engineer Scott, he'd been on the bridge, speaking via communicator with Lieutenant Kelso, when the phenomenon had spontaneously manifested. Scott had lost contact with Kelso, and his subsequent efforts to reach the other members of the landing party had also failed, blocked by the sheet of plasma, until finally he'd gotten through to Spock. At that time, the blaze of ions, free electrons, and neutral atoms had receded just enough to allow communications and transporter operation between the *Enterprise* and the ore station. As soon as Spock and Piper had beamed aboard, though, the mass of plasma had expanded back into place, shrouding the entire valley.

In light of those events, Spock concluded that Mitchell's abilities had developed to include the creation and manipulation of the obstructive matter in the atmosphere. If so, then the erstwhile helmsman likely had for some reason allowed Spock and Piper to transport up to the ship, though it appeared that he would not permit any of the crew to beam back down. In addition, the interference produced by the plasma prevented them from employing sensors to locate Mitchell, then transporting him from the surface of the planet and into whatever new prison they could construct for him—or into the lethal environment of space. Neither could they track the captain and Dr. Dehner in order to initiate their rescue.

Spock sat down at his sciences station and turned toward the communications console. "Mister Alden," he said, "has there been any change in the intensity of the interference?"

"There's been some fluctuation, sir," Alden said, his hand going to the silver receiver protruding from his left ear. "But not enough to allow our instruments to break through."

Spock considered this, wondering whether Mitchell needed a constant effort to preserve the plasma field, or if once established, it sustained itself. "Continue attempting to reach the captain," he told Alden. Spock looked back toward the main viewer, deciding what preparations to make. Captain Kirk's last orders, delivered through Dr. Piper, had been clear, but with the captain having been gone for hours, Spock needed to ready the crew for various contingencies.

This entire situation had begun when the ship had essentially followed in the path of the *S.S. Valiant*, an Earth vessel lost two centuries earlier, its commanding officer apparently ordering its destruction after it had encountered an unpredicted energy barrier at the edge of the galaxy. The *Enterprise*'s own trip through the unexplained field had left the main engines down, nine of the crew dead, and two others—Mitchell and Dr. Elizabeth Dehner—struck by some sort of charge. When Dehner, a psychiatrist assigned to the ship to study crew reactions in emergency conditions, had recovered, she'd seemed unaffected. Mitchell, on the other hand, had acquired a strange, silvery glow in his eyes, a radically amplified mental capacity, the facilities of telepathy and telekinesis, and the ability to generate bolts of electrical energy that he could wield as weapons. Perhaps more significantly, as his powers had continued to increase at an exponential pace, his personality had shifted from that of a fun-loving but capable Starfleet officer to that of a megalomaniac. He'd spoken of *using* worlds and of squashing his crewmates as he could insects. Spock had quickly determined that he would have to be stopped. Since then, Mitchell's words and actions had served only to buttress that judgment.

Spock reached across his panel and keyed open an intercom circuit. "Bridge to hangar deck," he said.

"Hangar deck," responded the member of the crew presently stationed there. *"Fields here."*

"Spock here, Mister Fields," he said. "Prepare the shuttlecraft *Darwin* for launch. Contact the armory and have them outfit the cabin with phaser rifles for a crew of six."

"Yes, sir," Fields said.

"Bridge out," Spock said, then toggled the channel closed. He did not at this moment intend to lead a rescue party down to the planet, as that would contravene Captain Kirk's orders. Still, with no means of determining the current status of Mitchell or the captain, Spock realized that he might have to act at a moment's notice. It would better serve to be as prepared as possible for such an alternative.

After the *Enterprise*'s damaging voyage through the energy barrier at the rim of the galaxy, Spock had counseled

Captain Kirk to take the ship to Delta Vega, for the dual purposes of recovering the main drive systems and stranding Mitchell on the unpopulated world. When the captain had initially refused to take such an action with respect to the helmsman, Spock had asserted that the only reasonable alternative would be to kill Mitchell. The captain had reacted sharply to that, even imploring Spock to *feel* for their shipmate, or at least to behave as though he did. Ultimately, though, Kirk had relented, choosing to intern his friend of a decade and a half at the ore facility while the crew repaired the *Enterprise,* then to maroon him there when the ship departed. According to Dr. Piper, when he'd begun his unaccompanied hunt for Mitchell, the captain had taken himself to task for allowing him to escape.

Since then, Spock and the crew had worked to find a means of counteracting the plasma cloud and the interference it caused. Among other efforts, they'd searched for points of minimum density, adjusted the modulation of both communications and sensor carrier waves, boosted the gain of each, and attempted to reflect off both water vapor in the air and rock formations on the ground, all without result. Spock had contemplated slicing through the ionized gas with the ship's phasers, but hadn't wanted to risk incinerating everything below it—including the captain and Dr. Dehner.

Dexterously operating the controls at his sciences station, Spock performed another scan of the plasma sheet, seeking out weaknesses in it. As he did so, he thought about the advice he had given to Captain Kirk—namely that he should execute his own closest friend. Spock remained convinced that the danger Mitchell posed could be neutralized only via his death, and yet he now found himself conflicted for having advocated such a view. He held respect for life as an axiomatic core of his personal philos-

ophy—and of morality in general—and he knew that the
captain did as well. But where Spock experienced no emotions, Captain Kirk did. For Spock, the decision that
Mitchell's life should be ended, like any decision, had
been derived by substituting the facts of the situation into a
virtual equation measuring the common good. He had not
had to factor out—or simply proceed in the face of—feelings of sorrow and regret, as the captain no doubt had.

Is there another way? Spock asked himself. He'd originally thought that abandoning the ship's second officer
on Delta Vega and then quarantining the system would
provide a solution, but as the breadth and depth of
Mitchell's superhuman powers had grown, that had become less likely. Now, with the mutated officer's demonstrated abilities—

On the display before him, the readings of the atmosphere above the valley changed abruptly. Numbers indicating massive temperatures, altered pressures, disrupted
wind flows, all fell in an instant back to within their normally expected ranges. Spock stood up and leaned down
to peer into his sensor monitor. The sheath of plasma had
vanished.

"Mister Spock," said Lieutenant Alden. "We're receiving an incoming transmission from Captain Kirk."

Spock straightened and turned toward the communications console. "On speaker," he ordered. Alden worked
his panel and a second later the captain's voice sounded
on the bridge.

"Enterprise," he said, and then he breathed slowly and
heavily, as though from exhaustion. *"From Captain Kirk.
Come in."*

Spock pressed a button on his console to tie in to the
captain's channel. "Spock here," he said. "Are you all
right, Captain?"

"Affirmative," Kirk said, still breathing in gulps of air. *"Gary and Doctor Dehner . . . are dead."* In the hesitation, Spock heard not only the captain's fatigue, but his emotional turmoil. *"Beam me back home."*

Now Spock hesitated. While he believed Captain Kirk, armed with a phaser rifle, could have killed Mitchell, and while that death might explain the disappearance of the plasma field, Spock had to be sure. "Captain," he said, "I would like your permission to perform sensor scans of the surface before transporting you up to the ship." He did not need to detail the obvious, namely that Mitchell's new-found abilities might well be allowing him to impersonate Captain Kirk. Before Spock permitted anybody to return to the *Enterprise,* he wanted to ensure that he would not be providing a masquerading Mitchell a means of fleeing Delta Vega—and worse, a means of reaching inhabited worlds.

"Understood," the captain said. *"I'll remain in my current location."*

"Acknowledged," Spock said.

"Kirk out," the captain said.

Spock addressed the communications officer once more. "Mister Alden," he said, "feed the coordinates of the transmission's source to the sciences console."

"Aye, sir," Alden said, and he began operating his controls.

Spock closed the channel on which he'd just spoken, then opened an intercom circuit. "Bridge to sickbay," he said.

"Sickbay, Piper here," came the reply.

"Doctor, report to the bridge at once," Spock said.

"I'm on my way," Piper said.

Spock signed off and closed the channel, then bent in toward his sensor monitor again. He would scan the planet's surface for Captain Kirk, as well as for the dead bodies of

Mitchell and Dehner. When Piper arrived, the doctor would be able to examine the captain's readings and determine their veracity. Even with Mitchell's powers, Spock didn't think he would be able to perfectly mimic Captain Kirk's cellular pattern.

Relieved but still cautious, Spock worked the sensor controls and began his own analysis.

Standing beside the sciences station, Spock observed Crewman Tamboline run through the diagnostic routine. Currently a second-class petty officer in the ship's services group, Tamboline had recently requested transfer into the sciences division. Captain Kirk had approved the application and Spock had taken on the task of training the young man.

In the command chair, the captain ordered the *Enterprise* away from Delta Vega and onward to Starbase 20. Spock looked toward the center of the bridge and saw Chief Engineer Scott, currently substituting for the vanquished Lieutenant Commander Mitchell, work the helm controls to send the ship onto its new course. As the impulse engines delivered a familiar thrum through the decking, the image of the planet disappeared at the bottom of the main viewscreen, leaving an open starfield ahead.

Other than the monotonous beating of the sublight drive and the occasional clicks and beeps of other equipment, the bridge remained relatively quiet, doubtless a reflection of the crew's somber mood. The captain had returned to the ship a day earlier, effectively bearing with him the news of the deaths of Lee Kelso, Gary Mitchell, and Elizabeth Dehner. Coming on the heels of the nine officers who had perished last week at the galactic rim, these latest losses had deeply affected many of the already traumatized crew. When Spock had taken his midday meal in the mess hall earlier today, he'd noted a decided moroseness among those present. Although last week's deaths had clearly impacted the crew at the time, the breakdown of the *Enterprise*'s main drive and the fantastic changes to Mitchell had provided unavoidable distractions. Now, though, with an extended period of inactivity as the ship headed to Starbase 20 for additional repairs, the crew had little to divert them from their grief.

Spock watched as the captain reached up with his bandaged right hand, a white cast running from the bases of his fingertips down past his wrist. Kirk switched on the microphone perched at the end of a semirigid metal cord that ran up from the side of the command chair. "Captain's log, stardate thirteen-thirteen-point-eight," he said. "Add to official losses Doctor Elizabeth Dehner. Be it noted she gave her life in performance of her duty." His voice sounded steady, matching the even demeanor he'd displayed since transporting up from Delta Vega. During the days of Mitchell's metamorphosis, Spock had noted signs of strain in the captain, but since being forced by circumstance to kill his closest friend by his own hand, Kirk actually appeared more settled. The control of emotion, whether internal or merely external, impressed Spock.

After glancing at the sciences station to verify Tamboline's ongoing diagnostic, Spock moved down from the raised periphery of the bridge and down to the lower, central section. He passed in front of Yeoman Smith, who stood behind and to the right of where the captain sat. As Spock reached the side of the command chair, Kirk completed his log entry. "Lieutenant Commander Gary Mitchell, same notation," he said, then switched off the recorder. "I want his service record to end that way," Captain Kirk told Spock, obviously speaking of Mitchell. "He didn't ask for what happened to him."

A pang of guilt darted through Spock's mind. The feeling itself disquieted him. After all his years learning and practicing Vulcan meditation and control techniques, he still had not fully mastered the restraint of his emotions. At the same time, he found an immediate use for his unwanted remorse. "I felt for him too," he admitted, recognizing the truth of the captain's assertion, namely that Mitchell had done nothing to warrant his fate. Spock also wanted to demonstrate his support for Kirk in what surely must be a difficult time for him.

"I believe there's some hope for you after all, Mister Spock," the captain said.

Spock glanced at him and allowed the corners of his mouth to curl up slightly. He felt no humor, nor did he find the content of Kirk's statement complimentary, but he did appreciate what he perceived as the captain's intent. Kirk had several times responded heatedly to Spock's suggestions on how to deal with Mitchell, and his words in this context seemed clearly meant to acknowledge the appropriateness and value of those suggestions.

As Spock regarded the main viewscreen, the captain said, "Take us to warp three when we've cleared the system, Mister Scott."

"Aye, sir," the engineer said from the helm.

Spock turned and headed back toward the sciences station, where he resumed his tutelage of Crewman Tamboline. A short time later, the throb of the impulse engines gave way to that of the warp drive as the *Enterprise* sped toward Starbase 20. The bridge personnel remained silent.

Spock exited the turbolift and walked through the unusually quiet *Enterprise* corridor. With the ship in dry dock, undergoing further repairs to the warp engines, the sounds and vibrations normally generated by the drive systems had now fallen silent and still. As well, many of the crew had taken advantage of the downtime to embark on shore leave on Vellurius, the planet about which Starbase 20 orbited. On his way here from main engineering, Spock had encountered only a single crewmember, Dr. Noel, who, judging from her civilian attire and the duffel slung over her shoulder, had appeared headed off the ship herself.

Spock arrived at his destination, cabin 3F 121. He pressed the button beside the door and heard the buzzer beyond the light blue panel, signaling his presence. "Come," he heard Captain Kirk say. Spock stepped forward and the door slid open before him.

"You wanted to see me, sir," he said as the door whispered closed.

"Yes, Mister Spock," Kirk said from where he sat at his desk. A data slate lay before him and he clutched a stylus in his hand. "I've just received a communication from Admiral Hahn." Mattea Hahn, Spock knew, currently served as chief of Starfleet Operations, the branch responsible for monitoring and supervising, distributing and coordinating, all ship and starbase activities and movements. "Because of the damage to the *Enterprise*'s warp drive and the extensive repairs still needed, she's decided that now is the appropriate time for the ship to put in for refit." During the course of the last few months, two other starships—the *Constellation* and the *Defiant*—had already undergone this latest overhaul of the *Constitution*-class vessels, which included improvements to the bridge module, science labs, and propulsion systems. "We're to travel to the Antares Fleet Yards, where the work is scheduled to take twenty-four days."

"I presume, then, that we are to spend less time here at Starbase Twenty than initially expected," Spock said.

"Yes," the captain said. "Just enough time for Mister Scott and his engineers to get the ship spaceworthy enough to make the long journey to Antares safely."

"I will consult with Mister Scott on how long those repairs will take," Spock said, anticipating the needs mandated by the change in plans. "I will ensure that the crew are made aware of the revised itinerary."

"Thank you, Mister Spock," Kirk said. "And let everybody know that they'll be able to take additional shore leave at some point during the refit."

"Yes, sir," Spock said. "Is there anything else?"

Kirk glanced down at the data slate in front of him, then back up at Spock. "Actually, there is," he said. Spock waited for the captain to continue. After a few seconds, Kirk looked back down at the slate. "I've been trying to write a letter to Gary's parents," he said. "They live on Earth, so I'm not sure when I'll get to see them next. Starfleet will send somebody to inform them in person about what happened, but . . ." He let his words trail off into silence.

"I understand," Spock offered.

Kirk looked up again. "Do you?" he asked. The question did not seem rhetorical, but Kirk went on without allowing an opportunity for a response. "Have a seat, Mister Spock," he said, gesturing toward the chair on the other side of the desk.

Spock crossed the cabin and sat down opposite the captain. "Sir?" he said.

"You know that Gary and I were friends for fifteen years," Kirk said. "We met at the academy, then served together aboard the *Republic* and the *Constitution*. I requested that he be assigned to the *Enterprise* as my second officer." He paused, his manner wistful. Spock waited, conscious of the toll that recent events must have taken—

must still be taking—on the captain. "You're aware of all that, aren't you?" Kirk asked.

"I am," Spock said.

Kirk regarded him for a long moment, then peered down at the stylus in his hand. He fiddled with the pointed writing instrument, turning it end over end, before finally setting it down atop the data slate. When he looked up again, he said, "As Gary began to change, most of my officers advised caution. Doctor Dehner even believed that his mutations, his powers, might be a good thing, might possibly lead to a better, advanced sort of human. But you, Mister Spock, you suggested something well beyond caution. You told me that I should either maroon my best friend on an uninhabited planet, or kill him."

Spock didn't know how to characterize the statement. The captain had delivered his assertion in a matter-of-fact fashion, but his words seemed as though they might have carried with them the hint of an accusation. A week removed from slaying Mitchell, did Kirk now suffer regret for what he'd done, and did he blame Spock for that? "After evaluating the circumstances, I provided you with the best counsel I could," Spock said evenly. "That is a requirement of my position as the ship's first officer."

"Yes, it is," Kirk agreed. He stood up and paced out from behind his desk. When he reached the corner of the cabin, he turned and addressed Spock. "Did you know that Captain Pike personally recommended you to be my exec?"

"I did not know that specifically," Spock said, "but I do not find the information surprising." He had served under Christopher Pike for more than a decade, during a series of exploratory missions aboard the *Enterprise*. By the time that Pike had been promoted to fleet captain and left the ship, Spock had risen to the dual stations of chief science officer and third in command.

"He spoke very highly of you," Kirk said. "He described you as extremely intelligent, capable, trustworthy, dedicated." Spock bowed his head in acknowledgment of Captain Pike's positive assessment. For his part, Spock held Pike in high esteem. "He also told me that you used to smile, widely and often."

Spock felt an eyebrow arch upward at the unexpected comment. A dozen years after the fact, he hadn't anticipated that this issue would arise. "Yes," he acknowledged. "When I was first assigned to the *Enterprise,* I did sometimes smile."

"But you don't really do that in the same way now," Kirk said.

"No," Spock said. The topic discomfited him, the subject matter of a relatively personal character.

"Why?" Kirk asked.

"Captain, I intend no disrespect," Spock said, "but may I ask the purpose of your inquiry?"

Kirk walked back across the room and stood beside the desk. "I have my reasons," he said, though not in a challenging way. "You and I have served together now for more than a year, and on many occasions, I've heard you proclaim your Vulcan nature. More than that, you've explicitly denied your human half. But smiling in the manner that Captain Pike described implies feeling behind it, and that would seem to fly in the face of such assertions."

"People certainly could have inferred emotion as the cause of my smiling," Spock said, "and I know that some did. It was primarily for that reason that I stopped."

"But why did you start?" Kirk asked.

Spock took a breath. "When I attended Starfleet Academy, almost all of my time outside of coursework I spent at the Vulcan compound in Sausalito. When I was posted to the *Enterprise,* I was the only Vulcan among the crew, and one of only seven nonhumans aboard. In my initial attempt to integrate with my shipmates, I chose to emulate some aspects of human behavior, including smiling."

"I see," Kirk said. He swung back around his desk and sat down again. "When we were on Delta Vega, I asked you why you thought you were right about Gary's mindset when Doctor Dehner, a trained psychiatrist, had come to a different conclusion. You contended that it was because she had feelings and you don't, that all you know is logic."

"I do believe that Doctor Dehner's emotions clouded her professional judgment," Spock said.

"As do I," the captain said. "But my point isn't about the doctor; it's about you. After I returned to the ship from Delta Vega, after Gary had been killed, you told me that you felt for him." The captain paused, seemingly to emphasize what he said next. "'Felt,' Mister Spock. That was the word you used."

The captain's display of logic—deftly linking together two incidents years apart, presumably in order to draw a conclusion—startled Spock. He could not deny Kirk's observation, but neither did he wish to discuss it. The captain must have perceived Spock's reticence on the subject as he did not pursue an explanation for the latter behavior.

"I don't need to know why you said what you did the other day," Kirk told him, "but I want *you* to know that on this ship, under my command, you never need to pretend that you're something you're not. I know that during this incident I urged you to try to feel for Gary, or at least act like you did. For that, I apologize."

"Thank you, Captain," Spock said. Once again, Kirk had surprised him. Though a decisive, action-oriented commander, he also appeared capable of balanced self-examination.

"I might still joke with you about emotions, Mister Spock," Kirk went on, "but I expect nothing from you other than that you prosecute your responsibilities to the best of your abilities." The captain leaned forward on the desk, once more plucking the stylus from atop the slate. "To that end, I want to recognize and thank you for your recent efforts. I didn't want to hear your recommendations about Gary, but they were the right ones. If you hadn't made them when you did, I don't know that I would've been able to . . . to do what had to be done when the time came."

"I did not make those recommendations lightly," Spock said, essentially pointing out that a lack of emotion did not imply a lack of consideration.

"Of course you didn't," Kirk said. "We've served together long enough for me to know that you perform your duties with great care." He leaned back in his chair, tossing the stylus back up onto the desk. "In fact, I'm going to need a good first officer now more than ever. Being as close to Gary as I was, I used to talk to him a great deal. Even if he didn't have your scientific acumen or the ability to provide insight on as wide a range of subjects as you, he did know me. And sometimes I didn't need his counsel anyway; just talking with him allowed me to better observe my own decisions, to pinpoint their weaknesses or confirm their strengths, but now . . ." He shrugged.

"I will endeavor to provide whatever support you need," Spock said. In his time aboard the *Enterprise* under Kirk's command, he had witnessed firsthand the friendship between the captain and Gary Mitchell. While Spock had never judged himself underutilized as the ship's second-in-command, he'd always understood that

Mitchell afforded Kirk a valuable resource. It made sense from a command perspective that, with his friend now gone, the captain would look elsewhere to replace that presence.

"Thank you, Mister Spock," Kirk said.

"Is there anything else, Captain?" Spock asked.

"Not unless you want to write to Gary's parents for me," Kirk said, tapping the base of the slate with one finger.

"If you would like me to compose a draft," Spock said, "I can certainly do so."

"No," the captain said. "Thank you, but no. I wasn't serious."

"I see," Spock said, then added, "I did not understand."

"Yes, well, that'll be all then," Kirk said.

Spock rose from his chair and strode out of the captain's cabin. As he headed to find Mr. Scott, he considered all that Captain Kirk had just said to him. During the thirteen months they'd so far served together aboard the *Enterprise,* the two men had, in Spock's estimation, worked well together. With recent events, though, and in light of the conversation just past, Spock thought that perhaps he and the captain had now come to a deeper understanding of each other, and to a deeper trust.

So thinking, he entered a turbolift on deck five, on his way to main engineering.

I

The Unimaginable Zero

Midwinter spring is its own season
Sempiternal though sodden towards sundown,
Suspended in time, between pole and tropic.
When the short day is brightest, with frost and fire,
The brief sun flames the ice, on pond and ditches,
In windless cold that is the heart's heat,
Reflecting in a watery mirror
A glare that is blindness in the early afternoon.
And glow more intense than blaze of branch, or
    brazier,
Stirs the dumb spirit: no wind, but pentecostal fire
In the dark time of the year. Between melting and
    freezing
The soul's sap quivers. There is no earth smell
Or smell of living thing. This is the spring time
But not in time's covenant. Now the hedgerow
Is blanched for an hour with transitory blossom
Of snow, a bloom more sudden
Than that of summer, neither budding nor fading,
Not in the scheme of generation.
Where is the summer, the unimaginable
Zero summer?

—T. S. Eliot,
Little Gidding, I

ONE

The transparent-sided lift glided soundlessly upward along an outer wall of the steel and glass tower. About the gleaming edifice sprawled Pil Stornom, the second most populous city on Rigel IV and the seat of the planetary government. High- and low-rise buildings vied with each other for their footings amid abundant parklands, all surrounding the red-tinted waters of the lake situated at the center of the modern metropolis. Under a heavy sky, citizens and visitors strode along pedestrian thoroughfares, while airpods darted about over their heads.

Spock had traveled here from Earth aboard the *U.S.S. Farragut*. He'd arrived yesterday, in time for a meeting today with Lanitow Irizal, the director of the Federation's Bureau of Interplanetary Affairs. Irizal himself had requested Spock's presence at the agency's headquarters, presumably so that the Vulcan could clarify or expand his testimony regarding the recent plot to assassinate the heads of state of both the Klingon Empire and the United Federation of Planets. Together with Captains Kirk and Sulu and the crews of the *Enterprise* and the *Excelsior*, Spock had helped thwart the conspiracy ultimately intended to maintain military tensions in the Alpha and Beta Quadrants. He had already been debriefed on several occasions by members of Starfleet Command and the Federation Council, with and without various combinations of his former shipmates by his side.

As rain began to spatter against the sides of the lift, Spock thought of his old crewmates—and in particular of

Captain Kirk. After the Khitomer affair, the decades-old
Enterprise had been decommissioned, at which time its
command crew had stood down from the ship together.
Most of them had then moved on to other tours of duty:
Dr. McCoy to Starfleet Medical, Uhura to Starfleet Intelligence, and Chekov to a ground assignment while awaiting
an opening for a ship's first officer. Mr. Scott had decided
to retire, acquiring a boat with the intention of leaving
Earth and settling in the Norpin Colony. And Captain
Kirk . . . to the surprise of virtually all of the captain's
friends, he too had chosen to retire. He'd spoken of the
overpoliticization of Starfleet, an opinion that Spock himself had fomented by volunteering the captain to meet the
Klingon chancellor's ship and accompany it into Federation space.

Jim had left Starfleet once before, thirteen years ago,
after the completion of the *Enterprise*'s mission to the
Aquarius Formation. Back then, none of the people who'd
known the captain had completely understood his pur-
ported reasons for retirement, nor had they believed that it
would last. It had taken four years and a failed romance,
but Jim had returned to the service, and eventually to the
bridge of a starship. Now, many of the captain's friends
believed that pattern would repeat, but such certainty did
not infuse Spock. The last time he'd seen Jim, at a hearing
last month before a trio of admirals investigating the conspiracy, Spock had perceived in his friend a deep and
abiding melancholy. Such an emotion had long been an
aspect of the captain's personality—and another thing to
which Spock had long ago contributed—but Dr. McCoy
had recently revealed that Jim had begun engaging in extremely hazardous pursuits: rappelling the Crystalline
Trench, diving the Alandros Caves, rafting down lava
flows. The combination of despondence and daredevilry

concerned Spock. Though he didn't know right now what he would say, he thought that he should seek Jim out soon and speak with him.

Outside the lift, Spock saw that the dark clouds that had blown in over the city this morning had fully opened up. Drops of precipitation beat down on the roof with a staccato rhythm as the car finally eased to a halt at the seventy-eighth floor, just three stories shy of the observation deck that topped the skyscraper. After straightening his uniform, Spock stepped out of the lift into a large reception area, the space decorated in earthy tones and adorned with numerous sculptures and paintings. He recognized the style of one carving as that of the artists in the New Dakar settlement on Ophiuchus III, and distinguished a canvas executed in oils as the work of Lura bn Zel from the planet Pandro. Spock gathered that all of the art had been collected from a variety of worlds, a symbolic expression of the BIA's charter to foster interaction and cooperation among far-flung civilizations.

At the far end of the side walls, doorways opened into corridors leading away from the foyer. Between them, opposite the lift, arced a large desk of ash-colored wood, behind which perched a Rigelian Chelonoid. Spock approached the bipedal reptilian, who had the gray-green hide, a blunt beak, and large, dark eyes characteristic of the species. Behind the Chelonoid hung a pair of banners. The one on the left displayed the seal of the Federation, a brace of stylized wheat stalks bracketing a circular starfield, white symbols on a navy blue background. On the right, a burgundy extent carried the emblem of the Bureau of Interplanetary Affairs, yellow-orange stars interconnected by a lattice of elegant, tapering curves.

"May I help you?" the receptionist asked in a low, hissing voice, nictitating membranes sweeping across his eyes as he peered up at Spock. At the front of the desk, what appeared to be a block of murinite had been engraved with the name TELSK. Spock identified himself and the object of his visit, then submitted to security scans of both his retina and his palm. After verifying his appointment, Telsk contacted Irizal's assistant, Rinsit. Another Chelonoid, Rinsit appeared in the reception area a moment later and ushered Spock through several corridors to the director's office.

Inside, Irizal stood from where he sat at a large desk, atop which lay the slender forms of half a dozen data slates, as well as a bulky tome spread open to a pair of densely printed pages. Past him, a glass wall presented an impressive vista of the city, currently shrouded in gray by the day's weather. Bookshelves lined the other three sides of the office, and Spock noted a sizable number of the bindings lettered in languages other than Federation Standard.

Irizal strode out from behind the desk to greet Spock, offering a bow of his head as he stopped before him. "Thank you so much for coming, Captain Spock," the director said. Though small in stature, he spoke with a deep, resonant voice. A native of Altair VI, he could be visually discriminated from a human only by the number of digits—six—on each hand.

Spock bowed his head in return. "It is my duty as a Federation citizen, and I am gratified to provide whatever assistance the Bureau of Interplanetary Affairs requests of me," he said.

The director laughed, a sharp, loud sound—"Ha!"—and said, "I certainly hope that's true."

"Indeed," Spock said, somewhat nonplussed by Irizal's reaction. "I would not have made the journey here otherwise."

"Of course, of course," the director said. "But you

might want to wait to find out what the BIA is asking of you before you agree to it."

"Given the present situation between Earth and Qo'noS, and the diplomatic nature of the bureau's work," Spock said, "I surmised that I was invited here to provide further context and detail about the assassination of Chancellor Gorkon and the attempt on President Ra-ghoratreii."

"Ah, I see," Irizal said. "That makes sense." He waved a hand toward an inner corner of the office, to a circular table surrounded by a quartet of chairs. "Why don't we have a seat and I can explain my reason for asking you here?"

Spock padded across the room and sat down. As he did so, he examined a platter perched on the tabletop, and which contained an assortment of sliced fruits and cheeses. He saw hourglass-shaped wedges of *soltar*, a red-skinned stone fruit indigenous to Vulcan, as well as prepared rolls of *gespar*, a traditional staple of Vulcan morning meals. Beside the platter, a ceramic pot offered up the scent of spice tea, yet another fare of his world.

"Please help yourself, Captain," Irizal said. He picked up a pair of small plates and placed one before Spock and the other before himself. "May I offer you a cup of tea?"

"Please," Spock said. He had stayed overnight at the Starfleet facility in the prefecture of Ankanner and it had taken him longer than he'd expected this morning to find a suitable location for his outdoor meditation, leaving him no time for a meal. As Irizal poured out two cups of the steaming russet-hued beverage, Spock reached to the platter and selected several pieces of fruit for his plate. Even if he had not just been told that he had been called here for a reason other than to discuss the recent conspiracy, he would have understood that now. Though he had never been ill-treated when speaking as a witness to those events, neither had he been indulged so.

After the director had finished serving the tea and taking some victuals for himself, he sat down and faced Spock. "I have to tell you, Captain, that I and others here at the BIA were most impressed by your performance as a Federation special envoy." Several months ago, a combination of over-production and insufficient safety standards at the Klingons' primary energy production facility on Praxis had resulted in a massive explosion. Half of the moon had been obliterated, sending poisonous fallout into the atmosphere of Qo'noS, the Klingon homeworld. With so much of the empire's resources committed to military operations, it did not possess the means to combat the calamity. At the urging of his father—who happened to be the Vulcan ambassador—and authorized by both the Federation Council and Starfleet Command, Spock had succeeded in initiating a dialogue with Chancellor Gorkon. Ultimately, the goal had been the negotiation of a lasting peace between the two powers, thus allowing the Klingons to manage the consequences wrought by the destruction of Praxis without having to sacrifice their security. Even after all that had subsequently taken place, those talks continued, driven by the empire's new chancellor, Azetbur.

"I was fortunate to find in Gorkon a receptive audience," Spock said. "He was a leader who comprehended and appreciated the value of peaceful coexistence even to the warrior culture of his people."

"Yes, I've read your reports about him," Irizal said. "Gorkon seemed like a remarkable figure. Nevertheless, your own efforts should not be minimized."

"Nor have they been," Spock said. As he sipped at his tea—slightly sweet, with a satisfying graininess to it—he recalled the commendation bestowed upon him by the Federation Council for his efforts, and the personal gratitude extended to him by the Federation president.

Irizal popped a cube of pale yellow cheese into his mouth. After he swallowed it, he said, "I understand that, after serving as envoy and completing your service aboard the *Enterprise,* you accepted a position with Starfleet Academy."

"I train cadets in certain areas of shipboard duty," Spock explained, "but my position as instructor falls under the aegis of Starfleet proper."

"I see," Irizal said. "I know that you've been a member of Starfleet for many years, Captain, but have you ever considered moving on from there, taking on new responsibilities and new challenges?"

"I have," Spock said. "I am continually reflecting on the choices I have made and the actions I have taken in my life. For right now, obviously, I have decided on this course."

Irizal nodded and took a bite out of a section of *soltar.* Spock chose an item from his own plate and ate it. "You are clearly satisfied with your current position," the director said after a moment, "but I've invited you here to Rigel to offer you an alternative."

"That has become clear to me," Spock said. "In what post do you envision me?"

"Federation ambassador," Irizal said.

The proposal intrigued Spock, but it also surprised him. Though he acknowledged that he had conducted himself proficiently during his brief tenure as a special envoy, and that he had accomplished the objective of opening peace talks with the notably recalcitrant Klingon authorities, he also knew that his education and experience had come in other areas. "I am a scientist and a Starfleet officer," he told Irizal. "I am not a diplomat."

"Aren't you?" the director asked. "I know that you've never formally trained in interplanetary relations, but after your commerce with Gorkon, I requested your service record from Starfleet. In the more than three decades you spent aboard the *Enterprise,* you participated in quite a number of diplomatic affairs, including the most demanding of such efforts, first contact."

"That is true," Spock said. From his earliest years as a science officer under Captain Pike's command, he had taken part in landing parties that had encountered alien species previously unknown to the Federation. Serving aboard Captain Kirk's *Enterprise,* that had continued to be the case, but in his additional position as the ship's executive officer, Spock had also been required at times to act in a political capacity.

"In addition to that," Irizal noted with a smile, "you would seem to have the pedigree for this sort of work." He clearly alluded to Sarek.

"The fact that my father has served with distinction for many years as the Vulcan ambassador is insufficient justification upon which to forecast my own performance in a similar role," Spock said. "Not only is there no genetic basis for the inheritance of diplomatic skills, but I have also learned very little from Sarek's experience since he and I have spent scant time together in the past forty years, and even less time discussing such matters."

"Forgive me, Captain Spock," the director said. "I see your point. I intended no offense."

"I have taken none," Spock said. "If I were to accept an ambassadorial position, to which planet would I be assigned?"

"Actually, in view of the breadth of your dealings with other cultures and how accustomed you are to frequent travel," Irizal said, "I envision your role as an ambassador at large. Your missions would be predicated on where you're most needed. President Ra-ghoratreii actually recommended you for the post, and after due consideration, I couldn't agree more. Last week, I informed him that I would be making this offer to you."

"Interesting," Spock said. The director and the president had considered their proposal well: the idea of conducting discussions with a multiplicity of societies appealed to Spock far more then the notion of being posted to one particular world.

"'Interesting,' as in you'd like to take the position?" Irizal asked.

"'Interesting,' meaning that your offer has provoked my attention and aroused my curiosity," Spock said.

"Then you'll consider it?" the director asked with obvious enthusiasm.

"I will," Spock said. He had never seriously considered pursuing such a career, but now that the opportunity had arisen, he would do himself a disservice if he did not grant it due deliberation.

"Excellent," Irizal said. "I'm sure you have questions, and I'd be happy to answer them, but I wonder if you'd like to see some of the missions on which the BIA would think about sending you, should you accept a position with us in the near term."

"That might prove illuminating," Spock said.

"Let me get the information," Irizal said, pushing his chair back and rising. He retrieved each of the six slates from atop his desk and carried them back to the table, where he picked one out and handed it over to Spock. "I don't know if you're familiar with the Frunalians," the director said.

"I am aware of their existence," Spock said, "but little else."

"I think you'll find them an intriguing people," Irizal said. "They have a science-oriented society, but also engage in institutionalized ritual, primarily with respect to a physical, mental, and emotional metamorphosis that every individual undergoes during their adult life. They call the process of transformation 'the Shift.'"

"Fascinating," Spock said. He peered at the display of the slate he now held. On it, he saw a city essentially hewn from solid rock. In the amethyst sky above it hung a colorfully banded world, the great sphere encircled by a planetary ring system.

"That's Orelt," the director said, jabbing a finger toward the slate. "The home of the Frunalians. It's a moon in orbit of a gas giant."

"And what would be the purpose of sending an ambassador there?" Spock asked.

"Our aims would be twofold," Irizal said. "First, we want to continue fostering a positive and open relationship between the Frunalians and the Federation. Second, surveys of the innermost planet in their star system reveal a field of stable rubindium. We'd like to negotiate for the rights to mine it." Discoveries of rubindium isotopes with a half-life greater than just a few milliseconds occurred infrequently, Spock knew. He asked several questions about the geologic find and then posed many more about the Frunalians themselves.

After that, Director Irizal moved on to the details of the other missions for which he believed Spock particularly suited. They spoke for the rest of the afternoon, about the Scalosian resettlement and the Treaty of Sirius, about the Alonis and the Romulans and the Otevrel. They talked of medical and scientific aid, of mutual defense pacts, of entente and détente.

Three hours later, Spock walked out of the headquarters of the Bureau of Interplanetary Affairs, no longer a Starfleet officer, but a Federation ambassador.

TWO

2267

The *Enterprise* trembled.

Captain James T. Kirk sat in the command chair at the center of the bridge, concerned for the safety of his ship and crew. Nearly a week ago, as they'd surveyed unexplored space, long-range sensors had recorded an aberrant and inexplicable reading. The crew had investigated the source of the anomaly to discover a fluctuation in the very fabric of the space-time continuum, something for which neither Spock nor any of his science staff could provide even a theoretical basis. Occurring within a relatively small area—less than a cubic kilometer—the phenomenon had initially appeared to be localized, but then sensors had identified a second such instability, slightly larger than the first. Inspection of the second fluctuation had resulted in the detection of a third, fourth, and fifth—all larger than the first two—and those had led to still others.

For days, the *Enterprise* crew had tracked the abnormalities across space, all the way to an uncharted planetary system filled with them. Spock had determined one of the inner worlds to be the central locus, and therefore the possible source, of the instabilities. Kirk had chosen to take the ship into the system, despite having to pass through areas of affected space, which acted upon the *Enterprise* like turbulence.

"Completing preorbital approach," said Lieutenant Hadley at the navigation console.

"Entering standard orbit," Lieutenant Sulu confirmed as he worked the helm station. Kirk peered at the main viewscreen at the front of the bridge and saw the copper-colored image of the world below. Blotches of white across the globe lent it a cold, unfriendly appearance. Sensors had revealed no indications of sentient life anywhere on the planet.

Again the *Enterprise* shuddered.

"Mister Scott," Kirk said, glancing over to the engineering station on the raised, outer portion of the bridge. "Shield status."

Standing beside the console, Scotty leaned in over Lieutenant Leslie's shoulder and studied the displays for a moment. "The shields themselves are holding, but for some reason it's taking extra power to control them . . . to control all our systems."

"It is the effect of passing through the unstable regions of space," Spock said from the sciences station. "They appear to be stationary, though, so once we have those about the planet mapped, we should be able to avoid them on subsequent orbits."

"Very good, Mister Spock," Kirk acknowledged. The captain understood and embraced the crew's mission to explore the unknown, but it made him anxious when the ship became so directly affected. Still, in addition to the scientific questions they raised, the fluctuating patches of space-time posed a potential threat to navigation in the region. The *Enterprise* hadn't passed through any of them while traveling faster than light, but doing so could have had an impact on the warp drive. Rather than simply quarantining the area, Kirk had instead opted to seek out the cause of the unusual areas.

"Captain," Spock said, and Kirk turned in his chair to see the science officer stand from where he bent over his hooded sensor monitor. "I am reading microchanges in the flow of time."

"What?" Kirk said, standing from his chair and making his way over to Spock. "Explain."

"Sensors are detecting microscopic pockets of space where the rate at which time passes is either faster or slower than in neighboring space," Spock said. "The alterations appear to be emanating outward from the planet in waves."

"Could these waves be dangerous to the ship?" Kirk asked. As though on cue, the *Enterprise* shook once more. Both Kirk and Spock reached out to the edge of the sciences station to steady themselves.

"I do not believe so," Spock said when the quaking ceased. "The pockets are too small, too widely spaced, and last too short a time for that to be the case."

Kirk looked over at the main viewer again, at the lifeless planet about which the ship orbited. "Can you determine precisely what is sending out these waves?" he asked.

"Scans are so far inconclusive," Spock said.

"Can we send down a landing party to find out?" Kirk wanted to know.

Spock's brow creased as he appeared to consider the question. "I do not know," he said. "While I do not believe the ship is in danger in orbit, it is unclear if a transporter beam could safely traverse the waves. Further analysis would be needed."

"Understood," Kirk said, and then stepped down to the lower portion of the bridge. Reaching up to the arm of the command chair, he activated an intercom circuit. "Kirk to transporter room."

"Transporter room," said Lieutenant Kyle, the words delivered with his English accent. *"Go ahead, Captain."*

"Mister Kyle," Kirk said, "I am considering transporting a landing party down to the planet below, but we are reading pockets of temporal flux radiating from there. De-

tails from Mister Spock. I want you to determine whether
or not it would be safe to beam down."

"Aye, sir," Kyle said.

"Kirk out," the captain said. He closed the channel,
then sat back down in the command chair. He waited pa-
tiently as the crew continued studying the unusual readings on and around the planet.

Periodically, the *Enterprise* quivered, the movements
sometimes barely noticeable, other times quite the opposite. Kirk continued to receive reports on the condition of
the ship's systems. Should the crew be put at greater risk,
he would not hesitate to break orbit and vacate the region.

After a time, as Spock scanned for and located the instabilities about the planet and Hadley adjusted the *Enterprise*'s orbit accordingly, the ship trembled less often and
with less force. As Kirk waited for his people to perform
their duties, he felt like standing and moving about the
bridge, but until the ship stopped shaking completely, he
decided to remain seated. "Mister Brent," he said, "status
of life support."

"Nominal, Captain," the lieutenant said from the environmental-control station to the left of the main viewscreen. "They're still drawing more power than normal,
but so far that's not an issue."

At midwatch, Yeoman Takayama produced a data slate
with a ship's status report. Kirk reviewed and then signed
it. The yeoman left the bridge to deliver the report to the
records section, then returned a few moments later.

The ship abruptly shuddered again, harder than it had
for some time. Then it happened a second time, and then a
third. Brent stood up and moved to a secondary station on
the other side of the bridge, where he checked the readings
there.

"Ach, that bumped up the power draw," Scotty grumbled. "We're still in the green, but we won't be if we start shaking again."

"Understood," Kirk said, just as the ship rocked once more. "Stay on top of it, Mister Sulu."

"We're holding orbit, sir," Sulu replied. "The helm is sluggish." Again the ship quaked, and then once more.

"Control circuits threatening to overload, Captain," Scotty said.

"Understood, Engineer," Kirk said. He pushed himself up out of the command chair and made his way back over to the sciences station. "Mister Spock," he began, but stopped when another wave buffeted the ship. He nearly lost his footing, and Brent nearly did too as the lieutenant crossed in front of Kirk on the way back to the environmental-control station. As the captain reached Spock, he said, "We can't avoid these areas of turbulence?"

"I believe we'll have them plotted in a few more orbits, Captain," Spock said.

Behind him, Kirk heard an electric sound and saw a flash of bright light. He turned quickly to see a shower of sparks erupting from the helm, Sulu flying from his seat. Kirk bounded back down to the lower section of the bridge, pressing the intercom button as he reached the command chair. "Sickbay, to bridge," he ordered. He passed the helm, from which smoke drifted upward. On the deck, Yeoman Takayama cradled Sulu's head in her lap. Unmoving and with his eyes closed, the lieutenant appeared to have lost consciousness.

"Switching to manual," Scotty said as he descended toward the helm. "Do we maintain this orbit?"

"Spock?" Kirk said as he examined Sulu.

"This is of great scientific importance, Captain," Spock said. "We're actually passing through ripples in time."

"Maintain orbit," Kirk said, standing back up.

"Aye, there," Scotty said as he sat down at the helm console.

At this point, Kirk realized, with the *Enterprise* clearly at some greater risk, he would have to contact Starfleet. He walked toward the communications station and saw Lieutenant Uhura standing just behind the command chair. "Open a channel to Starfleet Command," he said.

"Aye, sir," Uhura said, moving back to her station. Kirk followed her there. As he did, he saw the black armband still wrapped around the left sleeve of Uhura's uniform, which she'd requested permission to wear after learning of the death of her mother.

"Precautionary measure, Lieutenant," he said. "Broadcast to Starfleet Command my past week's log entries, starting with the unusual readings we had on the instruments and how they led us here. Inform Starfleet Command that apparently something or someone down on this planet—" Behind him, he heard the turbolift doors open. He turned to see McCoy entering the bridge. "Bones," Kirk said, pointing toward Sulu, and the doctor headed for the downed officer. Addressing Uhura again, he continued, "Can effect changes in time causing turbulent waves of space displacement." As he spoke, he went back down to the center of the bridge, to where McCoy now examined Sulu.

"Some heart flutter," the doctor said as he adjusted a hypo. "I'd better risk a few drops of cordrazine."

"It's tricky stuff," Kirk noted. "Are you sure you want to risk—" But already McCoy had applied the hypo to the base of Sulu's neck. The device hissed as it dispensed the powerful drug. Immediately, Sulu's eyes flickered open. The lieutenant pushed himself up, a confused smile appearing on his face.

"You were about to make a medical comment, Jim?" McCoy asked with dry sarcasm.

"Who me, Doctor?" the captain said, even more dryly.

At the helm, Scotty turned toward Kirk. "We're guiding around most of the time ripples now, Captain," he said.

"Good," Kirk said, and then he headed back toward the sciences station. They couldn't remain in orbit if it meant control stations around the ship would begin overloading. "Mister Spock?" he said.

"All plotted but one, Captain," Spock said. "Coming up on it now . . . seems to be fairly heavy displacement."

Two seconds later, the *Enterprise* jolted badly. Kirk grabbed the bridge railing to keep from being thrown to the deck. Amid the vibrations of the ship, though, he suddenly heard an unexpected sound: the long whisper of a hypo. Kirk whirled toward the sound and saw McCoy doubled over the helm. Even as the doctor stood up and spun away, the hypo continued to hiss. Finally, as it stopped, McCoy collapsed to the deck, to where an injured Sulu had lain only moments ago. At once, Sulu, Takayama, Uhura, and Leslie hurried to the fallen doctor.

"Bones!" Kirk called. He rushed across the bridge to his friend. "Get back to your positions," he told the crew around McCoy. Already the doctor had managed to get to his knees, though he remained bent over, his hands at his midsection. As the crew returned to their stations, Kirk kneeled beside McCoy to examine him. Spock, he saw, had followed him over from the sciences station.

"The hypo, Captain," Spock said, plucking the device from the doctor's hands.

"It was set for cordrazine," Kirk said.

Spock pulled the drug reservoir from the end of the hypo. "Empty," he said.

"Communications," Kirk said, "emergency medical team."

With no warning, McCoy bolted upright, his eyes wide, his face bathed in a sheen of perspiration, a wild yell issuing from his mouth. Kirk and Spock both stood back up at the doctor's side. "Killers!" McCoy screamed. "Assassins!" Slowly, he began to rise to his feet, his hands clutched to his stomach as though still holding the hypo. "I won't let you! I'll kill you first! I won't let you!"

As McCoy stood completely up, Kirk reached for his arms, concerned that the doctor might match his actions to the violence of his cries. Spock took Kirk's lead and reached for McCoy as well, but the doctor threw his arms into the air with surprising force, breaking the grips of his friends. He turned and dashed up the steps and toward the turbolift. The crew started after him, as did Kirk and Spock, but then at the turbolift doors, McCoy turned back in a threatening stance. Everybody stopped.

"You won't get me!" he yelled. "Murderers! Killers!" He dashed into the turbolift, the doors opening to reveal technician Wilson.

"Grab him," Kirk yelled as he and Spock raced after McCoy. But the doctor seized Wilson and hurled him from the lift, directly into Kirk and Spock. The doors closed, and by the time Kirk got there, the turbolift had already begun its descent from the bridge.

Kirk turned and saw many of the crew still on their feet, still gazing, stunned, toward the lift. Uhura stood by the command chair, and Kirk gestured to her. "Security alert," he said, and as the lieutenant moved back to her station to set the shipwide alert and inform security of the situation, the order seemed to rouse the rest of the crew from the shock of what they'd just witnessed. Scotty sat back down at the helm, while Leslie returned to the engineering panel.

"Captain," Sulu said, "I can take my station."

Kirk assessed him for a moment, but though the lieutenant looked well, he had just been treated for heart flutter. "Negative," Kirk said. "Yeoman Takayama, escort

Mister Sulu to sickbay and inform the medical staff about what happened to him."

"Aye, sir," Takayama said, and the two officers began toward the lift.

As Spock headed back to the sciences station, Kirk peered over to the engineering console. "Mister Leslie," he said, "how are the control circuits?"

"Showing normal loads now, sir," Leslie said. "Now that we're avoiding the areas of instability, we should be fine."

As Kirk walked toward Uhura, he saw Wilson standing there, looking to him questioningly. Obviously he hadn't come to the bridge expecting to be attacked. "Sir?" he asked. "We saw a warning light for the helm."

"We've got it on manual right now," Scotty offered. "See if you can reroute the secondaries."

Wilson looked to the captain again, who nodded. Once the technician started for the helm, Kirk addressed Uhura. "Lieutenant, contact security," he said. "See if they can tell where McCoy exited the turbolift."

"Aye, sir," Uhura said.

"Spock," Kirk said, continuing over to where the science officer now worked his panel. "What information do we have on cordrazine overdoses?"

"Checking now, Captain," Spock said. "There appears to be very little in the literature. It may take a few minutes to collate all of the available anecdotal data we have."

"All right," Kirk said. "In the meantime, I'm going to sickbay to see if anybody down there has any firsthand knowledge. You have the bridge." Kirk strode back to the turbolift, the doors opening this time to reveal an empty car. He entered, took hold of a control wand, and ordered the lift to take him to sickbay.

In his mind, he saw the feral expression on McCoy's

face, heard his delusional cries. Kirk knew of cordrazine from an incident that had occurred earlier in his career aboard the *U.S.S. Farragut.* After circumstances had resulted in a landing party having to hike three days over mountainous terrain in brutally hot conditions, an older officer had suffered a heart attack. The med-tech present had been left with no choice but to chance a minimal dosage of cordrazine.

The officer had died instantly.

When the turbolift doors opened, Kirk headed for sickbay, deeply concerned for his friend.

Spock sat at the sciences station on the *Enterprise* bridge and pored through the library record tapes, searching for whatever accounts he could find relating to cordrazine overdoses. As he'd told the captain, the medical database contained almost no such information. The scientific data did, however, expose the perils of utilizing the drug at all. While it had proven exceedingly effective in treating heart-related impairments in humans and several other species under the right conditions, it also had a long history of fatal applications. Incorrect diagnoses and inexactly calculated dosages had often resulted in death to the patient.

During the medical testing of cordrazine prior to the adoption of its use, the impact of an overdose of the drug had been believed apparent. Since it functioned as a strong stimulant for the cardiac muscles, an excess would likely damage the heart to the point of arrest, even in otherwise healthy patients. In most of the very few recorded instances of cordrazine overdose, that had been the case, with death typically occurring within seconds.

Obviously, that had not happened to Dr. McCoy. Spock did manage to find several reports that chronicled the fate of individuals who had survived having massive amounts of the drug injected into their bodies. In addition to stimulating the heart, cordrazine apparently could have an effect on brain chemistry. In an incident on Earth, in Stockholm, Sweden, a researcher had accidentally ingested a large quantity of the drug. Apparently believing himself under attack, he had barricaded himself in his lab. When colleagues had attempted to push their way inside to help him, they'd found that a trap had been set for them. A chemical explosion had killed seven people—including the original researcher—and injured twenty-three others.

In another incident, a disturbed individual had tried to use cordrazine to commit suicide, at least according to a note that he had left behind explaining his actions. Instead, he had survived, but had lost all knowledge of the people in his life. The condition had persisted for weeks, until he'd been found dead after putting a phaser to his own head.

In a third episode, a physician at the University of Alpha Centauri had suffered an overdose of cordrazine, though under what circumstances had never been determined. She had been found unconscious and taken to a hospital, from which she had subsequently vanished. Five months later, her corpse had been found halfway across the quadrant, in a public lodge in the city of Eglantine on Stygian III. An autopsy had failed to pinpoint the cause of her demise.

On Rigel II, a woman who danced regularly at a cabaret had been found lifeless in her dressing room. A postmortem examination had revealed that an extreme amount of cordrazine had been introduced into her body over a period of time. A criminal trial had later seen a jealous patron of the cabaret convicted of poisoning her with the drug.

In all, Spock found thirty-seven documented occurrences of individuals who had experienced a cordrazine overdose. Of those, only three had survived and returned to a normal life. *Eight-point-one percent,* Spock automatically thought, calculating Dr. McCoy's chances for a full recovery.

Poor odds, he concluded. *Poor odds indeed.*

THREE

2293

Alexandra Tremontaine walked along the wide hall that circled the complex of conference rooms located in the political center. Her low heels hammered along the slate floor, sending echoes reverberating through the open, empty space. She would reach the negotiating session late, nearly half an hour after it had been scheduled to begin. Familiar with the punctuality and the punctiliousness of the Frunalians, she could not imagine that the Federation delegation would have been able to delay the start of the meeting for more than a couple of minutes, if for even that long. Despite that she'd made the trip to Oreltē all the way from Earth and that she'd arrived only earlier today, she knew that the Frunalian ambassador, Jalira Tren, would not consider that sufficient reason for her tardiness.

In fact, Tremontaine counted on it.

She stopped before the pair of brushed stainless steel doors that led into the conference room being utilized for the summit. Before entering, she peered down at herself, smoothed the hunter green fabric of her conservative dress, adjusted on her bodice the small pin that described the insignia of the Bureau of Interplanetary Affairs. She consulted the data slate she carried, reviewing the names of the members of the Frunalian and Federation contingents. She'd met everybody present at one time or another, save for the new UFP ambassador, Spock. There had been ample time and opportunity to do so within the last couple of hours, but she'd decided that it would be more advantageous for her to appear at the conference fundamentally unknown to him.

Finally, Tremontaine deactivated her slate, then pulled open one of the doors and strode into the room. Inside, chairs rimmed the oval space, both along the walls and around a similarly shaped table at its center. A large screen dominated the long curve of one wall and currently displayed an image of mountainous, craggy terrain, which Tremontaine assumed to be an area on the planet nearest the Frunalian sun. A ruddy vein of exposed rock likely revealed the presence of the valuable and rare rubindium ore that the UFP had for some time now been seeking the rights to mine.

As Tremontaine paced toward the table, all five individuals present looked over at her from where they sat. Ambassador Tren stood up at one end of the table, and Ambassador Spock followed suit at the other. The one Frunalian aide and the two Federation aides—a Trill woman and a human man—remained seated. "Ambassador Tremontaine," Tren said. "Welcome back to Oreltē." Tren spoke her words evenly, but Tremontaine knew that the gracious greeting was in no way meant to excuse her lateness.

"How good to see you again, Ambassador," Tremontaine said. Tren stood several centimeters shorter than her own one-point-eight-five meters, although the fleshy comb that ran from the Frunalian's brow, across the crown of her head, and down her spine added to her height. That sensory appendage indicated that Tren had already undergone her Shift. She'd also lost both the ridges that had once risen from the backs of her shoulders, along with the entirety of the exomembrane that had covered her sage skin. As well, her four breasts had developed, all of them clearly defined beneath the formfitting metallic suit she wore.

"I'm afraid that this meeting started—" Tren glanced at a chronometer in the center of the table. "—twenty-seven minutes ago. Your appearance here at this time is a disruption." She did not sound angry or argumentative, but simply as though stating the facts as she saw them.

"My apologies, Ambassador," Tremontaine said. "As you know, I reached your world only today. I did not intend to get to this conference late, but I was unavoidably detained."

At the other end of the table, Spock spoke up, and Tremontaine peered over at him. "I'm certain that you can provide an understandable reason for your delayed arrival," he said. "Nevertheless, it is inappropriate for you to interrupt these proceedings." Lean and tall, about her own height, the Vulcan had a narrow, weathered face, rather handsome, she thought. He wore gray slacks and a loose, dark blue tunic, down the right side of which marched a series of silver glyphs.

"Actually," Tremontaine said, holding Spock's gaze, "my disturbance of this meeting is not only appropriate, but necessary." She turned to face Tren once more. "Ambassador, I bring word from the Federation that we are withdrawing from these negotiations."

"What?" the Frunalian aide said, coming up out of his chair. Tren fixed him with a glare and he quickly sat back down without saying another word.

Looking back at Tremontaine, Tren said, "I do not understand. Is the Federation no longer interested in mining our rubindium?"

"My understanding is that we're as interested as ever," Tremontaine said. "It is simply that these discussions have continued for quite a while, last year with Ambassador Pelfrey and over the last month with Ambassador Spock. By all appearances, the talks seem to be at an impasse. Consequently, the Federation believes that it can allocate its diplomatic resources to better effect elsewhere."

"Ambassador Tremontaine," Spock said with Vulcan calm, "I have received no word of this."

"I am carrying that word to you now," Tremontaine said. "I'm sorry that we didn't have a chance to speak before this session."

"I cannot offer an official response at this time," Tren said, clearly unprepared for the turn of events.

"How could we possibly expect you to?" Tremontaine said. "But I'm authorized to remain on Oreltē for several more days if you wish me to do so. When your government is ready, I will communicate your message back to the Federation." She waited for just a moment, and when neither Tren nor Spock said anything further, she turned on her heel and headed back toward the room's double doors. Before she could exit, though, the Frunalian ambassador called after her.

"Alexandra," Tren said.

Tremontaine stopped and looked around. "Yes?"

"Can there be no movement on this?" Tren asked. "All of us—" She raised a hand to include Spock and his two aides in her statement. "—have worked hard to reach an agreement, and even though we haven't to this point, we have made a great deal of progress."

"I'm sorry, Jalira," Tremontaine said. "I was given no leeway to allow continuation of these talks." She paused, as though considering the situation, as though searching for some means of accommodating the Frunalians. She peered for an instant at Spock, whose expression remained impassive. At last, she told Tren again, "I'm sorry." Then she turned and left the conference room.

Back in the quarters she'd been assigned at the Federation Embassy, Tremontaine waited for the fallout of the unauthorized action she'd just taken.

Spock rapped his knuckles on the dark wooden surface, then listened for a response. He heard nothing, but a few seconds later, the door opened to reveal the ambassador. "Mister Spock," Tremontaine said, raising her hand in the traditional Vulcan salutation. "I've been expecting you. Please come in."

As Tremontaine stepped aside, Spock held his hand up in reply, then walked past her and into the suite. The large sitting room had been laid out nearly identically to his own here at the embassy, though its appointments reflected human aesthetics rather than Vulcan ones. He waited for Tremontaine to close the door and come farther into the room.

"May I offer you something?" she asked.

"Only information," Spock said. The news that Tremontaine had brought with her, that the Federation had chosen to remove itself from talks with the Frunalians, had been wholly unexpected. Spock and his two aides had been on Orelté for a month, working daily to reach an accord on rubindium mining rights, and as Ambassador Tren had stated just a short while ago, they had made significant strides. To simply abandon all of that forward movement seemed wasteful to Spock, and unnecessary.

"Information, of course," Tremontaine said. "Well, to

begin with, we haven't been properly introduced. I'm Alexandra Tremontaine of Earth."

"Spock of Vulcan," he said, leaning slightly forward in an abbreviated bow. Tremontaine need not have identified herself. Even before she had entered the conference room earlier, even before Spock had been notified by the Bureau of Interplanetary Affairs that she would be joining his team, he'd been familiar with the ambassador—or at least with some of the work she'd done. Tremontaine had served the Federation in her current capacity for more than twenty-five years, in a career that had provided quite a few noteworthy accomplishments, including mediating an end to the war on Epsilon Canaris III, convincing the Gorn Hegemony to enter into a long-term ceasefire with the Federation, and establishing a far-reaching program that supplied medical aid to nonaligned worlds.

"Let's sit," Tremontaine said, and she moved around a low, square table to take a seat on an ornately crafted settee. Spock sat down on a matching piece opposite her. Although he had over the years viewed numerous holos of Ambassador Tremontaine in which she'd sported a variety of looks—short hair, long, blonde, brunette, redheaded, and in diverse styles—he had never before seen this particular configuration of her appearance: her lengthy fair-haired locks had been pulled back from her face and gathered behind her head in a complicated bun. She had bright blue eyes and delicate features, and physically, she reminded Spock of a woman he had once known in the cloud-city of Stratos. "So how is Jalira taking the news?" Tremontaine asked. She projected a confident air.

"If by 'the news' you mean the Federation's withdrawal from the negotiations," Spock said, "Ambassador Tren seems to be at a loss to understand it. I must confess that I am as well."

"I'm not surprised," Tremontaine commented.

"When I was informed that you had completed your dealings with the Medusans and would be joining our delegation here," Spock said, "I was told that the decision had been made as a result of your familiarity with the Frunalians in general and with Ambassador Tren in particular. Why then would you be sent here simply to terminate the conference?"

"I probably wouldn't be," Tremontaine said.

The assertion puzzled Spock. "I am uncertain how to interpret that statement," he said.

"I probably wouldn't have been sent to Oreltē just to pull the Federation out of these talks," Tremontaine said. "The reality is that the UFP position hasn't changed: we still want to mine the rubindium in this system."

"As you indicated to Ambassador Tren," Spock noted.

"What I mean is that I was not instructed to withdraw from the negotiations," Tremontaine said. "I was assigned here to assist you in reaching an agreement for those mining rights."

The revelation astonished Spock. "Then your announcement to Ambassador Tren was a lie," he said.

"If you must categorize it in such a way, I would suggest the term *prevarication*, or better yet, *subterfuge*," Tremontaine said. "But really it was merely a diplomatic tactic."

"I do not deem dishonesty a legitimate tool of diplomacy," Spock said. Although he had sometimes practiced deception in his life, most often as a Starfleet officer engaged in combat and other dangerous situations, he believed in the sensibilities of his people. As a rule, Vulcan culture held lying to be anathema. Further, the forging of relationships, whether between two individuals or two societies, required trust, and trust required truthfulness.

"In theory, Mister Spock—and perhaps even in practice—I agree with you," Tremontaine said. "But the reality is that I did not lie today." She stood up and made her way from the sitting area over to where a mahogany hutch stood against a wall. "Are you sure I can't offer you something to eat or drink?" she said.

"Quite sure," Spock said.

Tremontaine shrugged, selected a data card from a shallow drawer in the hutch, then slipped the thin red slab into a nearly invisible slot. Spock heard a muffled whir, not unlike that of a transporter, and then the sound faded back into silence. The doors of the hutch, engraved in graceful swirls, slid open to reveal the interior of a food synthesizer. On the materialization platform sat a porcelain cup. Tremontaine picked it up and the doors glided closed. She returned to the settee, but rather than sitting down, she stood behind it and peered across at Spock.

"You told Ambassador Tren that the Federation was withdrawing from the negotiations," he said to her, "but you just told me that you were not sent here for that purpose."

"That's true, but in neither instance did I lie," Tremontaine said, then paused to take a sip from her cup. Wisps of steam rose above its rim. "The BIA has given me a good deal of autonomy here, based upon my previous experiences with the Frunalians. I initially intended to come here and add my voice to yours, perhaps provide a different perspective. After reviewing your reports, though, I concluded that, even with the progress you've made, Jalira Tren remains a long way from granting us the rights to mine their rubindium. For that reason, and because the Federation *does* have other pressing needs for its diplomatic corps, I decided that this process needed to be either accelerated or abandoned. So unless Ambassador Tren in the next few days offers a compelling reason to resume the talks, they will be over, Mister Spock, and you and I will be leaving

Oreltē." She sipped again at her cup, then added, "But
Jalira will want to continue the talks, and at that point,
we'll be able to reach an agreement in short order."

"That," Spock said, "seems like arrogant conjecture."

"Oh, I disagree," Tremontaine said. She spoke with no
hint of having taken any insult from Spock's characterization. She walked back around to the front of the settee and
sat down again, placing her cup on the table. *"Conjecture*
is the formation of a judgment based upon incomplete information. That's not the case here. I have your reports of
the summit, as well as my knowledge and experience with
the Frunalians and Ambassador Tren. I decided on a
course of action not through conjecture, but through rational deduction. As for arrogance, well, I don't feel particularly self-important right now, but I'll accept your
observation. Fortunately, that's not relevant to the success
or failure of our mission."

Spock peered at Tremontaine, trying to take her measure. She did not speak without emotion, but she did maintain a levelness he found both convincing and compelling.
What he had at first viewed as conceit, he now judged as
self-assurance, the dividing line being the logic by which
she'd apparently arrived at her conclusions. Still, she had
acted unilaterally, and he questioned her about that. "You
reached Oreltē today several hours prior to today's session," he said, "sufficient time for you to seek me out and
detail your intentions. May I ask why you did not?"

Tremontaine glanced down at her cup on the table, then
reached forward and picked it up again. Spock perceived
her hesitation in answering as either uncertainty or regret,
and he thought she utilized the physical action of retrieving her cup as an attempt to camouflage the feeling. "For
that, I'm sorry, Mister Spock," she said, looking back over
at him. "I'm certainly aware of your long record of ex-

ploits aboard the *Enterprise* and the masterful job you did as a special envoy to Chancellor Gorkon. But for all of that, I didn't know you personally, and so I couldn't be sure how you would react to my strategy or how easy or difficult it would be for you to help me carry it out. I chose the path with the fewest unknowns, and therefore the path I could be most certain of traversing successfully."

"Reasonable," Spock said. It seemed clear that Ambassador Tremontaine had not acted without forethought.

"Thank you, Mister Spock," Tremontaine said. "I take that as a great compliment, coming from your disciplined mind."

Spock dipped his head in acknowledgment of the returned accolade. "Am I to take it then," he asked, "that your plan now is simply to wait for an official response from Ambassador Tren?"

"It is," Tremontaine said. "Later, I'll make arrangements for our departure, say, two days from now. That's something Jalira might check just to make sure that we're not bluffing."

Spock stood up. "It would appear that there is nothing else we need discuss then," he said.

"Actually," Tremontaine said, hastily setting her cup back down and rising from the settee, "even though I've read your accounts of the negotiations here, I think I'd like to discuss your experiences with you directly."

"Very well," Spock said. "Do you wish to do so now or shall we schedule another time?"

"Are you a vegetarian, Mister Spock?" she asked, the question an apparent non sequitur.

"I am," he said.

"So am I," Tremontaine said. "I know an excellent restaurant on the far side of the city. I was thinking that perhaps we could have our discussion over dinner."

Spock blinked. He could not be certain, but he thought that Tremontaine's invitation might be motivated by more the just her desires for sustenance and information; he thought that she might be attracted to him. It had been some while since Spock had noticed anything of this sort, and an even longer time since he'd been in any way involved with a woman. In addition to the dearth of opportunities over the years, owing to the rigors of his Starfleet duty and to his own solitary nature, there had also been the complications with Saavik.

Eight years earlier, after Spock had perished aboard the *Enterprise,* his body had been revivified and rejuvenated on the Genesis Planet, aging rapidly to maturity and triggering the *pon farr.* In order to prevent the unfulfilled mating urges from killing Spock, Saavik had bonded with him. Later, after he'd undergone the *fal-tor-pan* and his *katra* had been reunited with his restored physical self, the link with Saavik had remained. Although both of them had recognized the logic of her decision to do what she'd done, neither of them had been comfortable with the idea of allowing their connection to stand; Spock had been Saavik's mentor, she his student, and their joining had been born of necessity. Eventually, when the time had been right, the two of them had returned to Vulcan together, where they'd successfully undertaken the *rel-san-vek:* the dissolution.

Now, free of that encumbrance, Spock stood in Ambassador Alexandra Tremontaine's suite, faced with what should have been a simple choice to make. Having sensed Tremontaine's interest in him, accepting her request to dine together could easily mislead her into thinking that he reciprocated that interest. He would not wish to do that . . . except—

Except that this woman does intrigue me, Spock thought. He appreciated the clarity with which she'd analyzed the Frunalians' position, the decisiveness and confidence with which she'd acted, and the composed manner in which she conducted herself. "Yes," Spock said. "I'll join you for dinner."

"Wonderful," Tremontaine said. She did not smile, but Spock could still tell that his answer pleased her. He moved to the door and opened it for her, then followed her out. They exited the embassy, then walked across the city together, their conversation coming easily. At first, they spoke of the Frunalians and Ambassador Tren and stable rubindium ore, but over dinner the discussion moved on to other topics. Tremontaine asked about Spock's choice to join the Bureau of Interplanetary Affairs and about his service in Starfleet. For his part, Spock found himself curious about the ambassador's career, as well as what had driven her to pursue a vocation in diplomacy. By the time they retired to their own suites later that night, they had spent five hours with each other.

The next morning, Jalira Tren requested a resumption of negotiations, offering an extensively reworked proposal from which to recommence the talks. Three days later, Spock and Tremontaine departed Oreltē, the Federation mining rights to the Frunalian rubindium secured.

FOUR

2267

The sound of doors opening penetrated Lieutenant John Kyle's dazed mind. With his eyes closed, he heard voices and footsteps, and he realized that he had no idea where he was or how he had gotten there. As he stirred, he became aware of a sharp pain slicing through the back of his head.

"John, are you all right?" somebody asked. Kyle opened his eyes and saw Dave Galloway, a security guard, squatting down before him.

"I don't know," Kyle said. Past Galloway rose the transporter platform. Kyle remembered being on shift here, and that he'd being studying whether or not a landing party could safely beam down to the planet they currently orbited. He struggled to push himself up to a sitting position, and at his side, a second guard, Paul Bates, took his arm to help. "What happened?" Kyle asked, reaching up and rubbing the nape of his neck.

"We don't know," Galloway said. "We were searching for Doctor McCoy when we checked in here. You were lying on the deck, just coming to."

Kyle recalled the alert that had gone up about the doctor accidentally being injected with an overdose of a drug. McCoy apparently roamed the ship now in a paranoid delusion that he was being pursued by murderers. Kyle couldn't visualize the doctor in such a state of—

The lieutenant felt his jaw drop as a possibility occurred to him. He tried to get to his feet, but Galloway stopped him with a hand to his shoulder. "Easy there," the guard said.

"You don't understand," Kyle protested. "I need to check the transporter to see if anybody's beamed down."

"I can do it," Galloway said. He quickly stood and moved to the console.

"See if the transporter's been activated today," Kyle said.

Galloway worked the controls for a moment. "Yes," he said. "Nine minutes ago, there was a successful transport."

Kyle had been on the verge of confirming the ability to

beam down to the planet safely, but now he had direct confirmation. "Check the log. See who it was," he said, though
he suspected that he already knew the answer.

"Doctor McCoy," Galloway confirmed.

"Contact the captain," Kyle said, but already Galloway
had reached for the intercom.

"Bridge, security," he said. "Alert, alert."

"Bridge here," the captain responded. *"Go ahead."*

"Security, oh-five-four, sir," Galloway said, identifying
his patrol route. Kyle attempted again to stand, and this
time Bates helped him do so. "We just found the transporter chief injured."

Kyle staggered over to the console. As he reset the slide
controls, he spoke into the intercom. "Captain," he said,
"Doctor McCoy has beamed himself down to the planet."

"And the transporter at that time, Captain," Kyle heard
Spock say, *"was focused on the center of the time disturbance."*

"So whatever's down there, McCoy is in the heart of it,"
Kirk replied to the first officer. *"Set up a landing party.
Let's go get him."* Then, into the intercom, the captain said,
"Kirk out."

As quickly as he could manage with the pounding in
his head—the doctor must have struck him pretty hard—
Kyle swung around the console and began working the
controls.

"Maybe you should head to sickbay," Galloway said.
"We can get another operator down here."

"No," Kyle said. "You heard the urgency of the situation.
The captain will be here with a landing party straight away."

"John," Galloway protested.

Kyle looked at him with a serious expression. "Dave,
really, I'm all right," he said. "After the landing party
beams down, I'll have somebody take over for me."

"All right," Galloway said. "But if you—"

The intercom whistled, then transmitted the sound of Lieutenant Commander Giotto's voice. *"Security to Galloway,"* he said.

Galloway opened a channel and identified himself.

"The bridge just requested two security officers for a landing party to go after Doctor McCoy," Giotto said. *"I'm assigning you and Bates."*

"Acknowledged," Galloway said.

"Giotto out."

Galloway deactivated the intercom, then peered over at Kyle. "What did Commander Spock say was down there?" he asked.

"The center of the time disturbance," Kyle said.

"The time disturbance?" Galloway said. "And what does that mean?"

"I don't know," Kyle answered honestly. "I don't think anybody knows."

The wind blew cold across the planet's surface, although the sheer rock formations all around provided a considerable barrier. As the rest of the landing party spread throughout the area, searching for Dr. McCoy, Spock stood beside Captain Kirk and peered up at the unusual object situated at the heart of the archeological ruins. An irregular torus standing on edge, it had a dappled, golden surface. Spock almost could not believe what his tricorder reported about it.

"This single object," he told the captain, "is the source of all the time displacement."

"Explain," Kirk said.

"I can't," Spock admitted. "For this to do what it does is impossible by any science I understand." The captain gazed up at the object—it stood approximately four meters tall—then slowly started around it. Spock walked with him, checking his tricorder as he did so. "It is operating even now," he said, "putting out waves and waves of time displacement, which we picked up millions of miles away." The captain stopped when he'd made it halfway around the object.

"It's difficult to imagine that this single structure could do that," Kirk said.

"And yet it does," Spock said, verifying the fact with his tricorder. "I am at a loss both to explain how it is doing what it is doing, as well as to understand just what its purpose might be."

"It's functioning," the captain said, "and yet our sensors showed no sentient life anywhere on the planet."

"That is correct," Spock said.

"And these ruins, you said, were on the order of—"

"Millions of years old," Spock said, seeing the captain's point. If the inhabitants of this world had disappeared millions of years ago, whether dying off or departing in a mass exodus, then how could the object have continued to operate for all the time since then? Would it not require periodic maintenance, as well as a regular power source? Spock supposed that it might have employed solar or geothermal power, but his tricorder showed neither sunlight receptors on it nor any subterranean connections.

"To reach through an atmosphere and out into space, all the way to the *Enterprise*," Kirk said, "must have required a great deal of power."

"Incredible power," Spock agreed. As he reached out to touch the object, he added, "It can't be a machine as we understand mechanics."

"Then what is it?" the captain asked.

Beneath his hand, Spock felt a strong vibration, and he quickly stepped back. Suddenly, a deep voice boomed from the object: *"A question."* Light flashed through its circumference in time to its words. *"Since before your sun burned hot in space and before your race was born, I have awaited a question."*

Beyond the unexpectedness of the object's speaking, the response made no sense to Spock. Sol had formed approximately four-and-a-half billion years ago, the Vulcan sun even farther back in time. But the remnants of the civilization about the object dated from only millions of years ago. Had not a single individual in the history of that society ever asked a question here?

"What are you?" the captain asked.

"I am the Guardian of Forever," it said.

"Are you machine or being?" Kirk asked.

"I am both and neither," the Guardian replied cryptically. *"I am my own beginning, my own ending."*

"I see no reason for answers to be couched in riddles," Spock commented.

"I answer as simply as your level of understanding makes possible," the Guardian said. Though Spock did not doubt the sophistication of the object, he also perceived arrogance in its answer.

"What is your purpose?" Kirk asked.

"I am the confluence of all moments, all places," the Guardian said. *"I am what was, what will be. Through me is eternity kept."*

The captain peered with a creased brow over at Spock, clearly attempting to decipher the meaning of the Guardian's enigmatic pronouncements. Spock too tried to discern its intent. As Captain Kirk began walking again around the object, Spock followed, his mind working over the words that the Guardian had utilized in its replies. *Forever. Eternity. All moments, all places. Through me.*

As they reached the other side of the object, Spock formulated a theory. "A time portal, Captain," he said. "A gateway to other times and dimensions, if I'm correct."

"As correct as possible for you," said the Guardian. *"Your science knowledge is obviously primitive."*

"Really?" Spock said. Even if the Guardian was what it claimed to be, that did not diminish the level of scientific advancement that Vulcan and Earth and the Federation had achieved.

"Annoyed, Spock?" the captain asked with an amused air.

"Behold," the Guardian said. A mist fell from the top of the object to fill the empty space at its center. Within, images began to form: humans, barely clothed, carrying spears at the ready as they tramped through a tropical forest. Then the jungle scene vanished, replaced a moment later by another: pyramids rising in a desert setting, with people riding and leading beasts of burden. *"A gateway to your own past, if you wish."* The desert faded and a great white temple appeared, a crowd milling about before it.

Ancient Greece, Spock thought. *Or perhaps Rome.* More images came, one after another. Spock saw people in togas and—

"Killers!" McCoy's voice rang out. Spock turned and saw the doctor emerge from among the ruins, ducking between an upright column and a large slab of stylized masonry leaning against it. Uhura stood near him, apparently having flushed him out. The two security guards, Galloway and Bates, ran after him.

For just a second, McCoy headed toward where Spock and the captain stood before the Guardian, but then he sped to the right. Engineer Scott stood there, though, blocking the doctor's path. McCoy saw him and tried to reverse direction, but found himself surrounded. "Killers!" he yelled as Galloway drew closer. "I won't let you get me!" McCoy scrambled backward into a recess in the rocks. "I'll kill you first!" he yelled.

Galloway had his phaser drawn, Spock noticed, but he did not point it at the doctor. The captain's orders had called for minimal force in apprehending McCoy. Given the doctor's state, the physical effect to him of a phaser blast, even on a stun setting, remained unknown.

Finally, Galloway and Scott moved in, and McCoy attempted to rush through their midst. "I won't let you get—" As the two officers took hold of him, with Bates moving in as well, the captain and Spock raced over. "Assassins! Murderers! Killers!"

"Spock," Kirk said as he gestured toward the doctor. Spock immediately reached up and applied pressure to the appropriate points on McCoy's shoulder. The doctor stiffened and then collapsed. Galloway and the others lowered him to the ground, and Spock squatted down to check on McCoy's condition. He took hold of the doctor's wrist and felt for a pulse. It beat strongly—perhaps *too* strongly, no doubt a consequence of the considerable amount of cordrazine still in his body. They would need to—

"Spock," the captain said, his tone urgent. Spock stood up and stepped over to his side. "If that is a doorway back through time," he said, staring at the Guardian, "could we somehow take Bones back a day in time, then . . . "

"Relive the accident?" Spock said, understanding the captain's intention. "This time be certain that the hypo accident is avoided?" Kirk nodded to Spock, and then they both looked back at the Guardian, in which images seemingly out of Earth's history continued to appear and disappear. If they had truly found a time portal, then the captain's idea might have some merit, but— "Look at the speed with which the centuries are passing, Captain,"

Spock said. "To step through on precisely the day we wish . . ."

Captain Kirk seemed to consider this for a moment, and then he said, "Guardian," and moved toward the object. "Can you change the speed at which yesterday passes?"

"I was made to offer the past in this manner," the Guardian said. *"I cannot change."* As though testifying to the fact, the sights within its misted center continued to advance through human history.

After watching for a few seconds, Kirk said, "Strangely compelling, isn't it?" The captain, Spock knew, had a fondness for historical studies. "To step through there and lose oneself in another world?"

Spock glanced down at his tricorder and decided that recording the images might prove to be of some value. He worked the device to do so, but when he checked the data stream, he saw not just pictures being recorded, but the reality behind them. "I am a fool," he declared. "Our tricorder is capable of recording even at this speed. I've missed taping centuries of living history, which no man before has ever—"

Spock heard rapid footfalls in the sandy ground behind him, but before he could turn, McCoy sprinted past.

"Doctor McCoy!" Scott called.

"Bones, no!" the captain yelled. He took three steps and lunged after McCoy. But the doctor had been too fast and he leaped away, passing directly through the center of the Guardian. The mist and the images within evaporated as Kirk landed on the ground before the object.

McCoy had also vanished.

"Where is he?" Kirk said as he climbed to his feet.

"He has passed into what was," said the Guardian.

Spock heard the activation tones of a communicator behind him, and then Uhura said, "Captain, I've lost contact with the ship. I was talking to them and suddenly it went dead." She handed her communicator to Kirk. "No static, just nothing."

The captain operated the communicator's controls. "Kirk to *Enterprise*," he said. When he received no response, he held the device out toward Spock, who took it. "Scotty," the captain said, and the engineer retrieved his own communicator and activated it.

Quickly, Spock and Scott established a signal between the two devices, confirming their operation. "Nothing wrong with the communicator, sir," the engineer said.

"*Your vessel, your beginning,*" the Guardian said, "*all that you knew is gone.*"

Spock understood what must have happened, and the captain put the concept into words. "McCoy has somehow changed history."

"You mean we're stranded down here?" Scott said.

"With no past, no future," Spock replied.

"Captain," Uhura said, "I'm frightened."

"Earth's not there," Kirk said, as though attempting to grasp the enormity of the situation. "At least not the Earth we know. We're totally alone."

For a few moments, no one said anything more. Spock silently regarded the other members of the landing party, the only sound the low whine of the wind through the rocks. He wondered about the apparent paradox of what had just happened: if McCoy had indeed altered Earth's history in such a way that the *Enterprise* had never been built, or had at least not come to this world at this time, then how could the six of them be standing here now? Perhaps their proximity to the Guardian had prevented them from being affected by the change to the timeline, but whatever the case, they had no water, no food, and no means of leaving this place.

Except that McCoy just did *leave,* he thought. So could they, back somewhere into Earth's past. And if they could find McCoy, prevent him from altering the timeline—

"Captain," Spock said. "There is a possibility."

FIVE

2293

As they came to the last set of exhibits, she felt disappointed. Even though they'd spent the past couple of hours in the museum, the historical displays had so engaged Tremontaine that she hadn't wanted to reach their end just yet. Though she had known of the Alonis, and had even dealt with several of their representatives through the years, she'd never before this assignment visited their world.

An aquatic species, the Alonis resided beneath the violet seas that covered nearly ninety percent of their planet. They possessed a head and torso that resembled that of a humanoid, at least in shape and dimension, but their body narrowed down to a long tail rather than to legs. They did not have arms either, but short fins. With no fingers or thumbs, they would have been unlikely to develop an advanced, technological society had it not been for their short-range psychokinetic ability. With that skill, they had learned how to fashion water into essentially solid tools.

Tremontaine peered through the glass at the final set of displays, at the same time listening to an audio presentation via the miniature speaker affixed to the top of her ear. At the near end of a long chamber, a diorama depicted

Alonis scientists in a lab as they discovered the means of faster-than-light travel. Past that scene, a detailed scale model of an intricate underwater construction facility showed the fabrication of a prototype warp ship. Finally, at the far end of the chamber, she saw a mock-up of two Alonis clad in environmental suits encountering the crew of an Andorian vessel, making their people's first contact with an alien race.

"From the dawn of a civilization to the time they reach out into the universe, it's always a fascinating story," Tremontaine said. "But I find it particularly compelling in this case."

"Yes," Spock agreed from where he stood beside her. "The progression of exploration from ocean to land to sky to space is highly unusual."

"The way the Alonis have adapted to interaction with air-breathing races is so impressive," Tremontaine said. In quite a few locations throughout their vast submarine cities, the Alonis had erected structures to hold an atmosphere, specifically for the use of guests to their world. The tunnel in which Tremontaine and Spock now stood weaved its way through the mostly water-filled museum.

"We do regard ourselves as explorers," said Tel Renavir Morat, "not just of the physical universe, but of the many cultures that inhabit it." The chief of staff for the Alonis ambassador had accompanied Tremontaine and Spock to the museum, graciously leaving her natural environment in order to act as a guide for the Federation dignitaries. Out of a fluidic setting, Morat employed an antigrav chair for locomotion and wore a rebreathing suit that maintained a layer of water against the silver scales of her body. "We are as absorbed by the interior world as the exterior," she said, her words sounding slightly tinny as the translator in her helmet interpreted the chirps and snaps of her native language into Federation Standard.

"A most worthwhile perspective," Spock said.

Morat escorted Tremontaine and Spock past the final display and through a doorway, where they completed their closed circuit through the museum. There, the chief of staff bade them farewell until tomorrow, when the summit would resume. After returning their earpieces at the museum office, Tremontaine and Spock stepped up onto a transporter platform, informed the operator of their destination, and then a moment later descended another platform halfway around the world.

They exited the transporter station and emerged into the open air of Lingasha, the largest town on the primary landmass of Alonis. Night had already fallen on the tourist and diplomatic center, a place established expressly for off-world, nonmarine visitors. As Spock signaled for an airpod that would carry them back to the Federation Embassy, Tremontaine again felt disappointment. She realized that she hadn't wanted their outing at the museum to end not just because of how interesting it had been, but also because she hadn't yet wanted to part from her fellow ambassador.

"Mister Spock," she said, wary of breaching the formality with which they still addressed each other, even after all this time. They had worked together on Oreltē for only a few days, but after she'd completed a brief mission to Marcos XII, Tremontaine had been teamed with him for these talks on Alonis. Already a month old, the complicated and protracted negotiations for the construction of a Starfleet base here promised to continue for some time. During the past weeks, Tremontaine and Spock had spent a great deal of time together, mostly at the bargaining table, but also with their aides in preparation and analysis sessions outside of the conference. Additionally, they had eaten a num-

ber of meals together, typically working through those as
well. They had never really spoken on a personal level
here on Alonis, and only once back on Oreltē, during her
first night there. Their excursion to the museum today had
been the first activity they'd shared that had not been directly related to their jobs, albeit with Chief of Staff Morat
along as their guide. Now, Tremontaine decided that she
wished to be alone with Spock, away from the embassy
and their professional lives. The initial attraction she'd felt
for him back on Oreltē had only deepened as time had
passed. "Can I interest you in a nightcap?" she asked, recognizing the incongruity of using the honorific *Mister* as
she invited him out with her. "The Federation consul recommended a café where they have live music in the
evenings."

As the airpod approached, Spock said, "That would be
acceptable." Although his words hardly sounded enthusi-
astic, they also lacked any sort of coldness. Tremontaine
had known enough Vulcans in her life—some of them colleagues, some of them acquaintances—that she understood well their usual emotional control and outward
detachment. Spock seemed different to her than any of the
others she'd ever met, though. While he maintained his
own reserved manner, he also did not appear completely
stoic. She found his steady demeanor not aloof, but ap-
proachable and even soothing.

They boarded the airpod and Tremontaine told the operator the name of the café, which translated into Standard
as *Notes on the Water.* It took them only a few minutes to
cross town. As they entered the establishment, she heard
the strangely soulful strains of Alonis music, sinuous, extended tones that blended together in a way only possible
within a liquid medium. They walked through the small
interior of the place and then out the back, to where the

music played, and Tremontaine immediately wondered if she'd made a mistake in asking Spock here with her. Beneath a panoply of stars, the wide, dimly lighted terrace ran along a still inlet. Small tables sat against a railing that overlooked the water, in which spotlights penetrated past the surface and picked out the Alonis musicians, whose song played through speakers all around. The various elements combined to create a romantic ambiance.

Concerned that the setting might make Spock ill at ease, Tremontaine looked over at him, ready to tell him that they needn't stay. Before she could say anything, though, he pointed to the far corner of the terrace, away from the few other patrons present. "Would that table suffice?" he asked.

Pleased, Tremontaine nodded. They made their way over to the table and sat down, and an Antosian waiter quickly came over to serve them. Tremontaine ordered a glass of red wine, and Spock an Altair water. After the waiter had left, Spock asked her opinion of the museum, and they chatted for a few minutes about the exhibits they'd seen. When their drinks arrived, they sipped from their glasses, then sat back and listened to the evocative, almost haunting melodies drifting through the night.

When the performers finished their set, Spock said, "The Alonis music puts me in mind of whale song."

"Yes," agreed Tremontaine, who'd had the same thought. It had been a while since she'd heard such sounds, but back in 2285, virtually everybody on Earth had become familiar with them. At that time, a powerful alien entity had approached the planet, seeking to make contact with humpback whales, a species long extinct. Its communications had threatened the population of Earth, ionizing the atmosphere, vaporizing ocean water, and draping the globe in near total cloud cover. Along with Admiral Kirk and the former command crew of the *Enterprise*, Captain

Spock had traveled back in time to the twentieth century, where they'd retrieved a male and female humpback whale and brought them forward to the present. The ocean-bound creatures had then conversed with the alien, prompting it to reverse the damage it had done to Earth's environment. In the months and years that had followed, accounts of the incident had been widely reported, and the musical speech of the humpbacks had become commonly known among the general populace, Tremontaine included. Not wanting to bring up all of that, realizing that Spock must have heard questions and comments about it many times before, she instead asked, "Are there whales on Vulcan?"

"Not as such," Spock said. "There is, however, a species of large creatures that inhabits the Voroth Sea. In addition to being noted for their size, they are also known for their bioluminescent hides. They are fish, though, not mammals, and they bear only a passing resemblance to the whales of Earth."

"They sound interesting," Tremontaine said. "I'll have to make a point of seeing one the next time I'm on your homeworld."

"You have been to Vulcan before then?" Spock asked.

"A few times," Tremontaine said. "Mostly in an official capacity, but I also took two classes at the Diplomatic Institute in T'Paal."

"I am familiar with the institute," Spock said. "My father periodically lectures there."

"I didn't know that," Tremontaine said. "I never ran into Ambassador Sarek when I was there." It should have come as no surprise to Spock that she knew the identity of his father. As Federation representatives, she and Sarek had met on occasion, and sometimes had attended the same diplomatic events. "I've spoken with the ambassador on occasion, though we've never worked together," she added. "Of course, I'm certainly familiar with his reputation."

Spock drank from his Altair water, then said, "I am curious to know your understanding of that reputation, Ms. Tremontaine."

Ms. Tremontaine, she thought. *Mister Spock.* She took a sip of wine, then set down her glass. "Would you . . . when we're away from our bureaucratic roles, would you call me Alexandra?"

Spock seemed to consider this, and for a moment, she thought that he might object. Instead, he nodded and said, "Alexandra, then. If it is acceptable, I would have you call me Spock."

Tremontaine felt herself smile, a slight, closed-mouth expression that people who knew her well would have recognized as a sign of great delight. In her many years as an ambassador, she had learned the value of keeping a tight rein on her outward bearing, a choice that had spilled over into her personal life. "I would like that," she said. She paused, allowing herself to experience the moment, and then she returned to the question Spock had asked. "As for Ambassador Sarek, he is well respected, considered a strong negotiator with a sharp attention to detail. It's well known that a number of his successes—such as the Coridan accession, the Alpha Cygnus IX treaty, and the Koltaari reprisal—have occurred under adverse circumstances, but have proven absolutely vital to Federation interests. Because of that, your father is thought to be the best choice for the most difficult, most important missions."

"It is gratifying to know that his efforts are appreciated," Spock said.

"Well, I definitely appreciate Ambassador Sarek," Tremontaine said, then quipped, "For one thing, because he's dealt with the Romulans, it means I haven't had to."

She chuckled, hoping her attempt at humor wouldn't make Spock uncomfortable.

"From what I've been able to observe," Spock said, "it is the Romulans who are fortunate not to have had to face *you* at the negotiating table."

Tremontaine peered over at Spock. Had he just made a wry joke, or had he just complimented her? Or both? Amazingly, she thought she saw a glint—an *impish* glint—in his eye. "So tell me," she said, wanting to know more about him, "do you get back to Vulcan much? I assume you were raised there."

"I was born in the city of Shi'Kahr," Spock said. "I lived there until I entered Starfleet Academy. I do return there occasionally, most often to visit my parents, though with Sarek's work, they are often away as well."

"What does your mother do?" Tremontaine asked.

"She is a schoolteacher," Spock said, "though her travels with Sarek usually leave her little opportunity to practice her profession."

"What does she teach?" Tremontaine asked.

"On Earth, prior to marrying my father, she taught grade school," Spock said. "Once she moved to Vulcan, she began teaching human studies, including history, literature, and emotional analysis."

Tremontaine leaned forward in her chair. "Your mother lived on Earth?"

"She did," Spock said. "My mother, Amanda Grayson, is human."

"That's—"

—*interesting,* she thought, but did not complete her sentence for fear that she might offend Spock. Though not unusual for individuals of different species to enter into relationships, to marry, even to have children, Tremontaine hadn't known—why would she?—about Spock's mother being human. She wondered if his parentage had contributed to his Vulcan-but-not-completely-Vulcan persona, to his apparent lack of an impenetrable, emotionless veil. She also dared to think, for just an instant, what it all might mean to her. So many questions whirled through her mind, and she picked one. "You think of yourself as Vulcan, is that right?" she asked.

"I do," Spock said, "but I am also human."

"Does your mother live as a Vulcan?" Tremontaine asked. "Does she control her emotions, practice the—" She stopped, realizing the personal character of her questions. "I'm sorry," she said. "I don't mean to pry."

"But you do," Spock replied. "Or am I mistaken in thinking that you are interested in learning about me?"

Tremontaine felt herself flush. "Am I that transparent?" she asked.

"Transparent?" Spock said, raising an eyebrow. "No. But we have spent a great deal of time together in the past month, and I am perceptive."

"You most assuredly are," Tremontaine said with a laugh that utterly failed to cover her embarrassment. Silence settled between them, and Tremontaine felt terribly self-conscious. She hunted for something, anything, to fill the empty space, but her mind blanked. *For all of my political and communications skills,* she thought, *how can I be so bad at this?*

Mercifully, the musicians began to play once more, their notes lightening the weight that seemed to have fallen on her. She looked away from Spock and over the railing, at the spotlights reaching into the purplish blue waters to illuminate the Alonis performers. When she glanced back up, she saw Spock's gaze still on her.

He leaned forward and said, "It may help you to feel less uneasy to know that I am interested in learning about you, Alexandra." He sat back, then said, "Do you return to Earth often? I assume you were raised there."

Again, Tremontaine smiled, this time more widely. "I was born in the city of Montréal," she said. "In an area known as Plateau Mont-Royal."

They talked for a long time. She told him about her childhood in Québec, about her parents and her sister, about her abortive attempts to become a concert violinist. Spock asked many questions, and Tremontaine happily answered with the details of her life. He spoke of his own parents, of his half brother, and most revealingly, of his long reluctance to accept the human aspects of his nature. Eventually, though, Spock had come to know himself and to learn how to forge his duality into an integrated whole.

They stayed at the café until it closed, then hailed an airpod and flew back to the embassy. Like a gentleman, Spock walked Tremontaine to the door of her suite. She looked at his strong, handsome features, peered into his dark eyes, and felt enormously attracted to him. "Good night, Spock," she said.

"Good night, Alexandra," he said. He raised his hand between them, offering his paired middle and index fingers to her. Tremontaine had seen this before, among Vulcan couples, though she had never done it herself. Still, she recognized it as an act of physical affection, like a kiss, she thought.

Tremontaine slowly lifted her own two fingers and touched their tips crosswise to the tips of Spock's. A pleasant jolt charged through the point where her flesh met his, that first electric sensation shared between new lovers. And then she felt something more—no, she didn't *feel* it, it didn't affect her through any of her senses, but in—

In my mind, she thought. A tendril of existence not her own whispered along the core of her being. It seemed frightening, but in an exciting way, and Tremontaine didn't quite know how to react. She wanted to be open to Spock, though, and she strived to let down the mental barriers she hadn't even known she had until just now. She imagined her thoughts, her being, flowing free, slipping from the coffers of her mind. Her guard came down, slowly and ever so slightly, but when it did—

Spock's mind found hers. His being, his very essence, commingled with her own, allowed a glimpse of everything he was, allowed him to see her. For an impossibly short span, the two became one, the joining supremely satisfying and promising joys to come. Her mind reacted strongly, and her body too, fulfillment there and in the distance. The moment of contact extended and then—

Ended. Spock's fingers parted from hers, and his mind withdrew from her mind, their connection severed. But the echoes of their physical and mental touch lingered, like the remembered press of lips against lips, but more than that too.

"Good night, Alexandra," Spock said again.

"Good night, Spock," Tremontaine said, her voice drawn down almost to a sigh. With an effort, she turned from him and entered her suite. She closed the door and then leaned heavily against it.

Live long and prosper, she thought. Never before had that seemed like such a marvelous possibility.

In the chill just after dawn, Spock sat alone on a concrete bench near the center of the embassy courtyard. The large square area, located at the heart of the single-story edifice, boasted a colorful assortment of flora scattered across a green expanse of lawn. Several gnarled trees invested the space with age, and paved walking paths wound through the lush foliage.

He held his hands out before him, fingertip to fingertip, and his surroundings faded as he performed his morning meditation. The twitter of birds slipped away as he concentrated on the infinite, the misty gleam of the sun-drenched dew vanished as he focused on the void. His mind crystallized, taking shape about the dimensionless of a single point. Within, he found stability, he found peace.

And he found Alexandra.

It had been eight days ago that he had confirmed her interest in him at the *Notes on the Water* café, and that he had declared his own interest in her. Since then, most of their time together had been spent in conference with the Alonis ambassador and her chief of staff, as well as with their own aides. Outside the summit, they continued to work on finding a way to broker a deal that would see a starbase constructed in this system. But they had made a point of taking their evening meals together, and last night, with great discretion, Spock had stayed with Alexandra.

They had grown very close, very quickly, in a way that Spock didn't know if he'd ever experienced. His childhood betrothal to T'Pring had been arranged by their parents, a connection severed by the *kal-if-fee,* the challenge T'Pring had brought when they had been drawn together to commit themselves to, or to release themselves from, their marriage vows. His relationship with Leila Kalomi had been chaste, despite the love she had professed for him and the love for her he'd refused to admit, even to himself. Later, on Omicron Ceti III, under the influence of spores that broke down mental defenses, Spock had felt that love for Leila, had confessed it to her, and had spent a brief time exploring it with her. And neither his unanticipated but fiery liaison with Romulan Commander Charvanek, nor his joining out of necessity with Saavik, had occurred in circumstances that would have allowed the possibility of continuing those relationships.

But with Alexandra, Spock sensed the potential for much more. No longer the outcast child he had been on Vulcan, no longer struggling to deny his human, emotional heritage, he had arrived at a place in his life where he had found satisfaction—where he *felt contentment*. He knew himself and no longer needed to change that person in some substantive way.

Spock parted his hands and reset himself on the bench. Meditative peace eluded him at the moment, so he would need to reach deeper for it. Slowly, deliberately, he brought his hands together again and concentrated on the space formed within them. He closed his eyes this time and listened to the rhythms of his own breathing, his own heartbeat. He let the repetition of each carry his thoughts away, leaving behind the kernel of his mind. A shroud of lightlessness, of stillness, of silence, descended around him. He saw nothing, felt nothing, heard nothing, his very being settling into a revitalizing tranquility.

Minutes passed liked hours, the serenity renewing him.

"Spock," a voice said from outside his internal universe. He resisted it, not yet ready to surrender the calm he had found. "Spock," the voice said again, familiar and insistent. The living peace of his reverie dissolved, and Spock opened his eyes.

Dr. McCoy stood before him in his crimson Starfleet uniform, a red data card in one hand. Dark crescents below his eyes revealed that he hadn't slept well last night, and an overall look of fatigue suggested that he hadn't done so in quite some time. Spock perceived at once that something was wrong. Whether he had drawn that assessment from the unforeseen and exceptional quality of McCoy's appearance here, or from some telepathic sense of his troubled mind, Spock could not tell. "Doctor," he said, dropping his hands to his sides. "I thought you had been scheduled to return to a research position at Starfleet Medical. I did not expect to see you here on Alonis."

"I . . . yeah, I deferred my start date by a couple of weeks," McCoy said. "I needed some time . . . " He hesitated, and Spock waited for him to go on. "How are you?" he finally asked.

"I am well," Spock said, rising from the bench to face his old friend. "And you?"

"I'm . . . " McCoy reached up and rubbed at the side of his forehead, as though in pain. "I'm all right, Spock, but I need to talk to you."

"By all means," Spock said.

"There's just no easy way to say this," McCoy told him, the anguish in his voice corroborating his words. "Jim's dead."

In an instant, Spock knew that McCoy had been provided faulty information, and in the next, that his denial would not, could not, change reality. Rage burned within Spock, an undirected, white-hot fury that threatened to push him to violent action. At the same time, he knew he could do nothing. "What has happened?" he asked, actually shocked at the composed tenor of his voice. Although he remained outwardly calm, he knew that his façade could fracture at any moment.

"Jim was aboard the new *Enterprise*," McCoy said. "Starfleet asked him to attend the christening and the first voyage."

"I was aware of that," Spock said. "I read press accounts that indicated he'd accepted Starfleet's invitation."

"He and Scotty and Chekov went," the doctor said. "It was just supposed to be a press event, a quick jaunt around the solar system. The ship went out with a skeleton crew, no medical staff, no tractor beam—" As he'd spoken, McCoy's voice had grown louder. He turned away from Spock and thrust his arms into the air. "If you ask me, it was an accident waiting to happen. I don't know what Starfleet Command was thinking."

Spock wanted to prompt the doctor to continue telling him what had transpired, but he didn't. He concentrated on controlling his anger, his pain, his helplessness. And deep within him, he felt the smoldering ember of something he'd thought long dead: guilt.

McCoy turned back around. "I'm sorry, Spock," he said. "A pair of transport vessels got trapped in an energy anomaly and sent out a distress signal that they received aboard the *Enterprise*. It was the only ship near enough to respond in time. They managed to save some of the transport passengers before the two vessels were destroyed, but by then the *Enterprise* had become trapped as well. Scotty figured out a way to break the ship free, something having to do with the deflector dish, and Jim made it happen. But as the *Enterprise* escaped, it was hit by a burst from the energy field, rupturing the hull across three decks. Jim was . . . Jim was thrown out into space."

Spock could see tears forming in McCoy's eyes, and he suddenly had the urge to reach out and wrap his hands around the doctor's throat. *Misdirected anger,* Spock thought. *Destructive, pointless anger.* But in his mind's eye, he permitted himself to see his fingers clench about McCoy's neck, crushing the life from his friend. The foolishness, the emotional immaturity of the thought allowed him an outlet for his wrath. On the outside, he still managed to wear his stoic mien. "When did this happen?" he asked.

"Just a few days ago," McCoy said, and then he amended his reply, stating the exact date and time of Jim's death. "Starfleet Command's not releasing the news to the comnets until they've been able to notify Jim's nephews, which should be soon." With a heavy sigh, he moved past Spock and dropped onto the bench beside the walking path. "Remember how Jim told us that he knew he'd die alone?" he asked.

"Yes," Spock said. As his ire simmered, he recalled the time when the three had gone camping in Yellowstone National Park on Earth. Jim had fallen while free-climbing El Capitan, but Spock had been present and wearing jet boots, and he'd saved him. Jim had claimed that he'd known he wouldn't perish from the fall because his two friends had been with him.

"Damned if he wasn't right," McCoy said. "You can't get much more alone than in the vacuum of space." Spock turned and peered down at the doctor but said nothing. "Here," McCoy said, holding out the data card. "This contains accounts of what happened. I thought you might want to see for yourself."

Spock accepted the data card. "Thank you," he said.

"That's also got all of the details about the memorial service for Jim at Starfleet Headquarters," McCoy said. "It's being held next week. I don't know when you want to leave, but I thought I'd stay until you do so that we can go back to Earth together."

"That will not be necessary, Doctor," Spock said. His anger had dulled now, leaving in its wake a haze of sorrow and regret. Through all of that, though, he could see the impossibility of doing as McCoy wanted.

"What do you mean that won't be necessary?" the doctor asked, suspicion tingeing his words.

"You needn't wait to travel with me," Spock said, "because I will not be attending the memorial service."

"What?" McCoy said loudly, rising to his feet. "How can you not go?"

"I have a duty to perform here," Spock said.

"Doing what?" McCoy demanded. "Negotiating with the Alonis? Aren't there other ambassadors who can fill in for you while you're away?"

"Doctor, we are attempting to reach an agreement with the Alonis for the construction of a starbase within this system," Spock said. "This is of vital interest to the Federation, and a task to which I have been assigned for my obvious knowledge of Starfleet. There is no choice in the matter."

"There's always a choice in the matter," McCoy barked at him. He stopped for a moment and appeared to gather himself, then continued in softer tones. "Jim was your best friend for almost thirty years," he said. "But I'm not saying that you owe this to him; I'm saying you owe it to yourself. Whether you can see it or not right now, you need to be there."

"As I've explained," Spock said, "I need to be here."

"I can't believe what I'm hearing, Spock," the doctor said. "For that matter, I can't believe what I'm seeing." McCoy marched past him, then turned around and faced him from a distance. "I know you're a Vulcan, but I also know that you *feel* things too. You and I, we shared a great deal." He obviously referred to the incidents involving the Genesis Device, when Spock had reconfigured McCoy's brain to store his *katra*, and later, when they had endured the *fal-tor-pan*, re-fusing Spock's mind to his body in a process that had linked him and the doctor together in an intensely personal way.

"I will mourn Jim, of course," Spock said. "But of all people, the captain would have understood my commitment to my responsibilities."

"There are responsibilities other than those to the Federation and the Bureau of Interplanetary Affairs," McCoy said. "There are personal responsibilities, and you have them: to Jim, to the people who loved him, and most of all to yourself. You need to be at this memorial."

Spock did not respond, having already said all he intended to say. The doctor waited out the silence between them, then shook his head. "In case you change your mind, I'll be on the next ship headed in the direction of Earth," he said at last. He started to walk away, but then he looked back. "I have to tell you, Spock," he said quietly, "I'm disappointed." Then he turned and made his way to the nearest door.

Spock watched McCoy until he entered the embassy and disappeared from view. Afterward, he sat back down on the bench, closed his eyes, and sought the peace of meditation. It never came.

SIX

2267/1930

Uhura monitored her tricorder as it copied the second set of data from the Guardian of Forever. Though she understood the plan that Captain Kirk and Mister Spock had developed, she saw virtually no means of it succeeding other than by sheer luck. At the same time, she knew that they really had no other choice in the matter but to try.

Behind where she stood with Spock, she heard the captain talking with Scotty. "You keep rubbing the back of your head," he said. "Are you all right?"

"Aye," Scotty said, somewhat sheepishly. "Just a wee bump."

"What happened?" the captain asked.

"Ach, when Doctor McCoy ran toward that thing," Scotty explained, "Galloway and I ran into each other trying to stop him. Our feet got tangled and I fell backward."

To Uhura's surprise, the captain actually chuckled. "Next time," he joked, "remind me not to assign engineers and security guards to the same landing party." Uhura found Captain Kirk's levity, as well as his reference to "next time," reassuring.

After Dr. McCoy had leaped through the Guardian and altered history, Spock had attempted to find in his tricorder some evidence of the doctor's existence in Earth's past. At the time McCoy had disappeared, Spock had been recording the portal's output. He had been unable to locate any record of the doctor, though, because of the enormous volume of unprocessed, unindexed data conveyed by the Guardian.

Uhura compared it to having the numerals from one to a trillion each written on one of a trillion pieces of randomly stacked paper; there would be no swift means of locating a particular number without simply examining the sheets of paper one by one. You might have fortune on your side and find your number on the first page you inspected, but then again, you might also find it on the last. If you spent only one second per sheet, it would still take more than thirty-one thousand years to go through all of them. The tricorder could search data far faster than a person could page through pieces of paper, of course, but the Guardian had also provided far more than a trillion bits of information. With a superior computer, the data could be analyzed, refined, sorted, mined, and then efficiently searched; without such a computer, and without preprocessing the data, that search could take an eternity.

"Now," Spock said beside her, and Uhura operated her tricorder to stop it from copying any more data. Utilizing the images that he had earlier recorded—which fortunately had appeared within the portal at a far slower rate than the historical information the Guardian had broadcast—Spock had been able to isolate the period of time into which McCoy had traveled, essentially narrowing it down to sometime in the twentieth century. They had then asked the Guardian to replay both the Earth timeline that McCoy had changed as well as the unaltered timeline. When it had, they had recorded both sets of information onto Spock's tricorder and onto Uhura's. Theoretically, the devices now contained a record of the action McCoy had taken that had modified the flow of history on Earth. They simply had no effective means of finding it.

Uhura keyed a sequence of commands into her tricorder to verify the storage of both downloads. "All set here, Mister Spock," she said when she'd finished.

"Very good, Lieutenant," Spock said. He then turned and looked toward the rest of the landing party. "Captain," he said. "We're ready."

Kirk walked over to join Spock and Uhura. "There's nothing else that needs to be done?" he asked. "Nothing else that *can* be done?"

"No, sir," Spock said. Uhura shook her head. She too had put a great deal of thought into their predicament, and though she held little hope for the success of the strategy that the captain and first officer had formulated, neither had she been able to determine any other possible solutions.

"Very well, then," the captain said. "Guardian, will you show us the timeline of Earth's history again? The timeline that McCoy changed?"

Within the portal, the mist and images it had been

displaying for Spock and Uhura faded. *"Behold,"* the Guardian said a moment later, and once more, the mist appeared, and then the images.

While Spock monitored the Guardian with his tricorder, Captain Kirk turned and paced away, past Uhura and then past the others, obviously anxious for events to play out. Uhura joined Scotty, Galloway, and Bates as they too waited. Finally, the captain strode past them and back to where Spock stood before the Guardian.

"I was recording images at the time McCoy left," Spock reminded the captain. "A rather barbaric period in your American history. I believe I can approximate just when to jump, perhaps within a month of the correct time . . . a week if we're fortunate."

"Make sure we arrive before McCoy got there," Kirk said. "It's vital we stop him before he does whatever it was that changed all history." He then addressed the time portal. "Guardian, if we *are* successful . . ."

"Then you will be returned," the Guardian said. *"It will be as though none of you had gone."*

On her own tricorder, Uhura followed the flow of data coming from the portal. The amount still staggered her, and she showed the display to Scotty, who peered at it soberly. A moment later, Kirk walked over and faced them.

"Captain, it seems impossible," Uhura said. "Even if you're able to find the right date—"

"Then even finding McCoy'd be a miracle," Scotty interjected.

"There is no alternative," Spock said. Uhura knew he was right.

"Scotty," Kirk said, peering into the engineer's eyes, "when you think you've waited long enough . . . " The captain looked at all of them then. "Each of you will have to try it. Even if you fail, at least you'll be alive in some past world somewhere."

"Aye," Scotty said.

"Seconds now, sir," Spock reported. "Stand by."

"Good luck, gentlemen," Scotty said. Uhura could hear in his voice the difficulty he had in saying good-bye.

"Happiness at least, sir," Uhura offered. She wanted to say more, but really, what more could she say? The captain turned and rejoined Spock. Not knowing whether it would help or not, Uhura continued recording the output from the Guardian.

Spock studied his own tricorder. "And . . . now," he said, and he and the captain took one step and bounded through the portal. Within the Guardian, the mist and images faded again. When they had gone, so too had Captain Kirk and Mister Spock.

Uhura glanced up at Scotty. "How long do we wait?" she asked him.

"I don't know," he said. "I just don't know."

Neither did she.

They ran.

Behind them, Spock heard the sound of a whistle following them. Obviously some of the people who had witnessed him render the policeman unconscious had found a second officer to give chase. Beside him, Captain Kirk carried the clothes they had stolen.

They rounded a corner and sprinted past a line of men waiting outside a building. As they passed an alley, the captain stopped. "Steps down," he said, and Spock saw where a staircase appeared to descend along the side of the brick structure. "Come on," Kirk said, and he led the way into the alley and down the stairs.

At the foot of the steps, they came to a door. With the

captain's arms filled with clothes, Spock reached past him and pushed. The door opened and they hurried through it.

Inside, they both waited a moment, listening for the sounds of pursuit, but Spock heard nothing. They appeared to be in a darkened storage room, the dim illumination the result of daylight entering through a pair of small windows at the top of the back wall. Spock saw crates, furniture, stacks of paper, all festooned with cobwebs. The place smelled of dust and disuse.

On the other side of the door, a wooden stairway ascended to the floor above. Captain Kirk hurried over to it and peered upward, obviously waiting to see if anybody had heard them and would be coming down to investigate. Spock joined him there, listening himself, but hearing no activity on the steps.

As Spock looked about, further examining their surroundings, the captain set down the armful of clothes they had purloined. "You were actually enjoying my predicament back there," he said, no doubt referring to his own outlandish effort to explain away Spock's pointed ears, which the police officer had clearly noticed. Kirk had claimed Spock to be of Chinese ancestry, and that as a child, he'd gotten his head caught in a mechanical rice picker. "At times," Kirk went on, "you seem quite human."

"Captain," Spock said, trying to match his friend's obvious attempt to lighten the seriousness of their circumstances, "I hardly believe that insults are within your prerogative as my commanding officer."

"Sorry," Kirk said.

Together, they picked through the pile of clothes. The captain selected a pair of gray denim pants and a red and black plaid shirt, while Spock took blue denim pants and a gray denim shirt. They each would have coats as well, a brown one for Kirk and a black one for Spock, and a dark cap would also allow the Vulcan to hide the tips of his ears from a population who would not make first contact with an extraterrestrial species for at least another century.

As they began removing their Starfleet uniforms, Spock considered their situation. They had arrived back in time on historical Earth just a few minutes ago, and yet already they had stolen clothes for themselves and rendered a police officer unconscious. Either one of those events might already have altered the timeline that they had ostensibly come here to repair. In actuality, just their being seen by scores of individuals might lead to changes in history. Indeed, if the flow of time turned out to be a chaotic system, sensitively dependent on initial conditions, then the simple fact of their presence on Earth now, interacting with the environment, might well result in a temporal disruption. In such a case, they would have no chance of accomplishing their mission. They would therefore have to proceed under the assumption that time constituted a more robust natural system, in which it would take greater events to alter history.

"Should we hide our uniforms somewhere?" Kirk asked, holding up his gold shirt. "Or get rid of them?"

"I believe it would be safer," Spock said, "to have as little trace as possible of our future existence in this time period."

"Right," Kirk said. He peered around, then moved to a large iron structure in the far corner of the room. Spock watched as he held his hands out to it, then opened a small door in its side. "There's fire in here," he said. "We can burn our uniforms."

Once they had both removed their shirts and pants—they would keep their boots, they decided—the captain incinerated them. "It is against regulations to destroy Starfleet property," Spock noted as Kirk returned to continue dressing. "Technically, our uniforms did belong to Starfleet."

"Yes, well, technically, the Federation Starfleet won't

even be established for hundreds of years," Kirk said. "So it's not possible for us to violate regulations that haven't been written yet."

"Logical," Spock said.

As the captain pulled on his shirt, he said, "Have you checked the tricorder to see if it still works? Who knows what traveling through the Guardian might have done to it."

"I haven't," Spock said as he finished buttoning the front of his own shirt. He reached for the device, which he'd set down beside the pile of clothes. He quickly activated it and ran a basic diagnostic, confirming its operation. "The tricorder is functioning," he told the captain.

"Well, that's good, but . . . " He stopped and sighed, then said, "Time we face the unpleasant facts."

As Spock shut down the tricorder, he said, "First, I believe we have about a week before McCoy arrives." He set the tricorder back down and began buttoning his cuffs. "But we can't be certain."

"Arrives where?" Kirk asked. "Honolulu, Boise, San Diego? Why not Outer Mongolia for that matter?"

"There is a theory," Spock said as he began to tuck his shirt into his pants. "There could be some logic to the belief that time is fluid, like a river, with currents, eddies, backwash."

"And the same currents that swept McCoy to a certain time and place might sweep us there too," the captain said. He paced across the room.

"Unless that is true, Captain," Spock said, "we have no hope." He retrieved his tricorder once more and walked over to join Kirk. "Frustrating," he said. "Locked in here is the exact place and moment of his arrival, even the images of what he did. If only I could tie this tricorder into the ship's computers for just a few moments."

"Couldn't you build some form of computer aid here?" Kirk asked.

"In this zinc-plated, vacuum-tubed culture?" Spock said, incredulous. Although Spock did not know with precision the time to which he and the captain had come, he knew that they had arrived sometime during the first half of Earth's twentieth century, well before the advent of digital computers.

"Yes, well it would pose an extremely complex problem in logic, Mister Spock," Kirk said. Spock raised an eyebrow at the captain's obvious attempt to offer him a challenge. "Excuse me," Kirk went on as he turned away. "I sometimes expect too much of you."

Spock felt himself react to the captain's comment even as he began to consider how he might utilize the primitive tools and equipment available in this era to develop a means of improving the tricorder's search capabilities. Of course, they would either have to steal or find a means of purchasing what he would need. If they—

The lights hanging from the ceiling suddenly went on, and a woman's voice called down from the top of the stairs. "Who's there?"

The captain made no move to leave, and as Spock heard footsteps descending the stairs, he remembered that he needed to hide his Vulcan nature. He quickly moved back across the room to where he'd left the cap. He exchanged his tricorder for it, then slipped the black wool across the top of this head and down around the tips of his ears.

"Excuse us, miss," he heard the captain say behind him as the footsteps stopped halfway down the lower flight of steps. "We didn't mean to trespass. It's cold outside."

"A lie is a very poor way to say 'hello,'" the woman said. "It isn't that cold." She spoke with an English accent.

Kirk didn't reply for a moment, and Spock wondered how he would handle the situation. "No," the captain finally said. As Spock walked back over to stand behind him, Kirk added, "We were being chased by a policeman." The admission surprised Spock, as it might easily motivate the woman to want to turn them in to the authorities. Still, in his experience, he had observed the captain to have a keen perceptiveness about people, and he trusted his judgment now.

"Why?" the woman wanted to know. She wore a light brown, calf-length dress, mostly covered by a white apron.

"These clothes," the captain said, taking a slow step forward. "We stole them. We didn't have any money."

The woman—approximately one and three-quarters meters tall, with short dark hair that framed her face—tilted her head slightly to the side, an expression seemingly mixed of surprise and respect crossing her soft features. She gazed at the captain, as though considering how she should react to him. At last, she looked down and pushed her fingers across the banister, then glanced about the room. "Well, um, I could do with some help around here," she said. "Uh, doing dishes, sweeping, general cleaning." Her voice rose on the last word, clearly identifying her statements as an offer.

"At what rate of payment?" Spock asked. The captain peered back at him quizzically. "I need radio tubes and so forth," Spock explained. "My hobby."

"Fifteen cents an hour for ten hours a day," the woman said. "What are your names?"

"Mine is Jim Kirk," the captain said. "His is—" He hesitated, then simply told the truth. "—Spock."

The woman offered a nod at the information, but did not otherwise react to a name she must have found unusual. "I'm Edith Keeler," she said. "Well, you can start by cleaning up down here." She turned and started back up the stairs, but the captain called after her.

"Excuse me, miss," he said. "Where are we?"

"You're in the Twenty-first Street Mission," Keeler said.

A mission, Spock thought, realizing their good fortune in having chosen to conceal themselves in what turned out to be a charitable organization.

"Do you run this place?" the captain asked.

"Indeed, I do, Mister Kirk," Keeler said. She then continued on up the stairs.

The captain turned to face Spock. "Radio tubes and so on?" he said. "I approve of hobbies, Mister Spock." He reached for a broom leaning against a nearby wall. He handed it to Spock, then reached for a second one for himself. "Do you really think you can construct something that will help us extract the information we need from the tricorder?"

"I am not sure," Spock said. "I have begun to give the problem some thought, and it has occurred to me that I might be able to design a mnemonic memory circuit. It remains to be seen, though, whether or not I can use the components of the day to actually construct one."

"How can we determine that?" Kirk asked.

"It would help to first learn precisely what is available to us," Spock said. "Not only will I require the equipment out of which to build such a circuit, but also the tools with which to do so."

"Of course," Kirk said. "After we've finished here, we should scour the city, look for shops that have such items."

"Captain, it may be necessary for us to steal those items as well," Spock said, uncomfortable with the idea, but well aware of the importance of their endeavors.

"Well, we'll have some money from our efforts here,"

Kirk said, raising his broom to illustrate his point. "But we'll do what we have to do." Then, in a juxtaposition of action and goal that struck Spock as peculiar, the captain began to sweep. "After all," Kirk said, "we are trying to save the future."

SEVEN

2293

Tremontaine did not watch Spock because she did not wish to expose her concern for him in this venue. It would be unprofessional and inappropriate for her to display her personal feelings for him during a diplomatic negotiation, as well as behavior that would unquestionably make him uneasy. She did pay attention, though, listening to what Spock said and how he said it, noting his overall comportment, and taking in his appearance when in the normal course of the talks she looked at him. Aware that she hadn't known him all that long, and that she'd been involved with him for only a week and a half, she still believed that she could apprehend his pain.

"There is the issue of unfettered access to all parts of the base," said Tel Venatil Liss, the Alonis ambassador. Her translated words came through a speaker set into the center of the long table at which the Federation delegation sat. Across from Tremontaine and Spock and their two aides, a transparent wall offered a view of Liss and her chief of staff, Morat, as they floated in an adjacent, water-filled room. The conference center actually spread completely submerged along the sea floor, with a third of the structure built to sustain an atmosphere for the benefit of air-breathing dignitaries.

Tremontaine opened her mouth to respond, but Spock did so first. "A Starfleet starbase has many purposes and many needs," he said. "Because it will be an open port, it must be able to provide an environment and facilities suitable for a multitude of life-forms, and to defend itself against belligerent forces. Allowing anybody other than authorized base personnel unrestricted access to sections such as life support and shield control could compromise the security of the entire station."

Tremontaine's jaw tightened, a failure of her usual diplomatic composure, and she rubbed at her cheek in order to cover her flash of visible emotion. She and Spock had anticipated for some time an Alonis requirement for entrée to all areas of the starbase, and they'd devised an intricate argument for contending with such a problematic demand. His reply just now had been far from that mark.

When Spock finished, Tremontaine spoke up in an attempt to defuse what could quickly escalate into a contentious issue. "Ambassador Liss," she said, knowing that her words would be picked up, interpreted, and transmitted into the waters about the Alonis. "We've made progress on some very complex matters today, including settling on a list of potential sites for the base. Since it's already fairly late in the day, may I suggest that we adjourn until tomorrow morning?" In her peripheral vision, she could see Spock peer over at her, but he said nothing.

Liss twisted her body in the water to face her chief of staff. Tremontaine saw Morat gesture rapidly with her pectoral fins, the Alonis equivalent of a nod. Liss looked back toward the clear wall dividing the conference rooms. "Yes, we'll agree to recess until tomorrow," she said.

"Very good," Tremontaine said. "Until tomorrow then."

Tremontaine watched as Morat swam over to a control panel in the side wall. There, for just a second, the water shimmered in an odd way, clearly manipulated by the force of the chief of staff's mind. A second later, a light on the panel winked off, and then the transparent partition between the two delegations darkened to opacity.

Spock stood up and began gathering together some of the materials they'd brought with them today. At either end of the table, their assistants—Doran Slocumb, a human man, and Carissa Siddon, a Trill woman—did the same. Tremontaine collected the data slates and other items before her, then walked with Spock and their aides out to the conference center's transporter station. From there, the four beamed to Lingasha, then boarded an airpod for the trip to the Federation Embassy. Doran and Carissa chatted along the way, but neither Tremontaine nor Spock contributed to the conversation. In the distance, the Alonis sun descended toward the horizon.

As the low buildings of the coastal city passed below, Tremontaine thought about the last couple of days. When she'd first seen Spock two mornings ago, meeting him after his sunup meditation and heading together to the early conference session, she'd sensed that something might be amiss. As the talks had gone on that day, she'd become convinced of it. She and Spock had just spent their first night with each other, and so it had been easy enough to draw the conclusion that he had that quickly come to regret his choice.

At the midday break, Tremontaine had pulled Spock aside and asked if something troubled him. When he'd hesitated, she'd pointed out his inconsistent focus and newfound reticence toward her as indications that something clearly weighed on his mind. He'd then told her of the visit he'd received that morning from Leonard McCoy, and of the death of Captain Kirk. Though pleased to hear that nothing had changed between her and Spock, she felt terrible for his loss. She knew that he and the captain had been close friends for nearly thirty years, much of that time serving together in Starfleet. News of the incident that had claimed Captain Kirk's life had appeared on the comnets the next night, and not a single report had failed to mention Spock and the *Enterprise*.

The airpod stopped at the security checkpoint at the edge of the Federation grounds, then continued on toward the embassy, where it alighted on a pad beside the front entrance. The group entered the building, and once Doran and Carissa headed for their own rooms, Tremontaine walked with Spock to the wing that housed their suites. They didn't speak until they reached her door, where Spock told her that he'd see her tomorrow, with no suggestion of having dinner together or of reviewing the day's negotiations.

"Spock?" she said as he started toward his suite. He stopped, then slowly turned back to face her.

"Yes?" he said.

"Would you come in for a few minutes?" she asked. "I'd like to talk."

Spock regarded her with a passive expression no different than that which he normally wore, and yet she still thought that she could perceive the anguish behind it. *Am I really observing that?* she asked herself. *Or am I just imposing my own emotions onto Spock, believing that he must feel what I would feel if I lost such a close friend?*

Spock averted his eyes for a moment, and Tremontaine knew that he would turn down her invitation. "Please," she said, hoping to convince him.

"Very well," he said. She nodded, then reached for the

doorknob. She waited for the brief delay as security hardware and software verified her palm print, then pushed the door open after hearing the lock click free. Spock came in after her, and she felt grateful finally to be alone with him. She hoped that she could find a way to help him.

"Spock," she said quietly, walking over to stand before him. She raised her hand, two fingers out, wanting only to comfort him, to provide some refuge from the loss of his friend.

"Alexandra," Spock said, not reaching for her hand. "My mind is . . . disordered at the moment. It would not be a pleasant experience for you—" With her other hand, Tremontaine took hold of Spock's wrist and lifted it up to where she still held out two fingers.

"I don't care about pleasant experiences right now," she said. "I care about you. Let me help."

Spock looked at her without replying, his aspect unreadable. She could not tell if he would accept or deny her desire to help him, but he did not pull his hand from her grasp. Without taking her gaze from his, she brought his closed hand next to hers, then waited. After a moment, he unfurled his index and middle fingers, and Tremontaine pushed their tips against hers. A now familiar rush of energy surged through their point of contact. Tremontaine anticipated what would come next, the unfolding of her mind beside Spock's, the tenuous, evanescent connection like an imagined breath on the back of her neck.

She withdrew her defenses, did it more easily now than the first time and the times since, understanding now the existence, the possibilities of that internal connection. But as her thoughts revealed themselves, Spock's did not. She did not understand his absence, how he even *could* be absent from their link. Not knowing quite how to do it, she attempted to find him, to send her *self* in search of his *self*.

She sought Spock out and grew more concerned when she did not find him, until at last—

She encountered the wall. Stretching left and right, up and down, an infinite, impenetrable barrier. A sense of separation filled Tremontaine's being, and she grew distraught for Spock, seemingly lost to her right now.

And then an opening appeared in the vast barricade, a nebulous, glowing circle, seeming both real and unreal, a remembered dream, maybe, or a dream of a memory, but intimating access. Tremontaine pushed herself through it, into the shadowy area beyond. There, at last, she found Spock, his mind closed upon itself like a flower holding its petals tightly bound against a sudden frost.

Without hesitation, she let her mind drift toward his, seeking the coalescence of the two. She could feel his resistance, but also his need. All of her defenses down, she directed the filaments of her mind as best she could toward his own, which finally unwound just enough, at last permitting her being to interweave with his and—

The darkness within dragged her down, an anchor that threatened to hold her fast, to drown her in the depths of night. Tremontaine screamed silently, but then fought her fear, willingly accepted her overloaded descent into misery, tried to ease the affliction by sharing it. The awful weight of despair enveloped her, a bereavement complete and inescapable—

But not complete, no. Loss alone did not burden her, but also the terrible millstone of regret. How could she so easily have denied her closest friend his happiness, when she would not deny herself or others? Why had she not—

In no time, it all vanished, the strands of Spock's mind retreating in on themselves, leaving Tremontaine alone in the void. Utterly lost, she flailed about, and—

Spock pulled his hand away from hers, severing their

connection. Tremontaine worked to catch her breath, the experience of suffering his grief overwhelming. "Spock," she said as she stared into his dark eyes, her voice barely a whisper.

He looked away, then moved across the room, away from her. "I am sorry," he said without peering back around. "I didn't intend . . . " He turned toward her. "I did not mean for you to be so fully subjected to my pain."

"Spock," she repeated, still trying to gain her bearings. As though feeling posttraumatic stress, she wanted to collapse, to just sit quietly and find a way to overcome what had just happened to her. But she knew that she could not. Even across the room, she could see that Spock's face had become drawn. Allowing her access to his sorrow had also unleashed it on himself, undermining whatever techniques he had used to box it away. "I still want to help," she told him.

"There is nothing to be done," Spock said. "There is only reality. I will mourn my friend and move on."

Tremontaine took a step toward him, their physical distance making him seem so remote from her. He appeared exhausted now, and she knew that he had not slept well the past two nights, his slumber interrupted by troubling dreams. It amazed her that he could collect himself enough to present the illusion of normality.

Except that wasn't precisely the case, now, was it? Tremontaine thought. In conference, Spock had looked and acted as he always had, but his focus had been compromised. He'd more than once failed to follow up on details as the two of them had planned, and she'd had to request an early end to today's session in an attempt to avert any repercussions from his unexpectedly firm response to Ambassador Liss regarding Alonis access on the proposed starbase.

As though reading her thoughts, Spock said, "But there is the issue of my ability to remain effective in my role here."

Tremontaine nodded. "You shouldn't be here anyway," she said. "I heard on the comnets last night that Starfleet will be holding a memorial service for Captain Kirk next week. Surely you need to be there."

"I had thought to stay on Alonis," Spock said. "Because of the complexity and importance of these negotiations and my expertise from a Starfleet perspective, my presence here seemed of greater value."

To the Alonis and the Federation and Starfleet, Tremontaine thought, *but not to you.* She did not say that, though, not wanting to presume to tell Spock what would be best for him. Instead, she walked the rest of the way across the room and took his hand—not in any of the Vulcan ways he had shared with her, but simply holding his hand in hers. "You're leaving then?" she asked.

"I am," he said. "Starfleet and the BIA might object, as might the Alonis themselves. But my mind is not functioning at top efficiency right now, and so I fear my continued presence could actually damage the talks."

"Your withdrawal won't be an issue," Tremontaine promised. She doubted that any of the factions would fail to comprehend the enormity of Spock's loss or his need to attend Captain Kirk's memorial, though she supposed that some might be making the common error of mistaking Vulcans' strict emotional *control* for an emotional *dearth.* Regardless, she would ensure that Spock be granted the leave he required, bringing to bear the influence of her long and successful career, if need be.

"Thank you," Spock said. "If you'll excuse me, I need to book passage to Earth." He tried to pull his hand from hers, but she held on to it.

"Let me do that for you," she said. "Sit down and I'll make you some tea. While you rest, I'll find a way to get you from Alonis to Earth."

"Very well," Spock said again. She let go of his hand as he went to sit down on a nearby sofa, and then she headed toward the food synthesizer on the other side of the room. Thirty minutes later, she had found a transport traveling out of Ariannus that would get Spock to Earth in time for the memorial.

Tremontaine only wished that she were going with him.

The auditorium had filled to its capacity of one thousand, which did not include the several dozen dignitaries seated on the stage. The memorial had initially been planned for Starfleet Headquarters, but when it had become clear how many would attend, the organizers had opted to move the service over to the Starfleet Academy campus. Demand for a public commemoration would see another event held in a few days, on the grounds of the Cape Canaveral Museum, around the famed Pad B of Launch Complex 39. Here, though, people who had actually known James T. Kirk had gathered to remember him. Now, after two hours and numerous speakers, the ceremony appeared to be nearing its end.

Spock sat on the stage, between Starfleet Commander-in-Chief Smillie to his left and Dr. McCoy to his right. At the podium just ahead stood Robert Wesley, addressing the assemblage. Wearing formal civilian attire, Wesley had a well-lined face beneath a thicket of short gray hair. "Jim Kirk saved my life," he said. "With so many members of Starfleet here today and so many citizens of Earth, I know that I'm far from the only one who can make that claim." Spock knew that Wesley had been friends with Jim for more than four decades, since he had instructed the young

Midshipman Kirk at the academy. Ultimately attaining the rank of commodore and commanding the starship *Lexington,* Wesley had later retired from Starfleet and become governor of Mantilles, once the Federation's most remote inhabited world. "The man we honor today," Wesley intoned, "was a true hero. Even though he left Starfleet earlier this year, the very last act of his life, fittingly enough, was to save the crew and passengers of a starship—coincidentally a new starship named for the ones he'd so long commanded: the *Enterprise.*"

As Wesley began to detail the captain's long and distinguished record, Spock peered out into the audience, where he recognized so many of those attending. He saw in the front row Jim's three nephews, his only surviving blood relatives. Beside them sat the former members of the *Enterprise*'s longtime command crew—Captains Scott and Sulu, Commanders Uhura and Chekov—as well as Commander Dennehy and Lieutenant Commander Saavik. Earlier, Spock had seen numerous others who had served with the captain, including Jabilo M'Benga, Christine Chapel, Ryan Leslie, John Kyle, Arex, Janice Rand, Dawson Walking Bear, and Kevin Riley. He'd also noted the presence of several women with whom Jim had been involved romantically: Areel Shaw, Janet Wallace, Carol Marcus, Antonia Salvatori.

Amid all of those familiar faces, and still others, Spock felt alone. Despite being seated next to McCoy, with whom he had experienced so much, his sense of seclusion remained strong. *It is illogical,* he upbraided himself, but to deny the truth would do nothing to alter it.

"Captain Kirk's considerable list of accolades," Spock heard Wesley say, "includes three Starfleet Medals of Honor, the Grankite Order of Tactics, the Distinguished Service Star, the Lewis and Clark Corps of Discovery

THE FIRE AND THE ROSE

Cross, the Archer Ribbon for Conspicuous Bravery. . . . "

Spock had not seen or spoken to Jim for three months, since they had testified together at a Starfleet board of inquiry investigating the conspiracy that had resulted in the assassination of Chancellor Gorkon. At that time, on the threshold of resigning his commission, the captain's energy and emotions had seemed at a low ebb. After the admirals had completed their questioning, Spock had talked with his friend, presenting his opinion that the captain might best be served by reconsidering his decision to leave Starfleet. But Jim had been adamant about his retirement, citing not only the distaste he held for the politics that he felt had overrun the service, but also his own need for a life removed from the responsibilities of leading hundreds, and of making decisions and taking actions that could affect billions, even trillions, of lives. More than anything, Jim had said, he wanted to find peace.

Not long after that, as Spock had settled into the training position he'd accepted with Starfleet, McCoy had contacted him to reveal that the captain had taken up some very dangerous activities, quoting Scott as saying that Jim wanted to "run a bloody decathlon across the galaxy." Spock and McCoy had discussed the captain's perilous behavior, concluding that he sought such thrills in order to fill the void in his life left by stepping down from the command of a starship. But though he hadn't divulged it to McCoy, Spock had also thought that something else had contributed significantly to Jim's apparent courting of death: loneliness.

"In his career," Wesley told the audience, "Jim Kirk traveled from the heart of the Federation to the galactic rim, from the Klingon Empire to beyond Questar M-One-Seven, from Romulan space out to the Aquarius Formation."

From the time he had begun serving under Captain Kirk, Spock had perceived his commanding officer's wanderlust, his desire to explore. But after the death of Gary Mitchell, Spock had also begun to catch occasional glimpses of the captain's solitary nature. After the incident with the Guardian of Forever, those glimpses had become more frequent, Jim's sense of aloneness seemingly deeper. A quarter of a century later, after the captain had claimed to be departing Starfleet for good, his isolation had appeared nearly complete. He had proceeded to withdraw not just from his professional life, but from his personal relationships as well. According to McCoy, it had only been in the last week or so of his life—after Starfleet had asked him to christen the new *Excelsior*-class *Enterprise*—that Jim had renewed ties with some of his friends.

Ever since they'd parted company after the board of inquiry, Spock had anticipated contacting the captain, particularly after learning of his participation in such dangerous pastimes. But then Spock had been summoned by the Bureau of Interplanetary Affairs and had accepted their offer of an ambassadorial post. A month had passed, and then a second and a third. Only once before had he and Jim gone for such a long period with no communication between them: after the *Enterprise*'s five-year mission had ended in 2270, when Spock had resigned his Starfleet commission and returned to Vulcan to undertake the *Kolinahr* training. But their friendship had lasted through those two and a half years and then for two decades afterward, enduring many difficult circumstances. It had seemed reasonable to believe that it would continue into Jim's retirement.

But it hadn't. Spock had seen Jim at the board of inquiry, on one of the captain's last days in Starfleet. Then he had never seen him again.

At the podium, Wesley finished his tribute. "I was fortunate to have Jim Kirk in my life," he said. Then, with a lingering look across those present, he ended by saying, "We were all fortunate to have Jim Kirk in our lives." Applause followed him as he turned and walked back across the stage to his seat.

Spock waited as the Starfleet commander-in-chief rose and returned to the podium, from which he had guided the memorial. Many individuals had spoken throughout the morning. Dr. Gillian Taylor, a twentieth-century cetacean biologist who had helped the captain and the *Enterprise*'s command crew bring a pair of humpback whales into the present in order to avert Earth's destruction, had recalled meeting Jim, being charmed by him, and at last being enlisted to his cause. Admiral Westervliet Komack had remembered his own days as the flag officer in command of Sector 9 during the 2260s, a position he'd found fraught with challenges and filled with rewards simply because, at that time, Captain Kirk had reported to him. Helena Albrecht, former governor of Deneva, had talked of the terrible days when her colony had been invaded by deadly neural parasites, and of the days following, when the captain and crew of the *Enterprise* had destroyed the threat. Admiral Margaret Sinclair-Alexander of Starfleet Command had related tales of her service under the command of Captain Kirk, from whom she said she had learn so much. Rojan, the Kelvan leader who with a group of his people had fled the doomed Andromeda Galaxy, intent on conquering the Milky Way, had spoken admiringly of the captain's efforts to help them settle a world of their own, without the need of going to war with the Federation.

One after another, the speakers had recounted their experiences with Captain Kirk, explaining the tremendous impact he'd had on their lives. McCoy had spoken first, painting a portrait of Jim as a passionate man driven to explore space from an early age, as a fiercely loyal friend, and as a thoughtful, responsible, decisive leader. The doctor's obviously heartfelt and well-considered eulogium had set the tone for the proceedings, offering a friend's perspective of Jim as a person, and a respectful and laudatory view of him as a starship commander.

"Thank you, Governor Wesley," Admiral Smillie said after the applause had quieted. "Our final speaker before President Ra-ghoratreii concludes our ceremony will be Ambassador Spock of Vulcan. As many of you know, Mister Spock began serving with Captain Kirk almost thirty years ago, as his executive officer aboard the *U.S.S. Enterprise*—a role he permanently surrendered only upon the captain's retirement." The normally stern-mannered admiral smiled before continuing. "While their exploits together eventually became well known to the public," he said, "they have always been well known—and a constant source of irritation—to Starfleet Command." A swell of laughter rolled through the auditorium. The commander-in-chief waited for it to fade, then glanced over at Spock. "Ambassador," he said, then made his way back to his own chair.

Spock stood up, the black fabric of his Vulcan ceremonial robes settling about his lean figure. Unlike many of the orators today, he carried no notes with him. On the voyage from Alonis to Earth, he had written a suitable encomium for the captain and committed it to memory. But as he stepped up to the podium and peered out at all those commemorating Jim's life, Spock discovered that he did not wish to speak at all. He had no need to share his loss with others, already displeased with himself for having done so in the manner he had with Alexandra. Nor did he want to admit the sting of regret he felt for not having talked with his friend in the months prior to his death, nor to reveal the persistent remorse that had occupied him since the fateful decision he had so confidently made all those years ago.

As Spock's silence began to draw out, he saw some people shifting nervously in their seats, a mixture of sorrow and anxiety on their faces as they gazed at him. For their sake, he realized, he could not say nothing; for his own, he could not say what he had intended to say. "Commanding a starship," he said at last, recalling something he had once told Jim, "was James T. Kirk's first, best destiny." The captain had spent so much of his adult life on the bridge of the *Enterprise,* executing his duties to such a successful degree, that the statement verged on truism. "I have been, and always shall be his friend." Spock hesitated for a moment, debating whether those in attendance wished him to say more, but what else could he add that held any greater meaning than what he'd already said?

In silence, he returned to his seat. Dr. McCoy regarded him with a look of sadness, perhaps even of pity. After a few seconds, Spock heard scattered claps, but they did not blossom into applause, the brevity of his comments evidently startling people, including the Starfleet commander-in-chief. Admiral Smillie quickly hurried back to the podium. "Thank you, Ambassador," he said. "Now, to close our memorial, Federation President Ra-ghoratreii has asked to say a few words." As the president rose, the admiral once more retreated to his seat.

An Efrosian, Ra-ghoratreii had raised ridges that reached from the top of his nose and slanted across his forehead. He had long, silken white hair, a similarly colored moustache that fell from the sides of his mouth and chin well past the line of his jaw, and brilliant blue eyes

that could see only rough shapes. He wore a pair of spe-
cially designed pince-nez spectacles that transmitted
clearer images to his optic nerves, permitting him a better
awareness of his surroundings and thus allowing him to
move about more easily.

"Thank you, Admiral," Ra-ghoratreii said. "And I want
to thank everybody for attending. It speaks volumes that
so many people have chosen to be here today, from so
many different worlds and so many different circumstances. Though it may be redundant after the comments
of all those who have spoken this morning, I would be re-
miss if I did not mention my own experiences with Captain Kirk." As Spock listened, he noted McCoy continuing
to gaze at him. "I met James T. Kirk for the first time only
a few months ago. It was on the Klingon world of Khitomer, and the captain introduced himself by lunging
through the air and tackling me to the floor in order to
save me from an assassination attempt." Ra-ghoratreii
paused for a second, clearly for effect. "Needless to say, I
was very pleased to make his acquaintance." Laughter
again went up in the auditorium.

The president detailed the crisis surrounding the attempt on his life, and how Captain Kirk had helped both to
prevent a war between the Federation and the Klingons,
and to foster an active peace between the two powers. Ra-
ghoratreii then described what it had been like for him,
after the incident, to actually converse with the captain, a
heroic, larger-than-life figure he'd known about for so
long. He'd expected to be awed by the legend, he said, but
instead had been impressed by the man.

As the president started talking about other of Jim's
most important accomplishments, Spock pondered his
own immediate future, considering what he would do next.
The Bureau of Interplanetary Affairs wanted him to return

to the negotiations on Alonis as soon as possible, as did the Alonis themselves, but his own evaluation of his ability to adequately discharge his ambassadorial responsibilities at this juncture had only diminished since he'd taken leave. In the nights since McCoy had informed him of Jim's death—on Alonis, aboard the *S.S. Glasgow* en route to Earth, and in the apartment he still kept here in San Francisco—Spock had slept poorly, beset by uncharacteristically emotional dreams. In times of stress, Vulcans could go without sleep for weeks, and he now considered avoiding slumber in the days ahead. Perhaps a regimen of lengthy meditations over an extended period would help to settle his mind.

Spock listened as President Ra-ghoratreii brought his remarks to a close, reiterating his estimation of Captain Kirk as a legendary officer and as a great man. When he finished speaking, the audience clapped once more. The president bowed his head, then walked offstage to the left. As the applause quieted, a murmur of conversation grew in its place. People rose, both those out in the auditorium and the speakers up on the stage.

Spock got to his feet and strode quickly into the wing As he neared an exit, he heard his name called from behind him, once, then a second time. He considered not stopping, simply continuing through the door and then walking through the city to his apartment, having no inclination to speak with anybody right now. Such a response would be rude, though, as well as suggesting an emotional motivation. Spock turned and waited for McCoy.

"Spock, thank goodness," the doctor said as he reached him. McCoy's tired appearance had changed little since Spock had seen him on Alonis. "I thought those pointed ears of yours might not be working."

A rejoinder occurred to Spock—*Would that my ears did*

not function when I was within audible range of your voice—but he did not wish to encourage a prolonged conversation. "What can I do for you, Doctor?" he asked.

McCoy glanced at the people passing them, heading for the exit, and he sidled a few steps away from them. As Spock followed, the doctor peered at him as though evaluating him in some way. Then McCoy nodded back over his shoulder, in the direction of the stage. "It was a good service," he said.

"Yes," Spock agreed. "Is there anything else?"

"Well, it's good to see you too, Spock," McCoy said pointedly.

"Yes," Spock said again, and he turned to go.

"Wait," McCoy said, his voice rising for a second. "I'm sorry. I know this is difficult for you too."

Spock looked at him, unsure what sort of a reply the doctor expected. Surely McCoy had known him long enough *not* to anticipate an emotional response. "It is what it is," Spock said.

"I didn't get a chance to say so earlier," McCoy told him, "but I'm very happy that you decided to come." The doctor had arrived at the memorial just before the ceremony had begun. His eyes had widened in obvious surprise when he'd sat down onstage beside Spock, but there had been no time for them to speak with each other.

"As it turned out," Spock confessed, "I found that I could not stay away."

"I know what you mean," McCoy said. "Anyway, I also wanted to apologize for being so hard on you when I went to Alonis. I realize that we all deal with grief in different ways, and there's no telling how Vulcans do it." The remark sounded like a gibe, but McCoy's demeanor told Spock otherwise. When he said nothing, the doctor went on. "I liked what you had to say up there, Spock. In just a few words, you said the most important things. I know Jim would've appreciated it."

"Thank you, Doctor," Spock said. "But brevity is no measure of import or quality. I found your remarks quite compelling."

"Thank you, Spock," McCoy said. "That means a great deal coming from you."

Spock acknowledged the compliment with a nod. "If there is nothing else then—"

"Actually, there is," McCoy said. "I assume you're going back to Alonis."

"Eventually, yes," Spock said. While he intended to return to the conference as expeditiously as possible, he could not envision doing so for at least a week, maybe two.

"Then you're not leaving Earth right away?" McCoy asked.

"I have no plans to that avail," Spock said.

"Then I'd like you to come by Jim's apartment," McCoy said. The idea provoked an immediate response in Spock, an aversion that disturbed him as much for its existence as for its content.

"For what purpose?" Spock asked.

"In his will, Jim named me his executor," McCoy said. "There are a few items he left to you."

"Perhaps you can have them sent to me," Spock suggested.

"I can," McCoy said, "but . . . all of us are going to be there: Scotty, Sulu, Uhura, Chekov. We'll have a drink, tell some stories about Jim, talk about the good old days . . ."

"To which 'good old days' are you referring, Doctor?" Spock asked.

"All of them, Spock," McCoy said. "All of them up until the day Jim died." The doctor looked down for a moment, visibly overcome. He took a deep breath, then said, "We'd all really like you to be there. *I* would like you to be there."

Spock did not want to go, but McCoy's entreaty had moved him, yet another instance of his emotion overshadowing his logic. For many years, he had found a balance between his human and Vulcan selves, accepting his dual nature and learning to integrate them with each other. But now that equilibrium seemed threatened, and Spock wanted to withdraw into himself and find some way to restore it.

Fleeing a problem will not solve it, he told himself. If he had to avoid situations in order to maintain his logic, then his mental state would remain precarious. "Very well," he said to McCoy. "I will go with you."

"Good, Spock," the doctor said. "I'm glad."

Together they went outside and started across the Starfleet Academy campus, on their way toward Russian Hill and Jim's old apartment.

EIGHT

1930

Kirk walked beside Edith Keeler as she led him and Spock through the urban canyons of New York. Night, moonless and deep, had descended on the city. In many places, though, small attempts to combat the darkness prevailed: the illumination emanating from windows in the buildings they passed, the lights mounted on the ground vehicles that drove by, the cones of yellow light falling from the street lamps that lined the sidewalks.

Where it had not been cold this morning—despite Kirk's claims to the contrary when he and Spock had been discovered by Miss Keeler—the temperature had dropped considerably after sunset. Kirk kept his coat buttoned up to his neck and his hands buried in his pockets. Whenever he glanced over to their escort, he saw her breath puffing out before her in ephemeral clouds of white.

Keeler had a way about her, Kirk thought. Even simply walking through the wintry night, she projected a positive and vibrant air. This seemed true in spite of both the work she did—running a soup kitchen for the indigent—and the period in which she lived.

During the course of cleaning the basement today, Kirk and Spock had taken midday and evening meals upstairs, in the main room of the mission. There, they had seen a calendar hanging on a wall, displaying the days of June 1922, but then they'd consulted several different newspapers, all of which had identified the current month as January 1930. That placed them in an era of economic upheaval known as the Great Depression. And yet as they'd eaten their soup and bread this evening, Keeler had taken a few moments to address the penniless, hungry men who had come to her establishment in search of food and charity. She'd told them, essentially, that there would be better days ahead, not just for them, but for everybody. Incredibly, she'd spoken of the possibilities of atomic power and space travel, of eliminating hunger and disease worldwide, all accomplishments well in the future. To Kirk, her views made her seem as much out of place in 1930 as he and Spock were.

"Down this way," Keeler said, pointing left as they reached an intersection.

As they turned the corner, Kirk said, "I have to ask you, Miss Keeler, how can you be so sure that the days ahead are worth living for, when things appear so bleak right now?"

"Bleak?" she said, her delicate features visible at the moment in the reflected glow of a street lamp. "You mean because of the bank failures and the stock market panic?"

"Yes," Kirk said, sure that she must be referring to the events of the day.

"Oh, I don't know how bleak things are," Keeler said. "I suppose every day is bleak for somebody, no matter how good or how bad things are for the rest of the world. Poverty was widespread before the panic, it's just getting worse now. But at least we're not at war."

"But you sounded very optimistic about humanity's future," Kirk prompted her.

"Well, yes, I am," she said. "It seems to me that if mankind can produce Michelangelo's *David* and the plays of William Shakespeare, if it can give us the telescope and the microscope, sailing ships and aeroplanes . . . it seems to me that a society of such capabilities must surely be able to lift itself and its citizens out of poverty and starvation and disease."

"That is a noble view," Kirk said.

"We can be a noble people," Keeler replied.

"The history of mankind is also filled with tyranny," Spock said from behind them.

"Spock—" Kirk began to protest, but Keeler stopped him.

"No, you're right, Mister Spock," she said. "And it isn't just history. Mister Gandhi and the people of India are struggling right now to throw off the shackles of British imperialism."

"And you believe they'll be successful," Kirk said.

"Of course they will be," Keeler said. "It may take years or even generations, but they will succeed because our drive to be free is greater than our drive to conquer. Every day, every month, every year that passes will strengthen the resolve of the Indian people and weaken the will of the British politicians. Eventually, even the British people will favor the independence of India."

"An interesting analysis," Spock said.

"When you look at history," Keeler continued, "you do see tyranny. But you also see people climbing mountains, crossing continents and oceans, and flying across the sky." She paused for a moment, but Kirk chose not to fill the silence, instead waiting—anxious—for what she would say next. "Materialism is not a natural state for people, I don't think," she went on, "or at least it needn't be a *normal* state. People are better as explorers than as collectors, better as creatures of imagination than as creatures of possession."

"So you believe that the good in humanity will overcome the bad," Kirk said.

"Yes, I very much do," Keeler said, and she stopped walking. For a second, Kirk thought that he might have insulted her in some way, but then she pointed toward the building there. "This is where I live," she said.

Kirk peered up at the four-story structure, which even at night appeared to be in poor repair. Light streamed from several windows, though most appeared dark. Keeler started up a wide set of concrete steps at the front of the building, and Kirk and Spock followed. At the top of the stairs, she pointed to a dark archway above the front door. "I keep telling Mister Dubinski that he needs to replace that lightbulb," she said.

Keeler pushed through the door into a tiny vestibule, where a bare bulb hung down from the ceiling and shined on a row of metal boxes. Paint on the wall above and below peeled so badly that Kirk thought the bare spots outnumbered the beige chips that remained. Keeler flipped up the lid of the box marked 33, then closed it. "No mail," she said. "Thankfully."

After Keeler opened the inner door, they all moved forward into a narrow hallway. Here, the walls had been better maintained, with only a few places that showed chipped paint. Red carpeting covered the floors. A stairway on the left side of the hall led up to the second floor, while several doors lined the other side. Keeler walked to the first one and knocked.

"Are you sure it's not too late?" Kirk asked.

"I called Mister Dubinski earlier and told him we'd be coming," Keeler said.

Before long, Kirk heard movement within the apartment, and a moment later, the door opened. A heavyset man stood inside, a tattered red robe wrapped about him. It didn't appear as though he'd shaved in several days, and the stub of an unlighted cigar peeked out from the corner of his mouth. "Miss Keeler," he said, his accent swallowing the *r: Keeluh.* He gave Kirk and Spock a long look, then asked, "These the guys?"

"Yes," she said. "This is Mister Kirk and Mister Spock."

"They all right?" Dubinski asked.

"If they weren't," Keeler said, "would I bring them to the building I live in?"

"No, I guess not," Dubinski allowed. Looking back at Kirk, he said, "That's two dollars a week, in advance."

"Oh, yes, of course," Kirk said, recalling the cash that Keeler had earlier given to him and Spock. He reached into the pocket of his denim pants, pulled out two bills, and offered them to Dubinski. The landlord snatched them like a mouse stealing a piece of cheese.

"It's number twenty-one," he said, extracting a key from the pocket of his robe. "You need me to take 'em up, or do you wanna show 'em?" he asked Keeler.

"That's all right," Keeler said, taking the key. "We've disturbed you enough tonight. Thank you."

Dubinski grunted an acknowledgment, then closed his door.

"Charming fellow," Kirk remarked.

"Oh, he's all right," Keeler said as she walked back down the hall to the stairs. "A lot of places around here are charging two and a half and three dollars a week for a room." At the top of the steps, she went to the first door, onto which the number *21* had been affixed. She used the key to unlock it, then opened the door and reached inside to turn on a light. Then she stepped aside, obviously to allow Kirk and Spock to enter.

Inside, Kirk found himself in a single small room. The blue, patterned wallpaper looked old, but peeled in only a few places. He saw two narrow beds with their headboards against the far wall, separated by a low dresser. A second, taller dresser stood to the right of the door, and a closet had been built into the corner to the left. A table sat against the left-hand wall, below windows covered by sheer brown curtains.

"The loo is down at the end of the hall," Keeler said, still standing outside the apartment.

"The what?" Kirk asked.

Keeler chuckled. "Sorry, that's just my English showing," she said. "I meant the bathroom."

"All right," Kirk said.

"Here," she said, holding up the key that Dubinski had given her. "You'll need this."

Kirk walked over to the door and peered down at Keeler. As he'd told Spock during the talk she'd given at their evening meal, he thought her uncommon. Now, he gazed into her hazel eyes and found himself almost transfixed by her beauty—a beauty clearly not limited to the physical. He reached up and took the key from her, feeling a jolt as his hand briefly touched hers. "Thank you, Miss Keeler," he said.

She smiled. "You are very welcome, Mister Kirk," she said. "Good night." She turned and headed down the hall, toward the staircase leading up to the next floor. Kirk watched her for a moment, then withdrew into the room and closed the door.

"An interesting woman," he told Spock.

"Indeed," Spock said. He unbuttoned his coat, then removed it to reveal the tricorder hanging by its strap from his shoulder. He took it off and set it down on the table.

"We shouldn't leave that here when we go out," Kirk said. When they'd begun working at the mission that morning, they'd discussed searching the city tonight for shops that sold tools and equipment that Spock might be able to use to build a mnemonic memory circuit.

"Captain, may I suggest that I venture out alone tonight," Spock said. "You have been awake now for some time."

Spock needn't have told him that. They'd both logged half a shift on the bridge before McCoy's accident, and then had spent time down on the planet before leaping through the Guardian. They'd now been in the past for fourteen hours or so, which meant that they'd probably been awake for close to an entire day. But while Vulcans could do without sleep for protracted periods, human performance suffered without regular slumber. Still, the importance of their mission here provided him all the energy he needed right now.

"It's all right," Kirk said. "I've got a few hours left in me."

"Very well," Spock said. He picked up the tricorder from the table, hung it over his shoulder, and pulled his coat on again.

Together, they went back out into the night.

Spock sat at the table in the apartment, the late afternoon sun providing ample illumination for his work. Spread out in front of him, two dozen sheets of paper covered the tabletop, and another dozen lay atop the near bed. On each, he'd written a portion of the schematic he'd been designing in his head since their arrival in the past, four days ago. After the captain had acquired a sheaf of paper and two pencils from Edith Keeler yesterday, Spock had spent the night and all of today setting his plans down in writing.

Now, he wrote down the final markings on the final sheet, then stood up to survey his work. He stepped over to the bed and found the graphic representation of the mnemonic memory circuit's connections to the tricorder. From there, he traced his way through the entire diagram, verifying power requirements, confirming the logic flow of the data that would pass through it, and checking the over-all integrity of the layout.

Halfway through the process, as the afternoon gave way to the evening, Spock turned on both of the lights in the room, the one on the wall beside the door and the one on the wall opposite. By the time he'd worked his way through the whole schematic, night had fallen. His plan seemed sound, though whether or not it would actually function as he'd formulated it, he could not tell. In the few electrical components he and the captain had already pur-chased, he'd found some large variances from their stated ratings, making their usage problematic.

Spock collected the pieces of paper, carefully labeling the position of each. He then sat back down at the table and began to page through every sheet, in order to make a list of all that he would need. As he did so, he wondered if the captain had made any progress in his quest today.

Since their arrival in 1930, they had worked three full days at the 21st Street Mission, and a half day yesterday. While the captain had worked there this morning as well, Spock had taken the entire day to complete the design of the memory circuit. In the meantime, Captain Kirk had decided that, after putting in his time at the mission today, he would visit the New York Public Library. There, he would read through the city's newspapers of the last few days, searching for any indication of Dr. McCoy's presence in the past. It seemed like an effort unlikely to yield any results, but one worth making.

When Spock finished compiling an inventory of everything that he would need, he considered the issue of how to mount the components to fix them in place. He would need a solid surface, preferably wood so that he could attach them using nails or staples. Looking around the room, he spied the two dressers, and he went to the smaller one. He removed one of the drawers, then began to pry the back from it.

At that moment, somebody knocked on the door. Spock surmised that it must be either Edith Keeler or the landlord, Mr. Dubinski. He returned the drawer to the dresser, then donned his cap before crossing the room and opening the door. As he'd suspected, Keeler stood there.

"Mister Spock," she said. "If you're interested, I've gotten work for you and Mister Kirk for the next two days. It'll be ten hours work each day for twenty cents an hour. You'll be loading and unloading boxes from trucks."

"The higher rate of pay would be helpful," Spock said.

Though he and the captain had already decided that they would steal the components for the mnemonic memory circuit if they needed to, they both much preferred the idea of simply purchasing them. In addition to the simple immorality of theft, they would risk arrest by committing a crime, as they had already learned from taking the clothes they still wore. Not only could the fact of their being taken into custody conceivably alter the timeline, but if McCoy then arrived in the past, they wouldn't be able to stop him from changing history if they'd been taken to jail.

"Good," Keeler said. "Here, I've written down directions for you to get there." She held out a torn piece of paper. Spock took the information and made sure that he could read it. "You need to be there at seven A.M."

"Thank you," he said.

Keeler glanced past him into the room, obviously looking for the captain. "Is Mister Kirk here?" she asked. The mutual attraction between Keeler and the captain seemed readily apparent to Spock, although the two had spent little time together.

"He is not," Spock said.

Keeler smiled and nodded. "All right," she said. "Well, good night, Mister Spock."

"Good night, Miss Keeler," Spock said. As she headed down the hall, he closed the door. He then returned to the dresser, where he started to remove the wooden slats from the backs of the drawers.

Within an hour, the captain returned. He brought a brown paper bag with him, in which he carried food that he had purchased. Until today, they had taken all of their meals at the 21st Street Mission, but they had both agreed that they could do with some more substantial sustenance. As they sat down at the table to eat—various fruits and vegetables for both of them, as well as some sliced meat for the captain—Kirk asked about Spock's progress with the design for the mnemonic memory circuit.

"I have completed it," Spock said, "along with a list of all the components I will require." He picked up the paper and handed it over to the captain.

"There's a lot here," Kirk said.

"It is the minimal amount of equipment needed," Spock said.

"All right," Kirk said. "At midday tomorrow, we'll go to one of the radio repair shops we saw the other night."

Spock informed the captain of the job that Keeler had found for them for the next two days, and Kirk revealed that he'd uncovered no references to McCoy anywhere within any of the newspapers that he'd read. "I had another thought, though," Kirk said. "When McCoy arrives in the past, or if he's arrived already, he's still going to be under the influence of the cordrazine. If he runs through the streets screaming about being hunted by assassins, there's a chance that he might be hospitalized, or maybe even arrested."

"That is true," Spock said.

"While you work on the memory circuit," Kirk asked, "what do you think of me checking hospitals and police stations in the area?"

Spock considered the idea. "It might be reasonable to check hospitals," he said. "You could simply ask for Doctor McCoy by name, perhaps claiming to be his brother. I would be reluctant to approach the police, though. I am not sure how they would react to somebody asking about their arrest records or people they have in custody, and since we ourselves possess no identification—"

"Right," Kirk agreed. "Well, I'll begin checking hospitals tomorrow."

The next night, as the captain walked the city in search of a patient named Leonard McCoy, Spock began his attempt at building a mnemonic memory circuit.

NINE

2293

It had been a bittersweet afternoon. With the old crew congregated in Jim's apartment, scattered on chairs about the den, McCoy realized that they hadn't all been together in several years, at least not to speak of. They'd each ended up at Camp Khitomer at the same time four or five months ago, when they'd foiled the assassination of the Federation president, but those few minutes had been hectic and rushed, and there had been no opportunity even to talk.

Today, though, there had hardly been a silent minute. But for Spock, who had stayed mostly quiet, they had all taken turns recollecting tales of their former captain. With the floor-to-ceiling windows of the den affording them a spectacular view of San Francisco Bay, tears and laughter had mixed throughout the course of the get-together.

Uhura had remembered the grilling Jim had given her when, during the five-year mission, she'd requested reassignment from the command division to engineering and services. Captain Kirk had referred repeatedly to his belief in her leadership potential, and she'd come away from their meeting believing that his obvious disappointment in her choice would prevent him from authorizing a change to her classification. After her next shift, though, she'd found

new uniforms in her quarters—new *red* uniforms, the
color specifying the engineering and services division—
along with a data slate containing the captain's approval of
her request.

Pavel had given an uproarious account of the time he
and Jim, during the *Enterprise*'s return voyage from the
Aquarius Formation, had been stranded on the world of
the libidinous Nelestra. The leaders of the humanlike civilization had presented each of them with half a dozen
nubile and willing women. When the captain had explained that the women would not influence the establishment of diplomatic relations, the Nelestra leaders had
misunderstood and bestowed upon Kirk and Chekov another dozen beauties.

Hikaru had spoken of a number of his many hobbies
that he'd somehow coerced the captain into trying, and
Scotty had regaled them with a series of progressively
more outrageous drinking stories that seemed to take him
and the captain from one side of the galaxy to the other.
McCoy himself had told many a tale about his old friend,
from the very first time he'd met Jim to the last time they'd
spoken, less than a week before the captain's death.

Underlying every anecdote, though, had been the reality of Jim's absence. McCoy had enjoyed the reunion, but
his happy observation that it had been a while since
they'd all gotten together fell apart whenever he thought
of the reason for it: Jim was missing, and he always
would be. The apartment itself provided ready reminders,
since much of it stood empty. McCoy had boxed up most
of Jim's belongings and recycled much of his furniture,
though he'd been sure to leave enough for today's gathering.

As the day had worn on and the time had come for
everybody to go their separate ways, McCoy had distrib-

uted the few items Jim had specified in his will. Spock had received a trio of historic hardbound volumes, one on logic, one on philosophy, and one a poetry anthology. Scotty had been given a set of collectible Saurian brandy bottles, Hikaru a small collection of antique firearms, Uhura a songbook of traditional Earth ballads, and Pavel a pair of replica Russian sailing vessels. Each of them—including Spock—had seemed touched by the thoughtful remembrances.

Hikaru and Pavel departed first, followed by Scotty and Uhura. As Spock walked toward the door, McCoy reached for his elbow, finding it beneath the black folds of his Vulcan robes. "Would you mind staying a moment?" he asked. "I was hoping I could talk with you alone." Spock stopped, and the door glided shut.

"Yes, Doctor?" he asked. McCoy looked at Spock, but then suddenly could not bring himself to broach the issue of his nightmares.

Suddenly? he asked himself. In truth, he had been suffering from the terrible dreams—and unwilling to talk about them—for years, ever since he'd traveled back in time through the Guardian of Forever. Later, after Spock's *katra* had been stored in McCoy's brain, then removed and re-fused with Spock during the *fal-tor-pan*, the disturbing visions had intensified. Among other horrible scenes, he'd begun seeing images of his own death, as well as the hazy specter of a memorial service—a service held, he believed, for himself. Though McCoy's subsequent encounter with Sybok had caused his fractured nights to ease, that had lasted only a short while. At some point, the nightmares had returned, and with them, the wildly unsettling notion that he foresaw the end of his life—an end rapidly approaching.

"Spock, I wanted to . . ." he started, but again ran into

difficulty actually putting his troubles into words. "I wanted to thank you for coming," he said instead. "Not just to the memorial, but here to Jim's apartment too."

"Thank you for inviting me," Spock said.

McCoy felt incredibly awkward, so much so that he considered *not* asking his friend for the help he so desperately needed. But he knew that he could avoid this no longer. "Spock, would you mind taking a walk?" he asked, thinking that perhaps being in motion might make it easier to unburden himself.

"I was planning to go back to my apartment," Spock said. "I had intended to do so earlier so that I could meditate this afternoon."

"I'm sorry, Spock," McCoy said sincerely. "I didn't mean to disrupt your—" He had been about to say *grieving*, but thought that the word might offend his Vulcan friend. "—your personal time," he finished.

"Not at all," Spock said. "But unless there is something else you'd like to discuss, I will be leaving now."

"There is something," McCoy said. "But I think I'd like to get out and get some air while we talk."

Spock stared at him with an appraising look, then said, "Very well." He set down the volumes Jim had left to him while McCoy pulled on his dress uniform jacket, which he'd doffed after the memorial. Then he and McCoy exited the apartment.

They rode a turbolift down to the lobby of Russian Hill Tower, then emerged into the late afternoon sun. As McCoy composed his thoughts about what he would say, he strode in the direction of the marina, and Spock followed along beside him. As they neared a public transporter station, though, the doctor remembered a place he'd recently learned of and that he'd thought about visiting. Although he loathed traveling by transporter—for the memorial, he'd journeyed from Atlanta to San Francisco by tube—he made exceptions in exigent circumstances. Considering his current state of mind, having his molecules scrambled across half a continent didn't seem nearly as troubling to him as it usually did.

A few minutes later, McCoy and Spock stepped out of another public transporter and into a summer evening in Riverside, Iowa. The doctor had never been here before and didn't know if Spock had either, though surely it was no mystery that Jim had been born in the small farming community. McCoy quickly obtained an airpod and programmed it to take them to the address he'd found among Jim's papers.

After a short jaunt to the south of the town, the compact craft put down at the edge of a farm, where the paved thoroughfare that the airpod had followed met a dirt road at a T intersection. McCoy and Spock disembarked the pod, and beneath scattered clouds blushing reddish orange in the setting sun, they set off along the unsurfaced path. Rows of corn grew to either side, standing much taller than either one of them and lending the setting a claustrophobic feel.

"Jim spent most of his childhood here," McCoy said as they walked, dirt crunching beneath the soles of their boots.

"I knew that he'd been born in Riverside," Spock said, and McCoy inferred that he knew little else about Jim's early life.

"He didn't really talk much about it, did he?" McCoy asked.

"Not that I'm aware of," Spock said.

"I always had the feeling that Jim had a good childhood," McCoy said, "but that it ended far sooner than it should have. His parents died when he was a boy, and

then when he lived on Tarsus Four, he witnessed that mad-
man executing four thousand colonists." He paused at the
recollection of the tragedy, and at the thought of the hor-
rific scars it must have left on Jim.

After a moment, trying to lighten the mood, McCoy
said, "Not exactly something out of Mother Goose." He'd
expected Spock to respond in his typical humorless but
still amusing way, perhaps inquiring about what the female parent of an aquatic fowl had to do with anything.
But Spock had been unusually reticent throughout the
day—mourning in his own, Vulcan way, McCoy supposed—and he said nothing now.

They walked quietly for a few moments, and McCoy's
thoughts drifted from the horror of Tarsus IV and the
deaths of Jim's parents to the many other losses that Jim
had suffered in his life. The young Lieutenant Kirk had
idolized his commanding officer aboard the *Farragut*, but
had seen Captain Garrovick and two hundred other crew
members die when attacked by a strange gaseous creature. His best friend out of the academy, Gary Mitchell,
had died during his service aboard the *Enterprise*. His
brother and sister-in-law had perished on Deneva. His son
had been murdered by a ruthless Klingon commander.
Edith Keeler had died, and Miramanee and Rayna
Kapec—

McCoy shook his head, stunned as he realized the
scope of what Jim had endured in his personal life, which
did not even account for those Starfleet officers who had
lost their lives while serving under his command. When
Jim had mentioned knowing that he would die alone, had
he felt that, by the end of his own life, everybody he cared
about would already have passed away before him? How
difficult it must have been for him to have so many of
those closest to him leave.

Even some of those who didn't die left him, McCoy thought. Carol Marcus. Janet Wallace. And—

"Do you remember Ben Finney?" he asked, recalling the friend of Jim's who'd named his daughter, Jamie, after him.

"Yes," Spock said. "The *Enterprise*'s records officer for seven months during the five-year mission." Finney had been an instructor at the academy when he and Jim had become friends, and they'd later served together aboard the *Republic*. Finney's career aspirations of command had been dashed when he'd left open a circuit to the ship's atomic-matter piles, a blunder that could've led to a massive explosion that would have ripped through the *Republic* in just another few minutes. Jim, an ensign at the time, had discovered the mistake and corrected it, and bound by regulations, had logged the incident. Finney had been reprimanded and dropped to the bottom of the promotions list.

"He tried to destroy Jim's career," McCoy said. Years after the incident aboard the *Republic*, Finney had been assigned to the *Enterprise,* where he had faked his own death and framed the captain for it. "Jim faced charges of culpable negligence and could've been drummed out of the service," McCoy said, "maybe even done time in a Starfleet prison." During the captain's court martial, though, Finney had been found alive, hiding belowdecks aboard the *Enterprise*. "And yet when Finney stood trial for his own crimes, Jim gave testimony as a character witness on his behalf."

"Yes," Spock said. "Captain Kirk was . . . extraordinary."

"He really was," McCoy agreed.

They walked without speaking for a while, and up ahead, McCoy saw the solar-panel-covered roof of a house come into view above the corn. The sight of Jim's childhood home proved a powerful reminder that McCoy had said good-bye to his friend today, something he had not been seeking when he'd decided to visit this place.

He attempted to push away his cheerless thoughts, and in their stead, he tried to call to mind some of the lighter moments he'd shared with Jim and Spock aboard the *Enterprise*. Once, when the ship had put in for repairs at Cygnet XIV, the local technicians had programmed the library-computer with an affectionate and distinctly female personality, with a tendency to address the captain as "dear." Another time, they'd traveled to Sigma Iotia II, where Jim and Spock had improbably ended up posing as gangsters. And then there had been their visit to Space Station K-7, where the ship had become overrun by those highly prolific tribbles. McCoy mentioned all of those incidents to Spock, and then remembered another. "How about the time the computer started playing practical jokes on the crew?" he asked. Again he anticipated a dry retort, maybe something about there being nothing practical about jokes, but Spock simply acknowledged the comment and said nothing more.

At last, they reached the break in the cornfield where the farmhouse had been built. Between the one-story structure and the road stretched a large lawn. In the middle of the green span, two old trees stood guard, their leaves fluttering gently.

Jim grew up here, McCoy thought as he peered at the house. It seemed somehow inconceivable that the illustrious Captain James T. Kirk had ever been a carefree boy, running across the grass in his bare feet. It also seemed impossible and cruel that he was now gone.

"I've never been here," McCoy said. "And I take it that you haven't either."

"No, I have not," Spock said. Some quality in the Vulcan's voice suggested great emotion behind it. "Doctor, it is unclear to me why you have chosen to come here now, and why you have chosen to bring me along."

"I'm not really sure myself," McCoy admitted, looking over at Spock. "I found this address when I was cataloguing Jim's belongings in order to deal with his estate. I guess I thought that coming here might . . . I don't know . . . might somehow bring us closer to Jim." He knew that the explanation would hold no weight for Spock, and his next words confirmed that fact.

"That is not logical," he said, but then to McCoy's surprise, he added, "but I do understand the sentiment." The declaration served to underscore the grief that Spock must be feeling, Vulcan or not.

"It occurred to me that our visit here would be our own little memorial to Jim," McCoy said. "There's something sort of heroic and melancholic about it. Since Jim was nothing if not a romantic, I think he would've appreciated the gesture."

"Indeed," Spock said in obvious agreement, which pleased McCoy. The doctor stood silently with his friend for a few minutes, simply gazing at the farmhouse. He saw no movement in or around it, other than that of the trees and corn, occasionally nudged by a puff of evening air. Finally, Spock said, "Do you intend to do more than this?"

"What do you mean?" McCoy said.

"Do you, for example, plan to ask whoever resides here now if they will permit you to go inside the house?"

"No," McCoy said after a moment's thought. It had been hard enough this morning and this afternoon giving voice to his sorrow, first at the memorial and then with his friends in Jim's apartment. He did not wish to do so with strangers. "No, I don't think so," he continued. "This is sufficient, don't you think?"

"Yes," Spock said. "I concur."

McCoy turned to face back the way they'd come, and together, they headed for the airpod. They walked without speaking for a time as the curtain of night drew down around them. Soon enough, McCoy knew, he and Spock would reach the pod and take it back to Riverside. From there, they would presumably go to their respective homes. Spock had wanted to be alone ever since the memorial this morning—and perhaps even *during* the memorial. If McCoy wanted his assistance, he would have to look for it now; he could not burden his friend further by continuing to tell him he needed to speak with him, but then delaying actually doing so.

"To tell you the truth, Spock," he said at last, "I did intend to do more than simply see this place. I wanted to talk with you about a problem I've been having."

"I perceived that something in addition to the captain's death troubled you," Spock said.

"I've been having some very unsettling dreams," McCoy said. "Dreams about me dying." Several years ago, his nightmares had disturbed his sleep so much that he'd thought about asking Spock to teach him the methods of Vulcan meditation, but had resisted when his research had revealed the intimacy it would require. He felt it too much to ask of Spock.

"I would suggest that such a reaction to the death of a close friend is not uncommon," the Vulcan said.

"You're right, Spock," McCoy said, understanding that he had not made himself clear enough. "But I've been having these dreams since before Jim died. I've experienced these death dreams since . . . well, since the *fal-tor-pan*."

"The ancient ritual," Spock said, as though by rote. He said nothing more for a few seconds and then asked, "Have you consulted a psychiatrist?"

"I haven't," McCoy said. Several years ago, aboard the *Enterprise,* he actually had seen a psychiatrist, though not enough to mention to Spock. At that time, Sybok's calming influence had faded and McCoy's dreams had grown particularly troubling, a good night's sleep often impossible for him. But he'd attended only two sessions with Dr. Smitonick before walking out of the third. With seemingly no other recourse, McCoy had accepted Michal's prescription for pills that suppressed the storage of dreams in long-term memory. He'd used them with some success, but he did not like being medicated and so resisted using the pills on a regular basis. "I haven't really wanted to," he said, regarding psychiatric help, "because I don't think that would do me any good."

"But if these dreams are disturbing to you," Spock said, "would it not be appropriate to seek the services of a mental-health professional?"

"It would be if these were merely dreams," McCoy said, finally coming to the crux of his problem. "But I think they're memories."

"I do not understand," Spock said. "How can you have a memory of an occurrence—your own death—that has not yet happened? Unless you refer to the incident on the planet in the Omicron Delta region, when the knight on horseback attacked you with a lance."

"Sometimes I dream of that incident," McCoy said, recalling well the agony he'd experienced when his heart had been pierced and stopped beating. The advanced technology in use on the planet had been employed to repair his wounds and resuscitate him. "But I understand that, and it's not really what I'm talking about," he told Spock. "Sometimes it's a wounded man stabbing me. Recently, though, I mostly see a funeral in a cemetery, and I have the feeling that my dead body is in the casket." The

image had caused him severe emotional distress, not
least of all because it had convinced him of his impending death.

"But why would you categorize your own funeral as a
memory?" Spock asked. "Clearly that has never happened,
nor if it had, would you be able to recall it."

"Don't be too sure," McCoy said as they neared the airpod. "I suspect that you can remember your memorial service aboard the *Enterprise*." Before Spock's body had
been regenerated by the Genesis Device, before his mind
had been re-fused with his brain, he had been dead, killed
by radiation when he'd saved the ship from Khan. His sacrifice had been afforded full honors by Captain Kirk and
the rest of the crew—a memory that McCoy knew Spock
himself retained.

"Yes, but those were singular circumstances," Spock
said. "With my *katra* held within you, and you perceiving
the memorial service, ultimately those memories were
transferred to me via the re-fusion. Surely nothing like that
pertains to what you are experiencing."

"No," McCoy said. They reached the two-person airpod
and stopped before it. "But I began having nightmares
more than twenty-five years ago. For a long time, they
filled me with dread, but the images I perceived remained
indistinct, out of focus, and they didn't seem to be about
my death. After the *fal-tor-pan*, though, they became
clearer, enough for me to make out the images I described."

"Do you know precisely when you began experiencing
these nightmares?" Spock asked. McCoy appreciated the
question, suggesting as it did his consideration of his
problem.

"I do," he said. Around them, dusk had faded almost
completely. "We should get back," he said, thinking that

he and Spock could talk in the airpod. "It's getting dark." He pushed the glossy green touch pad set into the pod's hull, and it's gull-wing door swung upward. McCoy darted inside and Spock followed, working a couple of controls to close the hatch and turn on the interior lighting.

After they'd both taken their seats, McCoy said, "I started having these dreams immediately after you and Jim brought me back from the past through the Guardian of Forever."

"Am I to take it that you believe that there is a direct correlation between the two?" Spock asked.

"Yes," McCoy said, and it gave him hope simply to admit his suspicions out loud. He put his hands on his knees, elbows splayed, and leaned forward. "Spock, when I first went back in time through the Guardian, before you and Jim followed me, your present changed, indicating that I had somehow altered history."

"That is correct," Spock said.

"And once you and Jim traveled back to nineteen-thirty Earth," McCoy went on, "you determined that the way I had altered history was by preventing the death of Edith Keeler."

Spock's expression shifted for an instant, almost as though he had winced, but he said only, "Again, your description of events is accurate."

McCoy sat back in his chair. "But does that mean that, after I kept Miss Keeler from dying, I then lived out the rest of my life on Earth, three hundred years ago?"

One of Spock's eyebrows rose on his forehead. "Presumably so," he said, in a way that indicated the newness of the idea to him. "But because of the actions the captain and I subsequently took, that timeline no longer exists."

"But it *did* exist," McCoy insisted. "And I think I remember some of it. Or at least I have these impressions, these visions of incidents that have never happened in my own life, here and now, in our timeline."

"That is interesting, Doctor," Spock said, clearly giving McCoy's claims some thought. "What you describe, though—impressions of events that never occurred—does that not adequately express the nature of dreams?"

"I suppose so," McCoy said, disappointed by the observation, but committed to making Spock understand. "I know this is hardly scientific, Spock," he said, "but my dreams simply don't *feel* like dreams; they feel like memories."

"Doctor, how would it be possible for you to recall the events of a life that you did not live?"

"I don't know," McCoy said. He turned and looked out through the front viewport of the airpod, frustrated. He'd often asked himself these same questions, and so far he'd found no answers. "Maybe I'm wrong," he said, peering out at the cornfields, barely visible now in the darkness. "Maybe these are just dreams. But let's assume for a moment that they're not, that they are memories of that other life I lived." In Spock's reflection in the port, McCoy thought he saw skepticism. "Nobody ever really learned much about the Guardian of Forever or how it operated," McCoy argued. "Maybe the way it sent me through time is responsible for what I'm experiencing. Or maybe that other timeline does still exist somewhere, in some other reality, and I'm somehow connected to it subconsciously." He knew it all must sound preposterous, but also knew what he continued to go through. "If I am remembering that other life, then I'm worried that I'm also remembering my death in that timeline. Sometimes in my dreams I see a wounded man stabbing me, but I also see a funeral that I think is my own."

"Even if you are remembering your alternate life," Spock said, "how could you witness your own funeral?"

McCoy had thought of this himself, but he'd still been unable to dismiss his concerns. "I don't know, but I have the terrible feeling that I died prematurely," he said. "Maybe I was stabbed to death, but I find myself more and more concerned that I died from some disease or condition." Though it had happened many years before and he'd been completely cured, McCoy recalled well when he'd contracted xenopolycythemia and had been given a prognosis of one year left to live. He swiveled in his chair to face Spock again, trying to impress upon him the importance of all this. "I get regular Starfleet physicals and nothing has shown up, but I'm plagued by this horrible uncertainty. If I can, I just want to make sure that whatever happened to me in the other timeline won't happen to me here. I came to you, Spock, because I thought you might be able to help me." Extremely intelligent and knowledgeable, Spock also knew about the Guardian of Forever and the events that had taken place there.

"I see," he said. "Would it suffice, then, for you to know the cause of your death in the other timeline?"

"Yes, I think it would," McCoy said enthusiastically, buoyed by the implication that Spock had thought of a possible solution to his dilemma.

"Such information may exist and may be accessible," Spock said. "I took tricorder readings of the Guardian while it displayed both our own, unaltered timeline, and the altered timeline caused by your saving Edith Keeler. Those recorded readings may still exist."

"They 'may' still exist?" McCoy asked, disappointed by the conditional nature of Spock's claim.

"It is my understanding that the original recordings were stored at the Einstein research facility," he said, and McCoy felt immediately deflated. Station Einstein had been destroyed at the very end of the *Enterprise*'s five-year mission, when the Klingons had been on the verge of discovering and taking control of the Guardian. "It would seem likely, though, that Starfleet would have kept at least one other copy of those recordings in a separate location."

That made sense to McCoy, but the classified nature of everything surrounding the Guardian concerned him. "Do you think they'll allow me to review them?" he asked.

"Considering that you took part in those events and that you have a high security clearance," Spock said, "I believe they will."

"Who do you think I should approach about it?" McCoy asked, understanding that he would not simply be able to walk into Starfleet Headquarters, find an open terminal, and access the information he sought.

"I believe that copies of those tricorder readings would probably fall under the aegis of Starfleet Intelligence," Spock said. "I'm aware of at least one officer within that organization that you know quite well."

And that officer, McCoy knew, had just spent the afternoon reminiscing with them in Jim's apartment: "Uhura."

"Commander Uhura," Spock confirmed.

McCoy smiled nervously, hopeful that he would get the answers he needed, but reluctant to count on it until it happened. "Thank you," he said.

"You're welcome," Spock replied.

On the short flight back to Riverside, McCoy told Spock that he would be traveling from Atlanta to San Francisco a few more times in order to finish dealing with Jim's estate. He would make sure to deliver the books Jim had bequeathed to him, and that Spock had left behind in the Russian Hill Tower apartment. The Vulcan thanked him.

At the transporter station in Riverside, Spock stepped up onto the platform. McCoy said good-bye and thanked

him for listening and for his help, particularly at such a
trying time. Spock nodded but said nothing, and the fact
of his extreme reserve throughout the day recurred to the
doctor. He had noted more than once how uncommunica-
tive his friend had been today, something he'd naturally
attributed to the mourning process. He had been too involved with his own grief and his own troubles to give the
observation much thought, but now, as the transporter operator worked her console, McCoy worried about Spock.
Despite the Vulcan's apparent acceptance of his human
side over the years, McCoy had no idea what level of
emotional control—or *lack* of control—that implied, or
how easy or difficult it would be for him to deal with such
a powerful loss.

As the whine of the transporter rose and a coruscation
of white light formed atop the platform, McCoy could only
hope that Spock would be all right.

The incense burned with the aroma of the desert, dry
and rough, demanding. Enveloped by the parched odor
and with his eyes closed, Spock envisioned the Forge, the
vast, barren landscape steeped in Vulcan history. Home to
bone and ash and sandfire, the arid wastes had been the
site, eighteen hundred years ago, of Surak's great pilgrimage, which had ushered in the Time of Awakening. More
recently, just a century and a half past, the broken land
had also been where the Syrrannites had made their determined stand, out of which had sprung the modern Refor-
mation.

In his mind, Spock saw the desolate terrain, the uneven
rocks, the fractured ground. The phrase *hot as Vulcan* had
become a part of the vernacular throughout the Federation,
and the Forge gave it truth. Air burned in the stark setting,
flesh melted, blood boiled.

Spock sought refuge in the mental re-creation, utilizing it as a focal point upon which to concentrate. He let go of thoughts as they occurred to him, going back again and again to the severe cerebral tracts. Gradually, distractions fell away, leaving only the stillness of the sere Vulcan wilderness.

And then, unaccountably, motion interrupted the dead calm of the scene. In the distance of the imagined geography, in the foothills of the L-langon Mountains that bordered the Forge, Spock saw a lithe, moving form. Stealing among the rocks, the large predatory quadruped could not entirely hide the distinctive geometric markings on its back and tail, bright yellow shapes gilding its green hide. The *le-matya*'s head darted to and fro as it stalked whatever prey it had scented.

Perhaps pursuing a sehlat, Spock thought errantly, his meditative state faltering. His eyes still shut, he brought his clasped hands to his forehead and made an effort to center his mind by discarding the disruptive visualization. He turned his inner sight from the mountains and out across the cracked plain. He would not think of the *le-matya*, he would not think of the *sehlat*.

In his conjured vista, Spock allowed his gaze to follow the fissures jagging across the desert floor. Deep and dark, the widest of the earthen rifts pulled his attention into it and down, as though his mind's eye had become subject to gravity. He set his consciousness adrift as his interior view took him plunging past the steep walls, tracing their linear contours. Below hung a lifeless chasm, still and silent, like a bottomless grave waiting for the next victim of the relentless Forge.

But then sound drew Spock's notice, a bellow of animal fear. His internal perspective swept up and back to the foothills, where a large four-legged beast lumbered backward, the *le-matya* advancing toward it. Spock recognized the creature being hunted, with its brown fur and fifteen-centimeter fangs: as he'd suspected, a *sehlat*.

But not just any sehlat, Spock realized. *I-Chaya*. The pet he had kept so long ago.

The fearsome *le-matya*, with its poisonous claws and mouthful of razor-sharp teeth, lowered itself to the ground, its muscular legs poising to spring. Then it leaped forward.

No, Spock screamed within his own head, forfeiting the last vestige of serenity he still retained. He heard two voices echo his reaction. As the *le-matya* attacked I-Chaya, a child and an adult looked on—both of them Spock. The older Vulcan moved then, charging toward the deadly *le-matya*.

Too late, Spock knew. *Too late*.

He opened his eyes in his San Francisco apartment and pulled his clasped hands from against his forehead. His heartbeat had grown markedly faster and his respiration ragged, as though from strenuous physical activity—or from overpowering feeling. His attempt to level his emotions had failed utterly.

The death of Captain Kirk had significantly upset the balance Spock had for many years maintained between his Vulcan and human selves, the event bringing with it sorrow and an almost overwhelming guilt. His reaction had compelled him to abandon his professional obligations on Alonis, he had suffered nightly dreams filled with a depth of sentiment unfamiliar and discomfiting to him, and now his latest attempt to find peace within himself had instead dredged up memories of I-Chaya.

But also more than just memories of I-Chaya, Spock knew. The event surrounding the *sehlat*'s death—his second, revised death—bore directly on Spock's remorse. Not because of the loss of the pet, but because of what it meant he had done to Jim.

Spock stood quickly from the low stool in the alcove that he'd set up for his meditation. He turned toward the wall, where he had hung an "infinity mirror": a black octagonal frame held a perimeter of small lights between a transparent piece of glass and a mirror, causing a series of reflections in the mirror to resemble a tunnel of lights receding into the distance.

Spock put his fist through it.

The front glass shattered and fell in shards to the floor, the pieces landing with a clash. The mirror splintered but remained relatively intact, only a single thin wedge falling free. The tunnel effect of the reflected lights vanished.

As Spock pulled back his hand, he saw lacerations in his flesh, his blood flowing green from them. He wrapped his other hand around his injured fist and fixated on the physical pain. He needed something—almost *anything*—to help him pull his emotions into check.

By degrees, Spock's breathing calmed and his pulse slowed. Still holding one hand with the other, he walked into the refresher. After pulling a first-aid kit from the cabinet beneath the basin, he pushed his fist under the faucet and washed out his wounds. Using a protoplaser from the kit, he then healed his cuts.

Back in the main room, sparingly ornamented with Vulcan ceremonial trappings, the chronometer on the wall told Spock that he'd gotten back from his visit to Iowa little more than an hour ago. When he'd first returned to his apartment, he had with conscious intention given much thought to the predicament besetting McCoy. Curious about what the doctor would find if permitted to review the tricorder readings of the Guardian of Forever, Spock had striven to theorize some means by which memories of McCoy's life in one timeline might be accessible in another. Before long, though, he'd found that he could no longer keep his own problems at bay. The doctor's revelation that he'd been experiencing restless sleep and disturbing dreams had highlighted for Spock the truth of his own troubled nights, as well as his inability to adequately control his emotions.

"I am a Vulcan," Spock said, the words sounding less like a statement of fact and more like an attempt to convince himself of their content. The tenets of Vulcan philosophy provided for facing personal loss with equanimity, by employing logic to maintain emotional control and an overall state of quietude. Further, Spock had been taught by his father that the lives of the dead were to be mourned only when those lives had been wasted. Surely Captain Kirk's had not been wasted, even as it had ended, in an act that had preserved the lives of the crew and passengers of the endangered *Enterprise*.

But Spock had no control. He had no quietude. And he did mourn.

As he stood alone in his apartment, he felt as lost as he ever had. His strong emotions reminded him of when he and Dr. McCoy had traveled five thousand years backward in time on the planet Sarpeidon, when Spock's very nature had begun to devolve into that of the barbaric, passionate Vulcans of that period. He also recalled the polywater contaminant at Psi 2000 that had effected him in similar ways, depressing his powers of judgment and self-control.

But nothing physical caused the deterioration of his mental discipline now. He understood the logic of the situation, but logic failed him. Emotion alone drove him.

And the time had come for him to do something about it.

II

The Ground of Our Beseeching

Sin is Behovely, but
All shall be well, and
All manner of thing shall be well.
If I think, again, of this place,
And of people, not wholly commendable,
Of no immediate kin or kindness,
But of some peculiar genius,
All touched by a common genius,
United in the strife which divided them;
If I think of a king at nightfall,
Of three men, and more, on the scaffold
And a few who died forgotten
In other places, here and abroad,
And of one who died blind and quiet,
Why should we celebrate
These dead men more than the dying?
It is not to ring the bell backward
Nor is it an incantation
To summon the spectre of a Rose.
We cannot revive old factions
We cannot restore old policies
Or follow an antique drum.
These men, and those who opposed them
And those whom they opposed
Accept the constitution of silence
And are folded in a single party.
Whatever we inherit from the fortunate

We have taken from the defeated
What they had to leave us—a symbol:
A symbol perfected in death.
And all shall be well and
All manner of thing shall be well
By the purification of the motive
In the ground of our beseeching.

—T. S. Eliot,
Little Gidding, III

TEN

2293

In his office on the fifteenth floor of the Palais de la Concorde, Federation President Ra-ghoratreii sat in an armchair with a sheaf of papers in his lap. Glancing up from his work, he peered over to the far side of the large room, at the grand piano situated on a raised platform two steps above the floor. He briefly considered walking over and playing a tune on the ornately crafted instrument, thinking that doing so might revive his flagging attention, but he knew that today, as with most days, he had a tight schedule to keep.

Ra-ghoratreii stretched, then adjusted his position in the chair. He'd hosted a reception for the Gorn consul last night at Le Jules Verne restaurant in La Tour Eiffel, at which he'd stayed far later than he'd anticipated. As a result, he felt tired right now, even though the time had yet to reach midday.

Returning to the report, Ra-ghoratreii ran his fingertips over the surface of the uppermost hard-copy page, reading it by touch. He preferred the feel of the paper to that of his tactile data slate, which utilized an acutely malleable metal on which it raised characters. Alternatively, he could have looked at an oversized print version of the information by using his spectacles, or he could have listened to a computer recite it for him, but he favored doing it like this. He'd first learned to read in this manner and he still found it most efficient for him, maximizing both his comprehension and retention.

The report had been prepared by one of the deputy directors of the Bureau of Interplanetary Affairs. It provided an account and an analysis of the known political changes occurring within the new Klingon government. Since Azetbur had assumed the chancellorship after her father's assassination, she had faced down repeated attempts by members of the High Council and others to have her removed from her position. Some of the resistance to the new leader, Ra-ghoratreii understood, came from simple prejudice, a sexist attitude held by some Klingon males that women should not sit on the council, let alone in the chancellorship. But Azetbur also faced genuine political opposition as well. Even after the destruction of their primary energy-production facility on Praxis, many Klingons still believed the acceptance of Federation aid to be an act of cowardice, and the pursuit of a peaceful coexistence between the two powers to be a betrayal of the empire's honor and destiny.

Despite all of that, though, Azetbur had managed thus far to remain in office. According to observers, she had done so by several means. Federation aid, while distasteful to many Klingons, apparently paled when compared to the ignominy of living impoverished, hungry, and sick. Azetbur had also avoided the temptation to forcibly quell opposition views, instead engaging her adversaries in open debate. She had even accepted and implemented several of their proposals, effectively disarming them. Although she had won over to her cause only a handful of members on the High Council, those few wielded great influence.

Azetbur had also begun remaking her diplomatic corps. It surprised Ra-ghoratreii to read that Kamarag, Klingon ambassador to the Federation for more than a decade, had been recalled. His replacement would apparently be a man named Kage, whose record revealed virtually no political experience. In his youth, he'd been a soldier, but later in life, he had resigned the Klingon Defense Force to enroll in the Gorek Institute. There he'd studied civil engineering, a discipline he'd then practiced for twenty years before being recruited by Azetbur. Nothing obvious in Kage's background particularly recommended him for the role of ambassador, but he had evidently performed some work on the infrastructure of the First City, the capital of Qo'noS. Ra-ghoratreii believed it likely that Gorkon and his family had at some point become aware of Kage, perhaps even befriending him. Based upon the Federation president's dealings at Khitomer with the new chancellor, he suspected that Kage would turn out to be not some fawning toady, but an individual with a bright mind who shared Azetbur's vision for the empire.

Ra-ghoratreii read through the remainder of the known changes in the Klingon government, his fingers skimming down one embossed line of text after another. When he'd finished the report, he reached beneath the silver moiré fabric of his sleeve and touched the face of the chronometer he wore around his wrist. The numerals displayed in relief there told him he had a quarter of an hour before the next appointment on his agenda.

Without donning his spectacles—he had occupied this office for nearly five years and knew it well enough to navigate through it—Ra-ghoratreii walked over to his desk. He sat down behind it, his back to the gauzy white curtains that ran the width of the room and covered the tall windows in the outer wall. Even without his spectacles on, he detected the lack of bright light streaming through, telling him that the clouds covering Paris early this morning had yet to give way to the sun.

Ra-ghoratreii set down the report he'd just read, exchanging it for the dossier he'd had his secretary prepare for him. The collection of documents related to the person due in his office in just a few minutes: Ambassador Spock.

He quickly reviewed it, refamiliarizing himself with the Vulcan's background and record. His brief tenure as an ambassador had so far shown promise. Along with Ambassador Tremontaine, he had closed out negotiations with the Frunalians to allow the Federation to mine rubindium in their system, and then on his own had established a dialogue with the new colony on Archanis IV. He had then traveled to Alonis, where he had again joined Tremontaine, this time for talks seeking to establish a Federation starbase in the system. The proceedings had been going well, but Spock had departed Alonis to attend Captain Kirk's memorial last week. Soon after the service, he had requested a short meeting with Ra-ghoratreii, for the purpose, the president assumed, of establishing a timetable for his return to his ambassadorial duties.

The nature of Vulcans and their culture made it difficult for Ra-ghoratreii to assess how much more time Spock would need to mourn. Not even really understanding what that process might be like for the ambassador, the president had approached one of his advisers about it. But T'Latrek, a full Vulcan, had mentioned Spock's mixed ancestry, as well as the fact that even Vulcans contended with loss in different ways. Regardless, since the ambassador had asked for only ten minutes, Ra-ghoratreii had told his secretary to find that time in his schedule as soon as possible.

On his desk, the intercom issued an electronic buzz. *"Mister President,"* came the voice of his secretary. *"Ambassador Spock is here for his eleven o'clock appointment."* Ra-ghoratreii consulted his chronometer again, noting the punctuality of his visitor.

"Send him in," he said. He plucked his spectacles from where they hung around his neck and set them atop the bridge of his nose. He then looked up to the far left corner of his office as a pair of wooden doors there parted, in each a circle of frosted glass bearing the UFP emblem. Spock strode in, a slim data slate held in one hand. He wore traditional Vulcan habiliments, long brown robes that hung loosely on his sinewy form. "Ambassador," Ra-ghoratreii said.

"Mister President," Spock replied. He crossed the room and mounted the two shallow steps to the office's central platform, which contained Ra-ghoratreii's desk and the sitting area before it.

"Please sit down," the president said, gesturing to the four chairs that stood in pairs on either side of a low rectangular table. As Spock took a seat, Ra-ghoratreii stood and made his way around his desk, where he sat down opposite the ambassador. "Let me offer my condolences on the loss of your friend," he said. Though both he and Spock had spoken at the memorial, they hadn't talked with each other. "As Governor Wesley said, Captain Kirk was a true hero."

Spock nodded, but he did not otherwise respond to the observation.

"Our time is short, Ambassador," Ra-ghoratreii said, "so I won't waste your time with other pleasantries. What did you wish to see me about?"

"Mister President," Spock said, "I understand from BIA Director Irizal that it was you who recommended me for an ambassadorial post."

"That's right," Ra-ghoratreii said. "Your performance as a special envoy was exemplary. Your willingness to speak with Chancellor Gorkon and your ability to convince him to meet with me were of enormous consequence to the Federation. Once you stepped down from starship duty, it seemed a natural choice to offer you a diplomatic position."

"Because you personally recommended my appointment, Mister President," Spock said, "I believe it appropriate that you be the first to learn of my resignation."

What? Ra-ghoratreii thought but did not say. As a politician, he rarely reacted visibly to anything, preferring to maintain a veneer of composure. "Ambassador Spock, I am surprised," he said. "Do you not find the role—" He searched for the proper word, mindful that he spoke with a Vulcan. "—fulfilling?" he finished.

"It is not that, Mister President," Spock said. "I did find my ambassadorial responsibilities compelling and challenging. Indeed, if circumstances permit, I may seek such a position at some point in the future. For now, though, I cannot continue in that capacity." He raised the data slate he'd brought with him and took a small card from its input/output slot. "This is my formal, written resignation," Spock said, holding up the card. "Once I've left here, I will transmit a copy to Director Irizal."

Ra-ghoratreii made no move to take the data card, harboring a faint hope that he might convince Spock to reconsider. "May I ask why you want to leave?" he said.

"It has become clear to me that I cannot adequately carry out my duties at this time," Spock said.

"Perhaps you should leave such evaluations to others," Ra-ghoratreii suggested. "I have assessments that rate your performance very highly."

"That is gratifying to know," Spock said, "but regardless of any appraisal of my abilities, I have . . . personal business to tend to on Vulcan."

"I see," Ra-ghoratreii said. "If all you need is time away . . ."

"No, Mister President," Spock said. "It is more than that."

Ra-ghoratreii nodded. He knew that he would receive no further explanation from Spock. The Vulcan's claim of "personal business" had clearly been intended to forestall any debate about his resignation. "Very well," Ra-ghoratreii said. He stood up and opened his hand, and Spock deposited the data card in his palm. Ra-ghoratreii then walked from the sitting area and back around his desk, where he picked up his own data slate and deposited the card in its I/O slot. He touched a control specifying large-print output, and the screen filled with outsized characters. He quickly read through it.

"This seems to be in order," he said, looking across his desk at Spock. Ra-ghoratreii lifted his hand and offered the customary Vulcan gesture of greeting and farewell. "Peace and long life," he said.

Spock rose and returned the salute, but then replied with a traditional Efrosian valediction: "May you long hear the song of the future." He did not wait for a reaction, but turned and exited the way he'd entered.

Ra-ghoratreii sat down behind his desk and leaned forward, reaching to activate the intercom. An instant later, his secretary asked, "Yes, Mister President?"

"Find some time in my schedule and set up a meeting for me with the director of the Bureau of Interplanetary Affairs," he said. "I need to speak with him as soon as possible."

"Yes, Mister President," the secretary said.

Ra-ghoratreii sat back in his chair and sighed. He hated for the Federation government to lose somebody of Spock's caliber. And no matter the positive progress Ambassador Tremontaine had been reporting on Alonis, he wanted to replace Spock as quickly as he could.

He knew that it would be a difficult task.

Spock's sense of time told him the hour, but he checked the chronometer on the display of scheduled departures anyway. He recognized the illogic of the action, particularly when the readout confirmed what he already knew:

twenty-eight minutes remained before he could board the *Ri'Luje*, a transport headed to Vulcan. Of course, his inability to marshal his logical faculties and to sufficiently control his emotions had been what had driven him to embark on this journey in the first place.

Several hundred other passengers also waited in the large, chilly Port of Los Angeles lounge. Though Spock saw mostly Vulcans, he counted thirteen humans present too, as well as members of half a dozen other species. Three individuals—two humans and a Tellarite—wore Starfleet uniforms, though the *Ri'Luje* traveled under civilian registry.

Spock sat quietly as the minutes passed. It had been a week since he had visited President Ra-ghoratreii in Paris and officially relinquished his post as a Federation ambassador. Since then, he had put all of his affairs here on Earth in order. As he had pledged to do in his letter of resignation, he had submitted a report to the Bureau of Interplanetary Affairs spelling out his impressions and judgments regarding the ongoing negotiations with the Alonis. Director Irizal had contacted him directly to see if anything could be done to persuade Spock to continue his diplomatic service, and also to ask if the director or the BIA could provide any assistance with whatever personal matters had caused him to step down. Spock had appreciated Irizal's interest and offer of help, but had demurred on both counts.

In the days that followed, Spock had packed up the few belongings he would be taking with him to Vulcan, had put into storage several personal items he wanted to keep—such as the volumes Jim had left to him—and had recycled or given away what remained. He had given up his apartment, staying the last two nights at an inn hear the port while he waited for the arrival of the *Ri'Luje*, on which he'd booked passage to Vulcan. He'd considered contacting McCoy to inform him of his plans, but had decided against it, wanting to avoid being drawn into a conversation about why—

"Spock," said a voice to his left. He looked up to see Alexandra standing beside him. A charge rushed through him, reminding him once again how far his mental discipline had slipped.

"Alexandra," he said, satisfied that he'd kept any emotion from his voice. He stood up and faced her. She wore a lavender dress that complemented her blonde hair. "This is unexpected."

"I was told that you left the BIA," she said. To her credit, she spoke her words plainly, with no indication that she accused him of having failed her in some way. Although they had begun to grow close on Alonis, he had not been in touch with her since leaving there. "I was concerned," she said.

"How is it that you're here?" Spock asked, curious not only how she had located him, but what it might mean for the Federation—and for Alexandra herself—that she had left Alonis in the middle of the talks.

"I explained to Ambassador Liss the reason you had to leave the talks," she said. "I told her of Captain Kirk's death and of your long friendship with him. She understood and agreed to continue the summit without waiting either for you to return or for the Federation to send another Starfleet expert. Truthfully, I think she might have believed it provided her an advantage in the negotiations."

"Did it?" Spock asked.

"I allowed her to think it did," Alexandra said. "We made enough progress after that for me to present the full proposal that you and I had worked out. The day that the Alonis Parliament took up debate on it, Ambassador

Thivan arrived to take your place." Spock knew of Thivan, an Andorian and a former engineer who, while never a member of Starfleet, had been the lead designer on several space facilities. "Since the Alonis didn't expect to issue a formal response for at least ten days, I was able to get away."

"And you came to Earth specifically to see me?" Spock asked. He supposed that their encounter could have been accidental, but Alexandra's initial contention of concern for him seemed to indicate otherwise.

"When Thivan arrived to substitute for you in the talks, I contacted Director Irizal," she said. "He explained that you had resigned your post. When I asked why, he said only that it was for personal reasons and that you would be going back to Vulcan." Spock hadn't written in the letter he'd handed to Ra-ghoratreii and transmitted to Irizal that he would be heading back to his homeworld, but he had said so during his meeting with the Federation president. Clearly Ra-ghoratreii must have mentioned it to the BIA director. "When I heard that, I wanted to see you, to help if I could. I went to your apartment in San Francisco, and when I discovered that you'd just moved out, I decided to check the ships bound for Vulcan. The Ri'Luje was the first ship headed directly there."

"Logical," Spock observed with appreciation for her keen intellect.

"So tell me what's wrong," Alexandra said. "How can I help you?"

"You cannot," Spock said. Alexandra peered around at the other passengers present, then to the far side of the lounge. With a look, she invited Spock to follow her toward the corner, near a pillar, presumably to find whatever small measure of privacy they could in this public place. He walked over with her, and when she stopped and turned back to face him, she delicately raised her right hand between them, two fingers extended.

Once more, emotions churned within Spock. He felt desire for this woman, and guilt that came from knowing that he would now hurt her, and shame for all of it. He regarded her hand but made no move to touch her fingers with his own. "Alexandra . . . " he started.

"Spock," she said, lowering her hand. Again she masked her own feelings, though it seemed apparent that she wanted an explanation. He knew that he owed her that.

"Alexandra, I have . . . lost myself," he told her. "I am returning to Vulcan in order to remedy that situation. I will likely be there for quite some time. In fact, at the moment, I have no plans to ever leave."

"I see," she said, though Spock doubted that she actually did. How could she, as a human, possibly understand the depth of the difficulties he faced? "May I visit you there?"

"Alexandra," he said, "I am going to Vulcan in order to study the *Kolinahr.*"

"Is that an answer to my question?" she asked. "I don't know what the *Kolinahr* is."

"It is a course of study and a discipline by which Vulcans shed their emotions," he explained.

"'Shed their emotions,'" she echoed. "What does that mean, exactly?"

"It means that I will learn to perceive the world and to process information, thoughts, and sensory input without feeling," Spock said. "I will attain mastery of my emotions to such an extent that they will effectively be excluded from my life."

Alexandra nodded, obviously taking in what Spock had told her. "And this is a reaction to the loss of your friend?"

"It is more complicated than that," Spock said. "But it is

the case that Captain Kirk's death has highlighted a deficiency in my life."

"You view emotion as a deficiency," Alexandra said. This time, despite her passive expression, her words did seem to carry with them an accusation.

"I grew up on Vulcan as an outsider," Spock said. Despite his discomfort revealing the facts of his life, he cared for Alexandra and wanted her to understand why he had chosen this path. "I therefore found myself at a young age in the uncommon position of having to consciously select the world in which I would live, that of humans or that of Vulcans. I chose to live as a Vulcan."

"But you haven't really done that, have you?" Alexandra asked. "You spent years—decades—in Starfleet, serving aboard ships with predominantly human crews."

"That is true," Spock said, realizing that he might not be able to make Alexandra understand. Still, he wanted to try. "Once before, I left that life to pursue the *Kolinahr*. I nearly succeeded in achieving it, but unusual circumstances external to myself prevented me from doing so. After that, I accepted my twofold nature, as it were: an outwardly Vulcan bearing, and an inner life that, while mostly driven by logic, allowed for some level of emotion." That emotion included a long and painful run of remorse that he had buried through the years. Jim's death had helped him to see that he wished to hide from such feelings no longer; he wanted to eliminate them. "Recent events have reminded me of my long-ago choice to live as a Vulcan. I am making that choice again now."

Alexandra looked at him for a few moments without saying anything. He could read nothing in her countenance that told him how she felt. At last, she said, "I hope you find what you're looking for, Spock, that you achieve what you want to achieve."

"I hope the same for you," Spock said.

She started to step away from him, but then stopped and said, "Sometimes people don't always get what they want." Now Spock saw tension in her features, the mask she wore to cover her pain slipping down slightly. "And sometimes people want what they don't need." He did not know how to respond, nor did he think that she expected him to do so. "Good-bye, Spock."

As Alexandra walked away, he hated that he had hurt her and felt saddened that they would not learn more of each other, that their relationship would not grow closer. Those thoughts reinforced his need for the *Kolinahr*.

"Attention, passengers to Vulcan," a male voice announced over the public address system. *"The boarding process for the* Ri'Luje *will begin in five minutes. Travelers in boarding group one, please report to the transporter platform."*

As people within the lounge began to move, Spock continued to watch Alexandra as she walked away. She did not look back.

ELEVEN

1930

Kirk walked out of the radio repair shop with two full bags and almost no money. Other than the two dollars he had saved for next week's rent, he had just exhausted the remainder of the cash he and Spock had earned during the past week. One of the brown paper sacks he carried contained food, which he had purchased before entering the repair shop, while nothing but electrical components filled the other. With the money he'd had, he'd only been able to purchase perhaps a fifth of the items Spock would need to complete the memory circuit that the science officer had designed. With the few components they'd already acquired, Spock had begun actual construction of the computer aid three days ago, and what Kirk would bring him now would at least allow him to continue that work without interruption.

As he strode along the sidewalk through the midmorning bustle, headed for the apartment that he and Spock had rented, Kirk scanned the faces of the people he passed, peered around at those farther away, and looked for a familiar gait or posture. If Spock couldn't build a mnemonic memory circuit, or if he did but couldn't manage to cull from the tricorder the information they so desperately needed, then they would have to somehow find McCoy themselves. Even if Spock succeeded, they didn't know if it would be too late to do whatever they needed to do to prevent the doctor from changing history. Kirk remained constantly alert to all of that, and he searched for McCoy everywhere.

Bones, he thought, for just a moment setting aside his responsibilities to the crew of the *Enterprise,* to Starfleet, even to humanity itself. In some ways lost to him in the last week had been the plight of his friend. Since the timeline had been altered, Kirk's focus had necessarily been on restoring it, but right now he thought about Bones. Regardless of his leaping through the Guardian of Forever and back into time, McCoy would continue to suffer the effects of his cordrazine overdose. If Kirk and Spock found him and stopped him from changing the past—and therefore the future—their next concern would be getting Bones medical help.

Kirk shifted the bags in his arms and heard the hard ring of one vacuum tube against another. He knew that he needed to hurry back to the apartment so that he and Spock could then get back to the mission to help serve lunch. Edith Keeler had provided for the two of them during the first few days that they'd been here, and had found them higher-paying jobs for the past few days. Today, they'd worked early morning at the mission, and they would be returning at midday and in the late afternoon to assist with those meals. In the hours when they didn't work or sleep, Spock concentrated on the mnemonic memory circuit and Kirk did whatever he could think of to search for McCoy. So far, he'd been to the library to read through the local newspapers for any reference to the doctor, and he'd also checked at numerous hospitals to see if McCoy had been admitted as a patient.

When Kirk reached the apartment, he rushed up the front steps. In the vestibule, he hastily maneuvered himself close to the mailboxes so that he could open the one for the apartment where he and Spock now lived. He didn't expect to find anything, but he saw no reason not to verify that. The box was empty.

Seeing the number *33* on one of the mailboxes, Kirk thought of Edith Keeler. As he continued through the vestibule and up the staircase, he realized that they really hadn't spoken with each other all that much, other than when she had led him and Spock to this apartment building. He had listened to her often, though, paying attention to what she said to the men having a meal at the mission. He'd also heard her talking on an individual basis to some of those who'd gone there seeking help. Always, she put forth the positive—and, as it turned out, realistic—vision she held of humanity's future, applying it where she could to the lives of the despairing men who seemed to need hope even more than they needed a meal.

At the same time, Kirk had also witnessed a different example of Edith Keeler's strength. Twice, he had seen her turn out men who had apparently returned intoxicated to the mission for the third or fourth time. One in particular had stumbled in reeking of alcohol and slurring his words. When Keeler had asked him to leave, he had become belligerent, but she had shown no fear and no hesitancy. Kirk had moved to step in himself, emerging from the mission's small kitchen prepared to intercede, but by the time he had, Keeler had already walked the man all the way to the front door, through which she had then unceremoniously sent him. It had been just another detail that had added to Kirk's respect for her. He admired the difficult but important work she did, and he even thought that in a different time, in a different place . . .

As Kirk arrived at the top of the steps, he stopped himself. That way, he knew, lay madness. Still, he could not deny that in Edith Keeler he perceived a soul kindred to his own, in a way he never before had. And seeing what she envisioned for humanity's future from her vantage in these dark days of the twentieth century, between two devastating world wars, Kirk wondered, if Keeler could be shown the attainment of all the hopes she fostered for humanity, what then would she envision? If somebody saw their dreams achieved, they didn't stop dreaming. Kirk wished that he could see what her *next* dream would be.

Shaking off his own daydream, he crossed the hall to the apartment door. He took the handles of one of the sacks in one hand, then reached to turn the doorknob. When he entered, he immediately saw that Spock had made progress on the memory circuit. In addition to the collection of components he'd already assembled onto one board, which now sat on the table, a second set had now been cobbled together, mounted onto an upside-down drawer set atop the room's shorter dresser. Twists of wires connected one to the other, as well as to the light fixture on the wall and to the tricorder.

Kirk crossed the room to the short dresser, examining Spock's handiwork. The amalgam of parts emitted a high-pitched sound as it functioned, and an electric arc climbed repeatedly and noisily upward between two rods arrayed in a V formation. As Kirk set the two paper sacks he carried down on the near bed, he heard Spock switch off the equipment, which immediately quieted.

"Captain," he said from where he sat at the table, laboring over the tricorder with a knife they had taken from the mission, "I must have some platinum. A small block will be sufficient, five or six pounds. By passing certain circuits through there to be used as a duo-dynetic field core—"

"Uh, Mister Spock," Kirk said, "I've brought you some assorted vegetables, bologna and a hard roll for myself, and I've spent the other nine-tenths of our combined salaries for the last three days on filling this order for you." He picked up the sack of components he'd just purchased and placed it on the tabletop. Spock stood and reached inside, pulling out a pair of vacuum tubes. "Mister Spock, this bag does not contain platinum, silver, or gold, nor is it likely to in the near future."

Spock set the tubes down. "Captain," he said, "you're asking me to work with equipment which is hardly very far ahead of stone knives and bearskins."

"McCoy'll be along in a few days," Kirk said. "Perhaps sooner. There's no guarantee that these currents in time will bring us together. This *has* to work."

"Captain . . . " Spock said. Kirk walked back over to the bed and began unpacking the food from the other sack. "Captain, in three weeks, at this rate, possibly a month, I might reach the first mnemonic memory circuits."

A knock at the door interrupted Spock.

"Your cap," Kirk said as he put the food back in the sack and moved toward the door. Spock reached to pluck his wool hat from the table and ducked into the corner to pull it on over his ears. As Kirk reached the door, it opened, and Edith Keeler took a step inside. Kirk put his arm up to the door and attempted to block her view of Spock's electrical apparatus.

"If you can leave right away," she said, obviously excited, "I can get you five hours' work at twenty-two cents an hour." She hesitated then, a puzzled look appearing on her face. Behind him, Kirk heard the whine and crackle of the new setup, which Spock must have accidentally activated when getting his cap. "What . . . what on Earth is that?" Keeler asked.

Kirk searched for a response, but before he found one, Spock answered from directly behind him. "I am endeavoring, ma'am," he said, "to construct a mnemonic memory circuit using stone knives and bearskins."

To Kirk's relief, Keeler simply shrugged. He glanced over at Spock, then raised a hand and gestured toward the hall. Keeler offered him a smile and stepped out of the room. Kirk waited for Spock to gather his coat, and then the two of them followed Keeler out.

Spock waited with the captain until the hour before the evening meal would be served, when Keeler typically went into her office at the back of the mission. As they cleaned the main room, Rik—the silver-haired, mustachioed former vagabond who often helped out in the kitchen—set up to cook. When Rik himself went into the back to let Keeler know that he'd finished his preparations, Spock and Kirk moved quickly.

The captain moved to guard the door that led to the back hallway, to which Keeler's office, two storage closets, and the stairs to the basement all connected. Spock hastened over to the trunk sitting against the far wall of the main room, where he and Kirk had earlier seen a pair of watchmakers stow their tools. Keeler apparently allowed the two men to use the place as a makeshift workshop. In the three weeks he and the captain had been in the past, Spock had never seen them there, but this afternoon, he had immediately taken note of the tools they employed for the detailed work they performed on clocks and watches.

Now, Spock bent and rotated the numbered dial of the combination lock securing the trunk. With his superior hearing, he quickly disengaged the mechanism. He opened the trunk and saw the pouch in which the watchmaker had stored his tools. Spock picked it up and stuffed it into the folds of his coat, which he had brought over with him. He then closed the trunk and relocked it.

Rik returned to the kitchen a few moments later, as Spock and the captain wiped down all of the tables. They knew they would not be able to keep the tools, since Keeler would doubtless realize who had stolen them. Rather, Spock would use them overnight, then return them to their place in the truck in the morning, before the watchmakers would have a chance to find them missing.

When Spock and the captain had completed cleaning, they went down to the basement to stoke the furnace. Before they started, Spock pulled the pouch from within his coat. As he examined the tools, Kirk came over to peer at them as well. "How much do you think these will help?" he asked.

"They should allow me to work considerably faster," Spock said. Although they had purchased a couple of tools, he and the captain had spent most of their money on the electrical components required for the mnemonic memory circuit. "Using these," Spock said, "should allow me to pare days, perhaps even as much as a week, off the time it will take me to construct the circuit." After accepting that they would be unable to secure a block of platinum, Spock had estimated three and a half to four and a half weeks would be required for his efforts.

"Excellent," Kirk said quietly. Spock sensed the captain's tension. They had already been in the past longer than they had anticipated, with no indication of McCoy's presence here and no notion of whether they had already failed to prevent the doctor from altering the timeline.

Spock replaced the tools in the pouch, wrapped them again in his coat, and set it all down on an old table in the middle of the basement. He then moved to the furnace, where he picked up a shovel and began stoking coal. He worked quietly, the captain keeping his own counsel.

Then he heard the door to the stairway open above, and heavy footfalls pounded down the steps. Spock stopped shoveling coal and turned to face the stairs, as did the captain. They both watched as Keeler descended halfway down the lower flight, the hard set of her features readily conveying her anger.

"That toolbox was locked with a combination lock," she said, "and you opened it like a real pro." Spock found it interesting that she gazed pointedly at him, not even addressing the captain. When he did not respond, she walked down the rest of the steps and directly over to face him. "Why did you do it?" she asked.

"I needed the fine tools for my radio work," he told her. "They'd have been returned in the morning."

"Oh, I'm sorry," Keeler said, "I can't—"

"If Mister Spock says that he needs the tools and that they'd be returned in the morning," the captain said, "you can bet your reputation on that, Miss Keeler." Kirk smiled at her, and even Spock could see in it the affection he felt for her.

"On one condition," Keeler said, and then she stepped over to stand before the captain. "Walk me home?" The invitation surprised Spock, since Keeler normally stayed at the mission during meals. "I still have a few questions I'd like to ask about you two," she told the captain. Kirk raised both his eyebrows, as though proclaiming his innocence. "Oh, and don't give me that 'questions about little old us' look. You know as well as I do how out of place you two are around here."

"Interesting," Spock said, impressed by Keeler's acuity. "Where would you estimate we belong, Miss Keeler?"

"You, at his side," she said, "as if you've always been there and always will." Then she looked toward the captain. "And you," she said, "you belong . . . in another place. I don't know where or how. I'll figure it out eventually." She now returned his gaze with equal affection.

Spock lifted the shovel again. "I'll finish with the furnace."

"'Captain,'" Keeler said, as though completing Spock's sentence. She looked again to Kirk. "Even when he doesn't say it, he does." Once more, Spock took note of Keeler's perspicacity. He hadn't realized that he'd ever addressed the captain by his title anywhere that she could hear. Clearly, though, not only must he have done so, he must have done so on more than one occasion.

Keeler headed back up the stairs. When the captain started after her, Spock turned, bent down, and scooped a pile of coal from the floor and into the furnace. As he heard the sound of Kirk's boots on the stairs, he glanced over at him and watched him go. He had begun to grow concerned for the captain—not just as his commanding officer, but as his friend.

Although it still troubled Spock that he and the captain might themselves inadvertently change history, he had come to believe that, while they should still try not to be involved in any major event—however "major" might be defined—they simply could not control the uncounted ways in which their mere presence in the past changed it: the carbon dioxide they exhaled into the atmosphere; the air currents they altered with their movements; the people they met. He had concluded that they needed time to be even more like a river than they already hoped. Not only did they require that the same currents that had swept them to this point in the past would also bring McCoy here, but that, also like a river, time would not be affected by minor changes. A stone tossed into a river modified the movement of water around it, but downstream, the flow of the river remained virtually unchanged.

What troubled Spock now, though, did so on a personal basis. If the captain grew very close to Keeler, and they were then successful in restoring the timeline, he would have to face losing her. The Guardian had told them that if they could stop McCoy from altering history, they would be returned to their present. Clearly, Keeler would not be coming back with them.

Spock considered speaking with the captain about the situation, but felt uncomfortable about doing so. Instead, he would just have to hope that Jim's logic would overcome his romantic nature.

TWELVE

2293

Broken only by candlelight, the darkness within the Akrelt Refuge provided a haven from the blaze of the Vulcan sun. The stone blocks that formed the walls of the venerable structure, built out of the base of a canyon wall, still retained the cool of the morning. The underground spring that ran through the caves to which the sanctuary connected left a patina of dampness on surfaces throughout the complex.

T'Vora stood in an inner corner of the Refuge's main room, beneath its vaulted ceiling. Stationary atop a small landing crafted as a place for solitary meditation, she did not peer inward, but nevertheless found peace in the simplicity of her stillness. About her, in recesses carved into the walls at eye level, flames wavered at the tips of tall, tapering candles, casting her shadow darting about the floor.

In the near silence, T'Vora waited. Only the rhythms of her own breathing and the flutter of the fire about the wicks reached her ears. The time drew close, and she opened herself to the moment soon to come, listening for the sounds that would signal the arrival of the next aspirant.

In due course, she heard footfalls from outside, the harsh snap of heels against the steps leading up to the entry passage. She gazed toward the front of the room, where daylight crept in through an open archway. The silhouette of a man appeared there, his garments hanging long and loose about him. He took only a few steps into the room before halting.

"I am Spock," the man said, and then he identified his

father and forefather: "Child of Sarek, child of Skon." He made no apparent effort to visually survey his surroundings. Of course, it would require at least a few seconds before his pupils dilated in response to the decreased light within the Refuge. "I have come at the appointed time to meet with an elder." He spoke his words in his native tongue, but with the slight accent common to Vulcans who most often spoke Federation Standard.

T'Vora waited a moment, already testing, already probing. She sensed an uneasiness about Spock—

No, she corrected herself as she opened her mind. *More than mere uneasiness. Almost . . . desperation.* But in the next instant, it had gone.

T'Vora descended the steps of the platform to the floor and walked with a slow, measured gait to the center of the room. She stopped an equal distance from Spock, who stood before her, and from the reliquary, which stretched along the rear wall beneath a large bas-relief sculpture of T'Klass. "I am T'Vora," she said. "Elder and master." She knew the purpose of Spock's visit—he had requested it a month ago, when he had first returned to Vulcan—but she asked anyway, following the prescribed ritual. "For what purpose do you come to Akrelt?"

"I come to petition for my admission into the *Kolinahr,*" Spock said.

"Step forward with me, Spock," T'Vora said. She turned as he came abreast of her, and together they walked toward the rear of the main room. They climbed the dozen wide steps to a long altar of polished white stone, above which the graven image of T'Klass protruded from the wall. On either side of the figure, lighted torches illuminated the area.

T'Vora paced around the altar, upon which lay a collection of ancient artifacts, including items such as a *katric* arc, an IDIC pendant fashioned from dark rock, and a hand-wrought *Kolinahr* symbol. From the folds of her robe, she pulled a thin wooden rod, which she dipped into the flame of one of the torches. She then faced Spock across the altar's narrow dimension and lighted a cylindrical candle in its center. After quenching the rod and setting it down, she regarded the aspirant. "Beneath the visage of T'Klass, one of the first *Kolinahr* masters, in the presence of these relics that recall the shared past of all Vulcans, in this place raised by our forebears in antiquity," she said, "make your petition, Spock."

He peered upward at the monument to T'Klass, and then over the length of the altar, before finally looking back at T'Vora. "On the sands of our world, our ancestors cast out their animal passions," Spock recited, "saving our race by the attainment of *Kolinahr*. It is that which I seek. I make my petition to you, T'Vora, asking you to guide me in my quest."

"I hear what you ask," T'Vora said. In the time since Spock's request had been handed down to the Akrelt Refuge, she had begun her evaluation of him by researching his personal history. In so doing, a number of issues had arisen that called his fitness for the *Kolinahr* into question. As part of her responsibility as a master, she would have to probe for answers that would satisfy her concerns before she could sanction the petition.

"Spock, child of Sarek," she said, "you are also the child of Amanda Grayson of Earth, are you not?"

"I am," Spock said. His impassive expression did not change in the slightest degree, nor did T'Vora discern any shame in the admission.

"And you consider yourself Vulcan, not human?" she said.

"To deny my human heritage would be illogical," Spock

said. "My mother is human and therefore I am half human. But I have lived my life as a Vulcan, believing in Vulcan ideals and striving to fulfill them."

"And yet two decades ago, you failed to reach such an ideal," T'Vora said.

"That is true," Spock said, and T'Vora perceived his outward forthrightness as genuine. "I was admitted to the *Kolinahr* and studied for more than two years under the aegis of Master T'sai. I had completed all of the training and had passed all of the tests, needing only to conclude the final ritual in order to achieve my goal. That did not happen."

"Why?" T'Vora wanted to know. Here, Spock's privacy had not been breached. Master T'sai, since deceased, had noted only Spock's failure, but not the reason for it.

"During the final rite, a powerful consciousness called to me from space," he said. T'Vora allowed her eyebrow to rise, signifying what she considered to be the improbability and unusual nature of that which Spock described. "It was an entity with thought patterns of exactingly perfect order. It seemed a kindred spirit, one who had achieved what I had not, what I *could* not, even with the *Kolinahr*. The experience caused my emotional control to falter."

"What was this consciousness?" T'Vora asked, intrigued.

"It called itself V'Ger," Spock said, and T'Vora remembered the incident of the human machine that had, through unintended and unpredictable circumstances, amassed so much knowledge that it had gained sentience. "After failing the *Kolinahr*, I sought out V'Ger and communicated with it directly. I learned that, while it had come to a state of perfect logic, it was not satisfied. It wanted more. In effect, it was searching for that which many beings have, and which I had: illogic, the capacity to leap beyond the bounds of reason to find meaning and fulfillment."

"And this caused you not to return to the *Kolinahr?*" T'Vora asked.

Spock hesitated, the candlelight throwing inconstant orange light across his features. T'Vora anticipated some flicker of emotion, but detected none. Spock's uncertainty appeared to originate elsewhere, in his attempt to put into words what had driven him during the time he described. "I did not know how long it would be before I would be permitted—or *if* I would be permitted—to reenter the *Kolinahr*. But I wanted to move forward in my life and so I opted to return to Starfleet, to a life I had previously lived and that had gratified me. In making that choice, I also committed to attempting to accept my emotions, rather than to deny them."

"You selected the path of the *V'tosh ka'tur*," T'Vora said, the revelation unexpected. Spock could not still be one of the "Vulcans without logic," or surely she would have become aware of the feelings roiling within him. But then Spock rejected her characterization.

"No," he said. "The *V'tosh ka'tur* do not wish control of their emotions. I did, and I endeavored to integrate mine with my intellect. I wanted balance, as do the *V'tosh ka'tur*, but I wanted my logic to control that balance, to continue to be the overriding force in my being. I lived as a Vulcan."

"But among humans," T'Vora noted.

"Largely, yes," Spock said.

"And through the separation of your *katra* from your body and the *fal-tor-pan*," T'Vora said, "this remained the way of your life." Even before she had looked into Spock's past, she had been aware of his "death" and "rebirth."

"It did," Spock said.

"Why then do you seek to purge yourself of your emotion?" she asked. "You failed the *Kolinahr*, then declined to even attempt to resume your studies. Why now have you decided otherwise?"

"It has taken me this long to truly understand how detrimental emotions are, and that I lack the control I thought I possessed," Spock replied. "And also to realize that my place is in Vulcan society."

T'Vora observed an awkwardness in the aspirant's response, and she knew that she had come to the heart of his petition—of the *reasons* for it. "And what place have you taken in Vulcan society since your return here?" she asked.

"I have taken no place yet," Spock said, "other than that of candidate for the *Kolinahr*."

The response seemed incomplete to T'Vora. "What about as son to your parents?" she asked.

"I have resided in visitor lodging since arriving on Vulcan," Spock said. "I have not seen my parents." T'Vora did not need telepathic abilities to hear the self-reproach in Spock's answer.

"You have spoken to them though," she said. "They are aware of your presence here, of your petition for the *Kolinahr*."

"No," Spock admitted. His expression did not change, but T'Vora could see his shame unmasked.

She considered this. "In recent days," she asked, "what emotions have you not controlled?"

"Loss," Spock said, but he needn't have. T'Vora could suddenly feel the weight of the bereavement he carried within him, as well as his struggle to contain it.

"Caused by the death of your commanding officer for so many years," she said.

"The death of my friend," Spock said, and T'Vora almost reeled at what followed. The feeling flowed from the aspirant as surely as if an emotional dam had given way within him. Beyond the remorse at not having visited his parents, beyond even the grief for his friend, a terrible guilt permeated Spock's being, though its source seemed elusive.

T'Vora closed herself to the rush of emotion, reasserting her control over her own mind. She paused to settle her thoughts before continuing. "Spock, the *Kolinahr* is more than a way of life," she said. "It is a type of existence that, once achieved, cannot easily be undone. One must therefore enter into it for the proper reasons. You are not doing so."

"I can assure you—" Spock started, but T'Vora interrupted him.

"Do not assure me," she said. "It may be that within you lie the seeds of that which you speak: the need for control and the pursuit of life as a full Vulcan. But the *Kolinahr* is not a haven from what you feel with regard to your parents, or from the pain and sadness the death of your friend has brought, or from any of the other feelings churning within you. The purging of emotion is a serious matter, to be chosen on its own merits, for the proper, logical reasons." T'Vora reached forward, beside the rod she had earlier utilized to light the candle, and picked up a long silver implement with a bell at its end.

"Master T'Vora—" Spock began, but again she stopped him from speaking.

"No," T'Vora said. She reached forward and set the bell down atop the candle, extinguishing its flame. "Spock, child of Sarek, child of Skon," she said, "your petition for the *Kolinahr* is denied."

The house stood across the plaza in the heart of Shi'Kahr's residential district, as it had for seventy years, since before Spock had been born and brought home to this place. The entry gate, an open amalgam of straight lines and curving arcs that had been shaped from metal bars, captured in itself the geometric flow of the overall structure. The front wall swept in a semicircle around a courtyard, and at the rear of the house, a second story rose not unlike the great hemisphere of an observatory.

Spock regarded his childhood home from across the plaza, trying to recall when last he had been here. *Eight years ago,* he thought. After the *fal-tor-pan,* he had lived here in seclusion during his reeducation and reintegration sessions. Due to the trauma of having his *katra* disconnected from his body and then the subsequent shock of the re-fusion, he had spent most of that time here as though it had been the first time, as though he had not grown from infancy to his teens here.

Now, though, he remembered the house and his childhood and more. It had taken some time and a great deal of effort, but eventually he had recaptured all of his experiences and all of his memories from prior to the death of his body during the *Enterprise*'s escape from the Genesis Wave. He owed much to McCoy, he thought, and he suddenly regretted not contacting the doctor before he'd left Earth. McCoy had proven for many years to be a good friend, and Spock should have at least informed him of his departure, particularly given the problems with troubled sleep that the doctor had recently been having. He resolved now to get in touch with McCoy before too much more time passed.

A sleek airpod hovered through the plaza, pulling Spock's attention from his thoughts and back to his surroundings. He gazed again at the house in which he'd grown up, wondering if he would find his parents there. When last he'd heard from them, on the day prior to the memorial service for Jim, they had managed to send a

message from the Tholian homeworld. There, in his role
as Vulcan ambassador, Sarek had been nearing the completion of exceedingly delicate talks with several high-
ranking members of the Assembly. Both he and Amanda
had offered their condolences on the death of Captain
Kirk, as well as their regrets that they would not be able to
attend the commemoration. Sarek had also reiterated his
estimation that the captain had been a person of good
character, an assessment with which Amanda had whole-
heartedly agreed.

That had been a month and a half ago, likely time
enough for Spock's father to have finished his mission in
Tholian space. If so, he would likely be home now, as he'd
mentioned returning here with Amanda before beginning
his next diplomatic assignment. Through the years, Sarek
had typically interspersed his ambassadorial travel with
trips back to Vulcan.

Spock bent and lifted his duffel, slinging it across his
shoulder. As he started across the plaza, he felt a sudden
sense of disquietude. He had resided on Vulcan for the past
month without having visited his parents' home, without
even having attempted to let them know of his presence on
the planet. He had rationalized not doing so because of his
need to prepare for his *Kolinahr* petition and because he
hadn't been sure if Sarek and Amanda had even come back
to Vulcan. If they had been here during that time, though,
then when his mother learned that he hadn't contacted
them when he so easily could have—and she would learn
of it, for he would not lie to her—she would unquestionably be hurt. Sarek would accept and understand the logical reasons Spock would profess for his actions, but his
mother would not. And she would be right.

*Just as Master T'Vora was right to reject my petition for
the* Kolinahr, Spock thought as his boots thumped along

the plaza. His emotions had never in his adult life been in such a state of disarray for such an extended period, nor had his ability to manage his feelings ever failed so consistently. Perhaps T'Vora had been correct that he had seen the *Kolinahr* as a means of escaping the need to deal with recent events in his life—he would have to consider that possibility—but even short of that, he had certainly viewed the ritual purging of his emotion as a means of ending the turbulence within him.

At the front gate, Spock reached up and touched a signal pad set into the sky-red wall. If either of his parents were home, they would see his image on a display inside the house and invite him in by opening the gate. If not, then Spock's retina print would allow him access.

He had to wait for only a few seconds before the gates parted and swung inward. Spock entered the courtyard, the plants within in full bloom at this time of year. Bounded by tiny white blossoms, a winding slate path led up to the house through a lush expanse of grass. Other flowers of many varieties and colors decorated the outer edges of the courtyard, with several pairs of trees rising upward at either end of the space.

As Spock approached the house, he saw the front doors open. Sarek stepped out onto the path, clad in dark slacks and a brown tunic. His gray hair had grown longer than he normally wore it. "My son," he said.

"Father," Spock said, stopping before him, raising his right hand and offering the traditional Vulcan greeting. Sarek returned the gesture, then stepped aside.

"Enter and be welcome," he said.

Spock walked into the house, into the great room where Sarek and Amanda entertained when they hosted large gatherings. A complex fountain composed of many curves stood in the center of the area, set into a square pool. At the moment, water trickled from the numerous bowls in a leisurely flow, providing the setting a gentle susurrus of background noise. Low gray-blue plants ringed the periphery of the room, a subtle transition from the polished black floor to the azure walls. Simple cuboid seats sat scattered at irregular intervals, as did a series of abstract sculptures. Above, the usually transparent ceiling had been moderately polarized, obviously to temper the bright light of the sun as midday neared.

"May I provide you with a meal?" Sarek asked as he closed the front doors. "Or a beverage to slake your thirst?"

"Thank you, no," Spock said. He peered around, and neither seeing nor hearing his mother, he asked if she was at home.

"Not at the moment," Sarek said. "She has gone to the market for some fresh fruit." He motioned with one hand toward a cluster of seating cubes. "Would you like to sit?"

"Thank you," Spock said. He walked over and pulled his duffel from his shoulder, setting it down on the floor. He and his father then sat across from each other.

"It is acceptable to see you, my son," Sarek said. "Your mother and I have been concerned for your welfare."

The statement surprised Spock. "For what reason?" he asked.

"Not long after the death of Captain Kirk, we learned of your resignation from your ambassadorship," Sarek explained. "When we attempted to contact you on Earth, we found that you had relocated out of your apartment. The significant and unexpected nature of those changes in your life gave us pause, particularly when we did not hear from you."

"Of course," Spock said, realizing that he should have known that his father, in his position, would find out sooner rather than later that he'd quit his work for the Bureau of Interplanetary Affairs. "My apologies. I did not intend to cause you or my mother any concern."

"May I inquire as to why you stepped down from your diplomatic post?" Sarek asked.

"For a number of reasons," Spock said, not wanting to go into detail about the troubles he'd been having. "Primarily, though, I have decided on pursuing a different course for my life at this time."

"I am curious to hear about this 'different course,'" Sarek told his father.

"I came back to Vulcan to undertake the *Kolinahr*," Spock told his father.

Sarek cocked his head to one side, a clear indication of surprise. "That is also unexpected," he said. "When do you plan to present your petition?"

"I have already done so," Spock said. "I arrived on Vulcan a month ago and immediately requested a meeting with a master. I spent the time until then meditating, preparing."

"The *Kolinahr* demands much," Sarek said.

"I made my petition yesterday," Spock said. "It was rejected."

Sarek nodded, displaying no visible sign of disappointment. Despite that, Spock assumed that the news of his failure *did* dissatisfy him. Since Spock had been a young boy, his father had made it clear that he envisioned a Vulcan way of life for him. Sarek had ostensibly permitted him a choice to pursue either Vulcan or human philosophy, but at the same time he had made it plain which he considered superior. Though Spock had chosen to follow the path of logic, he had made other decisions for his life of which his father had strongly disapproved. After he had opted for a career in Starfleet rather than at the Vulcan

Science Academy, the two hadn't spoken to each other as father and son for eighteen years. Even after they had mended the rift between them, it had only been much later, after Spock's *fal-tor-pan*, that Sarek had allowed that his opposition to his son's enlistment in Starfleet had been in error.

"Do you intend to reapply for the *Kolinahr?*" he asked now.

"I do not know," Spock said. "I may consider it."

"What are your plans then?" Sarek wanted to know.

"I have none," Spock said. "But I am not functioning at peak efficiency. I am unfit to resume my duties with Starfleet or with the Bureau of Interplanetary Affairs, or to conduct myself in any other endeavor at this time. I require rest and an extended period of meditation."

"You are of course welcome here for as long as you wish to stay," Sarek said. "Your mother and I will be departing in three weeks for a summit I am attending on Andor, but perhaps that will provide you with an environment even more conducive to the rest and meditation you seek."

"Thank you, Father," Spock said. "I am—"

"Spock!" said a voice from the front door. He turned to see his mother standing there, a canvas sack depending from one hand. She wore a simple emerald shift that provided a dramatic contrast with her white hair.

"Mother," Spock said as he and Sarek stood. Amanda set the sack on the floor and walked hurriedly over to him.

"We've been so worried about you," she said. Normally not demonstrative in deference to Spock's own Vulcan predilections, his mother revealed her concern by uncharacteristically stepping forward and embracing him. Spock awkwardly raised his arms around her back. In the midst of his emotional crisis, Spock found joy in the act.

"I'm all right, Mother," he said. After just a moment, she stepped back and looked at him.

"I'm so glad," she said. "When did you get here?"

"I arrived at the house just a few minutes ago," Spock said. There would be time enough later to relate the entire story of his arrival on Vulcan, as well as the reason he had come.

"How long will you be staying for?" Amanda asked.

Spock glanced over at Sarek, and then said, "For some time, I suspect."

"That's wonderful," Amanda said. She looked up at Sarek and lifted two fingers to him, which he met with his own. The touch lasted only an instant, a personal but not intimate greeting between partners. Gesturing back toward the sack she had left beside the front door, she said, "I just got some fresh fruit over at the market. I was going to prepare our midday meal. Will you dine with us?"

"Yes, Mother," Spock said. "Thank you."

"Good," she said with a smile. She retrieved her canvas bag and headed toward the kitchen.

"I am going to assist your mother," Sarek said. "Why don't you take your things up to one of the guest rooms?"

"I will," Spock said. "Thank you."

As Sarek followed Amanda toward the kitchen, Spock picked up his duffel and started toward the center of the house, where a winding staircase rose to the second floor. Upstairs, he entered the first room he came to—the room in which he had lived as a boy. It did not appear much different now than it had all those years ago, though it now lacked the few items with which he had adorned it back then.

Spock set his duffel down on the bed and unpacked it. He put some of his clothes in the closet, some in the dresser, and he moved his toiletries into the refresher. After placing his personal data slate on the desk, he sat down on the edge of the bed and spent a few moments taking in his surroundings.

It all seemed so familiar—in some ways, *too* familiar. He had lived here for years, but never had he felt completely at ease on Vulcan. Though born and raised here, he had always been an outsider. Now, sitting in the room in which he had spent so much time as a child, he felt anything but at home.

THIRTEEN

1930

Kirk grabbed his coat and walked up the stairs after Miss Keeler, conflicted by what he felt. Her anger—unfairly directed at Spock for the theft of the tools, though she could not have known that—had wounded him. Regardless of her understanding of what he'd done, regardless of his justification for it, he had disappointed her, and that troubled him deeply. He and Spock had only been here in the past for three weeks, and yet in that time, Kirk had already developed strong emotions for this woman he barely knew.

When he reached the top of the stairs, he saw Edith waiting there with a small-framed man, perhaps in his forties, in a brown jacket. Kirk recognized him as one of the two watchmakers who'd been in the mission earlier. He must have returned here for some reason, and when he'd found his tools missing, he'd gone to Edith.

"Mister McKenna," Edith said, "this is Mister Kirk. It

was his friend who took your tools, but they tell me that they did not intend to steal them, that they would have returned them in the morning."

"And you believe that?" McKenna said.

"Actually, I very much do," Edith replied, and then she turned to Kirk. "Mister McKenna lost his watch shop last month," she said. "He's working down at the docks now when he can, but he still does watchmaking on the side when he has a chance. He's got no room where he lives, so I let him come here when the mission's doors are closed."

"That's very generous of you," Kirk said.

"Not at all," Edith said. "It's just something one does for a neighbor." She turned back to the watchmaker. "Isn't that right, Mister McKenna?"

"Well, yes, of course," he said. "And I'm much obliged to you, ma'am."

"You know," she went on, "it might also be neighborly if you would allow Mister Kirk's friend to borrow your tools overnight."

"Ma'am, I'd like to help but—"

"You do your work here because you have no place to do it at home, isn't that right?" Edith asked.

"Yes, ma'am, it is," McKenna said.

"Well, then, you won't miss your tools if Mister Kirk's friend is using them at night," Edith said. "That way you can keep doing your work here when you need to and everybody gets what they need." Kirk perceived the implied threat in her words, that if McKenna didn't permit Spock to borrow his tools, then she wouldn't permit McKenna to use the mission. The watchmaker must have understood as well because he quickly relented.

"Well, I suppose it'll be all right," he said. "Your friend's going to be careful with them, isn't he? Some of them are delicate."

"Which is precisely why my friend needs them," Kirk said. "He's doing radio work."

"I used to do that too," McKenna said. "Still have some sources if you need any equipment."

"Actually, we don't right now," Kirk said, "but we might. I'll let Miss Keeler know if we do and then she can let you know."

"All right then," McKenna said. "Guess I'll be on my way." He started down the hall toward the mission's main room, but then turned back. "I'll see you here tomorrow afternoon then, Miss Keeler?" he asked.

"You will indeed, Mister McKenna," she said. Finally, the watchmaker departed.

"Thank you," Kirk told Edith.

"You're welcome," she said. "I just wish you'd come to me about borrowing the tools in the first place."

"My humble apologies," Kirk said, bowing his head.

"You can apologize all you want," Edith said, "but you still promised to walk me home."

"I certainly did," he said. "Shall we go?"

"Let me get my cloak," Edith said, pointing down to the door that opened into her office. "I also want to put on a longer shirt. It's cooler out this afternoon than it was this morning." At the moment, she wore a brown, lightweight knit sweater with short sleeves.

She ducked into her office and closed the door. When she returned, Kirk saw that she had changed into a white blouse, and she held her purse in one hand. As they walked into the main room and over to the front doors, she set a white knit beret atop her head, then fastened her long, dark cloak about her. She told Rik that she would be going, but that Spock would help him with dinner for the men. Then she and Kirk stepped out into the late afternoon. Already the sun had begun to set.

For a while, the two of them strolled along the sidewalk without talking. They walked side-by-side, and the silence felt comfortable to Kirk, as if he knew this woman so well, and she him, that they didn't need to speak. The idea seemed absurd on the face of it, and yet he somehow sensed a connection with Edith.

After a few blocks, she said, "So, Mister Kirk, are you going to tell me where you're from and what you're doing here, or are you going to make me figure it out on my own?"

A smile played at the side of Kirk's mouth. "Jim," he said. "You can call me Jim."

Edith hesitated for a moment, and Kirk thought that she might protest. Then she said, "All right, Jim. And I'd like it if you called me Edith. But that doesn't change the fact that I want to know about you."

"Oh, I don't know," Kirk said. "Isn't a little mystery good for the soul?"

"So you enjoy taunting me," Edith said.

"No, I don't," Kirk said seriously. "But I think maybe you already know who I am." He knew that she couldn't possibly even imagine that he commanded a starship three hundred years in the future, but here in 1930, she looked to the stars in the same way that he had when he'd grown up on a farm in Iowa.

"Maybe I already do know you," Edith agreed. "Maybe a little bit. But do you know me?"

"Maybe a little bit," Kirk said with a chuckle. "But you've got a little mystery about you too. I could ask you some questions."

"Me?" Edith said in a surprised and obviously affected tone.

"Oh, don't give me that 'questions about little old me' look," he said, essentially repeating what she'd said to him earlier.

"Well, tell me, Jim," she said, "what questions do you have for me?"

"Let me see," Kirk said, trying to think of what he should ask. In truth, he wanted to know everything about her, but then something odd he'd noticed occurred to him. "You run the mission," he said.

"I try to," Edith replied.

"So you're responsible for everything in it," he went on.

"Yes, as much as I can be."

"All right," he said. "So why do you have an eight-year-old calendar hanging on the wall?" He'd noted it that first day he and Spock had been in the mission, and until he'd seen a newspaper, he'd thought they'd traveled back to 1922.

Beside him, Edith looked down, and when she didn't respond, he realized that something had happened.

"I'm sorry," he said quickly. "If I've asked something wrong—" He stopped walking and faced her.

"No, no, not wrong, it's just . . . " She peered up at him, as though forcing herself to face this moment. Finally, she started walking again. "I came with my father to this country almost eight years ago," she said. "In June of nineteen twenty-two. He was having a difficult time in England . . . really, he had been for a long while, since my mother died when I was a girl. But he finally decided that he wanted to make a new start for himself, and he thought that the United States would give him an opportunity to do that."

They waited as an automobile passed in front of them, then crossed the street to the next block.

"He also thought that this country would provide me more opportunities as well," Edith went on. "Women had been given voting rights equal to men here in 1920, and that hadn't happened yet in England. So he tried to convince me to come with him." Edith got quiet again for a few seconds, and then said, "He needn't have. I wouldn't have wanted to live with an ocean between us. So I came with him." Again, she looked up at Kirk with what seemed like great purpose. "He died only a few days after we arrived in New York."

"I'm sorry," Kirk said, genuinely sad for what had been an obviously terrible loss for her.

"Thank you," she said. "Anyway, that calendar was one of the first things we bought when we got here because it showed scenes of American history. I kept it because . . . I don't know why. I suppose because it seemed for a while like time just stopped for me. I loved my father very much."

Kirk wanted to say something to comfort her, but he knew that no words could ease whatever pain she still felt. Rather, he simply continued walking beside her, offering his presence however she needed it. After a few minutes, as dusk rose, the streetlamps came on around them. Kirk glanced up at one and then over at Edith. She smiled sweetly at him, and he took her hand in his. Once more, he felt the connection between them.

They passed a store selling radios, the strains of a song wafting out into the twilight. They came to another intersection and ran across the street in front of a horse-drawn carriage. Along the way, their hands parted, but it seemed natural. Everything seemed natural with Edith.

As they walked along the next block, Edith suddenly asked, "Why does Spock call you 'captain'? Were you in the war together?"

"We . . . served together," Kirk said, not wanting to lie to her.

"And you, um, don't want to talk about it?" she said. "Why?" She stopped and turned to face him. Kirk started to answer, but Edith continued to ask questions. "Did you—did you do something wrong? Are you afraid of something?"

He gazed into her eyes and saw a depth of caring

there—of caring for *him*—that he didn't know if he'd ever seen in anyone's eyes before. Then she placed a hand on his arm and said, "Whatever it is, let me help."

The words resonated for Kirk. His mother had instilled in him a love for reading at an early age, and he'd enjoyed books throughout his life. What Edith said brought one of his favorite tomes to mind. He put an arm around her back and started walking with her again. "'Let me help,'" he said. "A hundred years or so from now, I believe, a famous novelist will write a classic using that theme." He felt her own arm around his back now. "He'll recommend those three words even over 'I love you.'"

Edith stopped and looked at him again, a joyful smile on her lips. "Centuries from now?" she said. "Who—who is he? Where does he come from . . . um . . . where *will* he come from?"

"Silly question," Kirk said. "Want to hear a silly answer?"

"Yes."

He peered up into the sky and immediately saw the constellation of Orion. "A planet," he said, lifting his arm to point to the heavens, "circling that far left star in Orion's Belt. See?"

As Edith sent her gaze skyward, he dropped his hand back to his side and looked at her. After a few seconds, she turned to him. Slowly, they moved closer, and then their lips met, the touch of her flesh warm and soft and loving.

When they pulled back from each other, he saw again her beauty. He also realized the depth of his foolishness. If he accomplished his mission, he would leave this place and this time, returning to a place where Edith could never come. He knew that he should not love her, that he should stop right now and walk away without looking back.

Instead, he kissed her again.

* * *

After weeks of effort and helped along by the nightly use of Mr. McKenna's tools, Spock had finally completed a rudimentary mnemonic memory circuit. He had activated it a short time ago, executing a query both for any occurrences of the name Leonard McCoy in its various permutations, and for any discrepancies between the recordings of the two timelines. To minimize the volume of data searched, Spock limited it to the calendar year 1930. Now, at last, the tricorder signaled that some piece of information had been found.

Spock sat down at the chair he'd placed in the middle of the room. Before it sat the nightstand, atop which he'd set the tricorder. All around the room, on both beds, on the short dresser, on the table, equipment buzzed and whined as the electrical components performed a task for which they had never been designed.

On the tricorder's small display, Spock saw a catalogue of data, each entry simply denoted FILE. Knowing that he'd requested the list in chronological order, he selected the first one. For an instant, what appeared to be an image of a newspaper appeared on the screen, but then it blinked off. Spock touched a control, deactivating the display, then reached for one of McKenna's tools. He raised it to the manual monitor adjustment he'd exposed at the top of the tricorder. He tuned the display, then reactivated it. A moment later, the image reappeared on the screen.

It did, in fact, show a newspaper. Unexpectedly, an image of Edith Keeler appeared, her name spelled out in capital letters beneath it. Above, a banner read: SOCIAL WORKER KILLED. Below, the first few lines of her obituary stated that she had been killed in a traffic accident.

A mixture of emotions rose within Spock. He at first tended toward disbelief, even as he understood that this identified discrepancy strongly supported the concept that he and the captain had been swept to the same focal point in time as McCoy. He also felt sadness for Jim; even though the captain would have had to leave Keeler when they returned to their own time, this turn of events would be more difficult for him to bear.

But Spock had a job to do and he quickly settled his mind. He reached to the tricorder display controls to see if he could pan to the top of the newspaper page for a date. Slowly, the image began to move, but then he heard a sizzling sound in one section of the mnemonic memory circuit. A second later, the newspaper disappeared from the display in a coruscation of flashes and jagged lines.

Spock exchanged one of McKenna's tools for another, then stood and moved to the near bed, to the circuit components there. He reached down to where he believed the problem to be and made an adjustment. The sizzling stopped, and he returned to the tricorder. He couldn't be sure, but he thought that the data stored in the tricorder from 1930, from either one or both of the timelines, might have been lost. When he sat back down, he saw that his data search had resumed. For the moment, he let it run.

As he watched the display, the door opened and the captain entered. He had spent the evening working at the mission. "How are the stone knives and bearskins?" he asked.

"I may have found our focal point in time," Spock said.

Moving into the room and removing his coat, Kirk said, "I think you may also find you have a"—he sniffed at the air— "connection burning someplace."

"Yes, I'm overloading those lines," Spock said. "I believe we'll have our answer on this screen, Captain."

"Good," Kirk said.

"And Captain," Spock warned, "you may find this a bit distressing."

Kirk brought over a wooden box to sit on. "All right, let's see what you've got," he said as he perched so that he too could see the tricorder display.

Spock reached up with one of McKenna's tools and tuned the display again, keying it to show one of the search results. "I've slowed down the recording we made from the time vortex." Again, the image of a newspaper appeared.

"February twenty-third, nineteen thirty-six," the captain read. "Six years from now."

Spock knew at once that, in addition to losing data from the tricorder, he'd also lost part of the mnemonic memory circuit. He'd initially specified his search to include information only from 1930, but evidently that parameter had been lost when the search had resumed. Still, what appeared on the display confirmed his belief in the identity of the focal point in time to which they had been drawn. Beneath another labeled photograph of Edith Keeler, the headline read F.D.R. CONFERS WITH SLUM AREA "ANGEL".

"The President and Edith Keeler," read the captain, "conferred for some time today—"

Suddenly the image began to roll, and then sparks shot from the components positioned atop the far bed. Flames flashed upward, and the vacuum tubes blackened. Spock stood and reached for the links to the tricorder, quickly disconnecting them.

The captain rose and stepped over to the ruined components. "How bad?" he asked.

"Bad enough," Spock told him.

The captain seemed to think for a moment, and then as he crossed the room, he said, "The President and Edith Keeler—"

"It would seem unlikely, Jim," Spock said, knowing that he must tell him of the other possibility. "A few moments ago, I read a nineteen thirty newspaper article."

"We know her future," the captain said, excited. "Within six years from now, she'll become very important, nationally famous."

"Or Captain," Spock said, "Edith Keeler will die . . . this year."

Jim's expression grew hard.

"I saw her obituary," Spock said. "Some sort of traffic accident."

"You must be mistaken," the captain said, though without conviction. "They both can't be true."

Spock knew that, and he believed that the captain must know it as well. Again, he felt sorrow for his friend, and he covered it with action. He moved to the portion of the memory circuit that had just been destroyed. "Captain," he said, "Edith Keeler is the focal point in time we've been looking for." As he sat down on the bed, he picked up a new vacuum tube, then reached to remove one of those just overheated. "The point in time to which both we and Doctor McCoy have been drawn."

"She has two possible futures then," the captain said. "And depending on whether she lives or dies, all of history will be changed. And McCoy . . ."

"Is the random element," Spock said.

"In his condition, what does he do?" the captain asked. "Does he kill her?"

"Or perhaps he prevents her from being killed," Spock said. "We don't know which."

"Get this thing fixed," the captain said. "We must find out before McCoy arrives." He turned and headed toward the door. Without his coat, Spock could only surmise that he intended to go upstairs, to visit Keeler.

"Captain," Spock said, standing, "suppose we discover that in order to set things straight again Edith Keeler must die?"

The captain had opened the door, and now he closed it again. "Spock," he said, "we'll find McCoy, and we'll stop him from doing whatever it is he did—whatever he *will* do—to change history. That's why we're here. But in order to stop McCoy, we must know what action to take, and when."

"I'm afraid we just might have lost the ability to do that," Spock said. "I believe we lost some of the data we recorded from the Guardian. Once I repair the mnemonic memory circuit, I may be able to reconstruct the remaining information enough to estimate general happenings, but I don't know if I'll be able to isolate precisely what McCoy did."

"Do your best, Spock," the captain said. "In the meantime, if Edith Keeler is the focal point in time, then one of us should endeavor to be near her as much a possible."

"Agreed," Spock said. He did not feel the need to point out that the captain already spent a great deal of time with her.

FOURTEEN

2294

Amanda circled the piece as though stalking it, examining it from every angle, alert for any weakness. She paid attention to the textures of the materials and to the shadows the various components cast. Not dissatisfied with any of the details, she stepped back and regarded the work as a whole.

Upright blocks of dark clay bounded either side of a lighter, horizontal surface, which spread past the blocks into several other layers of different hues. The sculpture appeared abstract at first glance, which had been her aim. In reality, she had labored to create an impressionistic work not obviously so, in order to conduct her own personal experiment into the nature of visual art, words, and communication. She would display the piece with and without its title—*The End of the Maze*—and collect the interpretations of those who viewed it in each mode.

With her hands on her hips, Amanda stood alone in her studio, a geodesic structure attached to the house and with transparent walls that provided her the perfect light in which to ply her craft. She wore a ragged and very comfortable old dress and a white smock over it. The gray tones of wet clay covered her fingers, while other shades of gray, blue, and black streaked her smock.

Amanda walked over to the small table that contained the various materials with which she'd been working. One by one, she gathered them up and stored them in containers that would keep them fresh. After she'd put those away, she went to the small refresher at the rear of the room, where at the sink she began cleaning the tools she'd used and then her hands. When she finished, she would go find Sarek and Spock to ask them to come view her new piece.

As Amanda thought of her son, she smiled. He hadn't spent this much time with her and Sarek since before he'd gone off to Starfleet more than forty years ago. He'd stayed here for almost three-quarters of a year now, and Amanda had enjoyed just about every minute of it. She and Sarek had traveled twice during that time on his diplomatic missions, but both times they'd come back to Vulcan to find Spock still at the house.

When Amanda had first learned that her son had returned to Vulcan for the purpose of carrying out the *Kolinahr*, she had been deeply upset. He had tried once before,
two decades ago, to achieve the purging of his emotions,
and she had privately rejoiced when he hadn't succeeded.
Even now, she remembered all too well when Spock, at
the ages of five and six and seven, had come home after
his schoolmates had accused him of not being truly Vulcan. Amanda had watched as only a mother could as he'd
held his torment in, but she'd known how much the taunts
had wounded him. But she also knew that the hurt he'd felt
had its antithesis; not all emotions brought pain. Whether
he wanted it to be true or not, Spock had human blood
within him, and human feeling as well.

Her hands clean, Amanda dried them on a small towel
hanging beside the sink. After untying her smock, she
pulled it off and tossed it into a freestanding hamper. Then
she went to look for Sarek and Spock.

As she reached the door of her son's room on the second story, she saw him inside, his back to her. Before she
could speak, he turned from the dresser with a stack of
clothing in his hands. He walked over to the bed, where
Amanda saw his duffel open atop it. "You're leaving?" she
asked, stating the obvious.

"Yes," Spock said, glancing over at her.

Amanda felt disappointed, but also realized that this
marked a positive moment for her son. When he'd first arrived here, he'd been in a state in which she'd rarely seen
him as an adult. Though he had, as always, sought to hide
his feelings, to control them, he'd been unable to do so
very effectively—at least not in front of her. He'd been affected, emotive, obviously grieving for the loss of his
friend, but also showing signs of being more deeply troubled than that. He'd withdrawn from the rest of his life in

order to pursue the *Kolinahr*, but when he hadn't been permitted to do that, he'd come here, back home, openly in search of an inner peace that eluded him. He had spent his days here quietly, contemplatively, reading, walking, sitting in meditation. Amanda had eventually begun to see him reassert his Vulcan poise, and more important, to deal with the troubles within him.

"Where will you be going?" she asked as he moved across the room to the closet. Amanda imagined that Spock would return to Starfleet, though in the past months he'd also spoken positively of his experiences as a Federation ambassador.

As Spock reached for the clothes hanging in the closet, he said, "I am headed to Gol."

A knot of anxiety twisted within Amanda. Gol, the name of both an ancient Vulcan city and the high, fractured plain upon which it stood, remained the province of the *Kolinahr* masters. *No,* Amanda thought, willing back the tears that immediately threatened. "You're going to study the—" she said, but she could not finish the statement.

Spock stopped and turned to face her. "I am going back to the Akrelt Refuge to petition once more for my entry into the *Kolinahr*," he said.

"Does your father know about this?" Amanda asked. She and Sarek had spoken about this possibility, but over time had concluded that their son likely would not choose this path again.

"I have not told him," Spock said. "I only came to this decision within the past week. I requested a time to restate my petition before a Vulcan master, and today I received word that I would be granted an audience at the Akrelt Refuge tomorrow."

Tomorrow, Amanda echoed in her mind, the word almost as chilling to her as a death sentence. Still in the doorway to Spock's room, she looked down the hall and called out Sarek's name.

"Mother—" Spock began.

"You mustn't do this," she said, taking a step into the room. The terrible dread she felt came with a history. The time Spock had spent all those years ago undergoing the *Kolinahr,* working to rid himself of his human side, had been an agony for Amanda. And even though he'd failed to realize his goal, the experience had at first changed him. He had been more controlled, more distant, *colder.* It had felt sometimes as though she had lost her son, as though Spock had been taken away and a soulless replica left in his place.

But that had not lasted, and ultimately Spock had not only reverted to his distinctly Vulcan *and* human personality, but he had at last seemed to become comfortable with who he was. Now, though, if he managed to complete the *Kolinahr—*

"You called, my wife," Sarek said, and Amanda looked around to see her husband in the doorway. Sarek peered from her to Spock, and then to the duffel on the bed. "You are departing, Spock?" he said.

"I am," Spock said. He reached into the closet and gathered the few items of clothing hanging there. He took them to the bed, where he folded them over and loaded them into the duffel.

"Sarek, Spock is . . . " Amanda said, but she could not speak the words.

"I will be reapplying for the *Kolinahr,*" Spock said.

Amanda turned to her husband. "Sarek," she said, "we can't let him do that."

"Mother," Spock said, "this is the choice I have made for myself. I ask that you respect it. It is what is right for my life."

"I can assure you that your mother and I do respect the choices you make," Sarek said. "That does not mean that we always agree with them."

"This *isn't* the right choice for you," Amanda said, peering back at Spock. "It is one thing for a full Vulcan to rid themselves of their emotions, but you are half human. If you do this, you'll destroy a major part of who you are."

"Mother, please," Spock said. "Father, would you help explain why I must do this?"

"But your mother is correct," Sarek said. Amanda felt relieved and grateful that he admitted this. It had taken him many years to appreciate Spock's dichotomous character, and even longer to fully accept his son for the good person he'd become.

"Father," Spock said, his surprise at Sarek's declaration evident in his voice. "You have always supported me . . . in fact, have always *urged* me . . . to pursue a Vulcan way of life. The *Kolinahr* is considered to be our quintessential ritual, the achievement that allows but few Vulcans to reach a state of complete maturity."

"I do not dispute that," Sarek said. "But my son, you have already reached maturity."

Amanda watched Spock look away, apparently unprepared for his father's opposition. "There is no limitation on the age at which one may attempt the *Kolinahr*," he said.

"Nor am I suggesting that there should be," Sarek said. He walked into the room to stand beside Amanda. "What I am saying is that the battle you waged within yourself as a boy and as a young man has passed—has in fact been won."

"I have won no battle," Spock said, an assertion so preposterous that Amanda didn't know if even her son believed it. That he could make such a claim perhaps spoke to why he sought at this stage of his life to change himself.

"Spock," Sarek said, "when you were a boy of seven, in order to prove yourself as a 'true' Vulcan, you set out on your own, without preparation, for the Forge." Amanda recalled when Spock had been approaching the time for his *kahs-wan*, a Vulcan test of survival. Badgered by his classmates about not being really Vulcan, Spock had left home a month before the proper time, without having learned all that he needed to know in order to endure out on the Forge. Fortunately a visiting older cousin had followed him and brought him home, though not before Spock had faced a different test of courage when his pet *sehlat* had been attacked by a *le-matya*. A month later, Spock had taken part in the *kahs-wan*, at which he had succeeded. "You proved yourself then," Sarek told their son, "and you have continued to do so ever since."

"I do not understand how you can tell me that," Spock said. "You opposed my entry into Starfleet, in which I have spent a majority of my life, among humans. I failed the *Kolinahr* the first time and even failed the petition the second time."

"You have become who you are," Sarek said. "A good person born of a Vulcan father and a human mother. You practice Vulcan disciplines, honing your mind and your emotional restraint. You wear a truthful persona of logic and stoicism that covers a core of controlled feeling—controlled, but real feeling. *Human* feeling."

Amanda peered up at Sarek, pleased not only that he had come to this estimation of their son, but that he would reveal it to Spock. Her heart swelled with the love she felt for her husband. Looking back over at Spock, she said, "This is who you are."

"Yes," Spock said, nodding, and the expression on his face hardened, as surely as if he'd pulled on a mask. He bent down to the bed, sealed his duffel, and quickly hoisted it onto his shoulder. "But this is not who I wish to be." He strode purposefully across the room, past Amanda and Sarek, and out into the hall.

"Spock!" she called after him, but as she started forward, she felt Sarek's hands around her arms.

"You cannot go after him," he said. "We have told him what we could. Now he must find his own way."

As she heard Spock's footsteps descending the stairs, she knew that Sarek was right. And as she had all those years ago, when Spock had come home with a stiff upper lip, trying to hide his anguish at being deemed not truly a Vulcan, Amanda wept for her son. If he was accepted into the *Kolinahr* and completed it, she worried that, in a very real way, she would never see the Spock she knew ever again.

Beneath the stone countenance of T'Klass, Spock stood at the altar in the Akrelt Refuge. Unlike on his previous visit here, his thoughts did not race, his emotions did not whirl. The months of meditation and contemplation at his parents' home had helped to settle his mind, though that time and effort had not obviated his need to actively follow this course.

"On the sands of our world, our ancestors cast out their animal passions, saving our race by the attainment of *Kolinahr*," Spock said, declaiming the ritual statement. "It is that which I seek. I make my petition to you, T'Vora, asking you to guide me in my quest." When he had reapplied for the *Kolinahr*, he had not known whether he would be directed to meet again with T'Vora or this time with a different master. It seemed most logical that, having heard his initial request, T'Vora would be best suited to evaluate his recent progress, and therefore his fitness for entry into the ancient practice.

"I hear what you ask," the master pronounced opposite Spock, her lined face and dark hair illuminated from below by the orange flame of the candle sitting at the center of the altar. Behind her, hanging on either side of the T'Klass carving, a pair of torches gave humble view to this section of the sanctuary. "Spock, child of Sarek, child of Skon," T'Vora said, "for the third time in your life you come before a master asking to partake of the ultimate Vulcan sacrament. For the second time, you stand before me, asking for that which you have already been denied. Tell me, is there not illogic in that?"

"There is not," Spock declared. "To take the same action and expect a different result would be illogical only if the conditions surrounding that action remained static. In this case, though that which I seek has not changed, my circumstances have."

"And how have your circumstances changed?" T'Vora asked. She spoke in a tone that somehow matched the shadowy environs, while still retaining an air of command.

"When last I stood before you, Master T'Vora," Spock said, "you declared that the *Kolinahr* should not be employed as a haven in which to escape emotion. Since then, I have explored those feelings that in part drove me to the Akrelt Refuge nine months ago, and I have eliminated them as reasons for my return here now."

"You have eliminated the impetus provided by those emotions," T'Vora said, "but not the emotions themselves?"

"No," Spock said. "I control them now as I have in the past and far more than I did during our previous meeting. But yes, the emotions are present within me."

"If you can control your emotions as you say," T'Vora asked, "then what need have you of the *Kolinahr?*"

At last, Spock had been posed a question similar to one

he'd heard twenty-four years ago, when he had first pursued the *Kolinahr*. To this point, his experiences with T'Vora had been vastly different than his experiences with T'sai. "As I understand it," he said, "the *Kolinahr* encompasses more than simple emotional control. As you yourself declared, Master T'Vora, it is a type of existence. I believe it is one to which I am well suited, and one that will best permit me to fulfill my potential."

"And how do you see yourself fulfilling your potential?" T'Vora asked.

"As a functioning and responsible member of Vulcan society," Spock said.

"Yet, you are also human," T'Vora said. "The *Kolinahr* will not change that."

"To expect so would be illogical," Spock said. "But to accept that my being born of a human mother and a Vulcan father must define me or limit me in some way would also be illogical." He paused, trying to find a way to formulate his response in terms that would support his candidacy. "For virtually all of my life," he said at last, "I have viewed myself as Vulcan. I have come to realize that this perspective had not been entirely accurate. I wish to make it so."

T'Vora regarded him without speaking for several moments, and then she paced around the altar and over to where he stood. When he turned to face her, she said, "Your thoughts, Spock. Give them to me."

Spock lowered himself to his knees, then peered upward. T'Vora reached forward with one hand, the wide arm of her robe falling open as she did so. Her fingers found his face, their tips cool as they settled along his cheek and up to his forehead. "My mind to your mind," she intoned, "my thoughts to your thoughts." Spock felt the tap of another presence in his head and made an effort not to resist it. The threads of T'Vora's psyche floated about his own, insubstantial, nonthreatening.

And then they pushed forward, penetrating into him. He could sense the power of her mind, the sharp-edged focus, the perfect control, the Vulcan purity of it. T'Vora's thoughts invaded his, and he knew that he must not think of it as an assault. Still, reflex protected his consciousness, instincts of self-preservation steeled his defenses against the incursion into his thoughts.

With an effort, Spock willed his mental barriers to lower. He struggled, but then succeeded in allowing her the access she needed to measure his abilities. With even more difficulty, he laid his emotions bare. *The love he felt for his parents. His friendship for McCoy and Scott, Sulu and Uhura and Chekov. His affection for Alexandra. The sense of loss that had plagued him since Jim's death, and the intense remorse that accompanied it.*

T'Vora would see all of it. Spock knew that she had perceived his emotions before now, not only from speaking with him and observing him, but as a consequence of her sympathetic talents. Now, though, she would experience everything he felt in a raw, firsthand way. It shamed him to have his privacy breached so, but of course shame contradicted logic. He let the embarrassment go, and with it flowed a torrent of feelings, and with those, a slew of visual impressions. *The glowing, organic form of the Guardian of Forever. The soft, milky features of Edith Keeler. A Klingon face, unshaven, angry: Korax. The bridge of the* Enterprise, *a charred ruin, Jim and the crew within surely dead. An Andorian Starfleet officer named Thelin. I-Chaya dying in the desert. The great forms of humpback whales floating in a tank.* The vortex of images swirled through his mind, and with them the emotions they engendered: wonder, suspicion, pain, remorse.

What did I do? he could not prevent himself from thinking.

T'Vora severed the meld, leaving Spock alone but still vulnerable. He worked as quickly as he could to stem the flood that the connection with the master had unleashed. He had no sense of how long T'Vora had maintained their link. It could have been a second or a minute or an hour.

"You control much," she said.

"I—" Spock began, but he had difficulty forming words. Finally, he managed to say, "Yes." In the cool of the Akrelt Refuge, he became aware of the track of a tear drying on his cheek.

"Spock," T'Vora said, "I ask you to consider this. The *Kolinahr* is not universally positive even among full-blooded Vulcans. You have endured the training and discipline once before, and so you may think you know what to expect. But this time will be different from that one, because I will be your guide here in the Akrelt Refuge, and I am different from T'sai, and this place is different than the Riakin Sanctuary. But it will primarily be different because you are different. Years have passed, and you have experienced a great deal . . . things that no other Vulcans have during that period. You have had your *katra* separated from your body and then re-fused to it. Yours was the first *fal-tor-pan* even attempted since ages past. I cannot tell you how this will impact the *Kolinahr*."

Spock had already considered this, had even tried to research it. Nowhere in the literature about either the *Kolinahr* or the *fal-tor-pan* had he found mention of an interaction between the two. As T'Vora had said, it would introduce an element of the unknown if he continued along this path. But he had not come this far by being wary of the unknown.

"I choose the *Kolinahr*," Spock said. The effects of the

meld fading, his mind felt sharp. The path ahead seemed clear, the path behind littered with obstacles. He could only move forward. "I am ready."

"Let us trust that you are," T'Vora said. "Rise." After Spock stood up, the master instructed him to take the cylindrical candle at the center of the altar. As he did so, its flame wavered but did not go out. "Come with me," T'Vora said.

Spock followed as T'Vora paced around the altar to face toward the wall beneath the figure of T'Klass. "Step through," she said, pointing forward, though Spock could only see the dark stone blocks of the wall. Still, he did not hesitate. Logic dictated that the *Kolinahr* master must be obeyed; if Spock could not trust T'Vora, then he should not have accepted her as his guide.

He stepped toward the seemingly solid wall. *A holographic projection,* his scientific mind postulated, but the light of the candle reflected off the damp surface of the stone blocks. *A test then?* Spock wondered, thinking that perhaps T'Vora at the outset wanted to be sure that he would follow her directives.

But at the last instant before Spock would have struck the wall, a narrow entryway appeared. He hadn't seen or heard the blocks move, and yet he could not deny the opening before him. As instructed, he stepped through it.

On the other side, barely visible in the faint glow of the candle he held, a corridor stretched into the distance. He heard T'Vora's footsteps as she entered behind him. "Continue," she said, and Spock started forward again.

The narrow passage seemed devoid of ornamentation of any kind, though in the darkness, he could not be sure. After perhaps thirty paces, a gust of warm air struck him, and then a shadow along the left-hand wall revealed itself to be a large wooden door. T'Vora said nothing, and so Spock did not stop.

After another thirty paces, he felt a second rush of warm air, and then he spied a second door. This time, T'Vora told him to stop and enter. He did, the texture of the wood dry and rough against his hand as he pushed it open. It swung inward silently, revealing a dimly lighted cell perhaps three meters long and two wide. Spock gazed upward to the high ceiling to see several square holes through which daylight entered. That surprised him, as the Akrelt Refuge had been built out of the side of a deep canyon, with only the front of the structure protruding from solid rock. For there to be shafts reaching down here from so far above seemed unlikely.

Spock peered around the rest of the cell. To his left, the outline of a Vulcan IDIC symbol had been etched into the wall, filling it. Bedding lay on the floor below it. To his right, a series of different-sized niches had been carved out of the stone and filled with ceremonial statues. An open doorway also appeared to lead to a primitive refresher. Finally, in the far wall, another monument to T'Klass had been sculpted. Below it hung an unlighted torch. T'Vora told him to set it aflame, and using the candle, he did.

"Spock, child of Sarek, child of Skon," she said then, "your petition for the *Kolinahr* is accepted."

"I am honored," Spock said, facing her across the length of the cell.

"Beginning tomorrow," she said, "you will live here until either you succeed or you fail in your quest. It will commence tomorrow at dawn. You may bring what you wear and a single change of clothing. All else will be provided for you."

"I understand," Spock said.

"Then for now, go," T'Vora said.

Spock followed her as she made her way back through the corridor and out to the altar. There, he set the candle back down. After he took his leave of the master, he headed across the main room of the Refuge and out into the canyon. He would spend the night at the room he had taken in Gol, then return here at sunrise. He would begin again the quest at which he had failed so long ago. This time, he would achieve *Kolinahr*.

He would be truly Vulcan.

He would be human no more.

FIFTEEN

1930

Kirk walked through the darkness with Edith, hand-in-hand, after serving the late meal at the mission. Four days ago, Spock had informed him of an unthinkable possibility, and he had realized that while he would have to keep Edith under observation, he would also need to keep his emotional distance from her, for his own sake. He knew that, but so far, he'd been completely incapable of doing so.

"Edith?" Kirk asked. The day had been unseasonably temperate, and even after night had fallen, the air hadn't cooled much.

"Yes, Jim?" Edith said, the sound of her speaking his name like music to him.

"Tell me, why do you do what you do?" he asked. "At the mission, I mean." He appreciated what she had done for him and Spock, and also what she did for all those others in need.

"Because it's necessary," she said. "Because sometimes people need a helping hand."

"But why do *you* feel you have to provide that helping hand?" Kirk asked.

"Doesn't everybody feel that?" Edith said. "I'm not claiming that everybody does something about it, but don't people generally want to help their neighbors?"

"In a perfect world," Kirk said.

"No," Edith said. "In a perfect world, people wouldn't just want to help their fellow man, they'd actually do it. But that day will come."

"Why do you think so?" Kirk said, genuinely curious as to the source of her insight.

"Because we're all connected," she said. "We all live and die together."

"'Any man's death diminishes me,'" Kirk quoted, "'because I am involved in mankind.'"

"Yes!" Edith said excitedly. "John Donne. 'Meditation Seventeen.' I love that piece. That's one of my favorites."

Kirk smiled. He should have known she'd have an appreciation for Donne. "Do you know this?" he asked her. "'All I ask is a tall ship and a star to steer her by'?"

"No, I don't," Edith said, "but I like it."

"It's called 'Sea-Fever,' by John Masefield," Kirk told her, and then recited the first stanza.

"I must down to the seas again, to the lonely sea
 and the sky,
And all I ask is a tall ship and a star to steer her by,
And the wheel's kick and the wind's song and the
 white sail's shaking,
And a grey mist on the sea's face, and a grey dawn
 breaking."

"That's lovely," Edith said. They had reached their apartment building, and they started up the steps. At the front door, Kirk noticed that the light in the arch had been replaced. Inside, Edith pulled off her hat, then began to take off her cloak. He helped her with it. As she draped it over her arm, she asked, "Do you sail, Jim?"

"I like to travel," he said.

"I haven't traveled much," she said as she checked her mailbox. "I mean, I came over here from England, but that's about it. One day I'd like to see the world, though."

"Why don't you?" Kirk asked. Together, they walked into the front hall and began up the stairs.

"The mission," she said. "I'm needed here."

"Is that it?" Kirk asked.

"Well, what's the use of seeing new places," Edith said, "if you don't have someone to share them with?"

"It can be rewarding on your own too, but . . . I know what you mean," Kirk said. They reached the top of the stairs and walked along the second floor to the next flight up. As they ascended, Kirk asked, "If you did travel, where would you want to go?"

"I'd want to see every place," Edith said. "Greece, Russia, the Orient, Australia . . . the moon."

"The moon?" Kirk said. "You really believe mankind will leave Earth, don't you? That's amazing." He couldn't help laughing, both delighted and astonished by Edith's vision.

"Why?" she asked as they reached the third floor. "What is so funny about man reaching for the moon?"

"How do you know?" he asked her.

"I just know, that's all," she insisted. "I feel it. And more: I think that one day, they're going to take all the money that they spend now on war and death—"

"And make them spend it on life," Kirk finished.

"Yes," Edith said with a smile. She walked the rest of the way down the hall to her apartment. Kirk followed and they stood together by the door. "You see the same things that I do. We speak the same language."

"The very same," Kirk said. He knew that he should leave, that he should go back down the stairs to the apartment he shared with Spock. He knew that, but he leaned forward and kissed Edith anyway. Her arms came up around his neck, her cloak and purse flopping against his back. His hands went to her waist and pulled her close. They kissed each other deeply, passionately. He smelled the delicate scent of her flesh, heard the rush of her breathing.

When they parted, Edith reached into her purse for the key to her apartment. She unlocked the door, then pushed it open and stepped inside. When she looked back at him, he said, "Good night, Edith."

She said, "Come in?"

He gazed at her for a long time, knowing again what he should do, what he *must* do. But he still walked forward and into her arms, pushing the door closed behind him. They moved into each other's arms and kissed again.

It took a long time for them to get to the bed, and an even longer time to leave it.

Midnight had passed two hours ago, and still the captain had not returned to the apartment. Spock had heard his voice outside in the hall earlier, as well as that of Keeler. He'd heard their footfalls as they'd climbed the stairs to this floor, and then again as they'd mounted to the next. Spock recalled the decision he and the captain had made to keep Keeler under surveillance as much as possible, but he also knew that all this time the captain spent with her had as much to do with his feelings for her.

As Spock labored over the repairs to the mnemonic memory circuit, moving around the room the various components, his concern for the captain grew. Whether or not Edith Keeler died, Spock felt confident now that he and the captain would be able to stop McCoy. And when they did, they would return to the twenty-third century—which meant, regardless of Keeler's fate, Jim would lose this woman that he so obviously loved.

Well versed in the classics, Spock knew the quote by Alfred, Lord Tennyson: " 'Tis better to have loved and lost/ Than never to have loved at all." Perhaps the captain had considered this, and had made the conscious decision to enjoy whatever time he could with Keeler. Perhaps he believed that he would gain more from what would necessarily be a brief relationship than he would lose.

Spock reached to the tall dresser, to where he had added more equipment to the circuit. He had averaged eight hours of work each of the past four nights not only repairing the damage done, but augmenting his design with a layer of relays and buffers that should guard against overloads. He had confirmed that a significant portion of data from one of the timelines had been lost the other night as a result of feedback. He would make sure that did not happen again.

Taking an input power line from the equipment he'd placed atop the tall dresser, Spock strung a wire across the top of the doorway and over to the light fixture on the wall. He screwed an adapter into the empty socket, then plugged the cord into it. Returning to the tricorder on the nightstand at the center of the room, he activated that new portion of the circuit, testing its power consumption and stability. He heard a familiar buzz and whine, but nothing that indicated a threat to the new components.

Spock chose one of McKenna's tools and began adjusting the tricorder, tuning the added connection. As he did, he heard footsteps approaching out in the hall, and a moment later the door opened. The captain entered and closed the door.

Without even offering a greeting, he asked, "How long before we get a full answer?"

"I'll need at least two more days before I dare make another attempt," Spock said as he continued to adjust the tricorder.

"McCoy could've been in the city a week now for all we know," the captain said, clearly agitated. Spock thought that the pressure not only of righting the timeline, but of losing Edith Keeler one way or another, had begun taking its toll on him. For his own part, Spock also remained aware that the doctor might already have arrived in the past. "And whatever he does that affects her and changes history could happen tonight or tomorrow morning."

"Captain," Spock said, sitting back in his chair and momentarily halting his work on the tricorder, "our last bit of information was obtained at the expense of thirty hours' work in fused and burned circuits." It had taken him that long to replace the destroyed components.

"I must know whether she lives or dies, Spock," the captain said. "I must know what to do."

"Though we may not know precisely what action to take," Spock said, "we do have a general idea. We must stop McCoy from altering the timeline. To that end, we must find him, and when we do, isolate him from his surroundings, and most especially from Edith Keeler."

"Will that be enough, Spock?" the captain asked.

Spock put down the tool with which he'd been working and stood up. "Whatever McCoy did to change history," he reasoned, "he likely did not do so as a result of his absence somewhere. He was, after all, not present in the original timeline. It is therefore logical to conclude that if we can remove him as much as possible from interacting with the people and objects of this period, we will stand a good chance of preventing the damage he caused."

The captain nodded his head slowly. He appeared fatigued, but also strained. Spock could see the impact of his conflicting emotions. "Here, Captain," he said, moving around the nightstand upon which the tricorder sat. "Let me move everything off this bed so that you can get some rest."

Kirk waved off the suggestion. "That's all right, Spock," he said. "I don't think I can sleep right now. I was just going to take a walk, try to clear my head."

"Forgive me, Captain," Spock said, "but it is late and you have been up for many hours. I must point out that, in order for us to accomplish our goal, it would be wiser for us to be well rested."

Kirk shrugged. "I won't be well rested if I lie down and stare at the ceiling for hours," he said. "I'm going to take a walk . . . tire myself out just a little more." The captain attempted a small smile, but it did not touch his eyes. "I won't be out long, and I'll get some sleep when I come back."

"Very well," Spock said.

The captain opened the door and headed back out into the night. Spock watched him go, knowing how much turmoil he was experiencing. Spock would have his eased his burden if he could, but the facts were the facts, and there was nothing that he could do.

SIXTEEN

2294

In a small annex situated off the main room in the Akrelt Refuge, T'Vora sat in a straight-backed chair along the rear wall, observing. Seated beside her, Sokel also looked on. One of the two elders assisting T'Vora with Spock's *Kolinahr*, he specialized in facilitating a mind bridge between master and aspirant. Less invasive than mind melds, bridges allowed individuals to share singular thoughts or memories, compartmentalizing mental connections for the sake of both privacy and safety.

At the front of the annex, Spock sat facing Rekan, the second elder assisting T'Vora. At the moment, Spock showed indications of fatigue: a slight slump in his normally erect posture, an excess of blinking, a pallor recognizable even in the dim light spilling down from the apertures in the ceiling. T'Vora wondered if the weeks of logic exercises had worn on the aspirant, but then she noticed how enervated Rekan herself appeared. It stood to reason that if Spock's inquisitor tired, then so too should Spock.

"Given an n-dimensional hypersurface," Rekan said, her voice beginning to grow hoarse as she started another exercise, "with n invariant curvatures, K-sub-x, of the surface at each point, with x equal to the integers from one to n..."

T'Vora watched as Spock listened to the formulation of the mathematical problem. The solution to each question put to him, she knew, required no specialized knowledge beyond that which he already possessed. She wanted not

his knowledge and recall put to the test—though they necessarily were, by virtue of the content of some questions—
but his ability to reason logically.

"The aspirant is nearing exhaustion," Sokel said quietly
beside her.

"Yes, I see," T'Vora said as Rekan finished laying out
the particulars of the problem setup and posed an interrog-
ative. "We will end shortly."

The daily regimen of queries, ranging from very simple
to very complex and generally lasting from dawn until
dusk, had occupied much of the first two months of
Spock's *Kolinahr*. He had borne up well, displaying a
strong and focused intellect. As well, he had demonstrated
unflagging discipline, a testament to his commitment here.

"A preferred orthogonal basis," Spock said, responding
to Rekan.

"That is correct," the elder said. Then, without waiting,
she moved on to her next challenge. "You are standing on
Vulcan with a partner at one end of an unremarkable field
that is one hundred meters square. Ten thousand chairs
like this one—" She pointed to the simple wooden seat
upon which she sat. "—have been placed randomly in the
field. Your partner is a blind Vulcan with no ability to in-
teract telepathically to any degree. Without being permitted to touch your partner, you must direct him to walk
from one side of the field to the other. How would you accomplish this most efficiently?"

As Spock paused, obviously to consider the question,
T'Vora thought about it herself. It required only a moment's deliberation for her to see the correct answer, understanding that logic demanded she scrutinize not only
everything that Rekan had said, but also everything that
she had not. As she waited for Spock to find the solution,
she decided that this would be the last question of the day.

After a moment, Spock said, "I would verbally direct my partner across the field, while I walked ahead of him, moving any chairs in his path."

A simple problem, T'Vora thought, *but not if you allowed yourself to make assumptions on the information given.* Rekan's parameters stated that you could not touch your partner, not that you could not touch the chairs.

"That is correct," Rekan said. Before she could continue, T'Vora stood up.

"Kroykah," she said, bringing the proceedings to a halt. Both Rekan and Spock peered toward the back of the annex. "That will be all for the day," T'Vora said. "Rekan, Sokel, you are excused." Without a word, the two elders rose from their chairs and exited through the door at the rear of the annex.

T'Vora paced to the front of the room, where Spock stood to face her. Up close, she could see even more clearly his weariness. "How do you feel?" she asked.

"If the question is meant to evoke an emotional response," Spock said, "I feel nothing." T'Vora thought for an instant that he might have intended humor with his response, but discounted the possibility as he continued. "If the question is asked with respect to my physical and mental states, then I would say that I am fatigued."

"Is this due only to today's exertions?" T'Vora asked.

"From today's exertions, yes," Spock said, "but not *only* from them. The past weeks have been challenging, and I find myself growing tired faster today than, say, a month ago. I therefore conclude that the impact of the daily sessions has been cumulative."

"Do you understand why this is being done?" T'Vora asked.

"Not entirely," Spock said. "I can see the value in assessing my logical faculties, but in my estimation, I have already proven my fitness. Also, this is so far very different from the *Kolinahr* training I experienced with T'sai."

"Each *Kolinahr* is distinct, one from the next," T'Vora said, "among both aspirants and masters. Just as your experience with me is different than that with T'sai, so too is my experience with you different than that with any of my previous aspirants."

"While I do not question your methods," Spock said, "the uniqueness of each *Kolinahr* does not explain the intense concentration on my ability to reason."

"Your *ability* to reason is not at issue," T'Vora said. "But in seeking to purge yourself of all emotion, you must hone your logic, not only as a tool with which to reason, but absent feeling, as the singular means by which to conduct all aspects of your life."

"Yes, of course," Spock said.

"You will continue to sharpen your logic as your *Kolinahr* continues," T'Vora told him. "But you are ready to move on. Clearly among the tasks ahead you must inure yourself to all emotional catalysts. This necessarily demands that you deal fully with anything from your past that has left any residue of feeling within you."

"I understand," Spock said. T'Vora knew that no matter the method or approach, T'sai would also have addressed this with Spock.

"You obviously contended with such matters during your first *Kolinahr*," T'Vora said. "Since then, new events in your life have impacted you, and some may have reignited sentiments previously doused. You must face all of it, peel away your emotion responses until there is nothing left but memory and understanding, with no feeling whatsoever."

"I understand," Spock said again.

"Tomorrow you will rest and regain your strength,"

T'Vora declared. "We will begin on the following day to examine your life through the lens of emotion. All that you control must be studied and the restraint removed in favor of elimination."

"Yes, Master T'Vora," Spock said.

"Now go," T'Vora said. "Proceed to the refectory for the evening meal." Spock nodded in acknowledgment, then padded to the rear of the annex and through the door there. After he'd gone, T'Vora sat down in one of the chairs at the front of the room. She would sit for a while in quiet contemplation, as she would tomorrow as well. She needed to gather her strength in preparation for what was to come.

T'Vora had chosen to begin here.

Here, on the lower level of main engineering, aboard the Enterprise, *in the Mutara Nebula.*

Out in one of the deep, narrow fissures that sliced through the high plateau of Gol, Spock saw himself aboard the ship and no longer felt the heat of the Vulcan day around him. He had walked here with T'Vora and Sokel, away from the Akrelt Refuge, to this barren locale where he would, as aspirant, start to reveal his past. The three of them had kneeled in the dust, Spock and T'Vora in meditative poses, Sokel between them.

The master had chosen where to begin: Spock's "death" and "rebirth" and the emotions surrounding those events. Sokel had instructed Spock to access his memories of those times, to bring them to the forefront of his consciousness. He had done so.

The Mutara Nebula. The Enterprise. *Main engineering. The containment chamber.*

Out in the canyon, Spock had sensed something touch his thoughts, but he had detected no other presence. The recollections he'd brought forth had suddenly seemed . . .

bare . . . uncovered . . . available. Only then had he become aware of T'Vora's mind, not within his, not as with a meld, but connected to him in a secondary way. Sokel had opened himself as a conduit, joining but insulated from the two minds he had bridged.

And as he'd been told to do, Spock remembered.

Keenly aware of the seconds passing and knowing that he would also have to reseat the assembly's protective cap before the injector would function again, Spock concentrated as much as he ever had. With every thought focused on his hand, he willed every scrap of strength he possessed into fighting this one piece of machinery.

Spock knew that these memories had formed within a brain, within a body, soon dead, and would have been lost if not for the telepathic linkage he'd had with his own *katra*, which he'd stored within McCoy. As the time ticked away within his recollection—*twenty seconds left*—Spock allowed himself to summon what he'd felt, even as he'd contained his emotions as the events had unfolded. The sense of urgency with which he'd begun to take action had only grown in the preceding minutes, as had his desire for his death to come in the service of saving the rest of the *Enterprise* crew. It had *felt* illogical, but he had argued to himself that the needs of the many outweighed the needs of the few—or as Jim had noted, of the one. But he could not claim now that his actions had lacked emotional motivation; he had *fiercely* wanted to save the lives of his shipmates.

In his grip, the injector shifted, moving less than a centimeter. Spock pushed himself, and the component all at once shunted back into place. He bent down for the cap and lifted it with difficulty, his strength seeming to vanish. He set it atop the assembly, then pushed it back into place.

And still time had passed—*down to ten seconds*—and what had been a deeply felt need to preserve the lives of the *Enterprise* crew—and among those, the lives of his closest friends—had transformed into desperation. At some point Spock had worried about his mother, about how devastated she would be to learn of his death. And his concern had reached to Jim as well, knowing how many terrible losses the admiral had previously suffered in his life—losses to which Spock himself had already contributed.

He fell backward, his back slamming against the control panel in the bulkhead. He barely felt the impact, the sense of his flesh catching fire overpowering the rest of his physical awareness of self. He tried to open his eyes and realized that they already were open; he could no longer see.

With virtually no time left, he'd been unable to do more. Spock had cried out in his mind—*Did it work?*—frantic to know if he'd succeeded. And when in the next instant he'd felt the familiar vibration telling him that the *Enterprise* had gone to warp, carrying the crew and his friends away from what had been certain death, he had been elated. Looking back now, he could not deny it.

As he leaned heavily on the bulkhead, Spock turned toward the hard surface, then pushed himself away from it, trying to stand up straight. He immediately lost his balance, lurching to his left and collapsing to the deck. He reached down and attempted again to push himself up, but all of his strength had gone.

It didn't matter. As he let his upper body fall forward into the bulkhead, he knew that he had served the needs of the many. It is logical, *he thought.*

Then Spock waited to die.

In that moment, he had not feared death, but neither had

he accepted it. More than anything, disappointment had saturated his being. For his parents, for his friends, but also for himself. Spock had not accomplished all that he had wished to, and though he had in the past put his life at risk when circumstances warranted, he had discovered there in the containment chamber that he wanted badly to continue living.

Within minutes, he heard Jim's voice.

"Spock," the admiral called, the word echoing in the chamber, obviously emerging from the intercom.

Spock's body hurt as though disintegrating, every movement an agony, but he would move anyway. He had to act, had to unburden himself of this one final failure— for his own sake, and for Jim's. Slowly, he reached up along the bulkhead with his right hand, still in the protective glove he had taken from Scott's engineering suit. Mustering his best effort, he pushed himself up into a crouch with his left hand, also gloved. He would do this. He had to do this. The need filled him completely.

Somehow, he found the strength to stand.

Idly, he straightened his uniform jacket, then turned from the bulkhead. He could not see, but he knew the location of the intercom circuit outside the chamber, and therefore where Jim must be. Spock walked unsteadily in that direction, moving deliberately in order to maintain what minimal balance he retained.

He walked until he struck the transparent bulkhead on the other side of the containment chamber, at the curve of the entry compartment. As he staggered back, vague shapes and colors played across his vision, his eyesight not yet entirely gone. He eased to his right, to where the intercom and Jim would be.

"The ship," Spock managed to say, his throat raw. "Out of danger?"

"Yes," Jim said, the single word full of sadness. Spock could just make out the form of his friend standing opposite him on the outside of the chamber.

"Don't grieve, Admiral," he said, his voice low and harsh, the words rasping in his injured throat. He had already wounded Jim and did not wish to do so again, though that seemed unavoidable. "It is logical," he avowed. "The needs of the many outweigh..." He winced, his body seizing up in a paroxysm of pain.

"The needs of the few," Jim said.

Spock nodded. "Or the one," he added. His legs began to buckle and he steadied himself against the chamber bulkhead. "I never took . . . the Kobayashi Maru test . . . until now," he said, speaking of the Starfleet simulator in which a starship commander is faced with a no-win scenario. "What do you think of my solution?"

"Spock . . . " Jim said, the depth of his anguish plain.

Spock slid down the transparent bulkhead of the containment chamber, and on the other side, Jim followed him down. "I . . . I have been . . . and always shall be . . . your friend." He removed one glove, lifting his hand to place it flat against the clear partition, his fingers splayed in the traditional Vulcan salutation. "Live long . . . and prosper," he said, as he did neither. Jim reached his hand up to Spock's on the other side of the bulkhead.

Spock slumped and then died.

And then lived, in schism—

His body, revived by the Genesis Wave, awoke as an infant in the empty photon torpedo casing meant to be his casket. Growing unnaturally, at an accelerated pace driven by the protomatter utilized in the Genesis Device, he fled through subtropical vegetation, finding nourishment. But the planet and its climate changed rapidly, as unstable as Spock's own aging process. Blue skies turned *gray, sunlight to snow. Saavik and David Marcus—Jim's son—found him, and Saavik helped him through the* Pon farr.

But the descriptions of all that, the knowledge of all it encompassed, had come later. At the time, there had been only experience, sensation. His mind had been wiped clean, birthed again, and with no training, with no conscious decision to control his emotions, he had felt fear and sadness, loneliness and longing and anger.

The Klingons arrived, murdered David, and then . . . and then—

His katra, *stored within McCoy, became essentially inert after the death of Spock's body. But it haunted the doctor, the echoes within impelling him to climb the steps of Mount Seleya. McCoy faltered, at first not understanding.*

But Spock's mind, the essence of his being, had not truly lived, though neither had it perished. The understanding of the events that McCoy had experienced while carrying Spock's *katra* would also come later. But for McCoy himself, there had been sorrow and dread, confusion and panic and hope.

After his shipmates—his friends—recovered Spock's body, McCoy did go to Vulcan, did climb the steps of Mount Seleya, and then . . . and then—

The probing wisps of T'Lar's mind grazed the primitive consciousness within Spock's restored body. Her presence remained only for an instant and then vanished. When it returned, it did more than just brush past his mind . . . it searched through it. Spock recoiled, but T'Lar followed, attempting to soothe him, to convince him to let her help.

He had been terrified, Spock recalled. The memory, formed in such an indistinct time, would have proven elusive if not for the force of the emotion. But faced with the choice of being frightened or being alone, his unformed mind had sought assistance from T'Lar.

But T'Lar had not entered his mind again. McCoy had.

The dual nature of his mind . . . his minds . . . their minds . . . crippled him. He could no longer flee, and he could no longer let go. His psyche drifted, and with it, McCoy's. And then he sensed—

A tangle of images and sounds, tastes and scents and textures, of which he could not make the slightest sense. He felt lost . . . and yet not alone . . . alive . . . and yet unformed. He floated through the void, vulnerable and ready, a canvas upon which the universe could throw its infinitude of colors, an ether through which the universe could hurl its bounty of notes. He was nothing, waiting to be everything . . . or anything.

And then remembrance broke like a wave on the shores of time, bringing forth from the deep a clarity of perception.

In the desert of Gol, a sound broke the stillness. The touch of Sokel's bridge against his mind fled, and with it, Spock's connection to T'Vora. In the silence that ensued, he opened his eyes.

The day had faded, the Vulcan sun invisible beyond the rim of the canyon. The red sky had dimmed to a burnt orange. A light breeze had picked up.

Spock heard the movement in the dust and peered over to see Sokel scrambling to his feet, the elder's attention firmly on T'Vora. Spock looked at his *Kolinahr* master and saw her still on her knees, but doubled over, her palms to the ground, her arms trembling. As Sokel reached her, she gazed upward. To Spock's astonishment, she appeared dazed, and a trickle of blood flowed from her nose.

"Master, are you all right?" Sokel asked, taking hold of T'Vora's upper arms, steadying her. Spock pushed himself up from the ground and quickly found himself lightheaded. He reached up to his face, and when he pulled his hand away, he saw the green of his own blood on his fingers.

"Yes," T'Vora responded. "Yes, I'm all right." Recovering his stability, Spock walked over as T'Vora breathed in heavily, then exhaled slowly. Extricating herself from Sokel's grasp, she straightened up onto her knees. Sokel reached into the folds of his robes and pulled out several cloths.

"Your nose is bleeding, Master," he said, handing it to T'Vora. She accepted it and dabbed at her philtrum as Sokel offered a cloth to Spock. He took it and wiped at his own face, then at his hands.

Carefully, T'Vora stood up and regarded Spock. "I congratulate you," she said. "Rarely are aspirants so successful in recalling the emotions they have controlled, or in allowing me—or even themselves—access to them."

"It is that which I wish to purge," Spock said. "Without my recollections, without opening them up to scrutiny, how could I hope to do so?"

"What you say is logical," T'Vora said. "Nevertheless, it is uncommon. Perhaps it is due to your human extraction, or to your ability to emote, or to the uniqueness and intensity of your experiences."

Whatever the reason, Spock understood why masters conducted such efforts via a mind bridge and not a mind meld. A direct connection between Spock and T'Vora during such a powerful experience could have caused damage to either or both of their minds. Nothing such as this had happened during his first *Kolinahr*, but then, at the time, he had never before "died."

"Regardless of the reason," T'Vora continued, "this has been a very useful step in this process. Tomorrow, Spock, you and I will discuss what we experienced. This night and morning next, I wish you to contemplate all that we visited today. I must do the same."

"Yes, Master," Spock said.

"I will call upon you in the afternoon then," she said. "We will now return to the sanctuary."

Together, the three started through the canyon, back toward the Akrelt Refuge. As they walked, the stars began to appear overhead. They did not speak again that night, parting in front of the altar nearly an hour later.

In his room, Spock lighted a candle. He lay down on his bed, holding his fingers steepled together above him. Cautiously, he allowed into his thoughts some of the images and feelings that he had called to mind that day. As he reflected on all that he had been able to reveal to Master T'Vora, he suddenly realized why he had so readily been able to recollect emotions that, when they'd first occurred, he had suppressed. It was because this was not the only time he had remembered and experienced those emotions. Since Jim had died, much of this had filled his dreams.

SEVENTEEN

1930

"This is how history went after McCoy changed it," Spock said. Kirk sat beside him in the middle of their apartment, the two of them hunched over the nightstand and the tricorder atop it. Spock pointed to the small display. "Here, in the late nineteen thirties," he said as a crowd scene appeared. A pair of cable cars seemed to identify the setting as San

Francisco; the venerable vehicles still ran there in the twenty-third century. "A growing pacifist movement," Spock went on, "whose influence delayed the United States' entry into the second world war." On the screen, the scene shifted to a large, elegant room, in which men appeared to deliberate. "While peace negotiations dragged on, Germany had time to complete its heavy-water experiments."

"Germany," Kirk said, trying to recall the Earth history he'd learned in school, and at the same time trying to avoid any thoughts of Edith. "Fascism," he said. "Hitler." As though matching his words, the scene on the tricorder display shifted again, to images of brownshirts . . . Nazis . . . arrayed in great numbers and saluting, marching. Kirk heard somebody intoning their call to arms: *Sieg Heil! Sieg Heil!* And Germany . . . "Won the second world war," he said.

"Because all this lets them develop the A-bomb first," Spock confirmed, again pointing at the display.

A heavy breath escaped Kirk as the implications of it all threatened to suffocate him. *And Edith . . .*

"There's no mistake, Captain," Spock said. "Let me run it again." He worked the tricorder's controls. The image of the display rolled, then stopped on a newspaper article. Kirk read the title: PACIFIST LEADER KEELER TO SPEAK IN ATLANTA. "Edith Keeler," Spock said. "Founder of the peace movement."

"But she was right," Kirk said, recalling more recent history, the great strides that peace had brought to humanity after World War III. "Peace *was* the way."

"She was right," Spock agreed, "but at the wrong time."

Can there be a "wrong time" for peace? Kirk thought, but he knew the answer to that from firsthand experience. Peace *was* the way, but sometimes, as a last resort, force had to be used.

"With the A-bomb," Spock continued, "and with their V-2 rockets to carry them, Germany captured the world."

"No," Kirk said, the agony in his voice plain even to him. With Nazism ruling the world, would Zefram Cochrane even live, and if so, would he still create humanity's first warp drive? Would there be first contact with Vulcans? Would there be a Federation?

"And all this," Spock said, "because McCoy came back and somehow kept her from dying in a street accident as she was meant to."

As she was meant to, Kirk thought. How could that be? How could such a wonderful, loving woman be *meant* to die? It only reinforced the uncaring nature of the universe. *And to use Bones as the instrument of her salvation and death . . .*

"We must stop him, Jim," Spock said, his tone grave.

Kirk glanced at his friend, then slowly stood up. He felt the urge to flee, to find Edith and take her and run from this place—but he settled for pacing across the room. "How did she die?" he asked. "What day?" Would it be better to know, or not to know, he wondered.

"We can estimate general happenings from these images," Spock said, "but I can't trace precise actions at exact moments, Captain." Yes, Spock had already told him that. They'd lost some of the 1930 data from the tricorder. "I'm sorry," Spock finished.

"Spock," Kirk said, knowing that he needed help, that he needed his friend to say the words. "I believe . . . I'm in love with Edith Keeler." Spock already knew that, of course. Though he suppressed his own emotions, he could still see them in others.

"Jim," he said, "Edith Keeler must die."

Kirk felt as though a fist clenched around his heart.

Really, he had known this for days, but to actually hear Spock say it, to utter it so declaratively . . .

"Spock," he said, "I'm . . . going to do what has to be done. When the time comes, we'll stop McCoy, but . . . " He hesitated, as though he had a decision to make, but in truth, he had known this for days as well. "I'm going to spend whatever time I can with Edith."

"I understand," Spock said.

Kirk felt grateful for Spock's trust, but he also wondered if the Vulcan truly did understand, if he even could. Kirk knew that Spock had emotions, but that he held them hidden inside and tightly controlled. Strangely, considering the circumstances, he found himself feeling sorry for his stoic friend.

Kirk picked up his coat and headed for the door. "I'll be back later," he said. Then he went out to find whatever moments he could with the woman he loved.

Spock thought he heard something at the apartment door as he pulled on his coat and cap. He knew that the captain would be back soon from the mission, escorting Keeler home after the day's work there. Then, as the captain slept, Spock would move outside to patrol the building through the night. Now that they had extracted as definitive an answer as they could from the tricorder, they'd taken to doing this each night. When McCoy arrived in the past, they intended to find him before he could inadvertently alter the timeline.

Of course, another possibility had occurred to Spock. As the captain had suggested when they'd first traveled through the Guardian, McCoy could still appear in any part of the world. Perhaps, in his cordrazine-induced madness, he would kill or injure somebody, a person who then failed to telephone a friend or relative in New York.

Perhaps when that person in New York did not receive that call, they would then wait by the phone instead of going out and driving through the city. Perhaps that person would then fail to meet Edith Keeler in that fatal traffic accident, and history would still be changed.

The possibilities were infinite, Spock knew, and he could only continue to hope that time did indeed turn out to be fluid, and that they would have the opportunity to set the timeline right. If not, if time passed and Keeler did not die, if it became apparent that events had begun to enfold such that the Axis powers would win the second world war, what would he and the captain do? What *could* they do? Could they find a way to stop Keeler from founding the peace movement? Would that work to restore time, or would that simply complicate the alterations to it?

As Spock pondered the situation, he crossed the room and opened the door. He stepped out into the hall, intending to head to the mission, but then he heard Keeler's voice to his left. He looked over to see the captain ascending the stairs toward her, where she stood on the third-story landing. As she spoke, she took a step down and then fell forward. The captain reached out and caught her.

"How stupid," Keeler said. "I've been up and down those stairs a thousand times. I ought to have broken my neck."

The captain stared at her, and Spock surmised what he must be thinking. Although an injury or her death here did not match the obituary Spock had read about Keeler dying in a street accident, it seemed noteworthy that the captain may have just prevented her from falling down a flight of stairs. Of course, had the captain not been here, then Keeler might not have started back down the stairs in the first place.

As she leaned in toward the captain and kissed him,

Spock quietly opened the apartment door and stepped back inside. He waited just inside for a few seconds, until he heard the captain descend the stairs and walk down the hall. Then Spock opened the door again and went out to join him.

"Captain," he said, "I did not plan to eavesdrop."

"No, of course you didn't," Kirk said quietly, evidently shaken by what had just occurred with Keeler on the steps. He moved slowly past Spock to the stairs.

"I must point out that, when she stumbled, she might've died right there had you not caught her."

The captain stood still for a moment on the top step, then gazed up at Spock. "It's not yet time," he said, as though begging for that to be true. "McCoy isn't here."

"We're not that sure of our facts," Spock told him. "Who's to say when the exact time will come?" Spock trusted the captain to take the proper action when the time came, but he also wanted to ensure that his first re-action would not be as Edith Keeler's lover, but as the commander of the *U.S.S. Enterprise* and a citizen of twenty-third-century Earth. "Save her," Spock said, "do as your heart tells you to do, and millions will die who did not die before."

The captain simply looked at him and said nothing. Then he continued on down the stairs. The hour had grown late, and the captain had been scheduled to sleep now, but Spock listened as Kirk walked through the vestibule and out the front door.

Spock turned around and went back into the apartment. There, he waited for the captain to return, and beyond that, for the tragic events that he knew would soon follow.

EIGHTEEN

2295/2285/2269

The two of them had climbed the Two Thousand Steps and now stood atop the plateau, gazing out at the canyon from its edge. The ascent had tired T'Vora. At one hundred thirty-five years of age, both her physical and mental vitality had begun to erode. She still felt strong, but not as strong as she once had. Though time itself had doubtless taken its toll, T'Vora knew too that her station in Vulcan society had added to the normal deterioration of her body and mind. The rigors of the *Kolinahr* did not confine themselves to aspirants; masters too paid their price. And while an aspirant endured the *Kolinahr* once—or sometimes two or even three times—masters in some regard went through it time and again as they guided others on their paths.

T'Vora looked from the canyon and over at Spock. He stared out across the landscape, but she could discern that he did not see it. He looked not outward, but inward, as he most often did these days. In the year since he had taken up residence in the Akrelt Refuge and begun the *Kolinahr* under her auspices, Spock had been perhaps the most dedicated of the many aspirants who had ever come to her. Initially, and in some sense antithetically, his *desire* to purge his emotions had been extremely powerful. T'Vora had thought that this might be a consequence of his human heritage, but once they had started to move beyond his feelings, once they had delved deeply into the rational portion of his mind and peeled away his sentiment, his logical *need* to achieve the *Kolinahr* had been as great.

Because of this, T'Vora's interactions with Spock had

paradoxically been both undemanding and incredibly arduous. In terms of her bridging to his experiences, thoughts, memories, and emotions, his intense commitment to the course he'd chosen had provided an openness, a willingness to lower his mental barriers to allow her access. Again, T'Vora had at first believed that her ability to so easily observe the core of his mind had been due to his human genetics, but she had come to see that Spock possessed highly developed defenses, as strong or stronger than any full Vulcan she had encountered, for as much as he permitted her to see, he still held some things sequestered away from her.

At the same time, her virtually unrestricted view into Spock came with a cost. The force of so many of his experiences, from an emotional *and* a rational standpoint, made even bridging to them an onerous undertaking. More than with any other aspirant she had ever conducted through the *Kolinahr*, T'Vora had found it necessary to take time away in order to process what she had learned of him, and also simply to renew her own strength through meditation and rest.

Now, as she regarded him on the high plateau of Gol, at the edge of the Akrelt Canyon, she could see that this process had not been easy for Spock either. She understood well the severity of the *Kolinahr* to even the most prepared, best inclined aspirants. In this case, the lines in Spock's face had grown noticeably deeper; at the sides of his head, silver had begun to show in his hair, which had grown down past his shoulders; and his overall carriage reflected a weariness not present when first he had arrived here.

Of course, T'Vora had watched her own appearance begin to show similar signs during the past year. She supposed that, like other more traditional measures, the changes to their bodies could be used as a means of assessing the efforts she and Spock had so far put forth. Since the first time Sokel had initiated a mind bridge between them, those efforts had been significant. Month after month, T'Vora and Spock had explored Spock's emotional existence, from the impact caused by his father's disapproval of his human side to the loss he'd felt at the death of his closest friend.

They had begun with the unique, peering into his "death" and "rebirth," and it had proven a wise choice. From the moments leading up to his physical death through the *fal-tor-pan* that had reunited his *katra* with his restored body, Spock had experienced a plethora of different emotions, many of them relating to other times and events in his life. Analyzing and deconstructing these emotions, T'Vora and Spock had worked to recast all that he had felt in terms of logic. *All living things must die. Spock had made a reasonable and reasoned choice to forfeit his life to save those of his crewmates. He had reinforced the reintegration of his mind and body via logical Vulcan methods.* Under her direction, Spock had extracted his emotions from his memories, leaving behind an untainted canvas of fact.

But not completely untainted yet, T'Vora thought. For as much progress as Spock had made, he had yet a longer road to travel. Through their mind bridges, T'Vora had perceived in Spock a reservoir of remorse, collecting a series of regrets formed throughout the course of his life. As a boy, disappointing his father with his decidedly human behavior. As a man, realizing that he had hurt his mother, never telling her that he loved her. As a friend, failing Jim Kirk at the end of his life, allowing the captain's final months to pass without contacting him when his pursuit of dangerous avocations clearly indicated his unhappiness.

Spock had permitted T'Vora to see these and other instances of his shame, and with her help, he had worked his way through them.

And yet remorse remained within him, T'Vora was sure. Again and again during her interaction with Spock, it had hung in the distance, an island to which she could find no bridge. With so many other issues, she had not addressed it to this point. But with Spock making such major strides, the time had come at last.

"Spock," T'Vora said. He blinked once, very deliberately, as though hearing her from far away and willing himself back into the moment.

"Master?" he said, turning from the view of the canyon to face her.

"You have accomplished much since arriving here," she said. "I have especially noted your willingness to reveal that which you would see eliminated from your character."

"How better to achieve my goal than by working actively toward it?" Spock asked. His voice carried no inflection or hint of emotion that suggested his question contained anything beyond the literal interpretation of his words.

"That is true," T'Vora said, "but your efforts have been exceptional, and I commend you for them."

Spock bowed his head in response. "Your approbation holds meaning for me," he said.

"You have still more work to do in order to reach your ultimate destination," T'Vora said. "From this point in your progress, I know where that effort should begin."

"I am an apprentice under your tutelage," Spock said. "I look to you for guidance."

"As it should be," T'Vora said. "During our bridges, Spock, during our attempts to explore and understand your emotional existence, I have perceived in you a strong sense of remorse."

"My life has not been lived without shame," Spock agreed.

"As well I know," T'Vora reminded him. "We have contended with such issues in your journey so far. I speak not of that with which we have dealt, but of that with which we have not." She paused, giving Spock a moment to respond. When he didn't, she asked, "Do you know of what I speak?"

"I believe that I do," Spock said.

"From the first time we approached the issues surrounding your physical death aboard the *Enterprise* to the reintegration of your *katra* at Mount Seleya, I have been aware of what seems to be a singular regret, though it has remained isolated within you," T'Vora explained. "It seems to have existed before your death, and to have been exacerbated after your *fal-tor-pan*."

"After the *fal-tor-pan*," Spock repeated. "Yes. I know to what you refer. And it is a singular regret."

T'Vora held her hand out, palm up, gesturing toward the ground. Spock at once adjusted his robes and lowered himself to his knees, folding his hands together before him. Facing him, T'Vora did the same. "Tell me," she said.

Spock peered at her with his dark eyes, but he said nothing. The moments passed, the brilliant Vulcan sun tracking above them across the sky, the deep canyon snaking past them in both directions. T'Vora waited, understanding that what Spock would reveal had been a part of him for some time, and likely a profound wound that had never healed. T'Vora waited, and at last Spock began to tell her.

"I willfully violated a principle," he said.

* * *

On the main viewscreen, the image of Hiram Roth appeared, the human easily recognizable by his bald pate and cropped white beard. *"This is the president of the United Federation of Planets,"* he announced.

Seated at the operations station on the port side of the Klingon bird of prey's bridge, Spock noted the interference in the transmission that had been broadcast from Earth. Coupled with the lack of Federation vessels on assigned patrol stations and the number of overlapping distress calls that Uhura had intercepted, he deduced that some calamity had taken place in or around the Terran system. He did not have to wait long to have his suspicions confirmed.

"Do not approach Earth," President Roth said. Admiral Kirk moved slowly away from where Uhura sat to starboard at the communications console, until he stood before the command chair in the center of the bridge. *"The transmissions of an orbiting probe are causing critical damage to this planet."*

At his station, Spock quickly implemented a long-range scan.

"It has almost totally ionized our atmosphere," the president continued. *"All power sources have failed."*

On his console, Spock could see why. The probe itself appeared composed at least partially of energy, of a type Spock had never before seen. And although the nature of the probe's transmissions pointed to their use as a form of communication and not as a weapon, the prodigious strength of the signals would readily disrupt other energy sources in their vicinity.

"All Earth-orbiting starships are powerless," Roth said. *"The probe is vaporizing our oceans."*

The oceans, Spock thought. He worked his controls, re-examining his scan, and saw that none of the probe's transmissions focused on land.

"We cannot survive unless a way can be found to re-spond to the probe," Roth went on. Clearly the authorities on Earth had also concluded that the probe had not intended its transmissions as an attack. *"Further communications may not be possible."* Around the bridge, Spock saw, the crew seemed shaken: Sulu and Chekov at the forward helm and navigation stations, Uhura at communications, Dr. McCoy standing aft. As though stunned himself, Admiral Kirk gradually lowered himself into the command chair. *"Save your energy. Save yourselves. Avoid the planet Earth at all costs. Farewell."* The president's transmission shook from side to side, then degenerated into static.

In his chair, the admiral turned slowly around and peered over at the operations station. Spock returned his gaze. For a moment, Admiral Kirk raised his hand to his head, as though in pain. Then he looked to Uhura and quietly asked, "Can you let us hear the probe's transmission?"

"Yes, sir," Uhura said, also obviously affected by the threat to Earth. She touched a control, saying, "On speakers."

Spock listened closely as a strange whine played through the bridge. It modulated upward and downward, and it seemed as though the sound might contain multiple components, like several stringed instruments playing at once. Although he could not decipher its meaning, the complex structure of the message suggested an equally complex mind behind it. It also put Spock in mind of the language of certain other beings.

Admiral Kirk stood and walked over to the operations station. "Spock, what do you make of that?" he asked, leaning against the front of the console.

"Most unusual," Spock said, still listening to the peculiar sounds. "An unknown form of energy of great power and intelligence, evidently unaware that its transmissions are destructive. I find it illogical that its intentions should be hostile."

"Really?" Dr. McCoy said. "You think this is its way of saying 'Hi, there' to the people of the Earth?"

"There are other forms of intelligence on Earth, Doctor," Spock replied. "Only human arrogance would assume the message must be meant for man."

"You're suggesting the transmission is meant for a life-form other than man," Admiral Kirk said.

"At least a possibility, Admiral," Spock said, thinking of the beings of whom he had just been reminded. "The president did say it was directed at Earth's oceans."

The admiral seemed to consider this. He straightened, then walked across the width of the bridge to the communications stations. "Uhura," he said, "can you modify the probe's signals, accounting for density and temperature and salinity factors?" He had clearly understood what Spock had implied.

"I can try, sir," Uhura said. As she began working her controls, Spock stood and joined the admiral at the communications station. Dr. McCoy followed as well. In response to Uhura's manipulations of the signal, the sound of the transmission changed in stages. At last, she said, "I think I have it, sir."

"And this is what it would sound like underwater?" the admiral asked.

"Yes, sir," Uhura said.

To Spock, the sound now resembled a single voice, and one which he thought he recognized. "Fascinating," he said. "If my suspicion is correct, there can be no response to this message." Knowing that he would need to check his hypothesis, he excused himself and started toward the door at the back of the bridge, headed for the library-computer compartment located amidships. Fortunately, Spock and

Uhura had uploaded a Federation database to the Klingon vessel before they'd begun their flight from Vulcan to Earth.

"Where are you going?" the admiral asked.

"To test my theory," Spock responded. As he headed down the main dorsal corridor of the bird of prey, he heard Admiral Kirk and Dr. McCoy follow behind him. When he reached the library-computer compartment, he immediately instituted a search of the Terran zoological database, cross-referencing the audio of the probe's transmission as adjusted by Commander Uhura. The admiral and the doctor arrived a moment later and looked on as the computer hunted through the database, images of various Earth animals appearing on a row of displays mounted high on one bulkhead. It stopped when it reached the species *Megaptera novaeangliae*.

"Spock?" the admiral asked.

"As suspected," Spock said. "The probe's transmissions are the songs sung by whales."

"Whales," Kirk repeated, a measure of surprise in his voice.

"Specifically, humpback whales," Spock said.

"That's crazy," McCoy said. "Who would send a probe hundreds of light-years to talk to a whale?" The question seemed to Spock both supercilious and scientifically careless, though space had been so well explored in the region surrounding Earth that the probe likely had come at least as far as the doctor had suggested.

"It's possible," the admiral said. "Whales have been on Earth far earlier than man."

"Ten million years earlier," Spock noted. "And humpbacks were heavily hunted by man. They've been extinct since the twenty-first century. It is possible that an alien intelligence sent the probe to determine why they lost contact."

"My god," McCoy said. Spock assumed that the contempt he heard in the doctor's voice had been meant for those who would not only kill animals for no good reason, but also cause the extinction of an entire species.

"Spock," the admiral said, "could the humpbacks' answer to this call be simulated?"

"The sounds, but not the language," Spock said. Though the intelligence of Terran cetaceans had long been widely suggested, no interpretation of their vocalizations had ever been accomplished. "We would be responding in gibberish."

"Does the species exist on any other planet?" Admiral Kirk asked.

"Negative. Humpbacks were indigenous to Earth," Spock said, and then formulating a possible plan of action, he added, "Earth of the past."

"Well," the admiral said with obvious reluctance, "we have no choice. We must destroy the probe before it destroys Earth."

"To attempt to do so would be futile, Admiral," Spock said, recalling the nature of the probe's energy and its effect on other power sources. "The probe could render us neutral easily."

"We can't just turn away," Kirk said. "There must be an alternative."

Spock did not hesitate. "There is one possibility, but of course I cannot guarantee success," he said. "We could attempt to find some humpback whales."

"You just said there aren't any," said McCoy, "except on Earth of the past."

"Yes, Doctor, that is exactly what I said." Already Spock could see that the admiral understood the nature of his proposal.

"Well, in that case," McCoy began, but then he too realized what Spock advised. "Now wait just a damn minute," he said, but the admiral had already made his decision.

"Spock," he said, "start your computations for time warp."

T'Vora regarded Spock as he stopped speaking, each of them still kneeling along the rim of the Akrelt Canyon. She recognized the circumstances surrounding the scene that he had just described, recalling the reports of the alien probe that had threatened the humanoid population of Earth. She also remembered how the potential disaster had been averted: Admiral Kirk and the former command crew of the *Enterprise,* including Spock, had traveled three centuries back in time and brought two humpback whales—a male and a gravid female—back to the present. Once back in Earth's oceans, the whales had evidently communicated with the probe, at which point it had ceased its destructive transmissions and departed the Terran system. But for all of that, T'Vora didn't understand the reason Spock had related the events he had.

"It is unclear to me why you have told me this," she said.

"It was I who recommended to Admiral Kirk that we go back to Earth's past," Spock said. "It was I who counseled that we bring humpback whales forward in time."

"Your story made that clear, Spock," T'Vora said.

"The principle I violated is that which states that one should never alter a timeline," Spock said.

"But does one not do that each instant of their existence," T'Vora said, "by virtue of every decision they make, every action they take?"

"I refer not to the present, but to the past," Spock said. "I refer to timelines already in existence."

T'Vora knew almost nothing about time travel and she told Spock so.

"It is believed that the flow of time constitutes a complex natural system," he explained, "but one that is sensitively dependent on initial conditions. In physics and mathematics, this is known as chaos theory. In common parlance, it is often called the butterfly effect, an appellation taken from an illustration of the theory. On a planet such as Vulcan, the flapping of a butterfly's wings will change the state of the atmosphere, and the subsequent evolution of weather systems will diverge significantly from what it otherwise would have been had the butterfly not flapped its wings. Where perhaps clear skies would have prevailed, instead a cyclone will form."

"I understand," T'Vora said.

"In actual instances of time travel," Spock said, "it has been found that it typically requires a more significant event than the flapping of a butterfly's wings in order to effect an alteration in a timeline. Still, it has proven impossible to predict what will change history and what will not, or how a change will propagate through the ensuing years."

"But the concern is that by traveling back in time," T'Vora said, "it is possible to inadvertently alter the future."

"That is correct," Spock said. "The principle I advised Admiral Kirk to violate, and that I myself took part in violating, is one espoused by Starfleet, the Vulcan Science Academy, and all major scientific institutions within the Federation. It is also one in which I personally believe."

"But clearly your actions in retrieving the whales did not alter the timeline," T'Vora said.

"In actuality, they did," Spock said. "In the original timeline, those two whales were not transported aboard a Klingon vessel and taken three hundred years into their future because, for one thing, Admiral Kirk and myself and the rest of the crew had not even been born yet. The very fact of our presence in that time necessarily altered the timeline. The reason this does not seem to be the case is simply because no significant changes appear to have occurred."

T'Vora considered this. "Your actions did change the present, though," she said. "After you returned with the whales, the people of Earth were spared a catastrophe. Is that not sufficient justification for your actions, to have saved the lives of billions?"

"Would the Romulan Praetor think so?" Spock asked. "Perhaps a future war between the Empire and the Federation that would have produced a Romulan victory will now produce a Romulan defeat." Spock peered out across the canyon, the reserve he had cultivated in his time at the Refuge in obvious danger of slipping. When he looked back at T'Vora, she saw agitation in his expression and understood the enormity of the situation to him. "I am uncomfortable," he said, "with the notion that my action in violating a principle is justifiable because I approve of the outcome."

"Yes," T'Vora agreed. "I can understand that. But I would submit to you, Spock, that individuals can err, and that when such an error can result in the saving of billions of lives, it is perhaps far more understandable for that error to occur. As an isolated incident, I think that you may be according it too much weight."

"It is not an isolated incident," Spock said gravely. "Prior to that, I had willfully altered the past, and not for the purpose of saving billions of lives, but for my own personal gain."

The confession startled T'Vora, and only a lifetime of practiced emotional control prevented her from reacting visibly. After a moment, though, the unexpectedness of the revelation drove her to move. She parted her hands and rose to her feet. Spock followed her lead and did the same.

"Walk with me," she said, and she started along the path that traced the edge of the canyon. When Spock joined her at her side, she repeated to him what she had said earlier: "Tell me."

And Spock did. "There was an artifact," he began.

As the Guardian of Forever released him from its hold, having pulled him from thousands of years in the past and back to the present, Spock considered with satisfaction how successful the mission had been. When the *Enterprise* had initially been ordered on this assignment, he had grown concerned. In light of the events Captain Kirk had endured on their first visit here, Spock had feared for his friend's emotional well-being. As it had turned out, the captain had so far seemed to cope well with the circumstances.

For this mission, Captain Kirk, Dr. McCoy, Lieutenant Bates, and Spock had all been assigned to assist a team of annalists investigating Federation history via the Guardian. All four *Enterprise* crew members had been part of the contingent that had discovered the time vortex two years ago, and they had therefore been granted exclusive authority by Starfleet Command to actually travel into the past. No other individuals, not even the historians, had ever been permitted to pass through the temporal gateway.

In the days after the crew had originally encountered the strange and powerful artifact, the *Enterprise* had been relieved at the planet by the *U.S.S. Appomattox,* which had arrived to provide the military presence that Captain Kirk had recommended to Starfleet Command. After that, multiple efforts had been made to construct a research facility on the planet's surface. All such attempts had failed, the result of violent earthquakes that some suspected had been caused by the Guardian itself, though it would neither confirm nor deny any such explanation. Eventually, a research station, Einstein, had been built in orbit.

Now, as Spock arrived back on the planet from an observational mission to the dawn of Orion's civilization, he saw the rest of the *Enterprise* landing party, as well as a pair of historians from the research station. Captain Kirk and Lieutenant Bates stood with their backs to the Guardian, having just preceded Spock in their return from the past. Dr. McCoy, who had remained in the present, stood facing the time vortex alongside the two annalists. Dr. Grey, a human female, had a streak of orange through the top of her black hair. Dr. Aleek-Om, a tall, gold-colored Aurelian male, had two arms and two legs and stood upright, like a humanoid, but also possessed a beak and two large wings sprouting from his shoulder blades.

As Spock stepped forward between the captain and the lieutenant, he saw Dr. McCoy raise a hand and point in his direction. A look of surprise dressed the doctor's face. "Who's he, Jim?" McCoy asked.

Captain Kirk lifted his hands to his hips, and Spock couldn't tell whether the doctor's comment had amused or annoyed him. "What do you mean, 'who's he?'" the captain said. "You know Mister Spock."

"'Fraid I don't, Jim," McCoy said. The question could have been an example of the doctor's sometimes ill-considered wit, but it still drew Spock's concern. Before he could say anything, though, the captain opened his communicator and contacted the ship, simply ignoring what he must have judged a joke on McCoy's part.

"Kirk to *Enterprise*," he said.

"*Enterprise*," replied Lieutenant Commander Scott.

"Prepare to transport four back to the ship," the captain said, and then he moved away from the time vortex and the historians. Spock, McCoy, and Bates followed him over to a small cache of equipment that had been sent down from the research station. Kirk retrieved the three life-support belts that the *Enterprise* landing party had carried with them from the ship for possible use on the trip into Orion's past. An examination of their destination through the Guardian, though, had shown that the belts would not be necessary.

McCoy collected his medical tricorder from among the equipment, wrapping its strap about his torso. When Bates handed back Spock's own tricorder, which he'd given to the lieutenant when they'd been on ancient Orion, he also slung the device across his shoulder. The captain then handed one of the life-support belts to Spock and one to McCoy, keeping the third for himself. When Kirk distractedly circled his around his waist, the other two did the same. Spock thought that the captain's obvious preoccupation might indicate his own apprehension about what Dr. McCoy had said.

As Kirk gave the order for transport, Spock seemed to recall, though he could not be sure, that the landing party had beamed down to the planet with *four* life-support belts, not just three. Taking into account Dr. McCoy's comments, Spock began to consider more seriously the notion that he, Captain Kirk, and Lieutenant Bates might have inadvertently altered the past, and thus the present. Too late to say anything, he waited while the metallic shimmer of dematerialization formed before his eyes, then vanished as he re-formed aboard the *Enterprise*.

While the landing party descended from the platform, Spock spied another expression of surprise, this one worn by Lieutenant Commander Scott. "Captain, I was expecting it to be one of the historians with you," the engineer said from where he worked the transporter console. "But a Vulcan?"

"Explain yourself, Mister Scott," Kirk snapped, a clear indication to Spock that the captain also suspected that something had gone wrong.

"Sir?" Scott said.

"I don't know what's going on," Captain Kirk said as the doors of the transporter room parted, "but the first officer of this ship will be treated with respect."

From the corridor, an Andorian had entered, clad in a blue Starfleet uniform that bore the rank braid of a commander—although Spock knew that no Andorians currently served aboard the *Enterprise*. "Captain, I assure you," the unknown officer said, "no one has ever treated me otherwise." The implication of his response seemed clear.

"Who are you?" Kirk asked.

"Well, I thought sure you'd know Thelin by now, Jim," said Dr. McCoy. "He's been your first officer for five years."

Although the doctor had spoken casually, Spock no longer doubted the sincerity of all the comments that McCoy had made, and he said as much. The captain concurred. "Bones, Scotty," he said, "I'm asking you seriously: do you or do you not know Spock?"

"Honestly," McCoy replied, "I don't know him."

"I've never seen him before in my life," Scott said.

"And none of us have ever met Commander Thelin," Kirk said. He peered at Spock and then over at Bates, who nodded his agreement.

"Clearly something happened while we were down on the planet," Spock said.

"Yes," the captain said. He paced over to the transporter

console and reached across it, opening an intercom circuit. "Kirk to bridge."

"Bridge, this is Sulu," came the immediate reply. The captain glanced over at Spock, obviously taking note that Lieutenant Sulu remained fourth in command aboard the *Enterprise.* Thus far, the only change seemed to be with respect to the ship's first officer.

"Sulu," the captain said, "as quickly as you can, I want you to conduct a survey of the crew. Ask if anyone aboard has ever heard of a ship's officer named Spock."

"Spock?" Sulu asked, and then he spelled the name.

"That's correct," Kirk said. "Contact me as soon as you have the results."

"Aye, sir," Sulu said.

The captain signed off and closed the intercom channel. Looking around at the officers present, he said, "Bones, Scotty, I don't want you discussing this with anybody." After both men acknowledged the order, Kirk said, "Mister Spock, Mister Bates, Commander Thelin, come with me."

The captain led the group to a briefing room, where they assembled around a conference table. An idea occurred to Spock, and he asked if he could review the crew manifest. When the captain agreed, Spock handed off his tricorder to Lieutenant Bates, then sat down at the end of the table, in front of the computer interface located there. Across from him, he saw Commander Thelin's antennae move in a way he interpreted as consternation. Spock quickly keyed in a control sequence and brought up a display of crew files. As he quickly began browsing through them, Thelin spoke up.

"Am I to understand, Captain," he asked, "that you believe that you do not know who I am?"

"That's correct," Kirk said. "Earlier, Commander Spock, Doctor McCoy, Lieutenant Bates, and myself beamed down to the planet. Except for the doctor, we all took part in an observational mission to Orion's past."

"And at that time," Thelin wanted to know, "you believed that Commander Spock was the first officer aboard the *Enterprise*?"

"He *was* the first officer," the captain said. "I mean no disrespect, Commander, but there was no Thelin—there were no Andorians at all—among the crew."

"I take no slight from your comment, Captain," Thelin said. "But my recollection is that you, Doctor McCoy, and Lieutenant Bates transported down to the planet. I have not left the ship." After a moment, Thelin said, "Captain, with your permission, I would like to ask the records officer to check if there is a Commander Spock presently serving elsewhere in Starfleet."

"Yes, that's a good idea," Kirk said. "Also have him check on Ambassador Sarek of Vulcan, as well as the ambassador's family."

"Yes, sir," Thelin said. Continuing to read through the list of the crew, Spock heard a click as the Andorian opened an intercom channel. "Commander Thelin to Lieutenant Erikson." The records officer—the same individual Spock knew, or had known, to be in the position—responded, and Thelin told him of the research they needed done.

After Thelin had closed the channel, the captain asked, *"I don't remember you, Commander, but you remember me?"*

"Yes, very well," Thelin said. "You have been my commanding officer for several years." He hesitated, but then added, "We have also become friends."

"I'm . . . sorry," Kirk said, his voice growing quiet. "I truly do not know you."

"The situation is what it is, Captain," Thelin said. "Do you believe, then, that you caused a change to the timeline when you traveled back through the vortex?"

"That would seem to be the obvious conclusion," Kirk said.

"Indeed it would," Spock said as he finished scanning the crew manifest. "But the alteration appears strangely contained. I recognize every name in the ship's complement—all but that of Commander Thelin."

"But how can we have done anything thousands of years ago on Orion that would have resulted only in substituting one first officer of the *Enterprise* for another?" Kirk asked.

"It may be that other, more significant changes have been wrought," Spock said. "Changes that are not immediately apparent to us aboard the ship. I suggest that we have the computer compare the tricorder readings we took in Orion's past with the recordings of the same time period made earlier through the Guardian. In that way, it may be possible to detect the point of divergence."

The captain nodded. "Mister Bates," he said.

"Yes, sir," the lieutenant said, activating the tricorder that Spock had just given him. On that device, they had recorded events on historical Orion both directly and through the time vortex. Spock exchanged seats with Bates, allowing the young officer access to the computer interface.

"Spock," the captain said, "if your absence from the *Enterprise* is the only difference in this timeline, have you any theories that might account for so limited an alteration?"

"There is nothing in theory or in practice that would suggest—" Spock began, but he stopped when he heard the up-and-down call of the intercom signal.

"Sulu to Captain Kirk."

The captain toggled open a circuit. "Kirk here. What have you got, Mister Sulu?"

"We've contacted everybody aboard the ship," Sulu

said. *"Nobody has ever heard of an officer on the* Enterprise *named Spock."*

"Thank you, Mister Sulu," the captain said. "Kirk out." He closed the channel with a touch. "Well, then," he said.

Silence descended in the room, broken only by the intermittent clicks and chirps of the computer interface and the tricorder. Spock perceived a high level of anxiety in Commander Thelin and a great tension in Captain Kirk. He wondered if the current situation evoked uncomfortable memories for Jim, memories of what had happened during the events surrounding their discovery of the Guardian of Forever.

After a few minutes, Lieutenant Bates looked up from the computer interface, the tricorder held out before him. "Nothing," he said, frustration evident in his voice. "I can't find one thing we did when we were in the vortex that could possibly have affected the future."

"But something *was* changed," the captain said.

Spock agreed with that, but something troubled him. Even if the timeline had been altered beyond the *Enterprise,* the single change aboard the ship seemed wildly unlikely. "It seems, Captain," he said, "I am the only one affected. The mission, the ship, the crew—except for myself—remain the same."

"But *I* know who you are and no one else aboard does," Kirk said, clearly trying to make sense of the situation. "While we were in Orion's past, the time revision that took place here didn't affect me." Again, the intercom whistle sounded, and again, the captain opened a channel. "Kirk here."

The image of Lieutenant Erikson appeared on the multisided display in the center of the table. *"Sir,"* he said, *"we've checked the Starfleet records Commander Thelin asked for."*

"Your findings?" Kirk said.

"There is no Vulcan named Spock serving with Starfleet in any capacity," Erikson reported.

"Did you also research the Vulcan family history requested?" Thelin asked.

"Yes, sir," Erikson said. *"I can relay that to your screen."* The lieutenant's image vanished from the monitor, replaced a moment later by that of Spock's father. "Sarek of Vulcan, ambassador to seventeen Federation planets in the past thirty years."

Spock knew well the record of his father's service. "That is not correct," he said.

"It is in this case," Kirk noted.

"I wish to ask a question," Spock said. "What of Sarek's family, his wife and son?" There seemed to be no need to mention Sybok, Spock's half brother.

Once more, the image on the display changed. This time, a picture of Spock's mother appeared, though one clearly recorded some time ago. "Amanda, wife of Sarek, born on Earth as Amanda Grayson," Erikson said. "The couple separated after the death of their son."

Their son, Spock repeated to himself, and again he thought of Sybok, though Sybok had not been born to Amanda.

"The wife was killed in a shuttle accident at Luna Port on her way home to Earth," Erikson continued.

At once, Spock felt a terrible shock, though outwardly he controlled his reaction. He barely heard Erikson say that Sarek had not remarried. Though illogical, the impulse to scream rose within Spock, but instead, he merely closed his eyes. "My mother," he said softly. He struggled to push aside his torment and managed to do so by concentrating on the dilemma they faced. "The son," he said. "What was his name and age when he died?"

"Spock," Erikson said. "Age seven."

In the briefing room, all eyes turned to the Vulcan.

"Thank you, Mister Erikson," the captain said, and he switched off the intercom. The likeness of Spock's mother disappeared from the display. "Mister Spock, how?" Kirk asked. "How could our presence on Orion so long ago cause your death as a boy?"

"I do not know," Spock said. "While it may seem implausible, the chaotic nature of the flow of time may have made it possible."

"Still," the captain said, "it just seems incredibly unlikely that an alteration *we* caused in the timeline thousands of years ago would end up specifically affecting *you* like this."

"Yes," Spock said, and then a possibility suddenly occurred to him. "Perhaps we should examine this situation from another perspective. Could it somehow have been my *absence* from this timeline that caused the change?"

"I'm not sure I understand that," Thelin said.

"I'm not sure I do either," Kirk added.

"I'm suggesting that we did not alter the timeline when we went back in time," Spock said, "but that it was altered *while* we were back in time."

"The historians?" the captain asked.

Spock nodded. "Possibly."

The captain pushed back from the table and stood from his chair. "Mister Spock, we're transporting back down," he said. "Let's talk to Doctor Grey and Doctor Aleek-Om."

As Spock rose, so too did Thelin. "Captain, as the first officer of the *Enterprise* in *this* timeline, I request that you permit me to accompany you."

"Very well, Commander," Kirk said. "Mister Bates, recheck the tricorder readings of Orion and the Guardian.

This time, be alert for anything even remotely related to the planet Vulcan."

"Yes, sir," Bates said, and he turned at once back to the computer interface.

Spock returned with Captain Kirk and Thelin to the transporter room, and the trio immediately beamed back down to the planet. There, the two historians stood before the Guardian, though the time portal appeared inactive at the moment. "Doctor Grey," the captain called as he strode over to her. Spock and Thelin followed.

"Captain Kirk," Grey said, looking up from the tricorder she held.

"Doctor," the captain said, "we believe that an alteration has occurred in the timeline."

"Mister Spock?" Grey asked, peering from the captain and over at the Vulcan.

"Yes," Kirk said. "I know that you don't recall this, but Commander Spock traveled back in time with me and Lieutenant Bates. When we returned, though, nobody here knew him."

"Since you beamed back up to the *Enterprise*," Grey said, "we've been examining our recordings to see if we could determine the cause of what happened."

"You have?" Kirk asked.

"When we saw an unexpected traveler return through the time vortex," Dr. Aleek-Om said, "we understood that something had gone awry."

"Of course," the captain said. "Have you found anything?"

"Not yet," Grey said.

"We've examined our own tricorder readings, but we haven't pinpointed anything that we changed on Orion," Kirk said. "If we didn't change anything while we were in the time vortex, someone else must have. Was the Guardian in use while we were gone?"

"Yes, but it was nothing unusual," Grey said. "We were scanning recent Vulcan history."

"What time period?" Spock asked, suspecting that the span would include his death as a boy in this timeline.

"Twenty to thirty Vulcan years past," Grey said, confirming Spock's notion.

"Was there any notation on the death of Ambassador Sarek's son?" the captain asked.

Aleek-Om consulted his own tricorder. "Yes," he said at last. "The boy is recorded as dying during the maturity test."

"The *kahs-wan*," Spock said, recalling that he had been seven years old when he'd undergone the ritual. "A survival test traditional for young males."

"The date was—" Aleek-Om started, but Spock interrupted him.

"The twentieth day of Tasmeen."

"How do you know this?" Thelin asked.

"That was the day my cousin saved my life in the desert when I was attacked by a wild animal," Spock said. A template of what must have caused the alteration in the timeline began forming in his mind.

"This cousin," the captain said. "What was his name?"

"I do not recall clearly," Spock said. "I was very young. He called himself . . . Selek. He was visiting us, but I never saw him after that." Suddenly, what had happened seemed apparent.

"Spock, did Selek look . . . like you do now?" Kirk asked, obviously thinking along the same lines.

"I believe so, Captain," Spock said. "And I know what you're thinking: it was I who saved myself that other time."

"But this time, you were in Orion's past with us when the historians had the time vortex replay Vulcan history," Kirk said, spelling it all out. "You couldn't be in two places at once, so you died as a boy."

* * *

T'Vora stopped walking and turned to face Spock. Past him, the Vulcan sun had grown low in the sky, sending long shadows down into the canyon. "Is that what happened?" she asked him. "You, as an adult, had saved yourself as a boy, and then when that period replayed in the time vortex while you, as an adult, were thousands of years in the past, you died as a boy?" It not only seemed improbable to T'Vora, it seemed almost incomprehensible.

"That is an accurate description of what occurred, yes," Spock said.

T'Vora looked away, back down the path toward the Two Thousand Steps, and then she began in that direction. Spock walked along beside her. For a while, she remained quiet, trying to put what she'd been told into some sort of rational context. She also called to mind all that she knew about Spock's life. At last, she said, "It is self-evident that you did not die at the age of seven. I am also aware that your mother is still alive, and that she and your father have not separated."

"That is correct," Spock said.

T'Vora considered this. "You related the incident of the time vortex to me after stating that you had willfully altered the past," she said. "You claimed that you had done so in contravention of the accepted precept that held it to be wrong to change the timeline, and you further stated that you had done so for your own personal gain."

"I did," Spock said, though if he meant that he had told her those things or that he had actually done them, she could not tell.

"Am I to take it then," she asked, "that when this incident took place, you subsequently traveled into the past again, to the time that you were seven years of age?"

"Yes," Spock said. "Through the Guardian of Forever, I

visited the home of my parents in Shi'Kahr, masquerading as a cousin named Selek. When the seven-year-old Spock went out onto Vulcan's Forge, I followed him. When a *le-matya* attacked, I intervened."

"You saved your own life," T'Vora said, "but in so doing, you also restored the timeline that had been altered by the historians' work at the time vortex."

Unexpectedly, Spock said, "Perhaps."

"Perhaps?" T'Vora questioned.

"When I saved my younger self from the *le-matya*," Spock said, "events did not transpire precisely as I had re-called them from my own youth."

"The memories of a child, even a Vulcan child, are nec-essarily different than those formed by an adult, by virtue of the differing perspectives and life experiences of the two," T'Vora said. "Could that explain the disparities you perceived?"

"Not entirely," Spock said. "My recollection from my own youth is that my pet *sehlat* perished several months after my experience on the Forge, succumbing to a disease not uncommon to *sehlats* of advanced age. When I went into the past to save myself, my *sehlat* died out on the Forge, the result of poison it had taken from the *le-matya*'s claws."

"And yet when you returned to the present," T'Vora said, "you found that your mother had not died, that your parents remained together, and that you were once more first officer of the *Enterprise*."

"That is correct," Spock said. "As far as I can tell, the timeline has been restored but for the premature death of my pet."

T'Vora shook her head. "What you describe defies logic," she said. "If the timeline has been reset because you went back in time and prevented yourself from dying as a

boy, then why are the two memories you have of the incident—the one formed when you were a boy and the one
formed when you were an adult—different from each
other? Should they not be the same?"

"Logic suggests that they should," Spock said. "But the
manner in which the Guardian of Forever worked remains
a scientific mystery, and time travel itself poses many
problems that resist reasonable explanation. However, it
does seem unlikely to me that in the *original* timeline, I as
an adult saved myself as a boy. How could I, when at the
time my life was imperiled at the age of seven, I had not
yet become an adult? It seems to me that I may have restored *a* timeline, but not the *original* timeline."

They reached the point along the path where the Two
Thousand Steps reached the top of the canyon. "Daylight
grows short," T'Vora said. "We will descend to the canyon
floor and return to the Refuge." She began down the stairway that had so long ago been carved out of the rock wall
by Vulcans now lost to time and memory. Behind her, she
heard Spock's footsteps as he came down after her.

Along the great inclined span of the Two Thousand
Steps, T'Vora moved beyond the nature of the incredible
events Spock had described to the impact that those events
had left on him. He had related the tales of time travel in
response to her questions of the great remorse she perceived in him, but she did not know if she quite understood the connection between the two, between his choices
and his guilt. In one incident, he had seemed to have minimal impact on the timeline while helping save billions of
lives, and in the other, he had restored the timeline in
which he lived, again with minimal impact, saving his own
life and that of his mother. T'Vora could conceive that
Spock's violation of principle in so doing might have
caused him some self-examination and even some uncom-

fortable reflection, but she could not reconcile it with the deep-seated regret she had detected within him.

When they reached the canyon floor and began the march back to the Refuge, T'Vora raised the issue. "Spock, I have listened to the stories of your violation of principle," she said. "Considering the outcomes of those events, as well as your benevolent intentions in taking the actions you did, I cannot comprehend the level of remorse you claim this has brought you."

Spock did not answer for a moment, and T'Vora peered over at him. At last, he said, "It is not those two incidents alone that have caused me the guilt I still carry within me." His voice had lowered, as though he found the admission difficult to make. "It is those incidents juxtaposed with another . . . one in which I did *not* violate principle."

And for the third time, Spock told a tale of traveling through time.

INTERSECTION

Crucible

Spock set the last of the chairs upside down on the end of the table. Behind him, Captain Kirk pushed a broom across the floor, amassing the dirt that had been tracked into the mission since last night, when the two of them had performed the same chore. Spock peered over to the raised platform at the side of the room to where the captain, as had become his practice, had set down the dustpan and wastebasket.

As Spock went to retrieve the cleaning tools with which he had grown well accustomed during the past forty-seven days, he glanced over at the kitchen. There, he saw Rik—he had never learned the former vagabond's surname—with Edith Keeler, the pair washing the dishes from the night's final meal. Just then, Keeler turned from the basin and reached toward the serving counter to pick up several empty bowls. Spock saw her notice him peering in her direction, and she gave him a wide smile. He nodded in response, then returned to the task at hand.

Gathering up the dustpan and wastebasket, he walked over to the corner of the room, where the captain had finished sweeping. As they worked together in silence to dispose of the dirt and assorted refuse, Spock speculated about the state of mind of his commanding officer—of his friend. Over the course of the weeks that the two of them had been in Earth's past, Spock had witnessed Jim fall in love with Edith Keeler, and she with him. Even before the social worker's criticality to the timeline had become apparent, the romance had seemed futile, since the successful restoration of history would put an end to it. Spock harbored no doubts about what action the captain would take should the opportunity to right the flow of time arise: he would do it, regardless of his feelings for Miss Keeler. What did concern Spock was how the loss of such an obviously special relationship would affect Jim.

Once they'd done tidying up, Spock put away the cleaning implements, while the captain collected their coats. As Spock took his and pulled it on, he saw that Jim also held Keeler's navy blue cloak. "I'm going to wait for Edith," he said.

"Of course," Spock replied. Though he recognized the need to keep a close watch on Keeler due to her importance to the timeline, Spock also understood that Jim *wanted* to be with her.

"Has McKenna gotten those components you needed yet?" the captain said, asking about the transformer and vacuum tubes Spock had ordered through the watchmaker.

"He has," Spock said. "He told me that I could stop by his apartment tonight to pick them up, which is what I intended to do."

"Very good. The more information we have, the better," said the captain, obviously knowing that Spock would utilize the components to attempt to mine more meaningful data out of his tricorder. A forlorn expression crossed Jim's features for just a moment, but then he peered toward the kitchen, toward Edith Keeler, and his bearing changed.

"We'll be done in just a few minutes," Keeler called.

"Oh, that's okay, Miss Keeler," Rik said beside her. "I can finish up here. You can go."

"Are you certain?" Keeler asked.

"Sure, I don't mind," Rik said. "You go on."

"Thank you," Keeler said, and Spock saw her reach over and pat Rik on the arm. She picked up a rag and quickly dried her hands, then disappeared briefly as she ducked down below the counter. When she emerged through the swinging doors into the main room, she carried her handbag and pale blue cloche with her. She wore a wide-collared white blouse and a black skirt. After she'd set her hat atop her head, the captain helped her on with her cloak, then put on his own coat.

At the front of the mission, Spock held open one of the double doors for Keeler and the captain, then followed them outside. The temperature had cooled as night had fallen, and water had puddled in the street after an earlier rain. Dim circles of illumination penetrated the darkness, both from street lamps and the headlights of passing automobiles.

"Good night, Mister Spock," Keeler said, peering back over her shoulder.

"I'll see you back at the apartment," the captain said with a quick wave.

"Good night," Spock said. He raised his own hand in an awkward attempt to match the captain's gesture. As Jim and Keeler started toward the street, Spock turned to his right and started along the sidewalk. He would head for the building in which Mr. McKenna resided, and then—

Close behind him, a horn beeped twice, and Spock whirled quickly to see an automobile brake, its tires squealing as it lurched to a halt just in front of Jim and Keeler. The couple had stopped just past the curb, but now they hurried across the street in front of the stationary vehicle. The driver sounded his horn a second time in obvious annoyance, and then yet again.

As Spock continued on his way, he wondered if they had all just passed the point at which Edith Keeler had been killed in the original timeline. Had McCoy already arrived in the past and somehow influenced the moment? Had the captain's presence beside Keeler prevented the traffic accident that *should* have happened?

Spock considered the circumstances as he stepped into the street. He had to wait to cross until an automobile drove by—the same one that had stopped before Keeler and the captain. If that automobile had initially killed the social worker in the untainted timeline, if the critical event in history that McCoy had somehow changed had just passed, if Spock and Captain Kirk had failed to set right whatever the doctor had done, then he didn't know what else they could do to remedy the situation. Back in the twenty-third century, beside the Guardian of Forever, the captain had given instructions to the remainder of the landing party: once they thought that they had waited long enough, once it had become apparent to them that history had not reverted, they would have to try themselves to accomplish that which Spock and Captain Kirk had set out to do. *But if any of them had made such an attempt,* Spock thought, *then wouldn't they have appeared here in the past already? Wouldn't they—*

"Spock!" the captain suddenly yelled. Spock turned quickly and saw him hurrying by himself back across the street, leaving Keeler standing alone on the far corner, watching him go. Spock hastened back to the sidewalk and toward the mission.

"What is it?" he asked as he and the captain reached the front doors at the same time.

"McCoy," he said, pointing toward the mission. "He's

in—" He stopped speaking as he looked at the front doors, and Spock peered in that direction to see Dr. McCoy coming through the entrance. "Bones!" Jim called, rushing toward him.

"Jim!" the doctor cried, and he embraced the captain. An uncharacteristic swell of emotion coursed through Spock, and he too rushed toward McCoy, reaching for his hand.

"Bones," Jim said again.

McCoy pumped Spock's hand. "I am so happy to see you two," he said. "I didn't know where I was or how I got here—"

Jim peered back across the street, and now a look of horror suddenly appeared on his face. Spock followed his gaze to see Edith Keeler walking toward them, as though in a trance, seeming to take no note of the truck advancing in her direction.

Now, Spock realized. The moment had arrived.

Jim took three halting steps across the sidewalk, toward Edith.

"No, Jim!" Spock yelled, as McCoy also cried out.

At the curb, Jim stopped. "Edith—" he said in a harsh whisper. Keeler continued walking forward, still unmindful of her surroundings, moving directly into the path of the truck.

McCoy moved then. One step, another, and he reached the captain, brushing past him. But Jim raised his arm, then turned his body into McCoy's and held him back, prevented him from racing out into the street and pushing Edith Keeler to safety.

The brakes of the truck screeched along the wet roadway. At the last instant, Keeler came our of her daze, seeing the truck, screaming as it struck her. She was thrown to the ground hard, her head striking the tarmac with a violent, decisive sound. Keeler's body wilted at once, her life extinguished just that quickly.

Bystanders dashed to the fallen woman. Spock looked from the corpse of Edith Keeler over to where Jim still held McCoy. Jim's eyes were tightly closed, and for a moment, the life seemed to have gone out of him as well.

"You deliberately stopped me, Jim," McCoy said, his words delivered with quiet anger. Jim opened his eyes. Spock had never seen them filled with such agony. "I could have saved her," the doctor went on. "Do you know what you just did?"

Jim pushed away from McCoy and staggered over to the mission doorway. He leaned an arm against the jamb, his aspect distant. He had taken the proper action, done what he had to do, but at what cost to himself?

"He knows, Doctor," Spock told McCoy. "He knows."

Jim leaned his face against his fist, quaking with emotion. Spock had never seen him like this, and in that moment he didn't know if his friend would ever be the same again.

NINETEEN

2295/2270

Out in the easternmost reaches of Gol, the great statues lay in ruins. Where in ancient times the stone behemoths had towered over the volcanic plain, they had now fallen to rubble. Whether they had been toppled by the shifting of powerful seisms, the attack of advancing armies, or the simple decay of millennia, no one could say. The remains of an era long past antedated not only the cause of the ignoble fate of the huge effigies, but the identities of their builders and the reasons they had claimed for their efforts.

In the shadow of a massive, rounded slab of carved rock, T'Vora stood at a cairn she had earlier assembled, and at which she had devoted some time to memorializing whatever Vulcan ancestors had once trod these ravaged grounds. As sunrise unveiled the day, she peered from her umbral vantage out across the harsh geography. Steam rose from dozens of fumaroles littering the landscape. Though still early in the morning, the temperature had already begun to climb, and the vertical rise of the white vapor promised no cooling breath of shifting air currents.

In the distance, Spock approached. Yesterday, T'Vora had walked the Two Thousand Steps with him, ascending to the canyon rim, descending back to the canyon floor. It had proven a strenuous excursion both physically and mentally, most especially for Spock, who had revealed to her difficult details of his life. Consequently, T'Vora had decided on an ensuing period of rest and meditation today for both of them.

Through the night, though, T'Vora had not slept, instead contemplating all that Spock had divulged to her during their pilgrimage. Placing his accounts of those events into the framework of both his life and his emotional state had served to reinforce one judgment that T'Vora had made while undermining another. She had been fully and properly justified in rejecting Spock's petition for the *Kolinahr* when first he'd made it to her, but she no longer remained as convinced of her verdict in granting him aspirant status after his second petition. Because of that, she now confronted another determination, for which reason she had cancelled today's respite, leaving word for Spock to meet her out here on the Plain of Lost Antiquities.

As Spock neared, T'Vora stepped out from the shade and into the dawn rays of the Vulcan sun. She addressed him by name as he stopped before her, then began speaking without further preamble. "I am concerned that you have come to the *Kolinahr* for the wrong reasons," she said.

"Forgive me, Master T'Vora," Spock said, "but have you not already evaluated my impetus to the contrary?"

"Your query is without merit," T'Vora said at once, satisfied neither to be so questioned by an aspirant nor with the slack logic that the question demonstrated. "My acceptance of you into the *Kolinahr* made plain my assessment at that time of your suitability for it. My declaration of concern now clearly indicates that I am reexamining that assessment. And your query implies either that I have forgotten the former or that I have erred in the latter."

"Forgive me again, Master," Spock said. "I offer my humble apology for the folly of that which I asked."

"Very well," she said. "We will speak no more of it. But we will speak of my concern."

"As you wish," Spock said.

"During our time together yesterday, you related three tales to me when faced with my observation of a lasting remorse present within you," T'Vora said. "You stated that this remorse involved your willful violation of a generally accepted ethical principle—noninterference with the timeline—a principle to which you subscribe. You provided descriptions of two incidents in which you intentionally changed the past, contrasting them with one in which you explicitly worked to correct an alteration to history."

"As you say," Spock acknowledged.

"I initially inferred that you offered the third narrative as an illustration of your awareness of and dedication to the principle about which you spoke," T'Vora explained. "But upon reflection last night, and in considering the events of your life immediately preceding your pursuit of the *Kolinahr* with me, I have come to believe otherwise."

"I understand," Spock said. "It is an involved issue."

"You will explain it then," T'Vora said. "Come." She rounded back toward the large stone fragment—once a section of a sculpture's arm, perhaps, or of a leg—and padded back into the shade. Out of the direct rays of the sun, the air measured several degrees cooler. She motioned toward the small cenotaph of loosely piled stones that she had assembled. "About this totem that I have consecrated to the memories of our forebears," she said, "tell me what you must."

Spock did not answer right away, and T'Vora assumed that he gathered his thoughts before speaking. At last, he said, "In my life, I have been involved in a number of time-travel incidents, only three of which I have recounted to you. In all cases, I have had the opportunity either to alter or to preserve the timeline. Understanding and believing in the precept that history should not be changed, I have al-

most always acted accordingly. I have also counseled others to take action against their own personal interests in
order to maintain the integrity of the past."

"As you did with Captain Kirk on Earth in 1930,"
T'Vora said.

"Yes," Spock said. "But just two years later, during our
return to the Guardian of Forever for our mission of historical research, I traveled back in time for the intended purpose of altering the timeline specifically for my own
benefit. I saved my own life, as a boy, which in turn prevented the death of my mother. I do not know what other
consequences my actions caused, except for the fate of
Commander Thelin. He never served aboard the *Enterprise,* but was instead assigned as second-in-command
aboard the *U.S.S. Ticonderoga.* One year after his posting,
he was killed in an avalanche during a survey mission to
an unexplored planet."

T'Vora nodded. Without Spock having complete control of his emotions, she understood how such a reality
could weigh on him. She said nothing, though, not wish-
ing to interrupt the flow of the aspirant's thoughts.

"Years later, I encouraged another possible alteration
to the timeline when I suggested bringing Terran whales
forward in time from three centuries earlier," Spock continued. "I know that course of action apparently resulted
in the rescue of Earth's humanoid population, but I cannot
tell what other unintended consequences it had—or will
have." He paused again, and this time, T'Vora suspected
that he would finally crystallize the nature of the regret
buried so deeply within him. "I am not entirely comfortable with having violated my ethical standards by tamper-
ing with history," he went on, "particularly when I did so
for my own advantage. Nevertheless, I have learned to
live with what I have done. In the incident with Comman-

der Thelin, I at least appear to have restored *some* timeline; with respect to bringing the whales forward in time, I
at least seem to have contributed to a positive outcome for
the inhabitants of Earth. What troubles me considerably,
though, is that in my single-minded quest to restore the
timeline—a timeline I would later *intentionally* change—I
did nothing to ease the burden of my friend."

"Captain Kirk?" T'Vora asked.

"Yes," Spock said. "At no point during our weeks on
Earth in 1930 did I attempt to ease his personal burden. Although I recognized the terrible pain that losing Edith
Keeler would cause him, I did not even *consider* what I
might do to prevent or diminish that pain."

"But what could you have done, Spock?" T'Vora asked.
"Would you have sacrificed the proper flow of history for
the sake of one man?"

"After many years of contemplation, I have concluded
that it is illogical to regard any timeline as 'proper,'" he
said, peering down at the pyramidal pile of stones. "Still, I
am not suggesting that I necessarily should have abandoned attempts to correct the damage that Doctor McCoy
had done. But perhaps I could have been a better friend to
Captain Kirk, warned him away from the emotional turmoil that I knew he would face once we had accomplished
our mission. Or perhaps I could have found some way to
restore the timeline without Edith Keeler having to die."
Looking up again at T'Vora, he said, "I don't know. I only
know that I never even thought about how I could help my
friend."

It occurred to T'Vora to point out that Captain Kirk's
position of authority might have made it difficult for Spock
to do anything such as he now proposed, but she realized
that it didn't matter. This did not impact Spock intellectu-
ally, but viscerally. The emotions he still felt had been with

him for many years and needed to be dealt with on that basis. "This guilt that you feel, Spock," T'Vora said, "it has abided since you and Captain Kirk witnessed the death of Edith Keeler?"

"No," he said. "After her death, after our return from Earth's past, I was concerned for Captain Kirk, but I had no regrets. Later, though, after I changed the timeline to save myself and my mother, I began to feel the remorse of which I've spoken, and which you have perceived within me. And when I finally came to realize just how much the loss of Edith Keeler had affected Captain Kirk, just how much he had loved her, the remorse grew strong. It has lasted since that time."

"And when Captain Kirk was killed last year," T'Vora asked, "did that exacerbate your guilt?"

"Exacerbate?" Spock said. "No, but the captain's death called it to mind. Coupled with the loss I felt, it underscored the need in my life for mastery of my emotions and a complete commitment to logic."

"Spock," T'Vora said, "I denied the first petition you made to me because it seemed that you were attempting to employ the *Kolinahr* as a means of escaping your emotions, rather than choosing it solely on the basis of what it offered. After what I have learned yesterday and today, I am again concerned that this is the case."

"It is not," Spock stated categorically. "Master T'Vora, I first embarked on a journey to achieve *Kolinahr* a quarter of a century ago. I spent nine seasons in intense study with Master T'sai, until I arrived at the very brink of that which I had sought. As I told you, it was only the intervention of a powerful and perfectly logical consciousness, V'Ger, that pulled me from that path. I have now studied with you for nearly four seasons, and you are aware yourself of how much progress I have made. I mention all of this as evidence that I am capable of reaching my goal, and that I have earned the opportunity to do so."

A question rose in T'Vora's mind, and she posed it to Spock. "Why did you pursue the *Kolinahr* twenty-five years ago?"

Spock lifted an eyebrow. "For the same reason I do now," he said. "I came to understand my need to fully control my emotions and to function on logic alone, to be wholly Vulcan."

T'Vora had actually wanted to know if some event had precipitated that understanding for Spock in the same way that the death of Captain Kirk had led him to it last year. She determined that the answer would be of no relevance. Only that which had driven him to this *Kolinahr* mattered now.

"I have much to consider," T'Vora said. "All that you have achieved since coming to the Akrelt Refuge, all that I have perceived within you, all that you have told me. I will examine my concerns in the context of all that. I do not know how long it will take, but you may rest or meditate or study as you see fit until I render my decision."

"Your decision?" Spock asked, obviously not understanding.

"Yes," T'Vora said. "I must decide whether you will be permitted to continue with the *Kolinahr*, or have your aspirant status revoked."

The Klingon battle cruiser collided with the Starfleet vessel. From the sciences station on the *Enterprise* bridge, Spock watched the main viewscreen as the bulbous control section at the bow of the D7-class *Vintahg* struck the *U.S.S. Clemson* on the starboard flank of its single hull. The dorsal tube of the Klingon ship ruptured in numerous places, severing the connection between the forward superstructure and the wide, angled stern section that housed engines and weaponry. One of the two sleek warp nacelles that projected top and bottom from the *Clemson*'s long, elliptical body canted at a steep angle.

Then the rest of the *Vintahg* slammed into the *Clemson*. The Klingon vessel exploded first, but only by a fraction of a second. Clouds of flame bloomed about the two ships, dying in the next instant, smothered by the vacuum of space. One of the *Clemson*'s nacelles broke free and twisted away into the void, and then the vessel's main section burst completely apart.

Spock allowed himself a brief moment of dissatisfaction—of sorrow, really—for the many lives just lost. Around him, the *Enterprise* command crew quieted, their silence broken only by the thin voices of personnel broadcasting systems' statuses to the bridge. Finally, Ensign Chekov said, "Oh, no," his voice a whisper filled with dismay.

After the Einstein research station had transmitted its distress signal, but before the *Enterprise* had arrived in response, two other starships had also been destroyed. The *U.S.S. Minerva,* like the *Clemson* a Paladin-class vessel, still hung lifeless in space near the station, its crew dead, its broken hull emitting radiation. The *I.K.S. Rikkon,* another D7 battle cruiser, had been obliterated in battle, exploding just as the *Enterprise* had approached it. Now, a pair of Klingon warships—the *Goren* and the *Gr'oth*—remained.

On the ruby-colored world below stood the Guardian of Forever. There had been no indication of how the Klingons had learned of Starfleet's presence in this system, but according to Captain Chelsea of the *Clemson,* they believed that the strange emanations from the planet, the research station in orbit, and the two Federation starships assigned here, indicated a Federation attempt to develop a new weapon for use against the Empire. Though untrue, Spock also knew that the Guardian could be employed as a tool of aggression—to sabotage a ship in battle, to prevent a population from achieving warp drive, to stop an entire species from evolving in the first place. For that reason, it could not be allowed to fall under Klingon control.

In the center of the bridge, Spock heard the click of a button being pressed on the arm of the command chair. "Kirk to engineering," the captain said. "Scotty, what's happening with the weapons and shields?" Both systems had gone down when the *Enterprise* had struck a line of Klingon torpedoes seeded like mines across the ship's path.

"Captain, I've got one torpedo tube back online," said Mister Scott, *"but I don't know for how long. The deflector grid's got so many holes in it, we can't reenergize. We're doing the best we can, but we only have so many work crews."*

Spock knew at once what he needed to do. Any of several officers could substitute for him at the sciences station, but if they couldn't find a way to raise the shields, they would have virtually no chance of defeating the *Goren* and the *Gr'oth*. "Captain," he said, looking in Kirk's direction, "I can—"

"Go," the captain said, hiking a thumb over his shoulder toward the turbolift doors. "Use security or anybody else you need."

As Spock rose, he peered over at Lieutenant Haines, who presently crewed a secondary station near the engineering console. She glanced over her shoulder and nodded to him, obviously acknowledging what she knew her duty to be. On his way to the lift, Spock saw her secure her controls, then stand and head for the sciences station he'd just vacated.

"Scotty, Spock is on the way with some help," the captain said. "Get those shields back up. Kirk out." He closed the intercom circuit without waiting for a reply.

Spock entered the turbolift, turned, and reached for a control wand. "Position of the Klingons?" he heard the captain ask.

"Checking," Haines said. "The *Goren* is still in pursuit—" The lift doors glided closed, cutting off the rest of the lieutenant's words.

"Main engineering," Spock said, ordering the lift to his destination. He then reached for the intercom, activating it with a touch. "Spock to security."

"Security," a female voice responded. *"Delant here, sir."*

"Lieutenant, contact all security officers at nonessential duty posts," he said. During the *Enterprise*'s current call to battle stations, guards would be distributed throughout the ship, protecting both critical and noncritical systems, and providing a thorough defense against boarding parties. "Have them report to me immediately in main engineering."

"Aye, sir," Delant said.

"Spock out." He closed the channel, then waited for the turbolift to complete its journey.

Less than two minutes after he'd left the bridge, Spock entered main engineering. Already several security officers had arrived, distinguishable from the many red-shirted engineers present by the phaser pistols hanging at their waists. One of the guards, Lieutenant Carver, worked to congregate the others into a group by the main doors, and as Spock passed, he spoke up.

"Commander," Carver said, "Lieutenant Delant told us we were to report to you here."

"That is correct," Spock said. "Stand by. You'll be issued orders shortly."

"Yes, sir," Carver said.

Spock peered deeper into the engineering compartment. He spied Lieutenant Commander Scott standing at the long main console and hastened over to him. "Mister Scott," he said. "Status."

"No different than when the captain asked me a couple of minutes ago, Mister Spock," the engineer said without looking up. As he operated a series of controls, a technical systems diagram above the console shifted. On either side of him, members of his staff also worked.

"Shields are the priority," Spock said.

"I know that." The engineer stopped working various buttons and dials, then studied the schematic for a moment before finally turning toward Spock. "When the shields went down, it was because they got hit hard at multiple locations."

"The ship struck a line of torpedoes," Spock explained. "They detonated on impact."

"Aye, that'd do it," Scott said. "With the shields already weakened by the Klingons' disruptor bolts, those torpedoes overloaded the grid. At least thirty junction nodes burned out." He pointed up at the diagram, jabbing his index finger at several rectangles colored red.

"Can we bypass?" Spock asked.

"Ach, not that many of them," Scott said. "We'll need to replace at least two-thirds in order to raise the shields at all, and even then we'd only be able to bring them up to partial strength."

Amid the many noises crowding main engineering—the hum of the impulse drive, the snaps and beeps of controls being operated, the squeak of the doors opening and closing as additional security guards arrived, numerous voices—Spock heard the distinctive sound of a photon torpedo tube discharging, a fitting accent to what he said next.

"The *Enterprise* is in battle, Mister Scott. We must do whatever we can, as quickly as we can."

"Aye," the chief engineer agreed. "But it takes at least three people to replace one of the shield nodes. I've already got repair crews out on ten of them."

Spock turned and gestured toward the group of security officers, now perhaps thirty strong. "We have personnel," he said.

"Right," Scott said. "We can divide them up into groups of two, send each pair out with an engineer. That'd be the fastest way to go about it."

"Then let us begin," Spock said.

Scott called over Lieutenant Gabler and described the repair strategy to him so that he could coordinate it. Gabler quickly did so, gathering members of the engineering staff and assigning to each of them two of the security guards already assembled. The first teams began to depart at once.

"Mister Scott," Spock asked, "what is the status of the warp drive?"

"Down hard," Scott said. "If I had two days and no bloody Klingons knocking at our door, I might coax a few light-years out of them, but I couldn't even promise you that."

"In that case," Spock said, "what of the ship's weapons?" Through the deck, he detected subtle changes in the vibrations of the impulse drive, variations resulting from adjustments made to the ship's velocity. Although he thought it likely that the *Enterprise* still engaged the enemy, he also noted that, since he'd left the bridge, he'd felt not a single jolt of Klingon weaponry striking the ship.

"Most of the torpedo tubes are locked down cold and I don't know why," the engineer said. "As for the phasers, the couplings are burned out. We can replace them and reload the firmware, but we'll need to recalibrate, and the technicians I've got rated on the tuning algorithms are busy holding the impulse engines and life support together."

"I am able to assist with that," Spock said. "I am familiar with the tuning software."

Scott nodded, then addressed the engineer to his right. "Cleary, watch this board for me," he said, working to adjust the diagram once more. "Keep an eye on the number one impulse stack."

"Yes, sir," Cleary said.

Scott stepped away from the main console, and Spock followed. "We'll have to change the couplings here first," he said. They walked past the large impulse cyclers—four meters tall and nearly as wide and deep—that marched along one side of the compartment. They moved into the narrow passage between the cyclers and the bulkhead beyond, out of view from the rest of main engineering. There, several control stations sat interspersed with numerous access panels. In the far corner, Scott stopped and operated a console, calling up on a display a graphic representation of the phaser internals. He paged through several screens of information before finding the one he wanted. "Here we are," Scott said. "We'll need to replace these two couplings, as well as both of these." He ran his fingers across the display, first along one pair of connections, then another. "But I'll have to verify the condition of the hookups before we do."

"Understood," Spock said.

Scott then walked along the bulkhead, found the access panel he wanted, took hold of its two handles, and pulled it free. As he set the plate down, smoke wafted from within the bulkhead, carrying with it the scent of seared circuitry. The engineer waved it away, then peered inside. "The first seating doesn't look too bad," he said. He slid open the door of a neighboring equipment niche, from which he pulled out a Feinberg tester and a pair of insulated gloves. After verifying his observation, he set the tester aside, slipped on the gloves, and reached inside. A moment later, he pulled out a long metallic cylinder with dual prongs at each end. Much of the phaser coupling had been charred black. "We're lucky the power surge didn't fuse this in place," Scott said.

"Indeed," Spock said.

Scott set the coupling down, then found a replacement for it within a nearby equipment hold. As he worked to install it, Spock operated the control station to access the firmware insertion program, informing the engineer when he'd done so. Once Scott had fit the coupling into place, Spock uploaded the computer instructions into its memory. "Firmware transfer complete," he said. "Bringing up the calibration program."

"All right," Scott said, retrieving the Feinberg tester. "Let's start with a tenth of a percent variance."

"Setting one tenth of one—" Spock began, but he halted abruptly.

"What is it?" Scott asked, looking up from the tester. A second later, he answered his own question. "The impulse engines," he said. "They've stopped."

"Affirmative," Spock said. "The ship is no longer moving under directed power."

Scott strode back to the control station and deftly operated it. The calibration program disappeared from the display, replaced by a sequence of gauges. "We're not adrift," Scott said, pointing at the screen. "We're at station-keeping. The impulse engines are still online. They're just not being used."

"Perhaps we have been victorious in our engagement with the Klingons," Spock surmised.

"Let's hope so," Scott said.

Spock reached for the intercom above the panel and pushed its activation button. "Spock to—" Once more, he stopped in mid-sentence. This time, he heard a new sound, a hum pitched so low that it was nearly inaudible. To Scott, he said, "Klingon transporter." From their position in the passage behind the impulse cyclers, he and Scott could not see the invaders materializing.

Suddenly, the ship shook hard, sending Spock and Scott sprawling onto the deck. "What was that?" Scott whispered urgently as both climbed back to their feet.

"I am unsure," Spock replied. It made no sense that the *Enterprise* had taken a weapons strike from the Klingon vessels. They wouldn't be firing on the ship after they'd sent over a boarding party—and likely more than one.

Spock listened and heard sounds of confusion, and an instant later, the pulse of disruptor fire rose within the compartment, joined quickly by the whine of phasers. Klingon and Starfleet officers yelled, their voices accompanied by the rush of footsteps and the sounds of falling bodies.

Though unarmed, Spock edged toward the side of the nearest impulse cycler, intending to peer out from behind it to take stock of the situation. As he advanced, though, he saw a shadow on the deck ahead of him, and then a Klingon backed into the narrow passage, apparently looking to conceal himself behind the cycler. Spock lunged quickly forward and reached for his shoulder, found the proper spot, and applied pressure with his fingers. The Klingon tensed briefly, then slumped. Spock caught him and settled him to the deck, pulling the disruptor from his hand.

Out in the main section of the engineering compartment, the number of phaser and disruptor blasts began to diminish. Spock examined the Klingon weapon he'd just taken, searching for a stun setting. He could find none. He did not wish to shoot to kill, but if forced do so in order to protect his crewmates—

Spock heard the scramble of footsteps behind him, and he whirled to see that, behind the far cycler, another Klingon had taken cover. Scott turned as well, and when he saw the enemy soldier, the engineer reached down for the failed phaser coupling, evidently wanting to use it as a weapon. As he did so, though, the Klingon saw him and aimed his disruptor.

Spock did not hesitate. He raised his hand and squeezed the firing pad. A bolt of bright green energy flashed past the engineer and struck the Klingon full in the chest, sending him crashing backward onto the deck.

Scott stood back up, the coupling now held in his hands. "Thank you, Mister Spock," he said.

Spock nodded, then turned and stepped up again to the end of the row of cyclers. Now, though, the weapons fire seemed to have ceased. He waited a moment, then peered around the edge of the cycler.

He saw several members of the crew collapsed on the deck, either unconscious or dead. He looked around and spied other security officers partially hidden behind consoles and pillars. "All clear?" asked a female voice calmly, and Spock recognized it as belonging to a security officer, Ensign Labdouni.

"Clear from the second level," said another security officer, Crewman Lemli.

"We're clear by the main doors too," said a third voice, a tremor in it. Spock looked over and saw that the speaker had been Lieutenant Singh, an engineer and not a member of ship's security.

Slowly, the *Enterprise* personnel began emerging from wherever they'd taken cover, their phasers held at the ready. Spock stepped out from behind the cycler, the disruptor still in his hand but lowered to his side. Scott followed him.

All around the engineering compartment lay bodies—dozens of them. Spock counted ten Klingons and three or four times as many Starfleet officers. The boarding party had possessed the advantage of surprise, but they appeared to have been beaten back by sheer numbers.

Spock kneeled beside the first person he came to: Lieutenant Masters, a woman on his own staff and an expert on dilithium crystals. Her blue uniform had been singed black along her right shoulder, and blood had pooled in an open wound. Spock placed two fingers on the side of her neck, feeling for a carotid pulse. He found it, faint but there.

At a nearby console, he heard Labdouni calling for a medical team. Before him, he saw some of the other security guards performing basic triage on the fallen *Enterprise* officers, while still others disarmed and then checked the Klingons. His presence here obviously not needed, he stood and paced over to the nearest console. Scott, knowing his own duty, moved back over to the main engineering panel. Some of the equipment, Spock saw, had been damaged during the attack, likely necessitating the rerouting of some functions to auxiliary control.

At the console, he opened an intercom channel. "Spock to bridge," he said. When he received no response after a few seconds, he tried again. "Spock to bridge."

Still nothing.

Thinking that perhaps the intercom had been hit during the firefight, Spock tested it by attempting to contact another destination. "Spock to security."

"*Security,*" came the immediate response. "*Delant here, sir.*"

"What is the ship's status, Lieutenant?" Spock said.

"We've been boarded in two places," Delant said. *"The bridge and main engineering."*

"I am in engineering now," Spock said. "The boarding party has been overcome. What is the situation on the bridge?"

"Sensors show that ten to twelve Klingons beamed in, and then there was an explosion," Delant said.

Spock recalled when the ship had quaked just after the Klingons had transported into engineering, and he and Scott had been thrown from their feet. "The bridge crew?"

"We think they may have initiated the blast, sir," Delant said. *"There don't appear to be any survivors."*

Spock knew at once that Delant must be mistaken, that the bridge crew could not all have been killed. In the next moment, he realized that his denial would not change whatever had happened. He felt fury, but fought to push it away. He still had a duty to perform, a responsibility to the lives of the hundreds who would look to him for leadership if the captain had in fact been killed.

"What of the two remaining Klingon vessels?" Spock asked.

"The Goren *has been destroyed,"* Delant reported, *"and the* Gr'oth *is badly damaged. They've suffered heavy casualties, and most of their systems are down, including warp and impulse drive, weapons, and shields, and their life support won't last much longer."*

"How many Klingons left alive aboard the *Gr'oth*?" Spock wanted to know.

"Not more than a handful, sir," Delant said.

"Are their transporters still operative?" Spock asked.

"Indeterminate," Delant said. *"But they did manage to send the boarding parties over, so it's possible. We're monitoring for any transporter activity."*

Spock's attention wavered as he considered what more

information he required, and what action he needed to take next. The specter of the dead bridge crew hung in his mind, and again, he had to consciously struggle to get past it. "Have bridge functions been transferred to auxiliary control?" he finally managed to say.

"*Command and control functions redirected there automatically when the bridge was destroyed,*" Delant confirmed. "*Lieutenant DeSalle called in a couple of minutes ago and was headed there until we could determine . . .*" Delant faltered for a moment before continuing. "*Until we could determine the status of the chain of command.*"

"Understood," Spock said. Fifth in line to captain the *Enterprise,* DeSalle occupied that position behind Captain Kirk, Spock himself, Chief Engineer Scott, and Lieutenant Sulu. With Kirk and Sulu presumed dead on the bridge, and Spock and Scott under Klingon attack in engineering, DeSalle had made the proper decision in assuming command. But Spock knew that he must now do the same himself.

"*Inform Mister DeSalle that I'm on my way to auxiliary control now,*" he said.

"*Aye, sir,*" Delant said. "*Right away.*"

"Spock out." He moved to close the channel, but ended up striking the intercom so hard with his fist that its casing cracked. *I am in control of my emotions,* he told himself and then tried to will it to be true. He looked up to see if anybody had witnessed his lapse in self-control, but he saw nobody's attention directed toward him. Those present concentrated either on the wounded or on the ship's drive systems. Doctors McCoy and Sanchez had arrived, along with other medical personnel.

As Spock headed toward the main doors, McCoy glanced up and saw him. For just an instant, their gazes met, and Spock knew that they both thought the same unimaginable thing: *Jim is dead.* Spock looked quickly away and continued out into the corridor, on his way to take command of the *Enterprise*.

Chief Engineer Montgomery Scott sat in a chair at the center of auxiliary control, anxious to return to engineering, or even to work here on the many improvised relays that would be needed to repair the *Enterprise* enough just to get her to the nearest base. But with Captain Kirk gone and Spock temporarily off the ship, he'd been left in command. And before Spock had headed down to the shuttlebay for his short journey, he'd made it clear that Scotty would have to remain on the makeshift bridge and keep himself available for immediate command decisions, rather than climbing into a Jeffries tube somewhere.

Scotty knew his position in the ship's hierarchy, of course. He wouldn't have jeopardized the crew by staying down in engineering when he needed to be in auxiliary control. At the same time, he had to admit that he would've much preferred to be there than here.

Then again, he thought, *the last time I was there it was a bloodbath.*

Scotty still had trouble wiping the images from his thoughts. A dozen Klingons had transported into main engineering and had begun firing their disruptors. They'd all been stopped, more a function of good fortune than anything else, Scotty thought. The extra security guards Spock had ordered down to engineering to provide extra hands had helped limit the harm the Klingons had done. The boarding party had nevertheless managed to kill eleven of the *Enterprise* crew and wound another twenty-seven. They'd also damaged a number of engineering controls that, coupled with the destruction of the bridge, had taken many systems off-line, including the impulse drive.

Around Scotty, the second-shift bridge crew worked to keep the Klingon vessel *Gr'oth* under observation and to direct repairs aboard the *Enterprise*. Auxiliary control did not match the exact design of the bridge, but complete command and control of the ship could be effected from here. A series of workstations along the outer bulkheads surrounded a wide, curving console that stood at the center of the space. In a neighboring compartment, separated from the main control room by a grillwork partition, a long panel allowed access to engineering functions. Forward, a large viewscreen dominated the scene and currently displayed an image of the *Gr'oth,* its fractured hull partially penetrated by a fragment of the demolished research station.

Right now, the crew remained somber—as did Scotty's own mood. Under the direction of Captain Kirk, they had managed to survive, but at a terrible cost. The battle they'd come through had seen the destruction of two *Paladin*-class Starfleet vessels, and three top-of-the-line Klingon heavies had been destroyed, while a fourth Klingon D7 and the *Enterprise* had nearly suffered the same fate. The Einstein space station had also been reduced to rubble, but not before the seventeen researchers and security personnel had been transported to safety. Oddly enough, the *Enterprise* had suffered the same number of casualties: seventeen—eleven in engineering and six on the bridge.

All because of that blasted Guardian, Scotty thought. The enigmatic device—he had never believed that it could actually be alive—had been the reason for the construction of the research station, as well as for the constant vigil that the *Clemson* and the *Minerva* had maintained within the system. But the Klingons must have detected the vortex's temporal emanations and discovered Starfleet's presence here, because when they'd come, they'd come in force.

The Empire likely didn't know it, but in keeping them from gaining access to the Guardian of Forever the way he had, Captain Kirk hadn't simply saved the lives of the research station personnel and those of the *Enterprise* crew; considering the capabilities of the time vortex, he'd probably preserved the very existence of the Federation.

Even now, Spock had taken excessive precautions to prevent the Klingons from approaching the Guardian. Although only a handful of the *Gr'oth*'s crew remained alive aboard the broken warship, and although most of their systems—engines, shields, weapons—had failed, the status of their transporters proved impossible to determine. As a result, Spock had ordered the *Enterprise* out of the *Gr'oth*'s transporter range—they'd had to use thrusters in order to do so—and then had sent two shuttlecraft down to the planet surface to keep the Guardian under surveillance.

"Spock to auxiliary control," came the voice of the ship's first officer, now the acting captain.

Scotty peered over at Lieutenant Palmer, who sat at a secondary station set up for communications. He nodded to her, and she opened a channel. "Scott here," said the chief engineer. "Go ahead, Mister Spock."

"The shuttlecraft Columbus *is ready to launch,"* Spock said. *"Please open the hangar bay doors."* During the *Enterprise*'s continuing red alert status, the doors had been locked down and their control routed to the bridge—or at this point to auxiliary control.

At one of the secondary stations, Lieutenant Hadley glanced back over his shoulder at Scotty. "Go ahead," the engineer told him.

"Yes, sir," Hadley said, and he set to working his panel.

"Thank you, Mister Scott," Spock said. *"I will not be long. Spock out."*

As Palmer closed the channel, Scotty thought again that

Spock shouldn't be leaving the ship at all, not in the current circumstances. The engineer knew that a survey had to be done of the damage done to the bridge, if only to verify that nobody could have survived the blast that had destroyed it. When it had been opened to space, emergency bulkheads had sealed and locked into place. With the transporter presently off-line, that meant sending some members of the crew out onto the hull in an environmental suit or out in a shuttle. Spock had chosen a shuttle, but Scotty thought he should've chosen somebody other than himself to pilot it—though he did understand the first officer's need to see the devastation for himself.

And that need is very real, Scotty thought. In all the years he'd served with Spock, the engineer had never seen him in his present state. He still wore a calm Vulcan guise, but it barely covered the strong emotions he obviously felt. Scotty knew the commonly accepted phases of grief for humans—he'd been experiencing them himself—and he could see at least two of those in Spock: anger, bordering on rage, along with a deep sadness. Jim Kirk hadn't just been Spock's commanding officer for five years; he'd been his best friend.

"The shuttlecraft *Columbus* is away," Hadley reported from his station.

An ancient Gaelic blessing occurred to Scotty, and in a whisper that only he could hear, he offered it up. "Deep peace of the shining stars to you, Mister Spock."

In the distance hung the rusty globe upon which the Guardian of Forever stood. Spock brought the shuttlecraft *Columbus* from the hangar and along the starboard flank of the *Enterprise*. The roughly cylindrical secondary hull—battered by Klingon disruptors and torpedoes—passed from sight, and then so too did the dorsal connector atop its forward end. The great disk of the primary hull loomed in the shuttle's viewports as it climbed. The narrow edge of the saucer appeared, a paired set of running lights blinking there, one below, one above.

Spock adjusted the course of the *Columbus,* turning it farther to port. The shuttle angled in that direction and then straightened. Ahead lay the upper circular span of the *Enterprise,* and its center, the bridge module.

Or what remained of it.

As the *Columbus* glided forward, Spock looked away, gazing instead at the rest of the *Enterprise*'s saucer. Across its gray-white surface, bursts of blackened hull marked the places where Klingon weapons had reached their targets. Overall, he didn't know if he'd ever seen the ship in such a distressed state. As badly damaged as the *Enterprise* appeared, though, Spock marveled at how the captain had once more managed to extricate the ship and its crew from the most dire of circumstances.

Spock peered forward to see that the *Columbus* neared the ruins of the bridge. He programmed the shuttle's course to pass slowly above it. Situated at the top of the ship, in a superstructure that rose above the surrounding hull, the control center had always seemed oddly—and perhaps foolishly—placed to Spock. Arguably the ship's most important location, from which the captain and his command crew piloted and directed the operation of the vessel, it need not have been positioned where it would be so vulnerable, even with the added shielding that protected it. Buried deep within the heart of the ship, the bridge could just as easily have fulfilled its purpose, while at the same time being far less susceptible to external attack.

In this case, Spock told himself, *it wouldn't have mattered.* The Klingon transporters could have reached anywhere inside the *Enterprise,* and an explosion amidships could have torn out massive sections of multiple decks, doing far more harm than had been done here. Spock found arguments on both sides compelling, but he felt . . . muddled . . . his normally well-honed mind unable to cut through to the core of the issue.

But that didn't matter either, because Spock knew that none of those concerns had driven the placement of the bridge on Starfleet vessels. Symbolism had been of more significance to the Federation organization that held as its mandate exploration and scientific investigation first, and keeping the peace second. And never—*never*—would they be the aggressors in any conflict. Captain Kirk had often referred to Starfleet as "an instrument of civilization," and civilized peoples did not launch wars.

Below the *Columbus,* the shattered remnants of the bridge came into view. Spock operated his panel and stopped the shuttle. He stood and peered through the forward viewports.

The bridge had been completely opened to space. Spock studied the inner edges of the devastation, attempting to identify the various control stations, but he could discern none of them. The entire interior of the bridge had been blackened by the heat of the explosion, and much of what had been there had either been vaporized or blasted out into space. The helm and navigation console and the outer railings had been shorn from their mounts and could be seen nowhere. The command chair had also gone. Of the white dome that had covered the bridge, only a few scorched, twisted fragments had been left behind. A deformed section of rounded bulkhead marked where the turboshaft had once risen. The hull that had surrounded the rest of the bridge had exploded outwards, fracturing, leaving only charred, mangled slices of metal, like the fingers of some burned robotic claw reaching futilely for the stars.

As Spock surveyed the wreckage, one detail seemed utterly clear: nobody on the bridge could have survived the detonation. Although the icy depths of space would have subsequently dispatched anybody who had, Spock could not envision any of the crew enduring long enough for that to happen. The explosion must have killed them all— quickly, he hoped, and without pain.

Though he felt no motivation to move, Spock knew that he had to get back to the ship. As the acting captain of the *Enterprise,* the crew needed him. With an effort, he sat back down at the main console and engaged the shuttle's thrusters. The *Columbus* began forward, over the bridge and out beyond the saucer section, and then he aimed it to port.

Spock thought that he could have expected to feel the sadness he did, and that he might have even been able to accept it. He also understood his rage, but he would never have anticipated the extent to which his remorse had grown. Being so close to the Guardian of Forever seemed to strengthen the memories of it, and of what its existence had allowed to happen. Spock's guilt had begun a year ago, after he had used the Guardian to save his own life and that of his mother, and then truly realized how much he had failed the captain with Edith Keeler. Spock had been right in his evaluation of her importance to the history of Earth, but he should have *tried* to find some other way to restore the timeline—some way that would have permitted Captain Kirk his happiness. Now, with Jim dead, with any chance for him to find a lasting love gone, that regret seemed almost unbearable.

Alone with his thoughts, Spock worked the controls, heading the *Columbus* back toward the hangar bay.

* * *

McCoy sprinted toward the turbolift, his fatigue replaced by the rush of adrenalin. He carried a medical pouch in one hand and a tricorder in the other. After everything that had happened today, he almost couldn't believe what he'd just been told.

Earlier, McCoy had thought that he would remember this day for a long time, even if he attempted to forget it. The Einstein research station, destroyed. Two Starfleet vessels and their crews, also gone, and now four Klingon ships and their complements, with Korax plunging the *Gr'oth* through the atmosphere of the planet and directly into the Guardian of Forever. Considering the nature and obvious power of the Guardian, McCoy had been relieved when its destruction hadn't sent the entire galaxy into some sort of temporal instability.

The red doors of the lift parted and McCoy hurried inside. "Deck three," he said, hanging the tricorder over his shoulder and then activating the control wand. "Port of the central turboshaft."

After the lift eased into vertical motion, he let go of the wand and reached up to the intercom. "McCoy to M'Benga," he said. At the time DeSalle had contacted sickbay, McCoy had been checking on the condition of the crew members wounded today. Immediately after he'd spoken with DeSalle, he'd left sickbay so quickly— pausing only to grab up a medical pouch and a tricorder—that he hadn't even been able to inform the rest of the staff about what had happened.

"M'Benga here," responded the doctor. He sounded weary, and McCoy didn't wonder why after all of the casualties they'd had to treat today.

"Jabilo," McCoy said, unable to contain his excitement, "they found the bridge crew. They were trapped—"

"Wait. What?" M'Benga said. *"You mean they were found alive?"*

"Yes," McCoy said. "They managed to get off the bridge before the explosion, but the force of the blast jammed the turbolift they were in sideways into the shaft. They've been stuck between decks, unconscious. All but two of them are alert now, but they're all alive. I'm already on my way now, but we're going to need a medical team." As McCoy spoke, the lift slowed, then began to glide along horizontally.

"I'll arrange it," M'Benga said. *"Where are they?"*

"The central turboshaft on deck three," McCoy said. "DeSalle's shut the gravity down and they're floating them out."

"We'll be there as quickly as we can," M'Benga said. *"Out."*

McCoy thumbed the intercom channel closed. As he waited for the lift to complete its journey, he thought about Spock. McCoy had never seen the Vulcan as haggard as he had today, and he suspected that Jim's apparent death had pushed Spock to the brink of grief—and perhaps beyond. The news that the captain and the others had been found alive could only ease his burden.

The lift eased to a stop, and when the doors opened, McCoy exited onto deck three. He raced through the corridors until he reached the one that led to the central turboshaft. DeSalle and several security guards moved about in front of the open doors, seeing to the needs of the four bridge officers on the deck. Uhura, Haines, and Leslie all sat with their backs against a bulkhead, while Chekov lay supine.

McCoy ran over, and all eyes turned to him. He kneeled beside Chekov, who at a cursory glance seemed to have suffered the worst injuries. Blood coated the right side of his gold uniform, and he cradled one arm with the other. McCoy quickly retrieved a portable scanner from his tricorder and began to take readings. "I'm fine, Doctor," Chekov said.

"Now you let me be the judge of that," McCoy said, but already he saw the truth of what the ensign had claimed. Chekov's forearm had suffered a simple break, and the blood flowing from the gash in his shoulder had already been stemmed, likely by one of the security guards using a first-aid kit.

"Doctor McCoy," Uhura said, and when he looked over at her, she fixed him with a serious expression. "All of us are all right," she said, motioning to include all four of the bridge crew. "The captain and Sulu need you."

McCoy peered over at Haines and Leslie, in turn, and they both nodded their agreement. When he looked farther down the corridor, to where the empty turboshaft showed beyond the open doors, DeSalle waved him over. McCoy stood up and told the injured officers, "Doctor M'Benga will be here shortly with a medical team." Then he padded over to DeSalle.

"Doc," he said quietly, turning toward the shaft, "Captain Kirk and Lieutenant Sulu are still unconscious. The others seemed well enough to move, but we didn't want to do anything with the captain and the lieutenant until you had a chance to examine them."

"You did the right thing," McCoy said, patting DeSalle on the side of the arm. "Is anybody down there keeping an eye on them?"

"Ensign Stevenson," DeSalle said.

McCoy nodded. Stevenson primarily worked security, he knew, but she'd also done several rotations in sickbay. "Good choice," he said. He then stepped toward the end of the corridor and peered down past the deck. Emergency lighting had been turned on, and only a few meters below, he saw a car hanging at an angle, wedged into the sides of the turboshaft. It appeared precarious, but then McCoy recalled that they'd shut down the gravity in the tube.

"We cut through one side of the lift," DeSalle said at his shoulder, and indeed, McCoy could see into the car through the roughly rectangular opening. He spied part of a gold uniform, though he couldn't tell whether it belonged to Jim or Hikaru.

"I'd better get down there," McCoy said. He peered at the side of the shaft beside the doors, to the access ladder. He put his scanner back in his tricorder, tucked his medical pouch into the back of his waistband, then reached out and took hold of a rung.

"Careful, Doctor," DeSalle said. "Remember that the gravity's off."

"Right, thanks," McCoy said. He swung his foot onto a rung, then pulled his whole body onto the ladder. He gave himself just a moment to acclimate to zero gee—his stomach at once felt aflutter—and then he began to descend. As he'd been taught to do at the academy, he moved slowly and deliberately, keeping his focus on his movements. When he reached the car, he peered into the opening. "Ensign Stevenson?" he said, and although he hadn't spoken loudly, his voice echoed up the shaft. "It's Doctor McCoy."

"I'm here," Stevenson said. "I'll give you a hand climbing into the lift." A moment later, her face appeared in the opening.

McCoy stepped slowly from the rung. Just as he pushed himself onto the side of the car, he realized that in null gravity, the force he exerted on the lift would send it drifting in the other direction—in this case, down. Stevenson must have seen his startled look because she said, "It's all right. The car's wedged in pretty tightly, but just in case, we've also anchored it to the sides of the shaft."

"You thought of everything," McCoy said.

"We like to put the *secure* in *security*," Stevenson quipped. "Now, give me your hand." With one hand still on the ladder, McCoy reached down with the other. The ensign took hold with a firm grasp and said, "Just let go of the ladder and I'll guide you in." McCoy did so, and Stevenson conducted him expertly into the lift.

Once inside, he saw Jim and Hikaru. Both men lay in heaps at the lowest point of the car, where the floor met one of the walls. The small translucent window, through which riders could see the progress of the turbolift on its journey, had been cracked. An electric scent, like that of burning metal, filled the enclosed space. Patches of blood could be seen in several places, but not on either of the men.

Of the two, Sulu appeared in worse condition. His complexion had paled considerably, and his arm extended at an unnatural angle from his body. His respiration came in shallow, rapid breaths, and his skin felt moist and cool to the touch. While Stevenson steadied McCoy in the weightless environment, he took out his scanner and began examining the helmsman.

"He's in shock," McCoy reported. "He's bleeding internally. We need to get him to sickbay immediately."

McCoy heard the sound of a communicator being activated. "Stevenson to DeSalle."

"DeSalle here," came the reply.

"Is the medical team here yet?" she asked.

"Yes," DeSalle said. *"Doctor M'Benga just arrived with several nurses and orderlies."*

"Have a stretcher sent down here at once," Stevenson told him.

"*Will do*," DeSalle said.

"Stevenson out."

As the security guards had spoken, McCoy had turned his attention toward Captain Kirk. Unlike Sulu, who'd suffered a dislocated shoulder and two broken bones in addition to his internal bleeding, the captain's body seemed intact. Initially McCoy could find no reason for his loss of consciousness, but then he saw it: a slight swelling of the brain stem. McCoy ran a quick series of scans to confirm his diagnosis.

He turned to Stevenson. "Make that two stretchers," he said. "The captain is in a coma."

Spock strode through a wide, dimly lighted corridor on Starbase 10. Deep in the simulated night of the orbital station, few base personnel moved about, and even fewer visitors. Since exiting the quarters he'd been assigned here, Spock had seen only a small number of people, and not a single member of the *Enterprise* crew. After all that they'd experienced during the last several days—beginning with their battle against the Klingons and ending with their patched and barely functioning vessel limping here, to the nearest starbase—he assumed that they'd all retired to their guest cabins.

All of them, that is, but Dr. McCoy.

As Spock paced along, he considered what he himself had endured since the deadly encounter with the Klingons. The rapid flow of emotions—from grief to elation, from concern to hope—had been difficult to bear, partially due to their unexpectedness, partially to their volatility, but primarily because of the remorse underlying it all. In the hours since arriving at Starbase 10, though, he'd finally been able to recapture a sense of control that matched his outward composure. After seeing to the needs of the crew—rest being chief among those needs—and participating in an initial debriefing by the station's commander, Commodore Stocker, Spock had visited the infirmary. Captain Kirk and the other *Enterprise* wounded had been transferred there, where Dr. McCoy would continue to treat them, aided by Dr. Orondella, Starbase 10's chief medical officer.

Since the explosion of the bridge, the captain had remained in a coma—or at least he had until just a short time ago. Within the last hour, he had woken from three days of unconsciousness. According to Dr. McCoy, who had contacted Spock with the news, Captain Kirk appeared to have suffered no permanent damage to his brain.

Spock reached a T-shaped intersection and turned into a corridor that ran along the outside of the starbase. To his right, the transparent outer bulkhead provided a view of several ports that circled the biconic space station at its midpoint. He saw two Starfleet vessels—the *U.S.S. Diversity* and the *S.S. Selma*—and a Frunalian science scout currently berthed. Just visible around the curve of the station, the *Enterprise* floated in the pair of omegoid frames, set at right angles to each other, that formed the dock. Half a dozen power tethers had already been strung from the dock to the ship, but right now the *Enterprise* remained still and dark, like an injured animal that has wandered off to die.

But dead or not—and surely the ship would return to active duty once it had undergone extensive repairs—it had at least held together long enough to carry the crew to safety. After the captain's command decisions had resulted in the defeat of the Klingons, Lieutenant Commander Scott and his engineering staff had managed to restore the warp drive sufficiently for the ship to reach Starbase 10. Its five-year mission completed, the *Enterprise* had been on its way here prior to receiving the distress signal from the

Einstein research station, but it did not seem fitting to
Spock that it should end like this, with an exhausted,
wounded crew and a vessel barely spaceworthy.

A few moments later, Spock reached another T. He
turned left into the intersecting corridor, then right through
a pair of green doors and into the base's infirmary. Inside,
a long office reached both left and right, with quite a few
workstations on the outer bulkhead. Opposite those, several entryways opened into diagnostic, surgical, and recovery bays, while to the left, a pair of sealed doors led to
intensive care. Though still subdued, the lighting here had
not dimmed as much as that out in the corridors.

The only individual in the office sat at a workstation to
the right. An Andorian, he peered up from a data slate in
his hands. Dressed in a blue Starfleet medical uniform
that nearly matched the color of his skin, he wore the rank
of ensign and the insignia of a nurse. "Are you Mister
Spock?" he asked.

"I am," Spock said. "I was contacted by Doctor
McCoy."

"Yes," the nurse said, standing. "He said you'd be here
shortly. If you wait here, I'll get him for you." He set the
data slate down and walked past Spock to the far end of
the room. The wide doors there parted silently before him
and he disappeared into the intensive care section. Before
long, he returned and motioned Spock forward. "Doctor
McCoy asked that you come in," he said.

Spock trod over to the nurse, who then escorted him
into a central observational compartment, off of which
opened a dozen large patients' alcoves. A long multi-
person workspace stood in the middle of the area, where
two other medical professionals currently sat. The illumination remained low, though brighter light spilled out
from one of the far alcoves. A mélange of scents reached

Spock, some of which he associated with illness, some with healing.

The nurse led Spock through the compartment, stopping at the well-lighted alcove. Within, a variety of diagnostic and life support equipment lined the bulkheads. Dr. McCoy stood beside an oversized diagnostic pallet, examining the readings on the panel above it.

Captain Kirk lay on the pallet. An intravenous sleeve remained wrapped around his upper arm. The neural stimulator affixed to his temples had been removed, replaced now by a neurological monitor. With his eyes closed, the captain looked weak, but far less so than he had even earlier today.

"Spock," McCoy said quietly. "Come in." Dark circles arced beneath the doctor's eyes. Spock knew that he'd had little sleep over the past few nights, spending many of those hours in the *Enterprise*'s sickbay.

"I'll leave you to the doctor," the nurse said, and then he turned and left.

Spock stepped forward into the alcove. "I'm sorry to get you down here so late," McCoy said. "I should have told you not to come until the morning. As you can see, Jim's already fallen asleep."

"What is the captain's condition?" Spock asked.

"Even before we left the *Enterprise,* he showed some good neural activity," McCoy said, "and a few hours ago, it got even stronger. About ninety minutes ago, he regained consciousness. I ran some tests and he's showing good progress."

"Did you speak with him?" Spock asked.

"I did," McCoy said. "He was exhausted, but he was coherent. He knew who he was and who I was. He remembered being on the bridge and fighting the Klingon vessels, but not getting into the turbolift or the explosion. That's common, though, not recalling the time leading up to a head injury."

"What is your prognosis?" Spock asked.

"Complete recovery," McCoy said. "We'll probably keep him here another week or two, but he should be fine."

"Thank you, Doctor," Spock said. "For your work here and on the *Enterprise*."

McCoy tilted his head to one side. "Are you saying good-bye, Spock?"

"I am merely offering my gratitude for your exemplary efforts," Spock said.

"Well, then, you're welcome," McCoy said. "Come on, we should probably both get some sleep."

Spock peered at the captain, then back at McCoy. "I would like to stay for a few moments, if you have no medical objections."

"No, no medical objections, but . . . " McCoy did not finish his statement, but peered appraisingly at Spock. "No, it's all right," he finally concluded. "Just remember that even Vulcans need sleep."

"I do not intend to stay long," Spock said. "Good night, Doctor."

"Good night, Spock," McCoy said, and then he left. Spock listened to his footsteps, following them until the doctor exited the intensive care section. Then he looked over at the captain.

Yet again, Spock felt a billow of emotion—happiness for his friend's recovery—but now, he found it much easier collecting himself than he had at other times recently. He constricted his feeling, then replaced it with the logic of the situation. With the captain in an injury-induced coma for three days, his return to awareness and lucidity provided reasonable cause for relief.

Spock saw a chair by the captain's bedside, but he

chose not to use it. Instead, he simply stood in the corner, near where he'd entered the alcove. He brought his hands together before him, entwining his fingers, then bowed his head and closed his eyes.

In his mind, Spock envisioned the statue of Vektan in the T'Lona Sanctuary. He concentrated on the visage of the ancient Vulcan healer, revered for his teachings on applying the mind to aid the body in overcoming sickness and injury. Spock found power in the image, and peace in his meditation. His breathing slowed and his mind cleared.

Seconds passed, and then minutes, and then—

A sound stirred Spock from his reverie, like a wind sighing through a canyon. It came a second time, and he opened his eyes. On the diagnostic pallet, Captain Kirk had grown restless, his head moving sporadically from side to side, his arms twitching, though his eyes remained shut. He vocalized once, more a low moan than a word.

On the captain's temples, the neurological monitor gave no warning of any kind. Above him, the diagnostic panel recorded an increased respiratory rate, but no alarms activated. Still, unsure if the captain might be having a seizure, Spock sped out of the alcove.

At the workspace in the center of the main intensive care compartment, he addressed the two medical personnel there, a Denobulan woman and a human man. "Captain Kirk is not conscious, but he is moving about on his pallet," he said. "Since he has suffered trauma to his brain, I thought he should be checked."

Before Spock had even finished speaking, both people had risen from their chairs. "Let's take a look then," said the woman as both she and the man left the work space and started toward the captain's alcove. "I'm Doctor Lexit, by the way," the woman said as she walked. "This is Nurse Fenster."

Spock said nothing, the introductions incongruous to him under the circumstances. But as he followed the doctor and nurse into the alcove, Lexit said, "And you are?"

"Commander Spock," he said. On the pallet, he saw the captain still shifting around.

"Spock?" the doctor said as she bent over the captain and examined the neurological monitor. The nurse took up a position on the other side of the pallet. "First officer of the *Enterprise*, right?" Lexit asked before gazing up at the diagnostic panel. "I saw the ship in the repair dock. Looks like you were fortunate to get here in one piece."

Again Spock did not respond. He watched as the doctor picked up a scanner and tricorder and started to examine the captain, who murmured again, though nothing intelligible. "Trouble with the Klingons?" she asked.

"Doctor," Spock said, "I am not at liberty—"

"Nurse, four cc's of improvoline," Lexit said, as though Spock had not even spoken.

Fenster pulled open a medical pouch that hung from his waist. From it, he extracted a hypo, to which he then attached an ampoule. He adjusted the device's setting, then handed it across to the doctor. Lexit held the hypo up herself and rechecked the setting. "Captain Kirk is just dreaming, Commander Spock," she said. "All of his neurological and other readings are consistent with that and normal. We want him to rest more peacefully, though, so I'm going to give a small dosage of sedative." She reached down and injected the improvoline into the captain's arm, through the orange patient's jumpsuit he wore.

"Edith," Jim whispered.

Spock felt as though he'd been stabbed. All of the emotions he'd been experiencing in recent days, and all the way back to his second encounter with the Guardian, even back to his *first* encounter, came charging back. He could focus on only one thought: *What have I done?*

"Commander Spock, are you all right?" Lexit asked, staring over at him. Atop the diagnostic pallet, he saw, the captain's sleep had calmed, his body no longer moving about.

"Thank you for your attention to Captain Kirk," he said as evenly as he could, and not answering her question. "I will be returning to my quarters now." He left without waiting for a reply, hurrying back through intensive care and the infirmary's outer office. He hied through the corridors, heading for his guest cabin.

But beyond that, he didn't know where he would go.

III

The Timeless Moment, Never and Always

If you came this way,
Taking any route, starting from anywhere,
At any time or at any season,
It would always be the same: you would have to put off
Sense and notion. You are not here to verify,
Instruct yourself, or inform curiosity
Or carry report. You are here to kneel
Where prayer has been valid. And prayer is more
Than an order of words, the conscious occupation
Of the praying mind, or the sound of the voice praying.
And what the dead had no speech for, when living,
They can tell you, being dead: the communication
Of the dead is tongued with fire beyond the language of
    the living.
Here, the intersection of the timeless moment
Is England and nowhere. Never and always.

—T. S. Eliot,
Little Gidding, I

TWENTY

Through caverns sculpted by primordial forces and made their own by Vulcans now dust for ages, T'Vora walked. She kept her pace slow, each hand wrapped about the opposite forearm and buried within the arms of her white robe. Behind her, to left and right, Elders Rekan and Sokel trailed along on their way to the traditional destination. The triumvirate's footfalls echoed thinly in the damp space, the cool of the subterranean labyrinth a lie that would be exposed out on the Fire Plains of Gol.

On the cave walls, symbols passed. Etched into the rock here and out on the high plateau, they had been recorded in no other known place on all of Vulcan—not in the land, not on parchment, not in the memories of the scions leading from the mists of prehistory to the present. And yet the ancient icons had given up their meanings, studied through to understanding by masters past. That knowledge now passed from one generation to the next, but only within the circle of adepts.

It had been argued that keeping such information the sole province of the masters flouted logic, and that the notion of privilege defied the rights of the people in a free society. T'Vora agreed, though she had never been invited to offer her opinions in a public forum. She also knew that, apart from the principle involved, the actual content of the primordial characters lacked relevance to modern Vulcan society. The figures told no story, provided no insights, recorded virtually nothing about those who had engraved them, but for their egocentric dedication to their own passions. That aspect of their existence had survived beyond them, though, and its impact on Vulcan history had long been understood. The contribution of uncontrolled ardor to the near self-annihilation of the entire culture had been well recorded during the Time of Awakening.

From up ahead, T'Vora felt the hot, dry breath of the lava-riddled plain. Soon, she would know if she had succeeded. After an adult lifetime administering the *Kolinahr*, she did not doubt her strengths and capabilities, and now, after more than nine seasons with Spock, neither did she doubt his efforts as aspirant. But the issue, as always, would have nothing to do with their toils; rather, it would hinge on their collective judgment. Had Spock been right to petition when he had, and had T'Vora made the right choice when she'd accepted it? Had she decided wisely then a second time, when she had reconsidered his candidacy halfway through the process and allowed him to continue? It could be reduced to a simple equation: if their shared judgment had been wise, then Spock would achieve *Kolinahr;* if not, then he would not.

As T'Vora climbed around a rising, arcing length of the cave, the shadowy surroundings grew clearer. Daylight reached her and she felt the chill of the underground fall away completely. In the distance, she heard the low snarl of molten rock flowing in pools and rivers. The Fire Plains awaited.

T'Vora emerged from the mouth of the cave into the scarlet tint of twilight. She peered upward at the huge likeness of a master shaped from fire red stone. With its back to the caverns, the statue stood astride shallow, multishaped rock ledges that had been crafted into steps. Incised with the olden glyphs, the stairway led downward, where a ribbon of the stonework reached out into the edge of the sweltering Gol plateau.

Beneath the great figure, T'Vora stopped, as did Rekan and Sokel behind her. Out on the plain, at the end of the sliver of wrought masonry, amid pools of boiling water and cauldrons of churning, liquefied rock, Spock waited. Clad in a long, sleeveless ceremonial tunic atop a brown robe, he kept his head down and his hands together in a pose of meditation. T'Vora had directed him to spend the day here in contemplation of what would come next. She had not told him what that would be, because she did not know.

Now they would all find out together.

T'Vora pulled her hands from within the sleeves of her robe, spread her arms wide, and raised them high. "The journey we have taken together, leading this aspirant, ends here," she recited to the two elders from a litany now thousands of years old. "Here, on these sands where our ancestors cast out their animal passions." Spock, too far away, would not hear. She delivered the words not in the language she normally used, but in that of Old Vulcan. "At this hour, on this day, we seek to invite the aspirant to join us in a world of reason. A world in which emotion has been shed, and where pure logic dictates all that we are and all that we do." She lowered her arms to her sides. "Elder Rekan," she said. Rekan stepped forward and turned to face T'Vora. "You will judge first."

"I will judge first, Master T'Vora," Rekan said, also in Old Vulcan. The elder turned again, back toward the high plateau of Gol. Then she descended the stairs, the taps of her footwear swallowed up by the vast plain.

T'Vora watched as Rekan paced out to Spock. When she arrived before him, she spoke to the aspirant. Spock then lowered himself to his knees, folded his hands before him, and raised his head to the elder. Rekan reached forward, her hand going to his face, her fingers setting in place to allow her to meld with him.

The connection lasted only minutes, but T'Vora knew that the duration held no indication of consequence. Failure to achieve *Kolinahr* could be detected in an instant or an eternity; likewise, success. There could be no reasonable expectation regarding the span of time required. The elders and then T'Vora herself would take as short or as long as needed to arrive at their individual determinations.

Spock did not move from his knees as Rekan withdrew her hand from his face. The elder walked back across the blistering stone, then mounted the steps. Without a word, she took her place to T'Vora's left.

"Elder Sokel," T'Vora said, and he moved to face her. "You will judge next."

"I will judge next, Master T'Vora," he replied. As Rekan had before him, Sokel made his way over to the aspirant beneath the gloaming sky. He spoke to Spock, then established a mind meld between them. This time, the link continued for more than twice as long as it had with Rekan, but again, T'Vora drew no conclusions from that fact. She simply waited for Sokel to return to his place at her right.

"I will now judge," T'Vora declared, and she started across the scored volcanic rock. All around, steam rose from water bubbling up from underground. The scent of sulfur clung to the air like the dampness had to the cave walls. Farther afield, lava roiled within fissures and vents.

As she reached Spock, her gaze met his. His features revealed no hint of emotion. In his time as aspirant, his hair had grown long and his skin more rugged. Some of the ancient symbols preserved in the walls of the caverns and out on the steps and here in the ground ornamented his tunic. "Spock," she said, "the journey we have taken together ends here. You have been an aspirant these many seasons, but that too will end. Today you will achieve the

Kolinahr or you will not. Regardless of the outcome, you will depart the Akrelt Refuge tomorrow and return to a life without these demands that you have asked of yourself, and that I have directed." She awaited his response.

"I understand, Master," Spock said, offering the ritual reply. "I am prepared."

"Your thoughts, then," she said. "Give them to me." She raised her hand to Spock's face. His flesh felt hot and coarse beneath her touch, but the sensations faded quickly as she sent the tendrils of her mind in search of his. "My mind to your mind," she said, her eyes closing. "My thoughts to your thoughts."

This became the first test, the first area in which to judge. Although a mind meld necessarily required a lowering of mental defenses, it could also be accomplished—and most often was—with some barriers left in place. If still an emotional being, Spock would reflexively strive to maintain his guard at some points, despite that, in these circumstances, logic commanded otherwise. As a master, T'Vora could compel the release of all his thoughts, though of course she would not; as his *Kolinahr* master, though, she would need access to those thoughts, and if he could not make them available to her, it would reveal a deficiency of either his reason or his control.

But T'Vora encountered no resistance. Since she had not melded with Spock recently or often—though they had frequently bridged—she had allowed for some small measure of opposition. Instead, the filaments of her mind at once floated freely, interlacing with Spock's. It had happened that quickly, that easily. Far evolved from the last time that they had melded, his discipline impressed her.

T'Vora floated in empty space, and knew it to be filled. She looked for that which she most recognized: herself.

Memories surrounded her in the next instant, and she chose from among them the first.

There, in the Akrelt Refuge, beneath the sculpture of T'Klass, standing at the altar, at the reliquary atop it. "Do not assure me," *she told him as he made his petition to her.* "The Kolinahr *is not a haven from what you feel . . . the purging of emotion is a serious matter . . . Spock, child of Sarek, child of Skon, your petition . . . is denied."* She reached forward and set the bell down atop the candle, extinguishing its flame.*

T'Vora sensed no resentment, no disappointment. The recollection came without ego, without color. She detected remembrance and fact, but no feeling.

She probed further.

There, to the Enterprise, *to the* Kobayashi Maru *test, sacrificing the needs of the one for the needs of the many.*

Spock slumped, and then died.

And then lived, in schism—

His body, revived by the Genesis Wave . . . growing unnaturally, at an accelerated pace. His mind . . . wiped clean, birthed again . . . with no training . . . with no conscious decision to control his emotions . . . felt fear and sadness, loneliness and longing and anger.

T'Vora immersed herself in the emotions, and found them extant in name only. Spock remembered what he'd felt as a function of intellect, but no more than that. Death came as detail, and rebirth as well, the first a logical choice, the second a logical consequence.

She probed deeper.

There, in the house in Shi'Kahr, as a boy, Spock hurting his mother, unwilling to tell her that he loved her . . . even though he did. Striving to be Vulcan and denying his human heritage, struggling to show that he belonged.

There, on the Forge, even before the kahs-wan, *seeking*

to prove himself through his own test of maturity and survival. I-Chaya dying in the desert, but the boy Spock rescued by the adult Spock.

There, by the glowing, organic form of the Guardian of Forever, knowing that he had altered the timeline to save himself, to save his mother. The soft, milky features of Edith Keeler, whom Jim had loved, who'd had to die, and Spock had never even considered looking for another way.

There, in the courtyard of the Federation embassy on Alonis, McCoy arriving to tell him of Jim's death. The sadness, compounded by the regret of having failed his friend.

T'Vora swept along the chain of sentiment, from one to the next. Where before she had unearthed substance, now she found only shadow. Everywhere, understanding replaced feeling, reason replaced response.

She probed on.

Spock kneeled on the ancient stonework, fashioned so long ago that its origins could not be traced in even the oldest Vulcan legends. His vestments bore the same inscriptions as those carved all around him, though he could not read them. Only the masters understood the meanings of the arcane symbols.

As the day faded above him and the heat began ever so slightly to recede, Spock collected himself. The three successive mind melds had left him tired, though not exhausted, uneven, but not unsteady. Now, he took the time he needed to order his mind, to return his thoughts and memories to their normal, protected state.

Spock had arrived here early this morning, before dawn, as directed by Master T'Vora. As the sun had risen, he had reflected on his experiences since entering into the *Kolinahr.* He had survived the demanding disciplines, as well as the harsh trials that had taken him to those levels of consciousness beyond the reach of confusion, fatigue, and pain. He had learned emotional control in a way he never before had, not even during his first *Kolinahr* all those years ago. Beyond that, he had found the path *through* his feelings, extracting from them their factual essence, and then stripping them away.

As dawn had risen, Spock had slipped effortlessly into the mind-cleansing meditation he had also perfected in his time studying with Master T'Vora. He knew as surely as he could that, after he faced her and the elders today, the master would call on him to join them in the world of pure reason. He felt no pride in the impending accomplishment, nor would he when its moment arrived. But reaching the end of this trek satisfied him.

Throughout the day, the heat of Gol had risen, the only lull during the time when the shadow of the massive statue above the steps had crept across his location. Now, in the dwindling light of dusk, the temperature ebbing, Spock peered upward, not at the sky, but at the face of the great sculpture. Beneath it, Master T'Vora and Elders Rekan and Sokel waited. They had each come forward and melded with him, then returned to their places on the stairs. With the individual links, he knew, each of them had concluded their long evaluation of his fitness for the *Kolinahr.*

Now, Spock's own personal time of awakening had come. Or it had not. He would soon find out.

He lifted himself to his feet. Across inscriptions out of antiquity, he walked forward, climbing the low steps when he came to them. At last, he stood before the master.

T'Vora raised her right hand in the traditional Vulcan greeting, and Spock responded in kind. In her other hand, he saw, the master held a token, a set of colored geometric shapes fitted together to form the Vulcan symbol that denoted an existence of pure logic. Spock knew that it would either be given to him or discarded. T'Vora wore such an icon on a chain around her own neck.

Spock sensed the echo of events. The setting and situation closely matched his experiences of more than two decades ago, when he had first endeavored to attain the *Kolinahr* under the guidance of Master T'sai. Back then, though, he had reached this point only to find himself affected by the consciousness of V'Ger. He expected nothing of that sort to occur again, but even if it did, he deemed himself more capable now of withstanding it. The route he had taken this time in order to reach this point had proven more arduous, his labors more thorough.

The master stepped forward, as did Sokel beside her. "Our ancestors cast out their animal passions here on these sands," she said in the Old Vulcan tongue. "Our race was saved by the attainment of *Kolinahr.*"

"*Kolinahr,*" Sokel droned, "through which all emotion is finally shed."

"You have labored long, Spock," T'Vora said. "Now receive from us this symbol of total logic."

After ten seasons—more than three Standard years—of effort and a lifetime of striving to live up to some measure of the Vulcan ideal, Spock had finally achieved success in this exemplar of his culture's rites. He felt—

Nothing.

Spock lowered himself to his knees. Master T'Vora moved closer, then draped around his neck the chain holding the *Kolinahr* emblem. "We welcome you into our world, Spock," she said.

Spock stood up. He peered to either side of T'Vora at the two elders who had accompanied him on this path, then back at the master. "I recognize the contributions all of you have made to this accomplishment." He did not offer his gratitude. T'Vora and Rekan and Sokel had cho-

sen to be guides for aspirants seeking the *Kolinahr,* and
after his petition had been accepted—as it clearly should
have been—they had simply and logically performed their
duties. One did not thank logic.

"Come share a repast with us," T'Vora said. "We will
mark the transition of this leg of your individual journey to
the next." She turned and started up the steps toward the
entrance to the caverns. Rekan and Sokel went after her,
and Spock followed behind.

In the morning, considering himself more a part of Vulcan society than ever before, Spock departed the Akrelt
Refuge to began his new life.

TWENTY-ONE

2297

Sarek sat at the table in the dining room and regarded his
son with equal measures of appraisal and curiosity. Just
yesterday, Spock had returned from Gol, where he had for
the past ten seasons pursued and ultimately achieved the
Kolinahr. During his time away, Sarek and Amanda had
not heard from their son, a consequence of the isolation required for his training. Spock had arrived unannounced
late last evening, and he had spent most of today out of the
house, but in the short amount of time Sarek had been able
to observe him, he had noted the changes in his demeanor
with ease.

So too had Amanda. Last night, as she and Sarek had
prepared for sleep, she had commented on how distant

Spock now seemed. He had been unable to disagree, but had also suggested that it might take their son some time to become completely acclimated to his new mind-set.

Now, as the three of them sat down to the evening meal—Sarek and Amanda opposite each other at the small, square table and Spock between them—Sarek detected a definite tension in his wife. Spock, quiet and impassive, displayed no signs of having recognized this himself yet. No matter Spock's emotional control, though, Sarek expected that his son would perceive and understand Amanda's anxiety and act accordingly.

As Sarek took a bite of the *pok tar* he had prepared, Amanda peered over at Spock. "So what was it like living at the Akrelt Refuge all this time?" she asked.

"Austere," Spock responded without looking up from his meal.

"'Austere,'" Amanda repeated, and Sarek could see that the response had not satisfied her. He decided to intervene.

"How did you find the experience of training with Master T'Vora?" he asked his son.

Spock looked up for a moment, as though considering his reply, but then he simply said, "Instructive."

"Spock," Amanda rebuked him. "Just because you've got complete mastery of your emotions doesn't mean you have to answer us with single words."

"I intended no offense," Spock said. "I merely sought to respond with concision."

"Concision is not required in these circumstances," Sarek said. "Indeed, since your mother and I are interested in learning about your life and your recent experiences, concision might prove a hindrance to that aim."

Spock appeared to think about this, and then he turned to his mother. "I lived a simple, uncomplicated life at the Akrelt Refuge," he said. "I took morning and evening meals, often began and ended my days in meditation, and spent most of the rest of my waking hours training with Master T'Vora and Elders Rekan and Sokel."

"How did you find your training now as compared with your first *Kolinahr?*" Sarek asked. The experiences of *Kolinahr* aspirants had always intrigued him.

"I found my training this time both more extensive and more intensive," Spock said.

"Necessarily, I would assume," Sarek said, "since you had another twenty years of personal experiences with which to deal."

"That is one reason," Spock said. "Another was the rigor with which Master T'Vora conducted the training, and a third, the strength of my own need for it."

"I see," Sarek said. Over the years, he had occasionally heard mention of T'Vora's severity.

"Well, I'm glad it's over for you," Amanda said, a comment to which Spock did not react.

The three ate quietly for a few minutes, until Amanda said that she would bring out the second course and left the dining room. She returned shortly with a tureen of *v'spora*, a chilled dish comprising a mixture of fruits and tubers. She set it down in the center of the table, and after Spock and Sarek had served themselves, she did the same.

As they ate, Sarek asked, "Were you able to speak with Doctor Nivol today?" This morning, before Amanda had risen, Spock had spoken of his intention to seek a meeting with the director.

"Doctor Nivol?" Amanda said, obviously surprised. "Of the Vulcan Science Academy? Are you thinking of taking a position there?" She sounded pleased by the prospect of Spock remaining on Vulcan. Sarek thought that she had probably expected him to return either to Starfleet or to the Bureau of Interplanetary Affairs.

Spock addressed his mother first. "I am thinking of pursuing a position at the Vulcan Science Academy, yes," he told Amanda. Then, to Sarek, he said, "I did visit the academy today, but Doctor Nivol was unavailable to meet with me. I did, however, speak with her assistant, and I was able to schedule a meeting with the director for the day after tomorrow."

"Did the assistant provide any information about what positions might be open to you?" Sarek asked.

"He mentioned only that there would be several teaching vacancies once the current session ends," Spock said.

"Oh, you're looking to teach?" Amanda asked, a gleam of delight in her eyes. She had been an educator herself when Sarek had first met her, and she obviously took pleasure in the notion of her son pursuing the same vocation. Spock had previously trained young officers at Starfleet, but Sarek suspected that Amanda had not viewed that in the same way she would a teaching post at an institution such as the VSA.

"I am not," Spock said. "The director's assistant simply cited that those positions would be open. When I speak with Doctor Nivol, I will inquire about the possibility of my doing research at the academy."

"Do you have a particular area of study in mind?" Sarek asked.

"I do have an interest in temporal physics," Spock said.

"I do not believe that the academy has a department devoted to that field," Sarek said, "nor much expertise among its faculty."

"You are correct," Spock said. "For which reasons I will also contact the Physics Institute on Tiburon and the Ristoche Foundation for Scientific Research on Epsilon Hydra Seven."

"Really, Spock?" Amanda said. "You were awarded the

Zee-Magnees Prize in quantum physics for your work on time particles, for goodness sake. I'm sure the academy will take you on."

"Mother," Spock said, "just because the University of Alpha Centauri chose to recognize the work that Doctor McCoy and I did does not mean that the Vulcan Science Academy will or should create a position for me if one is not available, or if my field of study does not serve the institution."

"Well it should mean that," Amanda maintained. "With all the research you've done and all your experiences in Starfleet, you'd be an asset to them."

"Not if there was no institutional interest in that field," Spock insisted.

"I disagree," Sarek said. "It is in the best interests of the Vulcan Science Academy to engage successful, high-profile researchers such as yourself. In addition to the strong possibility that such individuals will continue to do important work, it also draws attention to the academy itself, perhaps attracting other skilled scientists and instructors to it."

"While that may be true," Spock said, "it is also no guarantee that Doctor Nivol will offer me a position."

"Spock," Amanda said, clearly trying to be supportive, "I'm sure you'll be able to find something at the VSA that you'll like."

Sarek watched as Spock coolly raised an eyebrow. "I don't think so, Mother," he said.

"You wait and see," she said. "You're father's right. If there's nothing for you when you meet with Doctor Nivol, they'll create something for you."

"I meant that, if I take a position at the Vulcan Science Academy," Spock said, "I will not 'like' it." Amanda reacted as though she'd been slapped.

"It is not necessary to correct your mother," Sarek said, recognizing that Spock's disrespect had been unintentional, but nonetheless disapproving of it. "If she speaks imprecisely, it does not follow that you cannot understand her meaning."

"I'm not convinced I spoke imprecisely," Amanda argued, and Sarek could sense her pain. He thought that she did not hurt because of what Spock had said, but because of his *Kolinahr*, his new manner, and all that implied. "If you don't think you'll *like* doing research at the academy, why would you want to do it?" Her voice rose as she spoke.

"I have learned through experience that I am gratified by performing research within areas of interest to me," Spock said.

"*Gratify, like,*" Amanda said. "It's semantics. You're talking about something that fulfills your needs. It's the same thing."

"I am an individual with certain intellectual tendencies and strengths," Spock said, neither his calm expression nor his even tone changing. "One of those strengths is a scientific mind with an ability to perform research in various fields. By doing so, I can add to the body of knowledge of Vulcan and of the Federation."

"Yes, and that *gratifies* you, but you don't *like* it," Amanda said, but then she quieted and looked away. Sarek saw her take a breath before she continued. "I'm sorry, Spock," she said. "Obviously I would never deny you doing what you wish to do. . . . " Her words trailed off, and Sarek thought that she had stopped speaking because she'd realized that, if she could have, she *would* have denied Spock something that he had wished to do: attain the *Kolinahr*.

"Mother, I did not intend to upset you," Spock said, clearly attempting to defuse the situation, though his reserve did not alter in the slightest degree. "I wanted only to point out the distinction between *liking* something and—"

"Yes, yes, you don't have emotions anymore, I understand that," Amanda snapped back. "You had them and controlled them for most of your life, but that wasn't enough; you had to rid yourself of them entirely." Once more, she took a moment to settle herself. Then she pushed back from the table and stood up. "Now you don't . . . you *can't* . . . like anything," she said softly, "and I suppose that means that you don't love anything either."

"Mother, I—" Spock started, but Amanda turned and strode quickly from the room. Sarek looked after her and listened to her footsteps as she ascended the staircase to the second floor, then turned to face his son. "Most illogical," Spock said.

"She is your mother," Sarek said. "There is nothing logical about upsetting her."

"She has spent the majority of her life on Vulcan," Spock said. "She married a full Vulcan who'd achieved *Kolinahr,* and she is clearly happy in that relationship. Why then should she reject the course I have taken? And how can any of this be a surprise to her?"

"You are mistaken in some of what you say," Sarek noted, "and the fact of your *Kolinahr* needn't be unexpected in order for it to displease your mother."

"I did not intend to upset her," Spock said.

Though Sarek believed his son, he said, "But you did."

"Am I to deny who I am?"

"No, Spock," Sarek said. "But I would suggest that you should not deny who your mother is, either."

"Human," Spock said.

"And emotional," Sarek added. "But not inferior to you or to me or to any Vulcan. Only different."

"Father," Spock said, "I did not mean to imply that mother is inferior to anybody."

"Again, your intentions do not alter the facts of how your mother perceived your comments," Sarek said. "And, I must say, how I interpreted them as well."

Spock nodded. "Yes," he said. "I will apologize to her."

"As you should," Sarek agreed. "But I also think that you should go. The choice you have made has been hard on your mother. In all the time you were gone, she was concerned for you. Now that you are here and she sees that you are safe, she has the freedom to feel the pain of losing you."

"She has not 'lost' me," Spock said. "But she wants me to be something that I am not."

"She wants you to be something you were," Sarek said.

Spock shook his head from side to side, as though unable to make sense of Sarek's words or his mother's actions. "Illogical," he finally said.

"But nevertheless true," Sarek told him.

"Yes," Spock said, and then he rose from his chair. "I will apologize to my mother. Then I will leave."

"Let us know where you go," Sarek said, also standing. "Your mother will continue to be concerned about you."

"Of course," Spock said. He pushed his chair back in, then rounded the table and left through the same door as Amanda had. A moment later, Sarek heard Spock going up the stairs.

Sarek sat back down at the table, though he did not continue eating. He would wait until Spock had spoken with his mother and then departed. Then Sarek would go upstairs and console his wife.

Spock stood in his third-story lab on the T'Paal campus of the Vulcan Science Academy. A door in one short wall led into the corridor, while a window opposite peered from the outskirts of the city toward the gleaming skyline of the urban center. A long display screen lined one side wall, while the other contained a narrower display and a door that connected to Spock's office. A table presently strewn with data slates occupied the center of the lab, beside a computer terminal that connected directly to the many VSA research databases located across the planet.

Spock gazed steadily at the end of the long display, at the final set of the hundreds of equations handwritten—along with copious amounts of text—in multiple columns across its entire length. He stood with his arms folded over his chest and a stylus clutched in one hand. "I am uncertain how to interpret this result," he said.

"From an applied perspective," said Dr. Vorant, "it does not appear valid." Two decades younger than Spock, with dark skin and dark eyes, the mathematician had come here at his request. Now, she stepped forward from beside Spock and pointed at several symbols on the display. "For this summation to approach infinity when this variable approaches one is not only counterintuitive, it appears to contradict the laws of the physical universe."

"That is how I read these final equations as well," Spock said. "The difficulty with that interpretation is that I have verified my calculations and reasoning six separate times." He motioned down the span of the display, all of it covered with a portion of the complex mathematics that he had developed over the course of the past two seasons.

Dr. Vorant paced away from him along the wall, peering at the equations. As she did, she raised a finger to her lips, a habit Spock had noticed during other encounters with her. "Manifold substantiations of a proof do not preclude an error having been made and overlooked," she said. "This is particularly true when the substantiations are performed by the same individual who wrote the proof."

"Of course," Spock said. "In this case, though, not only have I confirmed my result numerous times, I have also employed two completely distinct methodologies to achieve that result."

Vorant faced him from the far end of the lab. *"Distinct* methodologies?" she said. "From the start of your calculations?"

"Yes," Spock said.

"And for how much of the proof?" Vorant wanted to know.

Spock moved forward and reached for the controls at the corner of the display. He tapped a button to bring up a different screen. "This," Spock said after the display had blinked and redrawn with different information, "is the beginning of the proof utilizing the first methodology."

Vorant stepped back and studied the display. After a few moments, she said, "All right."

Spock worked the controls again, and once more the contents of the screen changed. "This is the beginning of the second proof."

Vorant scrutinized the display. "Yes," she said at last. "I can see that you've proceeded from totally disparate starting points, utilizing totally different tactics."

"The proofs also remain distinct through thirty-nine screens of one and forty-three screens of the other," Spock said. "The final eight screens are fundamentally the same."

"That would strongly suggest that, if there is an error, it would likely be found in those last screens, where the two proofs converge," Vorant said.

"Normally I would agree," Spock said. "In this case, though, the final eight screens contain the steps least complex, most straightforward, and easiest to validate."

"Obviously you require an independent observer to certify your result," Vorant said, walking back across the lab toward Spock. "Or to find the flaw in your calculations."

"That is why I requested you to come here," Spock said. "Would you be willing to provide such an evaluation for me?"

Vorant glanced back at the display. "Not right now," she said. "Not for this amount of work. I'm currently developing a solution for Valtuperan n-spaces. But if you are willing to wait for approximately three weeks, I will be able to examine your proofs then."

"That will be sufficient," Spock said. Although he'd been conducting research at the VSA in T'Paal for less than a Standard year, he'd already gained enough familiarity with the mathematics faculty to judge Dr. Vorant the most skilled among them. He would prefer to wait for her assistance than to immediately obtain somebody else's.

"Very well, then," Vorant said. "When I have completed my own work, I will contact you to obtain copies of the proofs."

After Vorant had gone, Spock redisplayed the last page of his proofs and again inspected the result. He understood that, even with his repeated checks and separate methodologies, he might well have committed an error—or errors—somewhere within his calculations, but he also thought it possible that he simply failed to understand how to properly interpret the result. Still, as he stood and studied the final set of equations, he could see no way to reconcile them from a practical standpoint. There seemed no reasonable way to give credence to an infinite amount of energy accumulating at a single point in space-time.

As afternoon faded toward evening, Spock remained in his lab and continued to ponder the issue. When through the window he saw the shadows growing longer on the ground, the last of the day beginning to fade, he deactivated the display and went into his neighboring office. From atop his desk, he retrieved his personal data slate, on which he had already downloaded his work. He then left the building and headed for his apartment.

As Spock strode from the campus and onto the pedestrian thoroughfares of T'Paal that surrounded it, the question of how to unravel the meaning of his result remained at the forefront of his mind. It took thirty minutes for him to traverse the two and a half kilometers to the low-rise building in which he resided, during which time he had made no progress with the problem. Once he had climbed the stairs and arrived at his second-floor apartment, he opted to put it out of his mind for the time being.

Entering his one-room unit, Spock set down his data slate on a shelf beside the front door, then crossed past his bed to the alcove that served as a kitchen. He prepared for himself a bowl of *plomeek* soup. As he sat down at a small table to eat, he activated the display mounted on a nearby wall, setting it to the Vulcan comnet so that he could learn of the day's events.

After supper, Spock laid out a mat at the foot of his bed, placing a candle to each side. He then lighted an incense pack inside a glass diffuser. Kneeling, he breathed in the subtle, dry scents of the desert and began his evening meditation.

Several hours later, his mind clear and freshly centered, Spock snuffed the candles and readied himself for slumber. He changed into his nightclothes and performed his ablutions before settling into bed. In the darkness, with his eyes closed and his mind at peace, as he began to drift to sleep, a new thought suddenly occurred to him.

Rousing himself, Spock turned on a light and crossed the room to pick up his data slate. He took it to the table and sat down, then called up the end result of his calculations. His interpretation, as well as Vorant's, had led them to conclude that, under the conditions Spock had theorized, an infinite amount of energy would occupy a single point in space-time defined by a set of chronitons and chronometric particles, clearly an impossibility. But Spock now wondered if his final equations could be describing two *identical* points in space-time, two sets of chronitons and chronometric particles that precisely matched each other. If some form of connection existed between those two points—

Spock pulled the stylus from its magnetic seating atop the data slate and began making notes on the screen. Once he'd codified his thoughts, he worked through a series of supporting computations. Two hours later, he had delineated preliminary verification of the new interpretation of his result. Rather than having infinite energy at a single point in space-time, two identical points connected to each other in some physical way—say, via a subspace tunnel— would allow the infinite energy to converge across the infinite number of points along that connection. It would mean the complete annihilation of everything between the two matching sets of temporal particles, but it remained consistent with the laws of physics. Although Spock saw no practical means of setting up such a set of circumstances, that did not detract from his conclusion.

His proof would still need to be authenticated, but with his revised view of his result and the new calculation to support it, Spock didn't believe that would present any difficulties. Satisfied with his work, he deactivated the data slate and returned to bed. Within minutes, he fell into a dreamless sleep.

TWENTY-TWO

2298

McCoy walked through the narrow corridor, surprised to find himself nervous as—

Nervous as a bridegroom, he thought with a chuckle. He couldn't deny that his palms felt sweaty and that a hollow tingle danced in his stomach. As ridiculous as that seemed to him, he supposed it made sense. He hadn't seen Spock in five years, since the day of Jim's memorial service at Starfleet Academy, since they'd walked along the farm where their friend had grown up.

Thinking of Jim immediately dampened McCoy's spirit. He'd been gone five years now, and sometimes that fact still didn't seem real. McCoy wished that the invitation he'd come to personally deliver to Spock, he could also have given to Jim.

He arrived at the correct door and looked for a signal beside it. When he didn't see one, he reached up and knocked. While he waited for a response, McCoy peered up and down the corridor. The modesty of the surroundings surprised McCoy, though he didn't quite know why. Perhaps he felt that way because Spock's apartment in San Francisco, while hardly luxurious, had at least been in a nicer, more modern building than this.

Before him, the door swung open. Spock stood there in dark slacks and a gray shirt. "Doctor McCoy," he said. Although Spock had used his title in addressing him for all those years, it now suddenly sounded absurd to McCoy.

"You know what, Spock," he said. "We've known each

other for more than thirty years and your *katra*'s even spent time in my noggin." He tapped at his temple. "I think it's time you started calling me Leonard."

Spock gazed at him without any visible reaction. "What can I do for you?" he asked. His voice possessed a cold, detached character, one McCoy recognized from when they'd all gone back to the *Enterprise* during the V'Ger incident.

"Well, to begin with, how about you invite me inside?" McCoy said, keeping his tone light. When they'd all returned to the *Enterprise* back then, Spock had just undergone the *Kolinahr* discipline. Four years ago, Spock had contacted him to reveal that he'd returned to Vulcan for the same purpose, and when McCoy had gotten in touch with Sarek a few weeks ago, the ambassador had confirmed that his son had now completed the training. But even if Sarek hadn't said anything about it, McCoy would've been able to identify that fact simply from Spock's manner.

Now, Spock stepped aside to allow him entry, though with less than a welcoming air. Several biting comments occurred to McCoy, but he said none of them. He hadn't come all the way from Earth to trade gibes with Spock or to offer observations about the Vulcan way of life. He'd come because, even after their recent lack of communication, McCoy still considered Spock his closest friend.

McCoy walked into the apartment and across the room. Again he found himself surprised. A kitchen nook and a refresher opened off the single, small room that had few adornments beyond a bed, dresser, and table. McCoy saw a number of candles on a shelf, what appeared to be an incense diffuser, and a couple of Vulcan idols. "I love what you've done with the place," he joked, unable to stop himself. When he turned to look at Spock and saw his stern countenance, though, he regretted saying it.

"Have you come for a reason, Doctor?" Spock said. The question sounded more like an invitation to leave than to stay. Spock hadn't even closed the door.

It's good to see you too, Spock, McCoy thought, but he chose instead to ignore his friend's completely stoic demeanor. "Actually, I have come for a reason," he said. "A couple of reasons, in fact. First, I wanted to tell you something I didn't get a chance to say the last time we talked." He paused, but Spock said nothing. "The advice you gave me about going to Uhura at Starfleet Intelligence for your tricorder readings of the Guardian . . . I did that, and she got me the access I needed. I reviewed the recordings and . . . well, it helped me a lot, Spock. I mean, it really changed my life for the better, and I wanted to thank you for that."

Spock said nothing, reacted in no way at all. When McCoy waited, though, he finally said, "You are welcome, Doctor."

McCoy thought back to his reunion aboard the *Enterprise* with Jim and Spock and the rest of the crew during the V'Ger incident, and he recalled just how distant and aloof the Vulcan had been when he'd first come aboard. As best McCoy had been able to tell, that had been a direct result of Spock's *Kolinahr,* and he could only assume the same here. Back on the ship, though, Spock had eventually thawed, and McCoy hoped that would happen this time as well.

"There is something else?" Spock asked.

"Yeah, there is," McCoy said. He felt very uncomfortable, particularly with Spock standing beside the still open door. "I'm getting married."

Once more, Spock did not react.

"In some ways, I have you to thank for that as well, Spock," McCoy said. "After I reviewed the recordings, I

was able to rid myself of the terrible dreams I'd been having, and also really deal with a lot of personal issues. My
life is a lot better now because of that." He waited a moment for Spock to reply in some way, but it had become
clear that the Vulcan would remain taciturn. "Anyway,"
McCoy went on, "I came all this way from Earth because I
wanted to ask you to be my best man."

At last, Spock's mien changed, one of his eyebrows lifting. "'Best man,'" Spock echoed. "That is a position occupied during a human wedding ceremony?"

"Well, not *all* human wedding ceremonies," McCoy
said. "There are a lot of different traditions. This is one I
like. A best man or best woman stands with a groom during the ceremony and is usually responsible for a number
of other items, such as holding the bride's wedding ring
and offering a toast to the newly married couple." McCoy
took a step closer to Spock, wanting to emphasize his next
words. "The best man is also typically the groom's best
friend."

Despite the extreme reticence Spock had already
demonstrated, McCoy expected him to respond to the declaration of friendship. After a moment he did, but not in
the way that McCoy had anticipated. "Doctor," he said, "I
think that you would be better served by selecting somebody else as your 'best man.'"

In all the years that they'd traded taunting remarks
with each other, that they'd argued both for argument's
sake and about real and important issues, McCoy couldn't
recall ever having been intentionally hurt by Spock. It felt
like that now. "Is that your real reaction?" he said. "Or am
I just out of practice when it comes to our usual banter?"

"Doctor, as with you, my life has changed since last we
spoke," Spock said. "I have attained the *Kolinahr.* For that
reason, I do not believe that I would be well suited to take

on the role of 'best man' for you. Nor do I wish to take on such a role."

McCoy felt deeply wounded. "Spock, I . . . I don't know what to say," he admitted. "I know we've had our differences, but I always thought . . . I always thought we were friends."

Without altering his expression at all, Spock said, "We were."

The past tense told McCoy all that he needed to know. "I guess that's the answer then," he said. "Sorry to disturb you." He walked back across the room and out into the corridor. He turned back, though, stopping the door with the flat of his hand as Spock closed it behind him. He peered at his old friend—his former friend, he supposed—and said, "Have a *happy* life, Mister Spock." Then he turned and left.

Near the center of the busy reception hall, a cluster of dignitaries surrounded Sarek and Amanda. Observing from one side of the large high-ceilinged room, Spock recognized among the group the Gorlan, Tellarite, and Vian ambassadors, as well as several noted scientists from various worlds. He watched for any indications of conflict between his father and Ambassador Gorv, aware that tensions often ran hot between Vulcan and Tellarite officials, but he saw none.

Spock had just arrived at the gathering, a first-night welcoming reception for the conference guests. Hosted at the Vulcan Science Academy's main campus outside of Shi'Kahr, and cosponsored by the VSA and the Federation Science Council, the symposium had been organized for the purposes of highlighting current scientific trends, sharing new research, and discussing how best to disseminate and further such knowledge throughout the Federation. To those ends, both scientists and diplomats from across the Federation and beyond had been invited to attend.

Spock knew that, for his mother's sake, he must speak with his parents. During the past year, since he'd completed his *Kolinahr* training, he had only seldom visited or even talked with Amanda. After she had displayed her disappointment in the choice that he'd made for his life, he had apologized for having hurt her, though not for the path he had taken. His mother had ostensibly forgiven him, but their relationship had never recovered to what it had been prior to his *Kolinahr*—nor did he expect it to, given the circumstances. Still, Amanda did contact him from time to time, and Spock visited his parents' home occasionally to dine with them. More often, Sarek came on his own to T'Paal to share a midday meal with Spock. At this point, though, he hadn't had any contact with either one of his parents for more than a month.

After a while, the people arrayed around Sarek and Amanda broke into smaller groups and the couple headed away, crossing the hall to one of several buffet tables. Spock immediately paced through the crowd after them, arriving beside them as they each picked up a dish and began selecting food for themselves. "Mother," Spock said. "Father."

"Spock," Amanda said, looking up. She smiled, but in a way that could not totally hide the sadness she obviously still felt for her son. "We thought you might be here."

"No doubt, you are here representing the academy," Sarek said.

"Of course," Spock said. "A number of VSA researchers are here."

"Are you well?" his mother asked.

"I am," Spock said. "And you?"

"Oh, we're fine," Amanda said. "I've got a little bursitis

these days—" She flexed her right shoulder, wincing as she did so. "—that I need to have Doctor Soji take a look at, but otherwise we're doing well."

"What is the status of your research these days, my son?" Sarek asked.

"It is proceeding slowly of late," Spock said. "As you know, I have achieved theoretical results since I began at the academy, but I have recently encountered difficulties in attempting work on practical applications."

"You find the work challenging then?" Amanda asked.

"Yes, I do," Spock said. He noticed, not for the first time, the pains his mother took to inquire about his life in ways that did not presuppose an emotional component; she had asked if he found his research challenging, for example, but not how he liked it. "And you, Father, how is your work progressing?" Spock said. "Do you have any upcoming ambassadorial missions scheduled?"

"Yes," Sarek said. "Next month, your mother and I will be traveling to the world of Verdanis, where I am to meet with the leader of the Terratins. You are familiar with the colony, are you not?"

"Yes, I am," Spock said. "A group of humans settled on a planet orbiting the star Cepheus, where spiroid epsilon waves contracted their molecular structure, reducing their physical size to approximately three-twentieths of a centimeter. The mutation impacted their DNA and became permanent with subsequent generations. When their planet was threatened by extreme volcanic activity, the crew of the *Enterprise*—of which I was a part—transplanted their entire city to Verdanis." Spock did not find a need to mention that the *Enterprise* crew themselves, for a brief time, had also been reduced in size. "I'm curious," he said. "How do you intend to interface with the Terratins?"

"It is my understanding," Sarek said, "that they have

constructed large—by their standards, gargantuan—accommodations for visitors to their world. In those facilities, they have also created sophisticated holographic communications equipment that will provide a means of interacting with them in a virtual way."

"Ingenious," Spock said. "And a logical solution to the practical issue of their relations with beings so much larger than they are."

"It's also better than the other alternative they offered," Amanda said. "They told your father that they could reduce him to their size, although I think they were joking."

"It is possible that they were not," Spock said. "When the—"

"Ambassador Sarek, Lady Amanda," a voice interjected loudly from directly behind them. They all turned—Spock's parents still holding partially filled plates of food—to see a portly Bolian clad in a many-colored tunic. To Spock's surprise, he clamped a hand onto the shoulders of both Sarek and Amanda. "I was hoping I'd get to see the two of you here."

"Ambassador Feliq," Amanda said at once. "How very nice to see you again."

"Ambassador, welcome to Vulcan," Sarek said with a bow of his head. "May I present our son, Spock."

"Spock," the ambassador blustered, and he took his hand from Amanda's shoulder and slapped it onto his. "Wonderful to meet you. Diplomat or scientist? Or are you just raiding the party to see your parents?"

"I am a researcher in temporal physics with the Vulcan Science Academy," Spock said.

"Temporal physics, eh?" Feliq said. "Are you sure you have time for that?" The ambassador threw back his head and guffawed, his cartilaginous tongue protruding from his mouth. When he settled back down, he said, "I didn't mean to interrupt your family reunion—"

"Not at all," Spock said, perceiving a means of withdrawing gracefully. "I was going to seek out some of the other guests." He bowed his head in deference to Feliq, then backed away, sliding his shoulder from beneath the ambassador's hand. As he turned and started across the reception hall, he heard his mother ask after the Bolian's wife and co-husband, but Feliq's response was lost to the purr of the other conversations all around.

Spock crossed to the far corner of the room, where he ordered a cup of spice tea from a server. Once he'd received it, he took a place against the wall and surveyed the large assemblage. He had not misled Ambassador Feliq when he'd told him that he wanted to look for other guests. Spock knew that the eminent Deltan quantum physicist Laujes had accepted an invitation to the conference, as had Saurian temporal theorist Ziresk Chot. Spock wished to meet and speak with both of them.

As he peered about the crowd, he saw two people, by appearances human, walking in his direction. Tall and dignified, the woman had short, spiky red hair and wore an elegant, calf-length black dress. The man, slightly shorter, had dark brown hair, cropped short, and wore a tuxedo. Both appeared human, though Spock recognized neither one of them. Nevertheless, they both strode directly up to him.

"Spock," the woman said in a soft, familiar way, and he identified the owner of the voice at once: Alexandra Tremontaine. He had not seen her in five years, since she had located him at the Port of Los Angeles when he'd been on his way back to Vulcan.

"Ambassador," Spock said. "Forgive me, I did not recognize you."

"Quite all right," she said. "It's been a few years." Glancing over to the man, she said, "This is Doctor Senofsky, professor of microbiology at Cambridge University, and more importantly, my escort for this evening."

"How do you do, Mister Spock," Senofsky said, raising his hand and politely offering a Vulcan greeting. Spock returned the gesture.

"Welcome to the Science Academy," he said.

"Spock . . . Spock . . . " Senofsky said. "Your name sounds familiar to me. May I ask what field you're in?"

"Currently, I am conducting research in temporal physics," Spock said.

"Hmmm," Senofsky said. "That doesn't ring a bell."

"Perhaps you would've been able to place him," Alexandra said, one side of her mouth curling upward, "if Spock had mentioned that he'd also traveled back in time to the twentieth century to bring a pair of humpback whales into the present."

A look of realization appeared on Senofsky's face. "Of course," he said. "Forgive me for not remembering your name."

"It is of no consequence," Spock said.

"Maybe not to you," Senofsky said, "but I and several billion other people owe you our lives."

"I did merely what the situation called for," Spock said.

"You're too modest, sir," Senofsky said. "Thank you." Spock acknowledged the doctor with a nod.

"What are you drinking?" Alexandra asked, pointing at Spock's cup.

"Spice tea," he replied. "It is of Vulcan origin."

"Not quite what I had in mind," she said. "Vulcan port sounds more like it." She turned to Dr. Senofsky. "Would you mind getting me a glass?"

"I'd be happy to," he said, and then he looked to Spock.

"If you'll excuse me." Again, Spock nodded, and Senofsky started away. Alexandra watched him go.

"He's a good man," she said, clearly referring to Senofsky. "We've been seeing each other for a few months now." She turned back to face Spock. "He's not the one, though. We have a nice relationship, but we just don't have that connection." She held up her hands before her and folded her fingers together, obviously attempting to illustrate her point.

Spock did not know how he should react, so he said nothing.

"You've changed," Alexandra said, a statement of fact that did not seem intended as an indictment. "I can tell."

"I have changed," Spock agreed. "I have completed the *Kolinahr.*"

"Yes, I can see that," she said. "I suppose it would be foolish of me to ask if you're happy now."

"You would simply be asking a question to which you already know the answer," he told her.

"Of course," she said calmly. "What would the logical equivalent be?"

Spock sensed a pain that Alexandra did not show, and he wondered if their link still endured. Whether he could actually discern her thoughts or because he simply understood her, he thought he perceived what she wanted to know. "I am living the life I wanted to live," he said. "I am satisfied by my work, and through the *Kolinahr,* I secured a peace within me that I had never before known."

Alexandra seemed to think about this for few moments, and then she unexpectedly smiled. "I'm pleased for you, Spock," she said. "Truly. Once, you allowed me a glimpse of the tumult within you. That you've managed to find peace . . . I'm really happy for you."

"Thank you," Spock said. He no longer possessed any

emotions for Alexandra, but he could still note how uncommon she was.

"Well, I'd better go find my date," she said. "I'm sure you and I will be running into each other during the course of the conference." She turned and left.

Two weeks later, the symposium concluded, but in all that time, Spock did not see Alexandra again.

TWENTY-THREE

2311

Amanda walked through the house, headed for the communications panel in the niche at the rear of the great room. Though still early in the day, she intended to contact Spock. She normally wouldn't attempt to reach him so early in the day, but her new plans would see her departing Vulcan later this morning, and she wanted to speak with him before she left.

As she reached the recess that housed the comm equipment, Amanda felt a pang of sorrow, as she still did from time to time when it came to her son. Most days, she tried to tell herself that her sadness stemmed from seeing less of him now, when he resided on Vulcan, than she had when he'd traveled the galaxy. She'd been making that claim, out loud and in her own head, for years now, ever since her son had returned to his home planet. Spock had always disputed her claim, missing the point that even she knew that her protestations held no water. But after Spock had completed his *Kolinahr,* their relationship had changed—for her, in a deeply painful way. In that regard, her assertion rang true: she saw less of her son now than previously, because without feelings, he had less to show her.

On her worst days, Amanda accepted that the Spock she had known for the first six decades of his life no longer existed. On her best, she clung to the notion that, *Kolinahr* training or no, the son she had raised into a man still lived within the emotionless shell he had cultivated. Regardless, she had striven, particularly in the last five or six years, to put aside her feelings—a distinctly Vulcan tactic—and improve her relationship with Spock. She had been successful, for the most part, and in the months when she and Sarek spent time at home on Vulcan, Spock had begun to visit them more often.

As Amanda sat down before the monitor, she worried about her son. For almost a decade and a half, since his return from the Akrelt Refuge, he had lived a mostly solitary life. He avowed that his research satisfied him, and she knew he believed that, but she wanted something more for him. Illogical, she knew, but true anyway.

She keyed in the sequence to reach Spock at his apartment. The screen blinked to life, displaying the logo of the Vulcan comnet. She waited while an indicator light confirmed the attempted connection. After just a moment, the screen flashed again, and this time, the image of her son appeared.

"Good morning, Mother," he said. Behind him, she could see on his small table a half-eaten plate of what looked liked *gespar*. Clearly she'd interrupted his morning meal.

"Good morning, Spock," Amanda said. "I'm sorry to be contacting you so early, but I didn't want to disturb you at the academy. Do you have time to talk?"

"I will be leaving for my office shortly," Spock said, "but I have time to speak with you now."

"Good," Amanda said, "because I wanted to share the good news with you before I left Vulcan."

"Is everything all right?" Spock asked. He spoke, as always, in a monotone and with an unchanging expression. Often, when Amanda found herself feeling down about her son's unemotional life, it had been Spock's wholly dispassionate manner that had provoked such a reaction. Now, she simply ignored it, focusing instead on her own excitement.

"Yes, everything's fine," she said. "Better than that, actually. I learned late last night that the Primrose Gallery in Paris has agreed to exhibit my latest artwork."

"That is a noteworthy accomplishment," Spock said, betraying no sign that he actually thought so, other than via the content of his words. "When will this take place?"

"The show will open in a little over two weeks," she said, "which means that I barely have enough time to pack up all of my work, transport it to Earth, and arrange its display. That's why I'm leaving in a few hours."

"Will Father be with you?" Spock asked.

"No," Amanda said, trying to keep the disappointment from her voice. "He's committed to hosting a delegation from Catulla here on Vulcan for two of the first three weeks that my exhibition will be running."

"Will he be joining you for the final week?" Spock asked.

"No, because he's got another commitment then," Amanda told him. "And that's the second reason I wanted to talk with you before I left. The day after I return from Earth is my birthday, and I've convinced your father that we should celebrate it with a party. After the Catullans leave and before I arrive home, he'll be preparing for it."

"A birthday party," Spock said. His impassive manner made it sound either as though he'd never before heard of such a concept, or as though he wanted nothing to do with it.

"Yes, a birthday party, and I want you to be there," Amanda told him. "I know it's not a Vulcan tradition, but since I'm going to be one hundred, I wanted to do it anyway. Honestly, Spock, with all the time you spent in Starfleet and among humans, you must be at least familiar with birthday parties."

"I am, Mother," Spock said, "although it has been some time now since I have participated in one."

"You don't really have to participate," Amanda said, "other than to show up at the house and wish me a happy birthday."

Spock paused for only an instant, in which time Amanda assumed that he weighed all of the factors relevant to his attendance at her party. Vulcans did not typically celebrate birthdays, and especially not with parties. There would be many people there, some of them nonhuman and emotional, necessitating unwanted interactions for Spock. The event would fundamentally be a waste of his time, which he could instead be devoting to his research. He would balance all of that, and probably more, against just one fact: his mother wanted him to attend.

Even on Vulcan, Amanda thought, *that calculus should add up in only one way.* In the next second, Spock confirmed that it did.

"I will be there, Mother," he said.

"Thank you, Spock," she said. "That will be the best present I could possibly receive." An awkward silence followed, as often happened between them. As usual, Amanda forced her way through it. "Well, that's all. I'll see you when I get back."

"Mother," Spock said, and he seemed to search for the

right words. "I hope that your exhibition is a success."
With the effort it required of Spock to decide what to say,
and with the detachment evident in his tone and on his
face, his wish actually hurt her more than it heartened her.

At least he chose to make the effort, Amanda told herself.
"Thank you, Spock," she said. She reached for the controls
and ended their connection. The ensign of the Vulcan comnet appeared again, and then the screen went blank.

Amanda sat at the comm equipment for a few moments, staring at the empty monitor. In her mind, though,
she saw neither the display nor the image of her son on it.
Instead, she saw Spock at the age of five, coming home
from school and trying so desperately to hide the pain he
felt at having his classmates deem him not truly Vulcan.
She had cried for him back then, understanding the depth
of his wounds. He no longer experienced those hard, hard
emotions, and that of course pleased Amanda. But it also
saddened her, because she knew that her son would also
never again experience the reverse: love and joy and all
those sentiments that brightened life.

Let it go, she thought, as she had so many times before.
Spock is who he is, and you can't do anything about it.

As Amanda rose from the comm equipment and started
for her studio at the side of the house, where she would
begin preparing her artwork for shipment, she also knew
that, in one way, none of what she thought about Spock
mattered. For however he chose to live his life, he was still
her son. Even if he couldn't love her, she still loved him.

At the table in his apartment, Spock carefully wrapped
the box in the decorative paper that he'd ordered shipped
from Earth. Though he no longer subscribed to the human
tradition of celebrating birthdays, his mother did. He knew
that she would be disappointed if he did not attend her

party—something that he had already agreed to do—and he knew further that a gift from him would make her happy. Consequently, it seemed only logical that he should arrive at her gala with a present in hand.

As he listened to the Vulcan comnet report current events on his wall-mounted display—a shuttle accident, a historic archeological find on the slopes of Mount Tar'Hana, the upcoming summit with the Tzenkethi—Spock also calculated just how to fold the colorful paper around the box. Several weeks ago, at the opening of his mother's art exhibition in Paris, he had contacted the proprietor of the Primrose Gallery to ask if any special materials had been created for Amanda's show. When Spock had learned that a commemorative program had been printed, he'd requested that one be sent to him. It had arrived last week, and he'd taken it to a local artisan and had it framed as a keepsake for his mother.

Spock finished wrapping the box, then prepared to leave for his parents' home. When he had spoken with his father yesterday, Spock had agreed to arrive several hours before the celebration so that he could assist with any final tasks that needed to be done. He had thought to wear casual clothes, but Sarek had informed him that Amanda wished her party to be an elegant affair, and so she hoped that guests would dress accordingly. He therefore gathered his ceremonial robes and tucked them into a carryall, along with his gift.

As Spock reached to deactivate the comm display, a red indicator light began flashing, signaling a break in the broadcast. His hand hovered by the controls as he waited to learn the content of the bulletin. On the monitor, a map of space appeared, depicting the Alpha and Beta Quadrants, with Federation and Romulan territories labeled and highlighted.

"From around an area of space that Starfleet identifies as the Foxtrot Sector," said a commentator, *"reports are telling of a catastrophic event."* The Foxtrot Sector, Spock knew, bordered the Romulan Neutral Zone and contained thirteen manned Starfleet outposts. A moment later, an inset appeared on-screen, illustrating those facts. *"Indications are that the entire sector has been decimated by some form of massive explosion. Initial estimates of the dead stand at four thousand."*

Spock found the news unfortunate, not only for the terrible loss of life, but also because of the devastating impact such an incident could have on galactic politics. Tensions had been running extremely high for some time now among the Federation, the Romulans, and the Klingons, and no matter what had caused the destruction of the Foxtrot Sector, it could readily serve as a flashpoint for the commencement of hostilities.

"Although neither the Federation nor Starfleet has yet issued a statement," the commentator continued, *"the Klingon Empire has claimed the cause of the destruction to be a Romulan ship that crossed the Neutral Zone into Federation space, where it attacked a Starfleet outpost. Klingon Chancellor Azetbur has branded the attack an act of terrorism and cowardice. There has been no response thus far from the Romulans."* The commentator paused, then concluded, *"More details will be provided as they become available."*

Spock deactivated the display with a touch. He considered contacting his parents about what had happened, but decided against it. If his mother had not yet learned of the events in the Foxtrot Sector, then he did not want to inform her. Such news could easily cast a pall over her enjoyment of her party, or even cause her to cancel it.

Picking up the carryall, Spock left his apartment and

walked the two and a half kilometers to the Vulcan Science Academy campus there in T'Paal. He made his way to the academy transporter, from which he beamed to the primary VSA facility on the outskirts of Shi'Kahr. Once outside, he found an airpod to take him on the short journey to his parent's house.

When he arrived, he approached the front gate and pressed the signal pad in the wall beside it. He waited for several seconds, but the gate remained closed. He peered through it into the courtyard and saw the front door of the house open, but he saw neither his father nor his mother. It also surprised him that he did not see any birthday decorations. He could only surmise that his parents had gone out this morning, perhaps to perform some last-minute errand needed for the party.

Returning to the controls beside the gate, Spock touched the pad that activated the retina scan. A beam of light flashed into his eye, verifying his identity. When it ceased, the two sections of the gate divided and opened inward. Spock followed the slate path that snaked through the courtyard to the front door.

When he stepped inside, he immediately sensed something wrong. In the great room, where Sarek and Amanda had always held all of their gatherings, Spock saw not a single preparation that would indicate that a large number of guests were expected later today. More than that, though, the house seemed . . . empty.

But not just empty, Spock thought. Empty in an unnatural way. He perceived . . . something . . .

"Father?" he called. "Mother?" He heard no response.

Peering around, Spock made his way across the great room, past the fountain at its center, and over to the communications panel in the recess at its rear. If his parents had needed to leave for some reason, he thought that perhaps they had left him a message. When he activated the comm display, though, he saw nothing.

Spock walked from the great room into the main living area of the house. He gazed into the sitting room to his left and saw nothing out of the ordinary, but also no sign of his parents. The hall that led to his mother's studio led away to his right, and Spock traversed it. He reached the doorway that opened into the geodesic addition to the house and looked inside. Several of the sculptures on which his mother had recently worked no longer stood where he'd last seen them, no doubt packaged up and shipped to Earth for her exhibition. He did not see Sarek or Amanda.

As he headed back down the hall, though, Spock heard a sound from behind him, a soft noise that he could not identify. He returned to the studio and listened for a moment. The sound did not come again, and he paced deeper into the room.

That was when he saw his father.

Hidden behind a work table at the center of the studio, Sarek sat on the floor, slumped against the wall. "Father," Spock said, taking a step toward him.

Sarek lifted his eyes then, and Spock saw an expression on his face he had never before seen there. His father's eyes looked hollow and didn't seem to focus. Spock could only describe his appearance as one of terrible sadness.

"Father," Spock said again, going over and crouching down beside him. "Are you all right?"

Sarek peered up at him, and finally he appeared to see Spock. "No, my son," he said. "I am not all right."

"Are you injured?" Spock asked. He reached for his father's legs, feeling for any obvious break.

"No, I am not physically hurt," Sarek said, taking hold of Spock's shoulder with one hand. "You have not heard the news?"

The news? Spock thought, and the bulletin he'd heard on the comnet recurred to him. "Are you speaking of the apparent terrorist attack in the Foxtrot Sector? It is a regrettable loss of life."

"No," Sarek said. "Your mother . . . "

"Where is my mother?" Spock asked. He knew that Amanda had been scheduled to return from Earth yesterday.

"Your mother . . . was killed this morning," Sarek said. A tear trailed down his cheek. "A shuttle accident."

The revelation startled Spock. Though he had detected something wrong when he'd first entered the house, he had never anticipated anything like this. He felt—

Nothing.

His *Kolinahr* training held.

TWENTY-FOUR

2311/2312

Beneath the fiery sky, on the plain of Vel'Sor, in the land held by his family for more than thirty generations, Sarek let go of Amanda. He stood at the center of the megalithic structure, atop a low platform, beside a circle of burning coals that represented so much: his wife's lost *katra,* their connection to each other, their life together. Even now, thirteen days after the shuttle crash that had taken her from him, after confirmation that she had indeed been aboard the doomed craft, Sarek battled his emotions with his logic, and he did not always win. In his many years, he had never faced a more difficult challenge.

Silently, he gazed about the circular grounds, at the dozen members of his extended family who had come here today and who now ringed the periphery of this ancient place. Behind them, red granite pillars rose out of the hard soil, topped by horizontal slabs of stone. The breeze blew hot here, the air a furnace even by Vulcan standards. The chimes scattered around the structure infused the environs with a continuous peal.

"What we have experienced here today," Sarek said, his voice sounding stronger than he felt, "has come down from the time of the beginning, without change." He addressed all of those present, but as he had for most of the long ceremony, he peered into the steady gaze of T'Pau. "This is the Vulcan heart. This is the Vulcan soul. This is our way."

Sarek bent and hefted the large ewer that sat beside the bed of white-hot coals, the searing temperature nearly blistering the flesh of his arms. Holding the antique container away from his body, he angled it downward. Water spilled from its mouth into the pit. The coals hissed as they drowned, gushing clouds of white steam rising upward. Sarek poured until he upended the ewer. Then, its contents spent, he set it back down.

"As it was at the time of the beginning," he said, "so it is now." He reached behind the irregular hexagonal shield suspended above the doused coals and took hold of the small mallet stored there. With a long, measured breath, he struck the metal surface, which tolled a deep, reverberant sound. "It is done," Sarek said. He dropped the mallet to the ground.

About him, the family moved. First, those attending T'Pau lifted her palanquin and carried her from the ritual site. The others followed next, all but Spock, who waited until only he and Sarek remained. Then, as tradition dictated, Spock crossed his hands atop his chest, and then he too turned and exited the grounds.

In this place where he and Amanda had joined together in matrimony, where they had brought their son at the age of seven to be bonded for the *pon farr* with T'Pring, Sarek stood alone and felt lost. *It is the natural order of things,* he told himself. *Each life begins, each life ends.*

For all his life, he had believed that his reason would always prove victorious over his emotions, but right now, his arguments to himself went for naught. Those emotions that he had for so long mastered would no longer be denied. Oddly enough, his logic prescribed that he accept the reality of his situation, which necessarily included the loss of control over his feelings.

Amanda gone, her katra *lost,* Sarek thought. He knew that her wishes had been that, upon her death, her organs be donated to the medical system on Earth for patients in need, with the rest of her remains given to a medical school for educational purposes. But effectively nothing of her body had been left after the crash.

Around Sarek, hot gusts blew, perpetuating the light clink of the chimes. He stepped down from the platform and crossed toward the square-arched entryway. The dirt grated beneath his shoes.

Outside the great stone ring, Spock waited. Custom held that, when possible, the immediate family of the deceased walk together from this place back to their home, but Sarek suspected that his son would have waited for him even were that not the case. Since Amanda's death, Spock had stayed at the house with him, taking leave from his position at the Vulcan Science Academy. He had assisted with numerous practical matters—contending with the guests to Amanda's party, preparing meals, rescheduling Sarek's upcoming ambassadorial agenda—but perhaps more important, he had provided a calming influence in a time of virtual madness.

As Sarek strode away from his family's ancestral land, Spock fell in beside him. "Father," he said, "though it is tradition, you need not walk all the way home."

"I am aware of that, my son," Sarek said. "My emotional control has failed me, not my logic." They had arrived here for the ceremony via public transporter from Shi'Kahr, and they each carried recall devices for the return trip. The rest of the family had arrived and departed in the same manner.

"It is a long journey," Spock said. "I am concerned for your health. You have been under tremendous strain, and with your surgically repaired heart—"

"We will walk," Sarek said, continuing along. "It is to honor your mother, a symbolic passage that avows that we leave her neither quickly nor easily."

"Very well," Spock said.

They moved along in silence, each with his own thoughts. During the time Spock had remained with Sarek at the house, it had mostly been like this. They had spoken little, no doubt because there had been little to say. Spock's *Kolinahr* training had allowed him to retain complete restraint of his emotions, and so there had been no need for Sarek to counsel him in any way. And although Sarek himself had been mired in sorrow, Spock's own perfect control made him an imperfect vehicle to discuss sentiment. Regardless of all that, what could either of them say anyway? Amanda was gone, and no words would alter that fact.

Minutes passed, and then hours. Sarek concentrated on the scrape of his footfalls as he and Spock walked along the trail that would eventually lead them back to the city. He focused on the sound, attempting to clear his mind, seeking a meditative state, but one image continued to vex his thoughts: an abstract sculpture that Amanda had recently completed. *Two and One,* she had called it. A pair of rounded, flowing forms joined at the base and formed from colored glass, it had been one of the many pieces she had brought with her to Earth for her exhibition.

Unreasonably, Sarek had grown to hate the work in recent days, leveling the blame for his wife's death at the inanimate object. Cargo would typically have been loaded onto a space vessel with the use of a transporter, but in the case of artwork, Amanda required—as did many people— that it be hauled to and from the ship aboard a shuttle. In general, people wished items that had been handcrafted to remain so, rather than at some point in their existence converted into energy and reconstituted back into an echo of its original material form. In her case, Amanda had not only insisted that her art be taken by shuttle to and from the vessels on which she'd traveled, she had wanted to accompany it during loading and unloading. The ship on which she'd returned to Vulcan had been delayed, arriving on the morning of her party rather than on the prior day. The shuttle carrying her to the surface had apparently suffered a total systems failure, and its flight path had taken it beyond the range of emergency tractor beams on the surface.

"Father," Spock said, his voice seeming loud as it broke the silence about them, "your breathing is becoming labored."

Though he had not been aware of it, Sarek now heard the rasp of his own respiration. He allowed himself to feel the fatigue in his muscles and joints, and he realized that he had pushed himself almost to his physical limits. The illogical idea of continuing to walk rose in his mind—

continuing to walk until he collapsed, his own life merci- fully ended so that he would not have to endure the un- bearable horror of missing Amanda.

Perhaps not so illogical, he tried to argue to himself. *Perhaps an elegant solution for ending his pain.*

Sarek stopped walking, the rational portion of his mind asserting itself. "We will rest," he said. Ahead, he saw the skyline of Shi'Kahr, still far in the distance.

"Will you not reconsider transporting back to the city?" Spock asked. "We have walked far from our family's grounds. We have fulfilled the tradition in honor of my mother. Our ways do not demand that you sacrifice your health in order to carry out a symbolic act."

Sarek turned to look at Spock. "You are right, of course," he said. He looked around and saw several large rocks beside the trail, and he moved to one and sat down. Spock walked over as well, but remained standing. "I will pay more attention to my body, and if it becomes neces- sary, we will transport back to Shi'Kahr."

"If it will suffice to meet your wishes," Spock offered, "I can complete this journey by myself, in your name."

Sarek regarded his son more closely, seeking in him any hint of compassion or sympathy or love. He saw only logic. If Sarek could not accomplish this goal and Spock could, and thereby spare both his father's physical and emotional health, then reason suggested that Spock should. "We have come full circle, you and I," Sarek said.

Spock did not respond.

"When you were a boy," Sarek went on, "you faced the issue of your identity in a way that most Vulcans do not."

"The hybrid nature of my existence forced me to such a point," Spock said.

"Perhaps," Sarek said. "Or perhaps I forced you to it."

"I do not believe so," Spock said. "At the time, my

emotions whirled within me, undermining my reason."

"As it does to all Vulcan youths," Sarek said. "Your mother and I wanted what was best for you, of course, as parents do. But where she trusted you to grow and make your own choices, I pushed you."

"You offered me guidance," Spock said.

"I think that because of your mixed parentage, I believed in the possibility that you would live more as a human than as a Vulcan," Sarek said, admitting this to himself for the first time, the flurry of emotion within him perhaps allowing him to see now what he had not before. "I do not disapprove of humans," he said, stating the obvious. "But I do think that Vulcan philosophy offers a better way. From a societal standpoint, we have done away with war and crime, and on a personal level, we achieve a peace of mind that humans seldom experience. I wanted that for you, my son."

"It is logical to have wanted the best for your child," Spock said.

"Of course," Sarek said. "But logic alone does not validate the correctness of a viewpoint. Your mother trusted and accepted the choices you made in your life. I did not."

"My mother did not accept all of my choices," Spock said.

"She did," Sarek said. "She simply worried when she thought you might have made the wrong choice." He paused, trying to recall the point he had sought to make. "In any event, we have now changed places, you and I. In your youth, you struggled to live the Vulcan example I set for you. Now I hunger for the peace your Vulcan discipline brings you."

"Forgive me, Father," Spock said, "but I do not understand why that should be. I understand the nature of the loss that you have suffered, but I do not believe that I am stronger in mind than you, or that my mental and emotional training could have been superior to yours."

Sarek raised an eyebrow. "You proceed from a misapprehension," he said. "I have never undertaken the *Kolinahr.*"

For a moment, Spock said nothing, clearly processing the information he had just learned. "I did not know that," he said at last. "I simply assumed that you had."

"I know," Sarek said. "But I did not find the need in my life. I controlled my emotions to a great extent, and I did train in the mental disciplines, but I did not wish to lose a portion of myself that did not threaten my existence."

"And yet, when I petitioned for my first *Kolinahr,* you did not stop me," Spock said.

"I did not think that I should," Sarek said. "If after your years in Starfleet, living among predominantly emotive species, you returned to Vulcan to purge yourself of emotions, it was logical to assume that you needed to do that. My opinion was no doubt improperly influenced by my concern that life outside of Vulcan society had not been in your best interests—a concern I eventually came to realize was misplaced. If you recall, when you petitioned for your second *Kolinahr,* I did not support it."

"No," Spock said, and then he lapsed into silence.

Sarek allowed the quiet to surround them. He felt strangely more settled now after speaking with his son, although he did not quite know why that should be. For now, he decided not to seek the logic in it.

After a few minutes, Sarek felt sufficiently rested and he stood up. The sky had begun to dim as dusk approached. "We should continue," he said.

"Are you sure that you will be all right?" Spock asked.

"Yes," Sarek replied. And for the first time since he had learned of Amanda's death, he actually believed it.

* * *

Spock deactivated the display in his lab and walked into his adjoining office. There, he prepared for his midday meditation by collecting several candles from a shelf and setting them on his desk. As he brought the incense diffuser over, though, a tone signaled an incoming transmission on his communications console. Spock sat down at his desk and turned to the monitor, working its controls to open the comm channel. The emblem of the Vulcan comnet appeared briefly, replaced a moment later by the image of Sarek.

"Father," Spock acknowledged. In the background, he saw the complicated arcing fountain that adorned the center of the great room of the house in which Sarek still lived. For a time, Spock knew, his father had considered relocating, but now, a year after Amanda's death, he had apparently decided against that.

"Spock," Sarek said. "I regret disturbing you during your workday, but I had hoped that I would find you on your midday respite."

"As you have," Spock said. "Your timing is most efficacious."

"I wished to let you know that I will be resuming my ambassadorial duties," Sarek said. Since the shuttle crash, he had withdrawn from public life, initially for the dual purposes of grieving for Amanda and recovering the control of his emotions. After he had regained his mental composure, though, he had chosen to continue mourning.

"Have you contacted the Bureau of Interplanetary Affairs?" Spock asked.

"Actually, Director Forsén contacted me," Sarek said. Forsén, Spock knew, had superceded Lanitow Irizal as the head of the BIA several years ago. "She asked if I would consider assisting a Federation subcouncil established to forecast short- and long-term effects of the Treaty of Algeron." The historic document had been signed by the Federation, the Klingon Empire, and the Romulan Star Empire in the wake of the Tomed Incident.

"I am sure that such an endeavor would benefit from your experience and expertise in such matters," Spock said.

"I concur," Sarek said with no hint of ego. "That is why I have agreed to return to my position as Vulcan ambassador and provide the subcouncil the aide it needs. I leave for Earth in two days."

"Why so soon?" Spock asked.

"The subcouncil has already been meeting for weeks," Sarek said. "I would depart immediately, but I need some time to prepare for my journey and to ready the house to stand vacant while I am away." The hesitation that followed lasted such a brief time that Spock doubted anybody but himself would have noted it. "Your mother used to take care of putting the house in order before our trips." Spock thought he could detect a trace of sadness within Sarek, but he could not be certain. Either way, it seemed clear that Sarek truly had recaptured his ability to rule his feelings.

"May I provide you with some assistance?" Spock asked.

"No, my son," Sarek said. "I appreciate your offer, but this is something I must do on my own."

"I understand," Spock said.

"Will you be available to dine with me this evening?" Sarek asked.

"Yes."

"That is good," Sarek said. "I will see you at dusk at my house then."

"Very well," Spock said. The conversation at an end, he saw his father reach forward. An instant later, Sarek's image disappeared, replaced by the Vulcan comnet logo. Spock reached forward himself and switched off the comm equipment.

Turning back to his desk, he saw the candles and diffuser arranged there. He lighted them all, then concentrated on the center flame. He regulated his breathing, using the desert scent to attempt to empty his mind.

Instead, he thought of Sarek. For half a season after Amanda's death, Spock had lived with his father, doing whatever he could to assist him. But beyond the practical matters of everyday life, Sarek had accepted no help. At first, he had permitted himself to experience the despondence that his wife's death had caused within him. Spock had suggested meditation and various mental exercises, and once even to meld with his father, but Sarek had declined all such recommendations.

At some point, though, Sarek had begun taking solitary walks through the thoroughfares of Shi'Kahr. Not long afterward, he had begun to appear less unsettled. Eventually, he had resumed meditation, at which point Spock had noticed marked improvements in his manner, and a clearly renewed containment of and power over his emotions.

In all, Spock had thought it a remarkable display of his father's mental capacity—made all the more so by Sarek's revelation that he had never undertaken the *Kolinahr*. *But then, if he had gone through the Kolinahr,* Spock thought, *he never would have suffered the turmoil he had after Amanda's death.*

Just as Spock had felt nothing. Just as he still felt nothing.

He closed his eyes and again tried to blank his thoughts. Again, his efforts failed. He recalled his years in Starfleet, and specifically that first period of time he'd served aboard the *Enterprise*. Back then, while maintaining his inner control, Spock had smiled in an effort to assimilate with his crewmates. It hadn't succeeded. When the crew had learned of his artifice, many had come to distrust him, understandably unsure which of his reactions they could believe. Spock too had found himself uneasy emulating behavior not his own, and in some ways, attempting to be something—some*body*—he was not.

But even after Spock had worked to regain the confidence of his shipmates, it remained clear that he did not fit in with them. Although always treated with respect and even kindness, Spock existed as a population of one, separate from the rest of the crew. Over time, he'd thought that a friendship might develop with the ship's human but stoic first officer, but despite her emotionless mien, she had shared virtually nothing in common with Spock.

After Captain Pike had been promoted to Fleet Captain and off the *Enterprise,* Spock had considered resigning his commission and returning to Vulcan, thinking that perhaps his father had been correct in opposing his entry into Starfleet. But while Spock had not entirely found his place within the space service, neither had he ever been completely at home on the planet of his birth. He had therefore resolved to stay aboard the *Enterprise*.

During the ship's five-year mission under the command of Captain Kirk, Spock had finally become comfortable with himself. He had cultivated friendships, particularly with Captain Kirk and Dr. McCoy. Only at the end of that time, when Jim's apparent death had caused Spock to bear the weight of his betrayal of the captain—of his friend— had he finally opted to return to Vulcan for the *Kolinahr.* When he had gone back to Starfleet, though, back to the *Enterprise* and to his friends, he had recovered the one place where he had ever truly found refuge.

Now, nineteen Standard years after his friend's death,

fifteen years after his successful completion of the *Koli-nahr,* and a year after the shuttle accident that had claimed his mother's life, he had found other refuges, spending his days in his office and lab at the Vulcan Science Academy, at his apartment here in T'Paal, and sometimes at his father's house in Shi'Kahr. He did not feel regret for failing to even search for a way to keep Edith Keeler in Jim's life, he did not feel sadness for the death of his friend, he did not feel grief for his father's loss, he did not feel sorrow for the death of his mother.

He felt nothing.

But he wanted to.

Spock opened his eyes. Before him, the candles still burned and a thin drift of smoke floated up from the diffuser. Out of habit, he peered at the center flame, looking to enter a meditative state.

How can I want *to feel?* he asked himself. *Is that not desire, something my* Kolinahr *prevents me from experiencing?*

It all seemed irrational. But Spock could not deny it. He *wanted* to mourn his mother. He wanted to mourn Jim. He even wanted the regrets he'd had because they'd been his own.

Spock suddenly remembered something that the captain had once said, when Sybok had wanted to ease his pain, to begin to remove from him the negative emotions that had built up within him during his lifetime. *The things we carry with us make us who we are,* Jim had said. *If we lose them, we lose ourselves.*

Had he been right? And had Spock lost himself by becoming *more* Vulcan, by embracing logic and stoicism *too* much? He recalled now that not only Amanda but Sarek had believed that he should not petition for the *Kolinahr.* His father had even claimed that Spock had already won the battle he had waged between his Vulcan and human aspects.

Spock leaned forward and extinguished the candle flames with a breath, then capped the incense diffuser. Standing, he quickly moved from behind his desk and into his lab. He activated the computer terminal at the center of the room with a touch. "Computer," he said.

"*Working*," came the response in a masculine voice.

"Access Vulcan cultural database," Spock ordered.

A ticking sound provided an audible indication of the computer's functioning while it processed his request. "*Ready*," it said a few seconds later.

"Are there any Vulcan rituals designed to reverse the effects of a successful *Kolinahr?*" Spock asked. He had never heard of such a thing, and he could not imagine the Vulcan masters conducting such a rite.

More ticks. "*Affirmative*," the computer said.

"How many?"

"*One: the* lot-san-kol."

"Is the *lot-san-kol* carried out or guided by the Vulcan masters or elders?" Spock asked.

"*Negative*."

Spock went back into his office and retrieved his personal data slate. When he returned, he placed it atop the computer terminal's transfer interface. "Computer," Spock said, "download all information available on the *lot-san-kol*."

When the download had completed, Spock took the slate into his office and reviewed it. He understood the process of the *lot-san-kol,* but did not know if it would be possible to accomplish. But he knew he had to try.

By the time he arrived at his father's house for the evening meal, Spock had already resigned from the Vulcan Science Academy and booked passage to Earth.

TWENTY-FIVE

2312

When McCoy heard the doorbell chime, he furrowed his brow. Having just finished up an intensive edit of his *Comparative Alien Physiology* text, and having the house to himself for the next few weeks, he hadn't been expecting any visitors. On this fine Sunday afternoon in the middle of a beautifully mild Georgia summer, he had planned on doing nothing more than tending his zinnias and perhaps enjoying a mint julep out on the front porch come the evening.

McCoy stuck his spading fork into the dirt, then pulled off his gardening gloves and rose from his knees. His joints felt a little creaky, but with all the work he'd been doing on the book, he hadn't had much of a chance lately to get out and exercise. Now that he'd finally completed the last round of edits, he hoped to change that.

He brushed the grass from the knees of his jeans, then climbed the back steps and opened the screen door. Inside, he headed through the kitchen and the hall to the foyer. As he swung the inner door aside, he spied the person standing out on the porch. McCoy stopped in his tracks, stunned. It took him a moment to recover. When finally he did, he stepped forward and opened the outer door.

Spock stood there. He wore dark blue slacks and a gray shirt. Behind him, down the front walk and past the two pairs of white oak trees after which the nineteenth-century plantation house had been named, an airpod had set down at the end of the lane.

"Doctor McCoy," Spock said. In just the two words,

McCoy heard the same icy, removed tone he'd heard when he'd last spoken with the Vulcan.

"Hello, Spock," he said. "I have to admit that I'm surprised to see you. It's been, what, thirteen years?" McCoy recalled well their last meeting, when he had visited Vulcan to ask Spock in person to be the best man at his wedding. Not only had Spock coldly rejected his invitation, he'd also made it clear that his new level of emotional control did not allow room in his life for old friends.

"Fourteen years, one month, eleven days," Spock said. Though his voice retained its inflectionless monotone, McCoy grinned at the memory of Spock's penchant for precision.

"Just as exact and annoying as ever," McCoy said, continuing to smile in order to demonstrate that he meant his comment in jest. "I suppose I should act the part of the southern gentleman and invite you in." He moved aside and gestured for Spock to enter.

"Thank you," Spock said as he moved past. McCoy closed both doors of the foyer, then pointed to the left side of the hall.

"Let's go in here," he said, parting the wooden doors and sliding them open. He led Spock into the room, which he had appointed in the detail of the house's era. A large fireplace dominated the center of the wall opposite the doors. Before it, two burgundy davenports faced each other, both at right angles to the hearth. A low oaken table separated the two pieces. "Have a seat," McCoy said, gesturing to the sitting area as he walked over to the bar cabinet in the far corner.

"Where is your wife?" Spock asked as he sat down.

"Away on Memory Alpha for a month-long conference," McCoy said. "Can I get you something to eat or to drink?"

"No, thank you," Spock said.

"Well, based on whatever reason you're here," McCoy joked, "am I going to need a drink?"

Spock peered over at him. "Possibly," he said.

The response gave McCoy pause. In just the few moments Spock had been here, he'd shown the same stern countenance, spoken in the same detached tone as when McCoy had last seen him. For that reason, Spock's suggestion that McCoy might need a drink seemed less amusing and more ominous.

Without pouring anything for himself, McCoy moved back to the middle of the room and sat down opposite Spock. "Why don't you go ahead and tell me why you've come," he said, "and then I'll decide whether or not it warrants any alcohol."

"First," Spock said, "I would like to apologize to you."

McCoy could not prevent himself from laughing. "I'm sorry, Spock," he said. "When I visited you on Vulcan all those years ago, you made it clear that your attainment of *Kolinahr* would no longer allow us to be friends. It wasn't just in what you said, but also in how you acted, how you spoke to me. Forgive me, but your demeanor doesn't seem any different now."

"It is no different," Spock said. "But that is why I have come."

"I don't follow you," McCoy said.

"I will explain," Spock said, "but I first want to apologize for hurting you when you asked me to stand with you during your wedding. My reaction was motivated only by logic, and not by the many years of our friendship."

"All right," McCoy said, confused. Despite what Spock had said, he'd offered no explanation for his behavior that McCoy didn't already know.

"After I completed the *Kolinahr*," Spock said, "I took a research position at the Vulcan Science Academy."

"Yes, I knew that," McCoy said. "I've actually read about some of your work in the literature: converging temporal loops, chaos theory, the infinite worlds paradox."

Spock nodded. "I have done little else beyond my research, other than occasionally spending time with my parents," he said. "Last year, my mother died."

As soon as Spock had mentioned his parents, McCoy recalled learning about the accident just after it had happened. "I heard about that," he said, his voice dropping to a soft level. "I thought about trying to contact you, but . . ." He remembered changing his mind over and over again about whether or not to reach out to Spock, until too much time had passed and he'd simply let it go.

"You made the correct choice in not contacting me," Spock said. "You would have been . . . disappointed . . . if you had."

"Look, Spock," McCoy said, "I don't pretend to fully comprehend the *Kolinahr* or even the Vulcan belief in suppressing emotions, and yeah, I was hurt when you wouldn't be in my wedding, but I never thought you were a bad person." The words pouring out of McCoy made him feel as though he'd been waiting to say them for a long time. "You and I have been through a lot together, Spock. All those years aboard the *Enterprise* . . . exploring the galaxy . . . life-and-death situations . . . losing Jim . . . almost losing you." McCoy leaned forward on the davenport. "You can't disappoint me, Spock, because I know too well who you are." He tapped at the side of his forehead, making obvious reference to having housed Spock's *katra* and having gone through the *fal-tor-pan* with him.

"That may make it easier for you to understand why I have come," Spock said. "I do not miss my mother."

McCoy sat back up straight as he tried to fathom what seemed like a non sequitur. "What?"

"When my mother died," Spock said, "I did not miss her, I did not feel sad. I still don't."

"But . . . Spock, I *know* you loved your mother," McCoy said.

"Yes," Spock agreed, "I did."

And suddenly McCoy saw Spock's point: he *had* loved his mother, but after the *Kolinahr,* he no longer possessed the capability of doing so. "I'd say I'm sorry, Spock, but if you've purged yourself of feeling, what does it matter?"

"It shouldn't," Spock said. "At least, it can't matter emotionally to me. But I have discovered that it *does* matter. I have concluded that I made the wrong choice in seeking the *Kolinahr.*"

McCoy shook his head, overwhelmed by the admission. "I think you're right," he said. "I think I do need a drink." When Spock said nothing more, McCoy stood up and walked back over to the bar cabinet. He opened its doors and peered inside, but then Spock spoke again.

"Doctor," he said, and McCoy turned back to face him. "Leonard," he said then, rising, "I need your help."

McCoy walked back over and stood before him. "Of course, Spock," he said. "Whatever you need."

"There is a process by which to reverse the *Kolinahr,*" Spock said. "I could find no record of it being practiced in modern times, but there is anecdotal evidence of it being used in centuries past."

"Wait a minute," McCoy said, holding up his hands and pacing away across the room. "A *Vulcan* process that isn't used in modern times? Haven't we been here before?" McCoy remembered standing on Mount Seleya and hearing T'Lar state that the *fal-tor-pan* had only been accomplished in the legends of previous generations. She had also revealed that the process would be dangerous to both himself and Spock.

"This is not the *fal-tor-pan*," Spock said, obviously understanding McCoy's implication.

"Maybe not, but . . . " He stopped. In other circumstances, he wouldn't have hesitated to help Spock, but now . . . "Spock, I have a wife," he explained. "I have an obligation to her. I can't put my life in danger and risk leaving her. I want to help you, but I just can't do that to her."

"I cannot tell you that there is no danger," Spock said. "But it would be only the danger associated with mind melds. Your life would not be at risk."

"A mind meld?" McCoy asked. He walked back across the room to stand by Spock once more. "That's it?"

"A series of them, but only mind melds, yes," Spock said. "I would tap into your emotions and the recollected feelings within your memories and use them to infuse my own thoughts, my own memories, essentially to . . . reanimate . . . them."

"That doesn't sound so bad," McCoy said.

"It will likely be very difficult," Spock said. "The effort will require a series of melds performed one after another, over the course of days."

"We can use lexorin between melds to combat the aftereffects," McCoy suggested. He had used the drug himself after Spock had transferred his *katra* to him.

"That will no doubt help," Spock said, "but the real difficulty will lie in the extreme degree to which your privacy will be invaded."

"My privacy?" McCoy said. "What about yours?"

Spock nodded. "This process will not be pleasant, and it will leave us with few secrets between each other," he said.

"As I said, haven't we been here before?"

"In the *fal-tor-pan*, our minds were linked and guided

by T'Lar," Spock said. "In this process, our connection will be more direct, more intense, and more personal."

McCoy turned and drifted across the room in the other direction, wiping a hand across his face. This didn't sound like something he wanted to do. But after all he and Spock had been through together, how could he say no? How many times had Spock saved his life, and how many times had the reverse occurred? For goodness sake, McCoy had held Spock's *katra* within him. What point would there be in denying him this?

At the other end of the room, he turned around to address Spock again. "Let me fill a prescription for lexorin," he said. "Then we can start."

McCoy wept.

The heels of his shoes rapped loudly on the concrete as he pounded along the empty city thoroughfare, the reports echoing off the nearby building facades. The moderate temperatures of the day had fled, and as he cried, the trails of his tears felt cold in the night air. He felt angry and deceived and—

Ashamed.

What had he done? No matter how bad the situation had become with Jocelyn, how could he have walked out, not only on his wife, but on his daughter? Had he learned nothing from his experiences with his father?

In the darkness, McCoy stopped walking. As he wiped his face dry, he thought about his own childhood. He had grown up alone, his mother dying as she had given birth to him, and his father abandoning him without even leaving the house. David McCoy had held his son responsible for the death of his beloved wife, and he had treated him accordingly. The injustice of the charge hadn't mattered, and whether David McCoy had blamed his son willfully or un-

consciously hadn't mattered either. Would Leonard McCoy do the same to his own child, deserting her not just in spirit, but in actuality?

But what should he do? Remain in an emotionally brutal relationship, teach his daughter by example that romantic love consisted of arguing and resentment and anger? He wouldn't be abandoning Joanna; he would be sparing her a childhood lived in a battle zone. He needed to leave, not just for his own sake, but for his daughter's as well. She would still have Jocelyn.

McCoy began walking again, putting more distance between himself and the place that, until just moments ago, he had called home. More distance between himself and Joanna. And whether or not he'd made the right decision in leaving his daughter, McCoy knew that he would feel shame for doing so for the rest of his life.

Spock watched all of this, and saw McCoy begin again to cry—

And Spock saw himself, not crying, but laughing. He hung by his arms and legs from a log wedged between two trees and enjoyed *playing*, and liked *the peaceful rural surroundings*, and loved *the beautiful woman who peered up at him with the most radiant of smiles*. Leila loved him, had loved him since they'd known each other six years earlier on Earth, and now finally he'd found the ability to love her, to admit—to her and to himself—to loving her.

But the ability to admit his love hadn't lasted. Spock abandoned Leila a second time, telling her that he would go on with his life, but not telling her—or himself—what he felt. The injustice of the situation didn't matter, and whether his love had been induced by the spores or merely revealed by them didn't matter either.

In the transporter room aboard the Enterprise, he said good-bye to her a second time. Her tears flowed, and the deep pain she felt released her from the effects of the spores as well. But still she loved him. And whether or not he'd made the right decision in leaving her, Spock knew that he would feel shame for doing so for the rest of his life.

McCoy watched all of this, and saw Leila begin to cry—

And McCoy saw himself crying too. He stood by himself in the soothingly decorated room, away from the people who managed the facility. As the casket closed on the still form of his father, McCoy provided mute witness to the fact. A man peered over at him and asked by way of a silent expression if they should continue. McCoy nodded, then looked on as his father's casket was slowly conveyed into the crematorium.

He had killed his father, deactivating the life support machinery that had kept him alive. He'd done so at his father's request, but as it had turned out, he'd done so only a short time before a cure had been found. And painful as all that remained, as McCoy observed the casket sliding into the furnace that would turn it and its contents to ash, all he could think of was how, at the end, he hadn't even been able to tell his father that he loved him. The casket vanished from view, but McCoy didn't move. For a long time, he stood there, the tears flowing silently down his face.

Spock watched all of this, saw McCoy crying—

And Spock saw himself crying too. He stood by himself in a briefing room aboard the Enterprise, away from the crew. As the ship spiraled in toward the dying planet, Spock had abandoned his post, his duty. He'd been called to the bridge, but he hadn't responded, couldn't respond.

He had wounded his mother, adopting Vulcan customs to the exclusion of human ones. He had done so partly at his father's urging, but also as a result of the accusations he'd endured from his schoolmates that he wasn't truly Vulcan. And difficult as all that remained, as Spock hid himself away in the briefing room, all he could think of was how he had never told his mother that he loved her. He moved to the conference table and put his head down, and he sat there sobbing, knowing how badly he had hurt his mother—

McCoy watched all of this, felt the ignominy of Spock's betrayal—

And McCoy saw himself committing an act of betrayal himself. He stood at the monorail station in San Francisco, a cold breeze blowing in from the bay. He saw Tonia lower herself to one knee, saw her raise her right hand, a jewelled ring held in her fingers. In eloquent words, she expressed her love for him, and then she proposed marriage.

McCoy denied her, and in so doing, hurt her badly. She fled from him, and he understood. He had known that she loved him, had known too that he loved her. How could he have let this happen, how could he not have at least tried to avoid letting this come to pass? For a moment that seemed like forever, he stood motionless, realizing the agonizing effects of what he had done to her.

Spock watched all of this, felt the ignominy of McCoy's betrayal—

And Spock saw himself committing an act of betrayal himself. He stood in a boarding lounge in Los Angeles, the air uncomfortably chilled. He saw Alexandra peer around at the other passengers, saw her invite him with a look toward a pillar in the corner. With delicate movement, she raised her hand and extended two fingers toward him, expressing without words her love for him.

Spock denied her, and in so doing, hurt her badly. She fled from him, and he understood. He had known that she loved him, had known too that he loved her. How could he *have let this happen, how could he not have at least tried to avoid letting this come to pass? For a moment that seemed like forever, he stood motionless, realizing the agonizing effects of what he had done to her.*

McCoy watched all of this, felt Spock's reciprocal agony—

And McCoy felt his own agony. He clutched the holo to his chest, unwilling to let go of the image of his mother. His father stood there, silent now, his posture accusatory. McCoy had never known his mother, and this one small token of her did not seem like too much to ask.

But whatever else had happened, he was still a son to his father, and right now, his father ached in a way that he could not understand, though he wanted to understand, wanted to help. But he could not hold on to the image of his mother. Unsatisfied but not knowing what else he could do, he surrendered it to his father and tried to feel nothing.

Spock watched all of this, experienced McCoy's sudden stoicism.

And Spock experienced his own stoicism. He clutched his hands to his chest, calling to mind the image of his mother. His father stood there, silent now, his posture defeated. Spock had never really known his mother, and being able to keep one small token of her, even just a mental picture, did not seem like too much to ask.

But whatever else had happened, he was still a son to his father, and right now, his father ached in a way that he could not understand, though he wanted to understand, wanted to help. But he could not hold on to the image of his mother. Unsatisfied but not knowing what else he could do, he surrendered it to his father and tried to feel—

Something.

And did. After all the denials of his human half, after

running repeatedly in his life from his emotions, from his very nature, Spock again felt something. And it poured forth in a torrent of feeling—

Disappointment and contentment.

Sorrow and happiness.

Regret and hope.

All the pain, and all the love.

"Spock!"

He was not Vulcan. He was not human. He was both.

"Spock!"

He opened his eyes and saw McCoy. A hand hung in the air just centimeters in front of the doctor's face, its fingers apart. Spock blinked and realized that the hand belonged to him. He lowered it to the davenport on which he now saw that he and McCoy sat, in the room of the old plantation house where for weeks they had returned again and again.

"Are you all right?" McCoy asked.

"I . . . I'm . . . " Spock stammered, not quite able to find his full voice yet.

"How do you feel?" McCoy wanted to know, and the words resonated for Spock.

"A long time ago," he managed to say, "my mother insisted that question held relevance for me."

"I know," McCoy said. "She was a good mother to you, Spock. Through it all, she loved you."

"I know," Spock said, which made the way he had withdrawn from his love for her that much more painful. But that was all right, because the ability to feel that also allowed him to feel this: "I loved her too. And I miss her."

"I'm sorry, Spock," McCoy said.

"No," Spock told him, understanding that this particular journey with McCoy—with Leonard—had come to an end. "This is what I wanted."

Leonard nodded with obviously precise awareness of the situation. "You're not just Vulcan," he said, "and not just human."

"I am, imperfectly, both," Spock agreed. "But I am whole."

"I'm happy for you," Leonard said.

"Thank you," Spock said. "For all that you have done for me, I am most appreciative."

"Welcome home," Leonard said.

TWENTY-SIX

2312

McCoy waited in the large, stylish atrium of the Federation Embassy. Sitting on a plush sofa near the top of the wide staircase that led down to the front doors, he realized that he had tired of traveling. These days, he preferred simply to stay at home when not busy with his various research projects. Maybe he'd logged too many light-years when he'd served aboard the *Enterprise,* or maybe he just loved the American South.

Whatever the reason, he hadn't particularly enjoyed traipsing halfway across the galaxy to Tzenketh, especially considering the aggressive stances that the Tzenkethi had begun taking with respect to various nonaligned worlds—and in some instances, close to Federation space. But after everything he'd been through with Spock—the weeks of intensive melding, the extreme sharing of their thoughts and memories and feelings—McCoy knew that he had to do this. His wife had agreed.

McCoy had waited for nearly an hour when he heard the front doors open, followed by the sound of footsteps on the stairs. At first, he didn't recognize the woman. She had longer hair than he'd expected, her sinuous locks reaching down to her shoulders, the color neither blonde nor red, but silver. But as she reached the top of the steps, McCoy distinguished her stature, her almost regal bearing, and her lovely features. He must have seen her sometime during the years in some comnet holo, representing the Federation somewhere in the galaxy, but the memories he retained of her were not his own.

As he stood up and approached her across the marble floor, she gazed over at him. She would assume that he hadn't managed to find his way here without proper authorization, but in an effort to ensure that he would not seem completely crazy, he had worn his Starfleet uniform. It seemed that retaining his active status paid dividends beyond the use of Starfleet Medical's research facilities.

"Excuse me," McCoy said.

The woman stopped and allowed him to walk up to her. She wore a lovely navy blue dress that perfectly balanced the silver of her hair. "Yes?" she said. "May I help you?"

"Ma'am, my name is Leonard McCoy," he said. "*Doctor* Leonard McCoy," he added, hoping that his title might also lend him credibility. "Are you Ambassador Alexandra Tremontaine?"

"Yes, I am," she said. "What can I do for you, Doctor McCoy?" She seemed serious and confident, but somehow also very open and pleasant. McCoy liked her at once.

"Ambassador, I'm friends with Spock," he said. On the voyage here, he'd rehearsed so many different speeches, but now, all of them went out of his head. "He and I served together for many years in Starfleet—"

"I know who you are," the ambassador said. She spoke

not in a challenging way, but simply stated a fact, clearly to ease McCoy's burden of identifying himself. He realized then that of course she would know him: when she and Spock had been together, they had shared intimacies that had taken them into each other's minds. McCoy didn't necessarily want to know that as well as he did, but the knowledge had come as a consequence of the *lot-san-kol* with Spock—and what McCoy had learned during their connections had been what had brought him here in the first place.

"Ambassador . . . " McCoy started to say, but then he peered over at the empty waiting area. "Can we sit for a few moments?" he asked.

They walked over and sat down next to each other on a sofa. "Ambassador," McCoy began again, "what I came here to tell you is none of my business, really, but Spock is my friend, and so I wanted to do this for him. He might eventually have come to you himself, but I don't know how long that would take. I'm painfully aware of what it's like to waste time in my life and I wanted to spare him that if I could. And spare you too."

"I suppose I should thank you for that," Tremontaine said lightly, "but I'm not quite sure yet what you're trying to tell me."

"For one thing, Spock has changed," McCoy said. "Well, not changed, but he's finally become the person he is, without reservation."

"A Vulcan in complete control of his emotions," the ambassador said.

"No," McCoy said. "He's come to realize that the *Kolinahr* was not the way for him. He has rejected it in favor of living comfortably with his emotions."

"All right," Tremontaine said. "And what does this have to do with me?"

McCoy took a breath, aware that he would now break Spock's confidence, but also knowing that, in the end, his friend would be pleased that he did. "Ambassador," he said, and then emended himself. "Alexandra," he said, "Spock still loves you."

And then he told her everything.

In the shining tower in Pil Stornom that housed the Rigel IV headquarters of the Bureau of Interplanetary Affairs, Spock sat as his desk in his office, reviewing the information on his data slate. He saw that the Tzenkethi had recently redeployed some of their space forces in what could be considered a provocative way. He suspected that they might be on the verge of attempting a physical expansion of their territory. It didn't appear that they would make any incursions into Federation space in the near term, but if the Tzenkethi succeeded in their efforts to grow, Spock knew that it would only be a matter of time before they looked toward the UFP with an avaricious eye.

He set the slate down and considered his return to the BIA. Since the *lot-san-kol* with Leonard, Spock had reevaluated many aspects of his life. Among them had been his work. He had been a researcher at the Vulcan Science Academy for a decade and a half, and while he had found his efforts in the field of temporal physics satisfying, he had also felt the need to move on to other challenges. His original service with the Bureau of Interplanetary Affairs had been short lived, but it had also been satisfying enough that—

The door to his office suddenly opened and a woman quickly entered.

"Alexandra," Spock said. An array of feelings coursed through him, and he let them come: shock, curiosity, excitement. He maintained his outward calm, but rose to his feet. "I am . . . pleased . . . to see you," he said, "but why are you here?"

"Your friend Leonard paid me a visit," she said.

Spock immediately understood the implications of that. He gazed at Alexandra, and she at him, for a moment that seemed to extend for a very long time. At last, he stepped from behind his desk and raised his hand, holding two fingers out.

Alexandra went to him.

EPILOGUE

Vel'Sor

Out beyond the city of Shi'Kahr, the megaliths encircled the ancestral lands of Spock's Vulcan forebears. Members of the extended family stood along the great ring and peered toward its center, to the low platform where Spock stood. There had been no Vulcan ritual for this, no ancient rite handed down through generations, but he had wanted to do this, and so had Alexandra. Even with his human heritage, Spock claimed the rights afforded to all Vulcans. He was both human and Vulcan, but the labels did not matter. He was who he was, and he would not allow his place within Vulcan society to be questioned. Nor would he allow Alexandra's place beside him to be questioned either.

That had been the way it had been with Sarek and Amanda.

Spock and Alexandra had already spoken the words they had wanted to speak, that the two of them had written together. As she had then left the ring, he had lighted the coals in the pit at the center of this place. The last time he had been here, for his mother's memorial rite, the burning embers had been extinguished in representation of her lost *katra*. Now, Spock had ignited them to symbolize new life.

He reached behind the shield that hung over the coals and took hold of the mallet there. He held it up, but then peered toward the square arch of the entry, to where Sarek stood beside it. Spock looked his father in the eyes, and Sarek nodded, his quiet, deliberate gesture an undisguised sign of his approval.

Spock struck the shield. It tolled a rich, echoing note that spread across the grounds. He dropped the mallet to the dirt and waited.

Within the arch, Alexandra appeared, a bundle cradled in her arms. She stepped down from the entry platform and across the land to the center of the ring. There, she held out to Spock the human infant that they had adopted.

Spock took his daughter in his arms. "On this day, at this hour," he told all those assembled, "we welcome to our family its newest member." He paused, and though he remained outwardly calm, within he felt a bittersweet joy.

And then he gave his daughter the name that he and Alexandra had chosen together: "T'Amanda."

ACKNOWLEDGMENTS

I began my acknowledgments in the first book of this trilogy with my editor, Marco Palmieri, and I have every reason to do so again here. For one thing, without Marco, *Crucible* would not have seen the light of day. Not only did he envision these books as a means of helping to celebrate the fortieth anniversary of *Star Trek,* but he gamely shepherded them through to publication. I always enjoy working with Marco because of the professionalism, skill, and creativity he constantly brings to his craft.

I would also like to thank Keith R.A. DeCandido for his timely and good-natured assistance. In this case, I wanted some details about the president of the Federation, and knowing that Keith had penned a deeply political *Trek* novel, *Articles of the Federation,* I suspected that he would be a good source for that information. Good call.

Thanks also to Mark and Bev Gemello, a lovely couple and great friends. Mark and I have shared much over the years, from playing baseball that first year at Tempe Diablo Stadium (and in so many other places thereafter), to the surprise party he threw for me in Sunnyvale, to our long and memorable trip through the National Baseball Hall of Fame in Cooperstown, to his standing beside me at my wedding, to the special trip he and Bev made last year for another very important surprise party. All this time later, if I'm managing a team, I know I can count on having the G–Man playing shortstop and batting third. I also know I can count on him and Bev for so much more than that.

Thanks also to Barb, Matty, and Faith Hahn for their wonderful friendship. They are an oasis in the desert, and I am so happy and privileged to have them in my life. Barb and Matty sang—beautifully!—at my wedding, and that's only where the talent in their family begins. Pay attention to the name Faith Hahn because you're going to hear it a lot in the coming years; she's going to be a star.

Of course, I can never think about acknowledging the people who help me without including Anita Smith, Jennifer George, and Patricia Walenista. They are all unique and magnificent women, and I count on them often and for many things. They could not be more loving and supportive, and my life is vastly better for having them in it.

Finally, there is Karen Ann Ragan-George. There are never enough words to adequately describe all that Karen means to me and all that she is, but I keep trying. Two of the words that work for me are those of her name. *Karen* descends from Greek and traditionally means "pure," and *Ann* arises from Hebrew with the meaning "grace." So Karen Ann is pure grace, a fine and apt description of a pure and graceful woman. (Incidentally, I believe *Ragan-George* is an old Deltan name that means "my sweet, sweet baby.")